THE SOMNIA

THE SOMNIA

Book Two of the Seer of York

by Alethea Lyons

BRIGIDS GATE PRESS

Overland Park, Kansas

www.brigidsgatepress.com

Printed in the United States of America

Also by Alethea Lyons

The Seer of York Series

The Hiding

Reawakening: A Collection of Short Stories

The Somnia

The Dreamwalker (*Coming 2026*)

Content warnings are provided at the end of this book

A thousand suns, a thousand moons
Forever dance through star-clad skies
They fly to fiddler's endless tunes
As mortals dream 'neath watchful eyes

Sleep casts his spell, allows no rest
His children haunt us from the womb
Torment and love from birth to death
A thousand sons, a thousand dooms

PREVIOUSLY ON ...

Harper Ashbury is walking through the Shambles when she bumps into a ghostwalker, a man giving ghost tours, and has a visceral vision of his death. She doesn't know how to interpret the sensations she experiences so continues with her day, shocked but not concerned. When his body is found the next day, she is guilt-ridden.

Harper researches the gruesome murder, using her job as an archivist in the cathedral's secret vaults to access illegal documents. The archbishop then orders Harper and her foster sister, Grace De Santos, to investigate as Grace's family are demonhunters.

The two women go to the place where the ghostwalker was murdered and Harper has a vision of his death. They're interrupted by Saqib Siddique, a forensic supernaturalist. Harper feels his skills could be useful and promises to keep in touch.

That night, Harper has a nightmare about a forest of eyes. She doesn't know it yet, but this relates to her past as she can't remember anything from before she was thirteen when Grace's father found her wandering in the mists of Swaledale. Feeling weary and scared, Harper tries to emulate a historical scryer and gain control over her visions. Instead, she accidentally summons a demon, Heresy. He tells Harper something is hunting her through her dreams and promises to teach her magic and conceal her in exchange for letting him stay.

When Harper reaches the cathedral the next day, the archbishop tells her that the deacon of the cathedral has been murdered. Saqib is already examining the body and has discovered both corpses are missing organs and have mysterious runes carved around the wounds.

While attempting to scry for the killer, Harper discovers the location of the next murder but finds it cordoned off by police tape when she arrives. Saqib examines the body and finds the same runes. Because all three victims are missing body parts relating to speech (vocal cords, lips, tongue), Harper believes someone is trying to silence people. The archbishop confirms her suspicions when he tells her that the deacon left him a voicemail just before he died stating he found something at the ghostwalker's guild house.

Grace and Harper break into the guild house but are caught. The two women speak to the guild master who reveals that these murders have happened before but won't give details. Heresy slips away and infiltrates the ghostwalkers' computer. He finds evidence files have been removed from the computer by magic. He follows the trail but is captured.

Harper experiences another vision of the forest of eyes and finds a corpse in a tree at the end of it. She recognises the location and sprints there, both afraid and hopeful of catching the killer. She encounters a supernatural creature but is unable to restrain them and they escape. Harper is sickened to find the body of a young woman whose eyes have been gouged out. The Queen's Guard arrest Harper but release her when the archbishop intervenes.

Heresy returns after Harper has a vision of her past, reiterating that something is chasing her through her dreams. He has discovered the murder victim the guild master mentioned was a woman whose body parts had been sold at auction. He and Harper search online and find a similar auction. Harper, Grace, Saqib, and Heresy go to stop it. Harper is taunted by the Auctioneer who tries to convince her to sell her eyes. Ze tells her that the body parts from the York murders were not taken to be sold but were taken by an ancient British supernatural. Harper fights the Auctioneer and escapes but fails to rescue zir prisoners which galvanises her desire to protect both humans and supernaturals.

Harper has a vision of a Viking village and realises the next murder will take place at a local attraction which has a replica village as its centrepiece. She meets the killer at the attraction and discovers it's the spirit of the River Ouse. The river escapes after claiming another victim.

During research in the cathedral archives, Harper learns of a spell called the Hiding that stops humans being able to perceive supernaturals. The runes in the spell match those on the victims. On her way home, she's stopped by a techno-witch, AJ Tailor, who has been sent by his coven to kill her. She accuses him and the coven of selfishness because they knew what was happening and did nothing to help either humans or supernaturals. AJ has a change of heart and joins Harper's team.

Harper and her friends catch the killer using a magical entrapment circle and Saqib's prototype device for detecting magic. Talking to the Ouse, Harper can tell the river is reluctant to murder people but feels duty-bound to complete the Hiding. The spell to trap the Ouse seems to go wrong, freezing the river which then shatters.

Having stopped the murders and disrupted the spell, they bear the guilt of the Ouse's death as well as knowing any supernatural deaths will be on their shoulders. They form a permanent alliance, pledging to use science, magic, and religion to protect all the peoples of York.

In the weeks after they stop the Ouse, supernatural incursions increase. Harper and the team find ways of compromising so they don't have to always kill, although some of the supes they encounter give them no choice. They form alliances in the supernatural community and learn how to relocate some supernaturals who are a threat, or a perceived threat, to humans. They also end up in an uneasy alliance with the Queen's Guard. They have some victories and some losses. Humans disappear into mirrors and faery circles and they can't get them back. Harper meets a strange violinist in the Shambles at Christmas who is cryptically threatening.

Unbeknownst to Harper's household, there's another creature that's linked to her by blood and dreams: a white cat called Zero. He's a dreamwalker and familiar. At his master's castle, he encounters a fetch—an omen of death—that foretells both his master's demise and Harper's.

CHAPTER ONE

Where the Bodies Lie

The streets of York swirled with mist as the Otherworld encroached upon the mundane. It churned around Harper's shoes, grasped her ankles, and slithered up her legs. She batted a hand through the miasma to clear a path but more flowed into the void. It clung to her, clammy as the fingers of a grindylow. Her footsteps faltered, uncertain despite years of familiarity, as her violet gaze swept the murky street. Supernatural Sight penetrated what the dying light could not.

Bizarre forms floated through the haze, silhouettes of beings only vaguely humanoid. Scuffs of boots and heaving breaths permeated the laden air. Straining to Hear, Harper turned slowly, trying to See out the corners of her eyes. She should've been alone. No one was willing to linger in the gloaming. No one human. No one sane.

Shadows flashed by and Harper gripped the hilt of her knife so tightly her bones creaked. Ice-cold fingers tap-tap-tapped down her spine. She spun, knife slicing a black trail through the silvery air. Mocking laughter rumbled beneath York's cobbled streets and through her soles. Whispers brushed her hair and tickled her ears.

Harper...

Harper...

Is this next time?

Have you come to play?

We're waiting ...

Myriad voices clawed past her eardrums and rebounded inside her skull.

Harper ...

Harper ...

Join us, Harper ...

We're hungry.

Her ears burned. Mist shone violet under her Sight. Blue eyes, slit like a dragon, gleamed, disembodied in the fog. Dim figures twisted through the mists to reach for her with clawed fingers.

Harper broke into a sprint, muscle memory guiding her sneakered feet down the right path. The shadow of Saint Peter's Cathedral emerged from the grey twilight. She burst through the south transept door, then pushed her back into it to shove it closed. The last wisps of mist curled around her ankles and dissipated.

Chest heaving, Harper rested her head against reassuring, solid oak. Cold iron bindings dug into her scalp, a comfort rather than the deterrent they were designed to be. Neither metal nor wood could truly keep the supernatural at bay—it let her pass after all—but the tightness in her chest eased. Her relief was unwarranted since she and Grace had hunted a deranged spirit through the cathedral only a few weeks earlier. The spectral apparition had believed itself to be of God, but its murdering spree had been anything but. They found its last victim in the tombs beneath the cathedral. Nowhere was truly safe.

The mists outside drifted higher than the rose window, blocking the last of the sunlight and the rising moon. Candles, ensconced on the walls, offered no light. Recently snuffed by an unseen hand, they released spirit-like smoke. Carved faces adorning the ceiling and pillars seemed to turn their faces as she passed. The dim light muted the brilliant colours of painted stone columns and shadowed the stone-slab floor; the richness of the cathedral reduced to monochrome.

A distant tolling breached the silence: not the sonorous voice of Great Peter nor the crystal call of the clarion bells. The Guard bell. Curfew. Once a guideline, now a rigorously enforced law. Harper patted her pocket, relieved by the crinkle of the pass granted her by the Council of Faiths. Their permission to be out after curfew gave her some leniency, although even that couldn't guarantee the Guard wouldn't haul her in for questioning again.

Already resigned to spending the night on the archbishop's office couch, Harper shifted her satchel on her shoulder and descended to the crypts, past the tomb of St. William and the night watchsen, and slipped through the gate that prohibited the public from wandering into dangerous areas.

Arriving so late was hardly ideal, but a murmuring book needed to be brought in immediately for containment and cataloguing. It was the first time she'd found something so blatantly magical in a normal bookshop, though if anyone else could hear it the bookseller would've called the Queen's Guard instead of putting it out for sale. If questioned as to why she thought the book was dangerous, she'd say the talking stopped. They'd believe her and put it somewhere safe, deep within the vaults. Once, she'd thought such artefacts were destroyed, which had been soul-wrenching, but now she knew the vaults went deeper. Now she knew magic was bound beneath the cathedral.

Her key, a filigree bookmark depicting the cathedral at one end and a cross at the other, granted her admittance to the Hall of Testing that guarded the cathedral's secret archives. Before entering, Harper texted her sister, Grace, to say she wouldn't be home that night. Mobiles didn't work as far underground as she was going.

Her heart quickened as it did whenever she entered the utter black of the Testing Hall. At home, she tried to tell herself her fear of the dark was irrational. Nothing was going to pounce on her bed and hurt her. But here … here danger lurked out of sight. If she failed the trial and was marked as a witch, she would be hanged—if she was lucky. She clenched sweaty fists and hoped it would be an easy test.

Lights flickered on from every angle, brilliant white like strings of fairy lights. They allayed the building panic but her exhale caught in her throat: they didn't illuminate the low-ceilinged hall with which she was familiar. Instead, the room stretched and the lights blurred together to conceal both ceiling and walls. Endless columns twisted to infinity.

Harper stepped forward.

A thousand Harpers stepped with her.

She cried out, covering her eyes, fearful of the magic she must have used to See such a thing. Yet there was no burning, no tingle or fizz in her retinas. Fingers splayed across her face, she opened one eye. The other Harpers copied her, layered images bending around each other to gape. She spun, surrounded, the door she had entered by gone without a trace.

Heart pounding, she lowered her trembling hands and twisted her fingers into the ragged end of her braid. She stepped towards one of the Harpers, who in turn stepped closer to her. Neither of them made a sound, save Harper's unsteady breathing. As they neared each other, mist bloomed between them and obscured the other Harper's face. When she reached out to waft the haze away, her fingers brushed against her doppelgänger's cold, hard hand. Harper bit back a cry despite tired logic knowing what she looked at. That small sound echoed around her, each Harper's yelp passing to the next like a disease until the vaulted room overflowed with high-pitched squeals.

"I'm an idiot," she told the image. Its mouth moved with her. The sound echoed, repeating, overlapping. Idiot. Idiot. Her voice sounded alien in the mouths of her mirrored selves. When the last word faded to nothing, she lowered her hand and her reflections copied her.

More by touch than sight, Harper worked her way through the maze. Surreal. Disorientating. Her heart fluttered in her chest. She no longer knew which way was forward and which was back. Mirrors trap your soul.

The voices from the street floated inside her skull.

Harper, come play with us.

The mouths of her reflections weren't quite in sync as her lips moved in a silent plea, begging whomever might be listening to show her the path.

Harper…

Harper…

Harper…

So many…

We'll eat them all.

Something golden flashed and she turned towards it, slipping between two Harpers who stretched their arms around her in an embrace. A chalice, unadorned by gems or inscription, hung in the air. As she neared, the image shattered. Hundreds of chalices appeared around her. They sliced through the voices, muting them. Harper cocked her head to the side, holding her breath, waiting. Silence.

A Grail test? Harper's first thought, fed by the movies, was to look for the plainest one, but it was all the same image, repeated over and over, like her reflection. *Only the pure can find the Grail.* Harper snorted at the thought, clapping a hand over her mouth and nose to muffle the sound. Although the magic singing through her didn't feel evil, she was sure the cathedral would view her as anything but pure.

The surface of the reflected chalice glinted in the sparkling lights. It sat on a thin plinth, little wider than the cup itself. Harper took a step to the side and the image turned with her, revealing a paten behind the false Grail. It too was of battered gold, with a hand etched on its flat surface, two fingers pointing heavenward. Instinct made her glance up. Nothing but lights stretched above as though they mingled with the stars.

She squinted at the reflections, trying to see past the dancing lights and deception. When it clicked, she slapped her forehead, a groan of frustration escaping. Too easy. Her fear made it harder than it should've been.

"This is my body, which is given for you," Harper quoted. "This cup that is poured out for you is the covenant in my blood." The room swallowed her words without echoes. A throaty growl grumbled beneath her feet and the mirrors slid apart to create a path. A few meters away, the chalice and paten rested on their plinths. Beyond them, a wooden door, the exit. Not an impossible Grail quest, just a reminder of one of the most well-known Bible stories. Harper huffed, irked she'd blown it out of proportion.

After closing the door to the Hall of Testing firmly behind her, she took a sip of water from the nearby fountain to steady her nerves. The corridor before her was well lit, even at this hour. It was not unheard of for archivists to be there after nightfall, especially with the early sunsets of winter and the vernal equinox still distant.

The curve of the corridor obscured its true length, which ran far beyond the footprint of the cathedral above. Not for the first time, Harper wondered to what extent the Queen's Guard were aware of the vast collection in the Church Archives. *She* wasn't aware of all its secrets. Possibly no one except the archbishop and the cathedral itself were.

Lost in musings, Harper counted the doors as she passed on autopilot. Some of the doors led to mundane areas—toilets, a kitchenette, stationery. Some were always locked and she didn't know what lay behind them. Private offices or collections, maybe. Doors six through sixteen led to crypts. Door seventeen was the First Vault, also known as the Main Reading Room. Her destination, Initial Evaluation and Classification, lay through the twenty-ninth door.

Once a natural cave, it had been converted to a cathedral morgue centuries before. Coolness, and its hidden nature, made it the perfect place to keep the dead from the prying eyes of the Guard. Harper breathed through her loose-fitting sleeve and pinched her nose closed. They had to keep the bodies *somewhere*, she just wished it wasn't *here*. Centuries of them: newer ones shrouded or coffined—the oldest now bare skeletal remains—lay line by line, in alcoves cut deep in the stone walls.

Carved prayers of protection, holy symbols, and quotes from scripture surrounded each crevice. Flecks showed where herbs, iron, and silver had been ground down and painted onto the stone. They preserved the sanctity of the holy and prevented the taint of the unholy.

While such protective measures previously had no effect on Harper as a witch, leading her to doubt their efficacy, over the past few weeks she'd noticed a change. Her skin tingled as she passed the recesses and the writings writhed, tormented, yet stilled when she turned to stare at them.

Her gaze caught the contorted face of a river hag, snared in the River Ouse the day before. Hair of pondweed stuck to mildewed skin. Even in death, Jenny Greenteeth lived up to her name. Fangs bared in a snarl caught by rigor-mortis-locked lips. Harper hadn't been part of the raid, let alone the one to kill her, yet guilt gripped her heart. The too-human face gave her an accusatory stare. The supernatural creature was responsible for almost a dozen deaths since the vanquishing of the spirit of the river, Usa. *Was Jenny evil, or merely at odds with humans? Was she any more evil than a cow might think we are?* Harper blinked back tears and kept moving. It was too late now.

Someone must've been examining Jenny for her body to have been left exposed. The freshest corpses nearest the door were usually locked behind iron doors. Tales of creatures like zombies and vampires were just that. Stories. Yet facing the corpse made Harper doubt the certainty with which the Council stated undead were fictitious. A chill hung around the alcoves. Inside, corpses—flesh still clinging to their bones—were kept cold by technology and stone with ventilation to reduce the smell.

It still struck the back of Harper's throat, putrid and rotting, summoning a memory: a girl in a tree, decomposing, voids instead of eyes. Harper clenched a hand over her stomach and clamped her lips closed.

Despite Jenny's body left on display, there was no sign of whoever was examining it. She averted her eyes from the other dead as she delved deeper into the cavernous hall.

Farther in, the alcoves were open. These held bones, long since stripped of meat. For some, it became their final resting place although most would be catalogued and sent to doors six through sixteen, or to the vaults. Those originally buried down here, back when it was still a cave beneath a tiny church, had been left in their berths even as the cave was expanded around them.

Parts of the original cavern still existed. Stalactites, no longer dripping or growing, hung as memorials to what once was. Calcite columns and rock formations naturally echoed a wedding cake as well as the pulpit and organ of a church. All were preserved with reverence and Harper was grateful the forebears of the cathedral had the foresight to work around them and not wantonly destroy.

The central areas of the hall contained cabinets with carefully monitored microclimates, housing everything from books to fossils, from artefacts to scientific equipment. Some were as large as Harper's bedroom, scattered with bookcases for mundane volumes and chained plinths for tomes containing magic. Other cabinets were no larger than her laptop. Rough-hewn stone passageways led elsewhere in the archives.

At the desk at the end, a familiar figure sat slumped over, her head on her arms. Harper glanced around. Falling asleep while there was a body exposed was not only sloppy but dangerous, especially to the superstitious archivists. She cleared her throat, once, twice. No reaction.

"Agnes?" Her voice echoed around the chamber, through the mouth of skeletons. *Agnes … Aaaaagnessss …* Harper swallowed and tried again, her voice a squeak. "Agnes?"

She shook the sleeping woman's shoulder. Agnes's woollen jumper bunched under her fingers as Agnes stayed stiff and unyielding. Bile rose to block Harper's throat as panic tightened her lungs. "*Agnes?*" She pushed the woman's shoulder again, harder. The archivist's head lolled to the side, dark hair falling back from her face. Harper screamed. Her head cracked against a glass case as she leapt back. Tears and stars blurred her vision. "No. No. No. Not here. Not here." The whispered words repeated over and over—whether her voice, an echo, or someone else's, she wasn't sure.

Her eyes burned as her vision cleared, Sight searching for hope. Agnes's empty sockets stared back, hollow pools in her pallid corpse.

Someone had started a new Hiding.

CHAPTER TWO

The Call of Music

Winter sun gleamed silver through the mists. It scattered over the River Ouse, mirroring invisible stars against the backdrop of black water. Grey stone banks jutted up to meet the cobbled path. It could've been a painting, save for the ripples trembling over the surface of the Ouse. The air was leaden. No birds sang. No bells rang in the north and no music drifted from the south. The metal roses adorning Lendal Bridge gave no colour, their Yorkshire white stark as snow. Only the chipped paint of a guardian angel placed at the apex broke the monochrome as ze gazed down in judgement at the dark water below.

Harper stared up at the angel from the north bank of the river. The seraphim held a shield, zir eyes downcast. In early November, the people of York had placed wreaths of holly and ivy upon the angel's bowed head, with dill and mint tucked into their fronds. The offerings were the vestiges of fear as the citizenry took their protection into their own hands. The Council of Faiths and the Queen's Guard both declared the murderous river spirit vanquished, but trust was a rare commodity.

As winter wore on, the offerings continued. While there had been few arcane incursions, as far as was commonly known, people stayed afraid. Too many disappeared, rumoured to be taken by magic or the Guard, for people to forget or move on. Armed soldiers walked the streets, curfew was rigorously enforced, and curtains twitched as neighbour watched neighbour. Church, mosque, synagogue, and temple had all seen attendance swell.

Harper glanced at Baker Tower on the opposite bank. A humanoid silhouette atop the tower held the thin shadow of a rifle. She crouched on the edge of the river and leant to touch the water. Mist curled between her outstretched fingers as they hovered over the surface of the river. Clenching her fist, Harper pulled back. The water was empty. It lacked a presence no one had known was there but which comforted and protected nonetheless. The river spirit. Dead. And with Agnes's corpse resting in the cathedral crypt pending investigations by Council and Guard, the Ouse's death seemed for naught.

"By my hand." Harper breathed the words into the cold air. Finding her friend's body yesterday stripped away any veneer of hope she'd done the right thing in stopping the Ouse. Guilt over the undine's death overwhelmed her guilt about Agnes. A tear trickled down her cheek. "I'm sorry."

She uncorked a vial of murky water and tipped it into its origin. It was right to do it here, the final place anyone had seen the Ouse's first victim alive. The splish of water was made louder by the ghostly quiet of the city. After the last drop plinked into the Ouse, the gentle tinkling continued. The windswept ginnels of the city sang with harmonics. The lone voice of a violin played a requiem. It burned her ears like her Sight burned her eyes. Magic. The music drifted over the water with the mist, a song from the North, calling.

"Hurry up, Harp. We'll be late." Grace's shout shattered the music like a hammer splintering a mirror.

Harper swallowed resentment at Grace's interruption. Her sister wasn't to know there was magic in the air. Not that it would've changed what Grace did. Not linked by DNA, the sister of her heart came from a long line of demonhunters and was therefore likely to say it was a curse she needed to protect Harper from. Harper barely reached the top of the stairs to the main road when Grace wrapped her in a hug. She let her sister's thick coat absorb her tears. The familiarity of Grace's coffee-and-vanilla-laced perfume loosened the knot that had been tight in her chest all morning.

"Done?" Saqib, their housemate and resident forensics specialist, held out his hand for the empty vial as the two women separated.

Harper passed it to him with a nod. "I know your machines couldn't detect any difference in the water before and after we vanquished the spirit, but it didn't feel right to tip it down the drain. I can't do anything for Agnes until the archives aren't full of people." Harper tapped the corner of her eyes to indicate she couldn't use her Sight to try and See the murder since the magic glimmering in them would be obvious. "At least I could do something for Usa."

"Do you think she knows?" Grace leant over the bridge, wrinkling her nose. "Is she watching from whatever afterlife she believed in?"

"What do supes believe in?" Saqib's soft curls bounced as he tilted his head.

"Probably the same as us." Harper glanced down at the still waters almost invisible in the mist. "Many, many things. In all the millennia of history between supes and humans, I can't believe no one ever asked."

"You could check the archives." Saqib's eyes lit up at the thought of discovery. "If anyone is going to know the spiritual beliefs of, well, spirits, it would be the Council of Faiths, and the cathedral archives have the biggest collection of supernatural materials in the North."

"Shht." Grace glanced at the silhouette atop the tower. The fog dampened sound but worry etched her brow. When the figure didn't move, her shoulders relaxed and her normal sarcasm edged her tone. "Because Harper doesn't know that having worked there for the last five years."

A faint blush touched Saqib's cheeks. "Sorry. Hey, when are you going to get me a guest pass, Harper?"

Harper stared down at the river, scarcely hearing their conversation.

"Harper?"

"I'm going for a walk. I'll see you at dinner." The music was gone, but something of the magic called to her. It stung her eyes and burned up her nose and in her ears. It hooked into her chest, snagged her spine. Northwest. Upriver. Beyond the horizon.

Harper was vaguely aware of Grace's hand warm against hers for a moment—the reality of the knuckledusters pressed into her palm her sister's way of saying 'stay safe.' Their voices receded, Saqib heading south to his lab at the police station and Grace begging for a lift to the veterinary clinic she worked at.

Harper headed back down to the river, steadied by a hand on the stone as her sneakers squelched on the rain-puddled stairs. At the base of Lendal Tower, faint outlines hovered in the mist. A tall ghostwalker in a cloak and stovepipe hat, and an audience, the ghosts of their gasps a susurration on the moist air. A short distance away, another faint outline shimmered under the bridge, almost submerged in the water. Usa waiting for her victim.

The urge to go North fought with a pull to the South as the ghostwalker's ashen form wandered down the riverbank. The North sang to her, beseeching her to turn. She'd been North, into the depths of the Dales where she'd been found. There were no answers in that place. There may yet be answers here, in the unprompted vision. Maybe somehow she would See something that would give a lead on Agnes's death. She ignored the ache in her chest. North didn't lead home as her heart hoped. She walked with purpose, hoping South would bring a resolution.

Eyes stinging with Sight, she followed the memory of the ghostwalker downriver. Solid patches of reality hurried past her on their way to the city centre, braving the mists, coats tucked around them. Harper's Sight remained locked on the past.

When she reached the place where the Foss joined the Ouse, she stopped, staring down their entwined waters just as the memory of the ghostwalker did. Land jutted between the two rivers and he stood at its tip, silent and still. Then the glimmer of the Ouse rose up behind him and took the form of a crystalline feminine figure. She reached inside his throat and ripped out his vocal cords. Vivid crimson splattered across Harper's vision, the burning in her eyes not quenched by her tears. She fell to her knees, biting back a sob. She'd Seen his death and failed to save him. Him and the others murdered by the Ouse. Usa killed them to protect her people, innocent supernaturals living in York. Supernaturals like Harper herself.

Pain punched Harper's gut and she doubled over, arms crossed over her belly as she cried. Magic burned through her. The call of the North and the Dales ripped her flesh with barbed prongs. It was many years since she'd wandered out of the mists roiling off the River Swale, but the anguish was still fresh. Music flowed from the hills, carried by the Swale into the Ouse, cascading downriver to assault Harper's ears. A tune she knew in her bones without knowing where or when she learnt it, one she'd played on her own violin. She couldn't help the family she'd lost there. She couldn't help anyone. "I killed her. All the deaths, at supernatural or human hands, they're my fault."

"Arrogant."

A voice cut through her grief with the twang of broken strings. Harper almost tripped over her satchel as she scrambled to her feet. She wiped her eyes on the back of her sleeve, the burning still strong as she studied the stranger's moss-green shoes and willed her eyes to dull to brown.

"Don't bother hiding from me. You broke that spell, remember?"

Despite her intentions, Harper looked up. Eyes of algae green regarded her, one brow raised. The stranger was a touch shorter than her, his face youthful and his eyes old. Gem-like blue hair streaked with the same green as his eyes curled around his shoulders and fluttered when the breeze stirred. His lips twisted in contempt. Despite the frosty January weather, he wore a thin sleeveless shirt, leaving well-muscled arms bare and a deep 'V' of chest on display. He glimmered with lilac fire to Harper's Sight.

"You're the violinist," she blurted out. "I saw you perform with the carol singers in the Shambles a few weeks ago." She'd been shopping for some Christmas sheet music, having dropped hers in the mud in the park chasing a will-o'-the-wisp, and almost missed the shop's closing time as she watched him play, enthralled. "You were brilliant. You're not hu …" She trailed off and twisted the end of her plait around her fingers. Discomfort wriggled under her skin at almost outing someone as a supe.

"Why, thank you." He flashed her a grin as he gave a sweeping bow and doffed his feathered cap. His crooked smile as he straightened made her heart skip a beat. She tugged her hair, reminding herself of the sneer lurking behind his charm.

"What do you mean, 'arrogant'?" Harper asked.

"To think that you, a paltry human witch of weak power and little control, are capable of destroying one of the oldest spirits of this land. You believe yourself responsible for Usa's demise, for the humans she sacrificed, and for those who have died or been taken since? *Arrogant*. Save your condemnation for the deserving, for those who commit the crimes, if crimes they are."

"I'm not to blame?" Hope lilted Harper's voice. He spoke with such authority that she wanted to believe him. No human could absolve her of her sins, but maybe another supernatural could.

"Blame?" The sneer returned to the man's face. "Blame is irrelevant. What is, is. You wandered out of our sister's mists. You do not blame her for leading you to the human land or your dissatisfaction with being here. What is, is. What will you do about it?"

"I'm trying." A child's whine, not the decisive tone of a woman in control.

"No. You are pouring salt water into Usa's purity and looking for someone else to take the responsibility from your shoulders. Leave blame to the wronged and the wrongdoers. Fight, Seer of York, Seer of the Dales. You took our fate into your hands. You owe us more than self-pity. So, I ask you again, what will you do about it?"

Harper clenched her fists. "I *am* trying. We all are. Trying to protect innocents on both sides. You shouldn't have to hide. You don't have to kill. Whoever has restarted the Hiding, it isn't necessary. There are other ways. Help us make York safe again."

"York was never safe, merely blind. Not everyone agreed a Hiding was needed. Some of those you have already met. Others you have yet to fight." The man smirked as he reached out and brushed a lock of hair behind Harper's ear. His fingers grazed her cheek, hot despite his meagre clothing. "You See much that you do not see. By un-hiding us, you have revealed yourself to greater powers than you know. Watch your back. There are some few of us who have a vested interest in your survival."

"Not as many as have a vested interest in my demise," Harper grumbled. The first few weeks after she disrupted the ritual had been beset by a new paranoia. Yet there had been no noticeable revenge attempts on her life.

"Fewer than you might think." The man chuckled.

"But someone is trying to hide you again. Do you know who it is?" Harper's look sharpened with suspicion as she swept her Sight-enhanced gaze over him. "Is it you? I won't let—"

"Let?" The violinist barked a bitter laugh. "You never stopped or allowed anything, Seer. Still, I will give you this for free. I am not taking up Usa's mantle."

There was a ring of truth to his words, although Harper wasn't sure why she wanted to believe him other than a false hope he was right and Usa's death was not her fault. So many books said supernaturals eschewed lying, but they emphasised that believing their words was foolhardy. Too often there was a double-meaning humans missed. She wanted to remain sceptical, but the music surrounding him settled around her, dimming her negative emotions. Harper flexed her shoulders but couldn't throw off the spell manipulating her even though she recognised its presence.

He turned his back on her with a casual wave of his hand. "Clear your eyes, Seer. Look beyond what you believe to be obvious."

"Wait. Help us. Please." The words slipped out despite knowing she couldn't trust him. The histories that spoke of fae double-speak were written by humans, biased humans. There had to be a way for both peoples to work together.

"I am. And I will," he replied without turning. "When the time comes, you will know what to ask me and I know the price you must pay for it."

"What does that mean?" Harper darted forward to grab his arm, but her fingers passed through his flesh like water.

"We will speak again, Seer, beloved of the Swale." He walked to the edge of the jutting piece of land, not stopping when he reached its end.

There was no splash, no ripple, as he descended into the gloomy waters of the River Foss as though it placed steps beneath its surface solely for him.

Harper rubbed her damp fingers together then straightened her spine. She hurried over the bridge leading back to the main road and turned towards the cathedral as Great Peter tolled twelve. Matching the cadence and rhythm, the song of the muezzin rose from the south.

She had work to do. The Foss, if that's who the musician was as she suspected, made a good point. Blame saved no one. She had to take action.

CHAPTER THREE

Witch Hunt

As Harper neared the cathedral, with only one extra book in her bag, courtesy of a stop at her favourite rickety second-hand bookstore on Minster Gate, she was drawn to a hubbub in the square at the West Front. A man with unkempt hair and ratty jeans waved a sign in the air. The mist was ankle-height and he stood above it on a step stool surrounded by a growing crowd of curious shoppers and lunchtime passers-by. A megaphone buzzed his words. Harper skirted the crowd until she could read the sign, written in a crimson, gothic font.

KILL THE EVIL

HIDING AMONG US

Harper staggered back, unaware of stepped-on toes or muffled curses, the crowd claustrophobic around her. Panic sank its claws into her chest and wrapped its fingers around her neck. It couldn't be. They couldn't know.

Harper closed her eyes, gulped deep breaths, and let the whispers of the crowd around her fade to a drone. A familiar tingle made her eardrums itch. Hearing didn't come as naturally to her as Sight, but soon his words became distinct. She opened her eyes, a chill blossoming from her heart as the crowd contorted into a sea of hate-filled faces and clenched fists.

"They say the demon who cursed our holy river is vanquished, but how many more haunt our city? You are frightened sheep content to be guarded by toothless curs."

A voice called out from the crowd, "The demon was exorcised and the murders stopped. The Queen's Guard did their jobs and they still guard us."

Harper scowled to hear the Guard given credit. While it was safer for her, Grace, and the others, not to be questioned on how they stopped the murders, it was galling to hear the Guard lauded. Regret twinged in her stomach, her guilt over the Ouse's death not assuaged by her conversation with the spirit of the Foss.

"Would you deny the strange happenings? People missing. Arcane lights in the night and whispers on the wind. Beasts unseen for centuries stalking the countryside. Only last night a fresh murder occurred with the same signature. Did they even catch the right killer?"

Harper swallowed the lump rising in her throat. *Had the Guard leaked Agnes's murder to keep people afraid?* Tears stung her eyes to hear her friend's death used for such dirty politics. She wouldn't be surprised if this rabble-rouser worked for the Guard.

"You must be vigilant and report the slightest suspicion. The demon almost succeeded because you trusted and no one raised the alarm. Arm yourselves with iron and silver. If even the holy river can be corrupted, then anything can be. Neighbours, friends, the very stones beneath our feet. Trust nothing. Shout a loud and clear warning of evil when you find it. Do not let the supernatural hide amongst us. We can see them. We can hear them. We can find them. And we can slay them."

He reached into his bag and tossed a pile of red papers into the crowd. The pamphlets fanned out to flutter into snatching hands. Harper flinched as one brushed her cheek. She didn't need to read it to know the evil it disgorged. The few voices of reason in the crowd were drowned out by jeers of the majority. Their animosity prickled Harper's skin and she wrapped her arms around her waist, trying to avoid being touched by the jostle of people. Their hatred set all the tiny hairs on the back of her neck on end. If the crowd discovered what she was, they'd tear her limb from limb in their rabid hatred. She shoved past jeering people with hard faces, her eyes blurred by tears, as the speaker continued.

"When you find the supernatural, you must strike it down without hesitation, without mercy. They would give none to you in their hell beyond the Veil where even God fears to go. The Council will not protect you. They have allowed these incursions. Again, I say arm yourselves. Protect yourselves."

Harper reached the cathedral steps and looked back. It was a mistake.

The man met her eyes, his lips curling in derision. "Hang the witch and burn the sorcerer. Seek out evil and destroy it utterly."

Harper froze, her feet stuck to the stone. She wondered how the crowd couldn't hear the drumbeat of her heart or the ringing in her ears, louder than Great Peter. Air rushed away from her. The man's voice still extorted violence, but Harper couldn't hear what he said. She was falling. Falling.

The ground at the bottom of the stairs cracked. Wider. Wider. Until a pit of cascading lava roared beneath her feet. Hands clutched for her ankles, blackened and charred. Voices lamented and wailed in agony. Her eyes rolled back and she fell to the ground. She screamed as every bone in her body splintered, shredding muscle and skin. A fissure cracked her skull in two, brains leaking into the molten rock. The stares of the saints around the main door pinned her there, like a stake through the heart.

"How dare you stand here in the shadow of God's house and spew forth hatred." Archbishop Marshall's thundering voice jolted Harper back to herself, and silenced both speaker and crowd.

Pain drained from Harper, and exhaustion surged in its wake. Beneath her was the ice-cold stone of the cathedral stairs. No lava. No clawing fingers. No one dragging her soul to Hell. She rubbed her head to probe for cracks or lumps. The vision of the ghostwalker's fall from the north tower that she'd experienced months ago shouldn't have been triggered again.

Folk stared up at the archbishop and Harper shuffled back, anxious to duck their gaze. He reached out and squeezed her fingers with the briefest glance in her direction. Although she could read worry in his eyes, the touch reassured Harper. Even if he discovered what she was, she was certain her sister's godfather would allow no harm to come to her. He, along with Grace's father, had been the one to 'cleanse' her of her so-called possession. The memory tried to force bile up her throat again. Even with nothing to exorcise, the experience had been torture. But faith in the archbishop was strong. He'd saved her life. He wouldn't let her die even if he believed her possessed again.

The mists parted before Archbishop Marshall as he descended the stairs and made his way through the crowd. He reached out—to touch a woman's arm, to pat a man's shoulder, to ruffle the hair of a child—until he stood before the man on the soapbox.

For all the man's perch gave him a good foot of height over the archbishop, he cringed back from the fiery glare. The archbishop's tone softened as he placed a hand on the man's elbow and guided him down to the flagstones. "I understand your concerns. Terrifying things are happening in our city, things that make us question God's wisdom and seek out new safeties, but this is not the way, my son. There is no place where God is not, no realm God fears, and no souls he does not love. To carry hatred within us is a slow death. Come inside, have a cup of tea, and talk with me. Maybe I can offer some balm."

Harper trailed after them as the archbishop led the shellshocked man into the cathedral. Archbishop Marshall glanced over his shoulder and winked as he ushered the man into his office. Harper's trembling legs took her deeper into the cathedral. She glanced up at the great East Window, its scenes of Revelations never reassuring.

"Merow." The soft tickle of fur against her ankles made her jump.

"Hello to you too. How did you get in here, kitty. Wait. You're not …?" She knelt to pick up the cat, then paused, eyeing it suspiciously. It tilted its head to the side, regarding her with crystal blue eyes. Something ached deep inside, similar to the call of the music earlier. She blinked, eyes misting, and the ache dispersed. "You're not Heresy, are you? Surely he wouldn't dare come here."

One of the self-proclaimed deception demon's more annoying qualities was his love of possessing innocent cats. As a vet, it infuriated Grace. As her sister was a demonhunter, Heresy annoyed Grace anyway though. Personally, Harper found his amusement at her failure as a witch to be his most annoying quality, but she was also forced to admit she'd learnt a lot from him and no one else was offering to teach her magic. AJ, the introverted techno-witch who was the fifth and final member of the household, point-blank refused to teach her unless it was unavoidable. There were still some in his coven who were uncomfortable with the fact he hadn't killed Harper as ordered. AJ walked a fine line between helping her and not overly aggravating his family. At least, that's what he claimed. Harper suspected he simply didn't like teaching.

She rubbed the cat's head. It purred and pressed against her fingers, allowing her to scoop it up. A black collar nestled, almost hidden, under thick, white fur and a silver disk hung from it bearing a triquetra but no name or address. A chill doused Harper, to see a symbol often associated with ancient magic. She dropped the cat outside the south transept door, away from the chattering crowd.

"Get along home with you," she hissed. "And tell your owner not to play around with superstitions. It'll get them killed, or worse." She pulled the heavy door closed before the cat could slip back inside. Then she hurried through the church, down into the crypts, and let herself into the Hall of Testing to enter the archives. She'd promised the Foss she'd do something, and this was what she knew best.

Harper settled into one of the many corners of the labyrinthine Third Vault, the home of books and artefacts believed to contain factual information about supernatural creatures and magical history of the human realm. There were no other archivists around and the lack of people let in a coldness she'd never noticed before. The archives had always been sacrosanct. No evil, human or supernatural, could reach into the deepest secret of the cathedral. Until yesterday.

Shelves stretched from the floor up into the arched ceiling. Cherry-wood planks adjoined seamlessly to stonework like trees growing through a ruined abbey. Ahead of Harper, bookcases curved and the paths between them cut off or bent sharply, fitting miles of shelves into a relatively compact space. Balconies of iron and oak were linked by sliding ladders and corkscrew staircases. New archivists had been known to get lost for hours and older archivists enjoyed scaring them with ghost stories of their missing predecessors. Or they used to. Harper suspected that would change with Agnes's death yesterday.

A book dropped onto Harper's mahogany desk, fluttering her research notes and sending up a billow of dust that made her eyes water and tickled her nose and throat.

"What." *Cough.* "Is that?" Harper rubbed her eyes on the back of her sleeve and Alfred's serious face swam into view. His glasses were specked with dust and his sleeves were almost silver with it. It wasn't an uncommon look for him and she wondered, not for the first time, when and where he changed clothes. She was fairly sure Alfred never left the archives, like some haunting spirit bound to holy ground.

"I hear you're working for the Guard now?" The flat betrayal in Alfred's tone stung.

"A marriage of convenience," Harper promised. She refused to condemn herself for working with the Guard *or* for using the opportunity to spy on them and help supernaturals. Alfred and the other archivists would approve of neither, but it was the right thing to do.

He sat down with a flump that stirred up more dust. A halo of it glowed around him in the lamplight before it settled. "I know in theory, yet it is still an unnerving thought. The archbishop did explain." Alfred shared a tired smile with her. "It must be difficult to live with. Have you found out any more about the missing people?"

Harper hung her head, loose hairs falling across her eyes. "No. Not the new ones on cases they've assigned Saqib nor the ones we think the Guard may have taken. I'm not even sure if the ones they have us investigating haven't been taken by them and the whole 'look into this, please' thing isn't a ploy to throw us off."

Part of her wanted to tell him she had solved some of the missing person cases. That one of the girls in question lived out her days in a mirror world. That four of the five people who disappeared in Rowntree Park were trapped in some faery dimension by an incarnation of the Pied Piper. To tell him that, she'd have to tell him how she'd found the magic, then she'd have to destroy it, and it wasn't that simple.

"Nothing is ever black and white." Albert's words interpreted Harper's thoughts too well. She huffed, crossing her arms over her chest. He did that far too often. "I have faith in you, Harper. More, I trust you. The archbishop allowed you to see higher than your clearance before—"

Harper suspected the archbishop was aware she had snuck into the Twelfth Vault, far over her clearance level, but she'd hoped Alfred ignorant of it. She watched him warily, waiting for condemnation, but his look hadn't changed and he continued seamlessly.

"—and I believe this book may be of use to you. Don't let it fall into the wrong hands." He tapped the dusty tome he'd dropped. It was bound in indigo leather with dirty brass corners and two brass clasps. The edges of the pages were gilt in the same colour. Harper rubbed the cover with her sleeve, fleetingly hoping it wasn't some kind of magic lamp book. Officially, any books containing magic were destroyed, but Harper had come to realise 'officially' and 'in reality' were further apart than she'd thought. The title under the dust read: **OF REALMS AND SHADOWS**.

"It's not been looked after very well." Harper sniffed in disapproval, then regretted it as dust burnt her nose.

"Some things are better left overlooked and with the appearance of being unimportant. Don't open it here," Alfred cautioned as Harper undid the top clasp. "It can only be safely read in a place that is the sole inhabitor of that space."

"Sole inhabitor? I don't understand." Harper frowned as she fingered a corner of the book. Not opening it around other people made sense, but that wasn't what he said. She thought of the fae woman in the paper shop on the Shambles. She'd assumed what she'd Seen there was always there, concealed from human vision by the remnants of the Hiding. But that spell was almost dissipated and the paper shop still looked like a paper shop. "You mean our reality isn't the only one on this side of the Veil and …" She froze. *Here?* The very thought was a sacrilege. "You're kidding? Right? Alfred, that's not funny. Keeping a book of magic is one thing but *using* magic?"

"I did not say magic was being used here," Alfred corrected. "But that doesn't mean there aren't things lapping at the edges of our reality that we must try to keep at bay. You have been trying to find out how Agnes could be murdered here. I fear this may be the answer, in which case it is not safe to trust in the sanctity of the archives until proof is gathered or new wards raised."

A cold finger of dread ran down Harper's spine. If this sanctuary had truly been breached, nowhere was safe. But the alternative was to believe someone with access, another archivist, murdered Agnes and somehow that wasn't better. "How can I know where it's safe to read it?"

"Your bedroom should be sufficiently mundane."

A little bit of Harper wanted to argue. It felt like an insult, although she wasn't entirely sure how. Still. It was a bit much from a person who never left the archives. "How can you know—"

"A last word of caution. Don't fall asleep on it. Lock it away before you go to bed." He looked straight in her eyes, a strange gleam in his, then stalked off without a backwards glance.

CHAPTER FOUR

Zero

A dirty, white cat skulked in the shadows outside The Grand. Zero didn't care that it was one of the fanciest hotels he'd ever been to, nor that the doorman was a poorly disguised member of the Queen's Guard. He didn't even care about the tangled snarl of magic he could sense somewhere on the upper floors. All Zero cared about was the fact his fur was dusty and scruffed up and his master wouldn't let him fix it. Because his master *did* care about all those other things and dirtied his white familiar on purpose so he wouldn't stand out.

Makes me look like a stray. Zero trotted around to the back of the hotel, where the alluring scent of salmon threatened to steal him away from his master's duty. He pawed at the kitchen door. Although his stomach growled like a tiger, piteous mewls escaped his throat. When one of the pot washers peered out, Zero mewled again as he widened bright, blue eyes and flattened his ears. It wasn't difficult to look pathetic. He quashed the corresponding feels that rose in his chest.

"Aww, hello, kitty." With a quick glance over their shoulder, the pot washer knelt to scratch behind Zero's ears. "Are you here for some milk? Let me see what I can sneak for you." The door closed in Zero's face and he scowled at it.

Fish? Chicken? Ham? He mewed at the door.

While he liked milk, and loved cream, it most certainly didn't like him. He hadn't eaten in almost two days and he wasn't yet fully recovered from the New Year's rituals. His master healed him of physical damage, but there was always a price: the pain remained. He wanted real food. Actually, what he *wanted* was to open a portal into the hotel, but his master had warned that any magic might alert the Queen's Guard or the magic users he was there to observe. So, he had to go through the excruciating 'poor kitty' routine to beg his way in.

The door opened again and a saucer of milk was set on the back step. Zero dutifully licked up a few drops while the Bringer of Milk patted his head. Then a few more. It *was* good despite the tummy ache he'd have later. That was a side effect of many things his master made him eat and they didn't taste as pleasant.

"Are you lost, kitty?"

Zero swallowed a hiss as the pot washer tugged on his collar to check for a name or address. They wouldn't find one, not one a mundane human could read anyway. It was difficult not to scratch them away as the unfamiliar touch incited waves of nausea and sent static jolts through his magic. Only two humans had ever touched it and not made him ill. Whatever kept the collar on liked to make sure it stayed locked around Zero's throat.

His body calmed when the human released him and returned inside. Zero enthusiastically dived into his milk again, like the wasted-away stray he imitated. When he finished the milk, he pawed the door again and mewed for more. This time, when it opened, he slipped through the crack between the door and their ankles before they could shut him out. Their bitten-off yell made him flinch as he darted between cooks and cleaners. No crash of pans followed, nor knives slicing too close for comfort. He narrowly dodged boots as big as his body, but they weren't aimed at him. Zero slipped through the swinging doors to the dining room, blessing the selfish preservation instincts of underlings everywhere that kept his benefactor from rousing their fellows to a cat hunt.

He skirted the near-empty dining room. The scent of salmon was strong here. *Shush, tummy. Greedy Cat.* The few patrons were absorbed in their breakfasts or staring at those skinny bricks humans found so fascinating. Zero had never gotten close enough to a human using one to find out what they were. When he was sneaking wasn't the time to indulge curiosity. In humans' dreams the bricks emitted strange images and cacophonous sounds. Mentally filing it as a human oddity to be explored another time, Zero stuck close to the walls. Pot plants, bags, and the general human predisposition against looking down enabled him to pass unseen.

The black-and-white tiled floor was cold under his paws. He tried to avoid stepping on the black ones, more to add some tiny measure of fun to the mission than for the practical purpose that it might contrast with his fur. The spiky design in the centre of the main lobby warranted further investigation but the person at the front desk remained diligent at their post. Zero wondered why the Guard had never destroyed the inactive magical inlay.

He hid beneath the panelled wood front desk for almost an hour as the attendant's muttered cursing and echoing sneezes grew worse and worse. There was a twinge of self-reproach: they must be allergic to cats. Sensible humans were. It was a natural warning something 'supernatural' was about. When someone eventually checked in for the top floor, Zero was glad to slink away, smuggling himself between bags and coats on the bellhop's trolly to hitch a lift. *Lazy Cat.* Trying to remain concealed and trot up all those stairs was not something he wanted to do unless he had to. The lift was much better. He pawed at a dangling zipper accessory.

When they exited the lift, Zero wiggled out and dropped silently to the carpeted floor. Nearby magic bristled his fur and he once again resisted the urge to groom. There was limited time until the bellhop unpacked and turned around. There were five rooms, one eliminated by the bellhop having opened the door. So close, it was impossible to miss the reek of magic from 505. Not just any magic. Blood magic. It zinged in his arteries, pumped to every extremity of his slight body.

This is bad. Why would the Guard set a trap using sanguimancy? It's against the Accords. Master will be furious. Zero shivered. Unhappy master was something to be prevented at all costs. Including risking being caught by the Guard or whomever they'd laid this trap for. Including risking death.

With a quick glance to ensure the bellhop was still unloading bags, Zero tapped the door twice with his paw. A swirling black vortex opened, barely big enough to cram his head through. Ears pricked for stray sounds and nose sniffing, he checked for inhabitants before squeezing the rest of his body through. There didn't appear to be anyone around, human or folk, although the scent of magic was strong enough to mask subtle odours.

Zero skirted the edge of a seven-pointed star etched on the carpet in trails of salt. *Maybe for purification or possibly to keep something in or out?* The design was unfamiliar, which was unusual enough without the elements of it that niggled at him. They should only be present in a summoning spell *or* a banishing spell. To see both sets of symbols in one spell was nonsensical. Whoever drew this didn't understand magic at all. *So how are they messing around with blood magic?*

The source of the magic's metallic tang was seven copper bowls lined up on the TV console each filled almost to the rim with blood. Zero hopped up to sniff. Not fresh, but not old either. Probably gathered over two or three days to avoid fatigue or obvious signs of blood loss. Then imbued with magic in advance, but only three of the bowls' blood matched the signature of the magic saturating it. Which implied not everyone performing the ritual could wield blood magic proficiently, or maybe even at all. Yet if there were three genuine sanguimancers, how could the crafted spell be so sloppy? *The more I know, the less I like this. Master is going to be very angry. There was only supposed to be one actual witch here, and a recently awakened one at that.*

He studied the magic from a vantage point on top of a cupboard. The pattern was needlessly complex. It sounded more like art than a serious spell. *If I adjust a few of the lines, I can make it something useful. Master needs witches. If I adjust the spell, it will banish them home for zir to question them without me having to use any of my own magic. The Guard can have the others, the pretenders. They don't need to know master sent me to check up on them.*

His master's game of appearing to be on both the Guard's side and that of other folk was a tightrope walk. It let zir control unsanctioned magic via the Guard's unyielding persecution while keeping magic alive and performing the rituals needed to ensure bountiful crops and moderate weather. Neither side could ever be allowed to exterminate the other. Fortunately, cats have excellent balance.

The drop from the top of the cupboard was a bit too far for comfort, so Zero slid his front paws down the side a ways before springing for the bed. It caught him like a hug and he rolled onto his back, head smooshed into the blanket, and wiggled around. To his relief, it knocked some of the dirt off. He didn't need it anymore. While it was much more luxurious than his master's bed, it smelled impersonal. The lack of scent made him feel very far from home. He rolled over and hopped down to examine the spell. A few redirections in the salt lines strengthened the banishing elements and instructed the magic on where to portal the witches. Everything else in the star was pretty decoration that he was fairly sure would do nothing.

Zero had just finished his adjustments when a beep at the door sent him scurrying into the bathroom. He slid on the tiles as the door clicked open, then scrambled up the side of the bathtub so he could cower behind the shower curtain against the white porcelain.

"Did you hear something, Edie?" A low-timbre human voice moved closer as it spoke. Zero's ears flattened against his head and he scrunched himself as small as he could. The air swished and fluttered the edge of the curtain as the bathroom door opened, but no one came in.

"It's your imagination, Stu."

Zero recognised this voice. The Guardswoman who was the inside sen on the job. His master had made him spy on her for almost six weeks as she infiltrated the supposed coven. *How did I miss three sanguimancers joining them?* The ache in his bones was psychosomatic, but also a warning. His blood would be the ink in which lessons would be learnt. He'd failed his master, but his master was kind. Zero would be taught to do better next time.

The door closed with a loud click. *Great. Shut in. No one better want a shower.* He eyed the taps with distaste and distrust. *You know what you did,* he hissed at them in his head.

Waiting until everyone assembled and night fell was tediousness interspersed with the occasional few minutes of gut-tightening terror of being caught—everyone apparently had a horrible bladder and needed the toilet as soon as they arrived. The time to groom made him less itchy but it wasn't fun. Boredom was one of Zero's least favourite things and a little bit of him wished to get caught just for something to do. But that would aggrieve his master and he would have to undergo further training in 'how to stay still' and similar. Boring *and* ouchie. He would've preferred a cupboard where he could pull down clothes and make a cosy den in the back corner, but the tub was clean, dry, and nothing was actively trying to hurt him so long as he remained unnoticed. Zero concluded it could be worse.

When the air sharpened and time stretched, he knew the ritual had begun. The last person through shut the bathroom door, so he risked a small portal to return to the top of the cupboard. Crouched low, still but for the twitching at the tip of his tail, Zero watched.

Seven humans stood at the points of the star and an eighth in the middle. Zero added unsanctioned human sacrifice to the list of crimes the magic users were potentially committing. As they were not documented in his master's annals, any magic they did was a crime, but blood magic and death magic were far worse than something small like a protection spell. His mind shied away from the implication that his master *did* sanction some human sacrifices.

Magic gleamed in the air like threads of rainbow wire tying the witches to each other and the spell. The seven around the edge each held a copper bowl of their own blood. Their chant was nonsensical but key words wrote themselves in the magic as they tumbled from witless lips. Within the trap of a fake spell, real magic knocked on the air, and something answered. The modified spell gleamed as the casters dripped blood over the salt. Zero was relieved none of them noticed his changes, although it reinforced his concerns about powerful idiots.

The last drop of blood saturated the salt, and the chanters fell silent. The star glowed. All of it, not merely the parts Zero adjusted. He cursed in cat. It shouldn't be possible. It wasn't real magic.

The world held its breath. One second. Two. Then the screaming started.

And then it stopped.

Screams echoed through the forest like the screech of out-of-tune violin strings. They ricocheted between trees as if the terror emanated from the knotted bark. They scattered the gelatinous orbs crowding Harper and sliced her skin like whirling shuriken. She hunkered down, hands over her ears. Tears froze on her cheeks. *Please wake up. Please wake up.* But a part of her didn't want to let go. She buried her fingers deep in her ears. Fear scrambled her brain and froze her bones. *Please stop. Please make it stop.*

The screaming cut off abruptly. It left her breathless, though the screams hadn't been hers. Had they? It hurt to swallow.

Something snapped closed around her neck. It tightened deep, scraping against cartilage. Nails cut into flesh as she clawed at a non-existent noose. They'd caught her. The forest above darkened. Each breath took more effort until, energy spent, she could draw no more. Her hands dropped to the ground. Her head lolled back. Eyes closed.

In the moment of peace, the noose vanished, but she didn't gasp for air. Harper lay on the moist grass, chest still, and let herself die. Fighting never helped. Maybe death would bring her home.

Her whole body juddered, like someone slammed on the brakes in a car doing seventy, only she hadn't been moving. Harper opened her eyes. Snow hung in the air, a twinkling mirror of the night sky above. Time had braked, not movement. Then the snow fell upwards and gathered into clouds until the stars and moon vanished. A light sprinkling of it remained on the ground.

Flakes of ice crunched underfoot like slivers of bone as Harper climbed the tree-clad hill. She didn't know when she'd stood, the dream blinking time back and forth, broken and incongruous. Footprints ran down the hill the other way as though she'd walked this path before.

Harper's consciousness drifted somewhere higher than her body while at the same time sitting behind her eyes. The Harper up in the sky knew Heresy was supposed to protect her from these dreams and her premonitions of the Hiding should now be over. The Harper behind her eyes knew none of this. The Harper behind her eyes was scared.

She clutched her arms around her, drawing the wafting material of a white cotton dress tight around her too-thin frame. Bare feet caught on jagged rocks and twigs. Drips of red marred pristine snow. Blood pooled in the descending footsteps. Harper held one foot over them. Same size. Same shape. But going the wrong way. She resumed her trudge up a Sisyphean hill. Her soul grew heavier as she plodded on. *Don't go back. Don't go back. Don't go back.*

The straining song of a violin blew the beat of words away. It tugged at her soul like the music floating down the Ouse had done a few days earlier. Louder here, the dream told her she was closer to its source. Almost close enough to touch if she but wished it hard enough …

CHAPTER FIVE

Shaken to the Core

The crash of shattering glass woke Harper. She sat bolt upright, arm extended, fist tight. "I had it. I had it," she whispered, wide-eyed. "Please, God. I had it." Whether she believed in her sister's deity didn't matter. At that moment, she needed Her. "Please give it back. Please." But if God answered, the answer was …

"No." A silken smooth voice slithered around her neck and into her ear. "You do not need to go so far as to deify me, Harper dearest. My magic may be far superior to yours, but that is no excuse for blasphemy. Tut tut. What would Graceless say?"

"Heresy, shut up." Harper slapped the self-proclaimed deception demon off her shoulder. She tucked her legs up and cocooned herself in a blanket. Head on her knees, she swallowed a sob. Hairs on her arm prickled. Heresy was little more than a ball of static soot in his natural form and his reassuring pats tickled.

"As appalling as some of your magic is, bringing this *book* home may be one of your most ill-advised actions to date. Rather impressive." Heresy said the word 'book' as though the offending tome were covered in slime.

"What are you talking about?" Harper raised red-rimmed eyes.

A tendril of smoke waved towards her bedside table where the book Alfred entrusted to her lay open. It had taken three days of fretting for her to work up the courage to unlatch it. The results had been anticlimactic, so she'd used her Sight.

"Magic made me fall asleep?" Harper glanced out the window. It was dark already but that didn't mean it was late, the winter solstice had been less than a month ago.

"You said the archive gremlin warned you," Heresy said in his 'I told you so' tone.

"Don't call him that." Harper glared at him. "He warned me to be careful with it and not to go to sleep. How on earth would he know to warn me not to use magic on it? Especially passive magic. If he knew to warn me of that, I would've been arrested already." Harper stretched then rolled her shoulders. It wasn't Heresy's fault she'd been stuck in that nightmare again. It wasn't his fault that—

"You woke me up!"

"Of course I awoke you, Sleeping Unbeauty. I have told you many times before, you do not want to be caught by the thing hunting your dreams. This book took you closer to it."

Fear and hope warred in Harper's chest, prickly as heartburn. "This book is about other realms adjacent to or overlapping ours, despite the Veil and over four hundred years of history disputing it. Does that mean the thing hunting me is in a realm next to ours?"

"Sometimes you are the stupidest witch I have ever met."

Harper bit her tongue. Maybe Heresy didn't have eyes because his sarcastic comments had been accompanied by so many eyerolls that they'd permanently disappeared into his cloud-of-ash body. After taking a deep breath so she could force herself to speak evenly, she asked, "What am I missing, Heresy?"

"A very significant word."

"Please, Heresy?" Harper couldn't keep the exasperation out of her tone.

"What do you think the dreamscape is, dearest seer?"

"Well, normally it's a manifestation of subconscious, sleeping thoughts, right? And when I have a vision, it's a magical projection of an event."

"You sound so very certain of that." A white-fanged Cheshire Cat grin split Heresy's body.

"Are you saying dreams are a different realm?"

"Are you saying they are not?"

Before Harper could formulate an academic argument, a tremor rippled through the room. Books fell with a loud thud and the pencil holder on her desk rattled.

"Was that you, Heresy?" Harper clutched at the bed. She pointed at the broken glass littering the floor. "You broke the vase to wake me up, right? Am I being so dumb that you need to break more things?" *And since when can you shake the house?*

Heresy's grin faded. He rolled closer to Harper and tucked himself behind her ankles. "That was not me. The thing that hunts you in the dreamscape is near."

Harper leapt out of bed, tugged on slippers so she didn't get stabbed by broken glass, slammed the book shut, and shoved it in a drawer. "What the heck, Heresy? It's attacking the house?"

A door slammed downstairs followed by AJ's muffled cursing and Saqib's laughter. The familiar sounds grated. *Didn't they feel that?*

"Harper?" Saqib shouted up as though nothing untoward were happening. "Grace? You home yet?"

"I'm here," Harper called back. *What do I tell him?* She scooped Heresy up in the palms of her hands and held him at face level. "What do I do? It knows my address? What's powerful enough to find me in a dream and then try to knock the house down?"

Heresy poked her nose. "It has not found you and I doubt the buffoons downstairs noticed a thing. It is like … what is the crude thing you humans do? Carpet bombs. The hunter showers the area with attacks in the hopes one will hit you, but they don't react to anyone else. Close enough to affect your belongings, but not other sentients. Not other than me since we have a blood pact. Now you are fully awake and the book is closed, it seems to have ceased its assault. Still, I shall increase the concealment spells around the house. It cannot follow you in the wakening. None but the most powerful dreamwalkers could do that. You should be safe enough out there, but do not sleep near this tome again."

"Come down. I've found something interesting," Saqib called.

"Coming," she shouted back. "Heresy, if it can attack the house, maybe it *is* a powerful dreamwalker."

"If it were, then it would not have to resort to such crass magic." Heresy dismissed her concerns before he dribbled between her fingers and sank through the floorboards. Harper hoped he was doing as he said and increasing the protections on the house. She clattered downstairs to find Saqib elbow-deep in the fridge selecting vegetables for dinner. When she opened her mouth to tell him what happened, the words stuck in her throat. *Heresy said he couldn't feel it. Why scare him when the thing wants me? If they don't know, they can't stop me if it turns out to be the only way home.*

Harper buried the thought before it finished running across her brain. It was hunting her. But the dreams Heresy warned against were the sole glimpse she'd ever had of the road home, a path witnessed through her premonitions about the Hiding. In a way, it had been a relief that stopping the ritual took away the choice of pursuing them. Now it seemed she was mistaken: the visions of her forgotten past could be accessed in other ways. She bit her lip and decided to keep it a secret unless it threatened the others. At least until she'd had time to make a rational decision. Heresy said they were safe for now.

"What did you find?" She popped the kettle on then sat at the table, watching Saqib chop up cauliflower while onions fried and potatoes boiled. "Anything about Agnes?"

"It's tricky to perform a thorough investigation, because of course the Council doesn't want the Guard to know where the body was found. The archbishop let me have a look at the cataloguing hall, but there's so much there, it's hard to tell if any of the uncatalogued items were involved. I couldn't find any evidence of tampering to gain access though. Since a lot of the security is electronic, I recommended AJ take a look, but he's wary of entering the archives. I pointed out that if you can go undetected he should be fine, but he's still not said he'll go. Anyway, the medical report indicates Agnes's lividity hadn't changed so she was most likely killed where you found her. Liver temperature indicated she hadn't been dead long, even accounting for her being somewhere chilled."

Harper pulled her knees up against her chest, heels balanced on the edge of her chair. "Do you think they might've still been there when I"— she swallowed the lump wedged in her spine—"when I got there?"

Saqib froze. "Don't dwell on ifs, Harp." The *thunk, thunk, thunk* of chopping resumed. "We have enough to deal with. Anyway, in her case it's more like what I didn't find. No writing. I checked using all the methods we used before on the Ouse's victims but there was no writing around Agnes's eyes. I expected to see the same as on the woman you found in the tree."

She nodded but his words did nothing to settle her heart or warm her goosed arms. "What did you find?"

"Since Agnes was on holiday, we're not sure exactly when or where she disappeared from. I've been looking at CCTV from around the cathedral on her last day working and on the evening you found her. Grab the stills out of my bag. The photos of the cataloguing chamber are in there as well." He jerked his chin towards a rucksack tossed on another of the kitchen chairs.

Harper withdrew a stack of photos. "What am I looking at?"

"Use your Sight," Saqib suggested. "I know you couldn't use it at the scene with so many people there. I'm curious to see if it picks up anything unusual, whether it's related to what I found or not. I couldn't do much with the CCTV, but I've tried some different ways of taking and developing the photos from the vault. Nothing popped as supernatural to my eyes, even stuff we know is supe stuff. But maybe it's like the lights that let you see the Ouse and the combination of our talents will reveal something."

"You make me sound like a science project." Harper smiled but inside doubt twisted through her. The scent of pine hung in the air despite the aromas of roasting spices, and the chill of snow seeped between her toes. Nonetheless, she summoned the magic, fire roaring behind her retinas as she flicked through the pictures. When she looked up, Saqib hastily turned back to his prep, pretending he hadn't been watching the strange violet glimmer of her gaze.

Unexpectedly, Harper could See flickers of lilac light around some of the cases. Saqib was closer to detecting magic with his tech than she'd thought. Harper wasn't sure if that was a good thing or not. While it would undoubtedly be useful for their cause, it could be disastrous if the police, let alone the Guard, discovered it.

She turned her attention to the CCTV stills. At first there was nothing, then a bright spot caught her attention. The white tufted ears made her squint, bringing the photos closer.

"You noticed the cat too?" Anxiety strained Saqib's tone. He so desperately wanted his experiments to work. And to solve the case, Harper acknowledged out of fairness to her friend.

"Yes. I also saw a white cat near the cathedral the next day, so it might live near there. Are you sure it isn't Heresy?" Harper squinted at the photo again. He was probably settled in the peephole of the front door, strengthening the illusions around the house. Even if she did ask him, she didn't trust him to give an honest answer.

"Certain. A white cat has also shown up in CCTV footage near two other disappearances elsewhere in Yorkshire. Not all the disappearances of late are related, but I'm starting to think these are linked. At the time of one of the kidnappings I know exactly where Heresy was because he was playing a computer game with AJ and me. We think the cat might belong to whomever took the women."

"AJ let Heresy near a computer?" Harper raised an eyebrow. The techno-witch and the spirit didn't get along. If Heresy couldn't find a cat to inhabit, his next favourite haunt was a computer. He especially enjoyed messing with AJ's, but thus far AJ was winning the rivalry.

"It's good to have an extra person in the squad. They're getting used to each other, so long as Heresy doesn't try to break game physics too much."

"You said you think two of the other disappearances are linked to Agnes's murder?" Harper circled back.

"I've received the physical evidence and footage this morning. Two women who were missing for two weeks then found dead. It took a bit for the police to ask me to help so either the supernatural element wasn't clear right away, or they didn't want to admit it."

"What is the supernatural element?" Harper asked.

"I haven't received the autopsy reports for these two yet, just crime scene photos and some trace physical evidence. I'm being politely blocked by the Guard, but as the Chief asked me to investigate, there must be a suspicion of supernatural activity, at least."

"Do you think they're …" The words clogged Harper's throat and she struggled to breathe. "Do you think they're also missing organs? Like the others from the Hiding ritual last year?"

Saqib stiffened, then he took a deep breath and his shoulders slumped. "Those people weren't missing for days beforehand, but yeah, that's what I'm afraid of."

They were interrupted by Saqib's phone buzzing on the table. Harper snatched it up before it could vibrate itself off the edge. "Doctor Siddique's phone, who's calling please?"

His back was to her, Saqib's shoulders shook with silent laughter at her prim and proper telephone voice.

"Hello. Is that Ms. Ashbury? It's Detective Derek Wright."

"Hi, Derek. Saqib's been filling me in on the other murders. Have you got an update on the case? Can I put you on speaker?"

After gaining his consent, Harper put the phone on loudspeaker and placed it on the countertop next to Saqib. She pulled herself onto the counter, heels drumming a muffled beat against the cabinet as she listened in.

"What's going on, Derek?" Saqib paused his prep work.

"I'm at the Grand Hotel. I think you should get down here."

"Another missing woman?"

"What missing woman?" Grace walked in, shaking her hair free of raindrops as she draped her coat over the back of a chair and nudged it towards the radiator.

Harper put a finger to her lips and pointed at the phone.

"Go on, Derek," Saqib said. "It's just my housemate. She's a De Santos, you can speak freely in front of her."

"Oh … well … um … yes. Nice to meet you, Ms. De Santos."

Harper rolled her eyes while Grace smirked. She could never get used to the mix of awe and fear Grace's family name invoked, although Grace was always quick to use it to their advantage.

"In answer to your question, Saqib, I don't know," Detective Wright continued. "There's definitely something missing. I don't like to say too much over the phone. Get down here before the real crime scene techs show up. I guarantee you'll want to see this and I have a feeling your brand of forensics is going to be more useful."

With that, he hung up. The three housemates exchanged a glance.

"Guess dinner's cancelled again." Grace frowned.

Saqib threw the already prepped vegetables into the slow cooker. He grabbed a tin of tomatoes and placed it next to the uncut veg and the spice mix. "AJ will have to finish it off. Grab your stuff, we better get going. I'll grab my emergency kit."

Fifteen minutes later, the three of them reassembled in the kitchen, Harper and Grace with a variety of weapons, from Harper's machete to Grace's crossbow. Saqib was laden with three large bags of scientific equipment and a tripod strapped across his back.

As they struggled to manoeuvre Saqib's stuff out the door, a velvet voice piped up from the peephole. "Are you going anywhere fun? May I attend? The house is sufficiently protected with AJ staying behind and the wards we set up."

"There will be police there, Heresy," Saqib replied. "Maybe Guard too. Best you steer clear, mate."

The door harrumphed at them, wisps of smoke escaping from the peephole as Heresy pouted. Harper was grateful for the small porch and the fact their house faced York's ancient wall rather than a lace-twitching neighbour.

"You can come." Harper ignored the incredulous looks from the other two. "Just stay out of sight. If we need to hide something magical, you can help."

"This is a bad plan." Grace closed the door with more force than necessary. "A very bad plan."

CHAPTER SIX

Bloodbath

It wasn't a long walk, but with all of Saqib's equipment, the lingering drizzle, and the likelihood of coming home after curfew, they drove a route convoluted by bus lanes and one-way systems to park a couple of blocks from the largest hotel in the city centre. It wasn't a place Harper anticipated trouble. The Guard paid close attention to places where rich folk stayed. What was also strange was the darkness. The streetlamps were out as well as every light in the hotel. Harper clung to Grace's hand.

"What's going on, Wendy?" Saqib asked a grim-faced police officer standing at the black-and-yellow caution tape. The blue-and-red flashing lights of police cars were some relief to Harper although they made the shadows jump and flicker as though hiding lurking creatures.

"Bad shit." Wendy waved them under. "Got a 999 call a little after curfew, concerns of a fight, so the local guys showed up. They called it in to us. It's a bloody mess, Saqib, no pun intended. You have to see it yourself. It's weird. Derek's waiting for you inside."

"Thanks, Wendy." Saqib gave them a smile as the trio headed into the hotel. "Top floor, right?"

"That's it. Good luck." Wendy saw them off with a curt nod.

The lift was inoperable so they hefted Saqib's gear up the service stairs. Even the emergency lights were off—the only illumination came from the torches they carried. The bag over Harper's shoulder banged against the railing. She bit her lip, swallowing a yelp. Every nerve fizzled, telling her to defend, to run. Her clammy palms gave no purchase on the smooth banister. The static of Heresy on the back of her neck didn't help. She clenched her jaw and climbed higher, cursing the lack of light.

Grace put herself at the front, as usual, and pushed the door open. Light trickled down the stairs. With it came the smell of blood. Despite the magically enhanced stench, Harper was relieved to reach their destination—the police had set up several large lights running off a portable generator and the area was almost as bright as daylight.

At the top of the stairs, Saqib opened his bag and removed gloves, hairnets and shoe covers, and passed them out to Harper and Grace. Derek was waiting down the corridor. When he saw Saqib, a thin smile twitched his mouth before disappearing again.

"Hey, Derek." Saqib shook his hand, then gestured towards the closed door of room 505. "In there?"

"Yeah." Derek wiped his brow on the sleeve of his suit.

"Nice to see you again, Derek." Harper clasped his sweaty hand before putting on her gloves. Grace gave him a sharp nod.

"I wish it were under better circumstances," the detective said. "You know the rules. Chief says you get to check out anything really odd."

"Anyone been in here other than you?" Saqib asked.

"A couple of local officers, the hotel manager-on-duty, the bellhop who called it in. I'll get their details so you can check the database to eliminate their prints."

"Great, great," Saqib muttered, only half listening as he got to work. Once he was satisfied there was no further evidence to collect from the hallway or the door itself, he eased down the handle and the door creaked open.

"Blood," Grace said, her jaw tight as the metallic tang became obvious even without magical assistance.

"Yeah, be glad you can't smell it like I can." Harper gritted her teeth. Behind the scent of iron, she caught something else: a sugary vanilla smell with a tinge of smoke. "Marshmallows?"

"This wasn't some bonfire party gone wrong." Saqib's voice was unusually strained, the door open no more than a few centimetres.

"Saqib, are you alright. You've gone pale as a—"

"Don't say it, Grace," Saqib warned. "Don't say 'ghost.'"

Harper leant around him and pushed the door open farther. It squelched.

Grace silently crossed herself with a trembling hand.

The room beyond was red. Blood red. Here and there a glimpse of opulent wallpaper survived, but not much. Viscoid material slithered down the walls onto the clogged carpet. Dark fluid dripped from the chandelier, its crystals turned to rubies. Frozen, carmine vortices were smeared on the mirrors and television screen. Harper's stomach forced its way up her throat. She closed her eyes, nails dug into her palms to ground herself without taking deep breaths.

"Where are the bodies?" Saqib looked over at Derek who was leaning against the wall watching them.

"There were none."

"You're saying someone walked out of here with several corpses?" Harper asked, unable to tear her eyes away from the scene.

"Or walked in with a huge vat of blood, which seems equally unlikely. But that's Saqib's department, I'm gonna go have a coffee outside." When he reached the stairwell, Derek called back, "Let me know when you're done. Chief wants an update as soon as."

Saqib grimaced. "Right, let's get to it then."

Harper and Grace stood back as he got to work photographing the scene and taking a variety of samples from the blood-soaked room. With Derek gone, Heresy oozed through Harper's hair to sit on her shoulder. He bristled with excitement, sending small shocks down Harper's spine until she shrugged him off.

"Do you think someone brought in bags of some blood-like substance and exploded it to make a scene?" Grace asked hopefully.

Saqib held up a vial. "The test is positive for haemoglobin, so this is definitely blood, although I'll have to get it back to the lab to find out if it's human. If they had exploded a central mass, like from a bag of blood, there would be a void left by the culprit. This is pretty evenly doused everywhere."

"If someone died here surely there would be more than just blood." Ignoring the churning of her stomach, Harper peered closer at the wall nearest to her. She was very glad the detective called *before* dinner. She wasn't sure she'd want any when they got back, especially not the blazing red curry Saqib had started. It would be a while before she could eat tomato soup too.

"Normally I'd say 'yes,'" Saqib said. "With this much blood loss and no corpse, I would expect to find other fragments of human remains. There's also no pattern to this blood. If someone slit their throat, for example, there would be splatter patterns."

"Really, Saqib." Grace's skin had a green tinge. "Do you have to say 'splatter'? Euch." With a grunt, Grace disappeared back down the corridor.

"Such a weak stomach, dear Graceless." Heresy chortled.

"For once, I agree with him." Saqib raised an eyebrow. "A vet and a De Santos repulsed by a bit of blood?"

Harper clenched her fist over her stomach. "This is not 'a bit of blood.' She's fine when she can do something. Fight something. Heal something. But as soon as the action is gone, she turns green. Could there be patterns, but there's just too much blood to see them?"

"This blood is too smooth." Saqib pointed at the wall. "It's almost like it was poured on. You try." He turned off his equipment and stepped back.

Harper took a deep breath, and instantly regretted it. Summoning her Sight, she surveyed the room. "There's something. It's hard to make out under all this blood. Pass me a pencil and pad?"

Saqib handed over his notebook. Harper's eyes never wavered from the scene before her as she sketched until she glanced down at the floor for the first time.

"Saqib."

His head snapped up at her shocked whisper. "What is it?"

"Step back."

Saqib backed up until he was almost touching the wall. "What?"

"That's a banishing circle, I did a course on how to recognise transportation magic at uni, plus Heresy's been teaching me. I don't know what it's supposed to banish but based on all this blood I'd guess something bad. Why would someone transport something to a hotel to banish it? Why not do it wherever the thing already was? Seems risky." Harper continued sketching as if her hand had a mind of its own. "Do you recognise it, Heresy?"

"The specifics? No. Overall? Some. For all it is ornate, it is but a minor spell. Most of the drawing is superfluous, although in those parts there are elements of summoning. They should have done nothing, but it is peculiar. We may have found someone who is a sloppier witch than you, Harper. Or should I say, 'was'?"

"All this blood doesn't mean it's a higher-level magic?" Harper asked.

"Most of the blood is post-magic. It happened after the spell was completed." Heresy *hmmed* a bit, then added, "There is blood magic present under all this mess. Powerful idiots." He snorted.

"Saqib, could the casters have survived losing this much blood?" Harper checked dubiously.

"*If* this is human blood, then they're dead. There's too much blood here for even a dozen people to have contributed to it and survived."

"Whatever they intended to banish may have escaped." The spirit drifted closer, keeping one tendril wrapped around Harper's wrist as he suspended himself over the ritual. "It should not be possible for this to have summoned something, but it should also not have been possible for Harper to summon me. When the circle opened to banish whatever they were getting rid of, something else may have forced its way back through. Like a very large cat through a very small hole."

"A *homicidal* cat. I can't see anything." Saqib fiddled with his lights, trying different wavelengths without success. "Damn, and I thought I had something when we could see the Ouse's runes."

"You would not," Heresy scoffed. "It's been drowned in blood. Drawn in blood, activated by blood, closed by blood."

"So why the fright?" Saqib breathed a sigh of relief. "If it's closed now …"

"It doesn't mean it won't reopen," Harper cautioned. "If it does, heaven knows where it'll send you. I've been practicing—"

"And failing."

"Shut up, Heresy," she snarled. "I've been practicing and I know it's not open, but I don't think it's locked, based on what I studied at uni. The circle's still there, beneath the death."

"This is a seven-pointed star." Heresy balled up on Harper's shoulder again, then waved a tentacle of soot. "They would have stood here, here, here, seven summoners, all offering their blood to open this circle."

As he pointed, Harper Saw glimmering figures dressed in white, ghostly outlines waving their arms, lips moving in a silent chant. She spoke as if in a trance as she walked around the edge of the room. "I can See their shadows. I … I recognise one of them. Edith. She was in my class at uni. It was a small class; few people are permitted to study occult and supernaturals. She wanted to join the Guard."

"Guess you didn't stay in touch," Saqib said.

Harper's eyes flicked back and forth, searching for small clues as the vision unfolded before her. "They each held a basin of blood. There's one person in the centre. They look human. The one they intended to banish, maybe? The person doesn't seem to be fighting it. The circle opened. Something came out. Something …"

Saqib wrapped an arm around Harper's waist as she stumbled. She gulped oxygen, faint and dizzy, a great weight on her chest. Her eyes darted around the room, seeking the darkness that disrupted her vision.

"Harper, what is it?"

"Something came through. They didn't banish the person in the middle they … they …" She clenched her fist over her mouth and leant heavily on Saqib.

"Let's step out a sec and—"

"No." It came out sharper than intended. "Sorry. No. I need to See the rest."

Twisting her fingers through her hair, and with Saqib's arm around her waist, Harper surveyed the room again. The vision played out slower this time. A hulking shadow appeared in the centre of the star, though all the rules of magic Harper knew said it shouldn't be there. In a matter of moments, it had seven of the eight humans trapped in its muscular arms. The eighth arm reached for Edith. Who wasn't there.

Harper had lost track of her in the seconds it took the demon to gather its prey. Her attention snapped back to it as lightning crackled and humans screamed. Their bodies charred, consumed by the grasping fingers of electricity. Their flesh flaked away to be absorbed by the demon's body. A dazzling flash of lightning blinded Harper and a thunderous clap of silence sucked in their screams. In less than a minute, they were gone.

The demon spun, seeking prey. Its face was visible for the first time: part bird, part snake, just as its body was part human, part winged beast.

Harper bit her fist to hold back nausea and terror. She had to See where it went. It would be up to her and Grace to prevent it finding more victims. It took a step towards her and Saqib, and Harper backed away on instinct. Heresy chuckled, unable to see her vision, just her reactions. As the demon's foot touched the centre of the star, the magic glowed silver and turquoise. Harper squinted as the brilliant light overwhelmed her Sight. When the glow faded, the demon had vanished.

Harper leant her head back to stretch the tension out of her neck. "It's gone. I don't know where, but the thing that killed these folks is gone."

Saqib half slumped against her in palpable relief.

"I could have told you the demon was no longer in the room," Heresy huffed.

Harper looked over the scene again. Near the back of the room, the vision-remnant of her classmate stood again. She stared straight at Harper and Saqib as though she knew they would be there. Midnight hair flowed to her waist. Her white robes were splattered with gore. Blood leaked from black cavities where her eyes had once been. Harper blinked and the woman disappeared.

"C'mon, Heresy." Harper spoke without looking, fixated on the spot where Edith had stood. "Let's make sure this thing is locked before anything else comes through or disappears. Maybe we can suss out where that demon was banished to, and by whom."

"Your command is my wish, dear Harper." Heresy lengthened and gave her a mock bow.

It was the wee hours of the morning before Harper, Grace, Saqib, and Heresy saw home again. They collapsed in the kitchen for tea and a late-night snack.

"It was so disgusting." Grace mimed retching. "All blood and gore and ick."

"I'll see if I can find out what it was in the archives," Harper said. "Unless Saqib finds something first."

"I'll let you know when I get the lab results. I'm going in early tomorrow."

"We should head to bed then." Harper yawned.

"It's bedtime already?" A messy-haired young man walked into the kitchen and tossed a silver envelope onto the table before making himself a cup of coffee. The other three stopped and stared at the crossed halberds under a gilt crown embossed on the envelope.

"When did this arrive?" Harper forced the words through dry lips.

"Not long after you left. Must've been hand-delivered." AJ glanced at the three around the table, all staring at the envelope still. "No big deal, right? Aren't you working with them? If they knew what we were, they wouldn't've sent a polite letter, they'd've bashed the door in."

"True." Saqib drew out the word. "Trrrruuuuue."

"It's not a good sign." Grace ripped the envelope open and a single sheet fell out.

Dear Ms. Ashbury,

Please attend at Fulford Road Police Station on the morning of January 11th at 9 a.m. as church liaison, as appointed by Archbishop Simon Marshall.

With utmost sincerity,

Lieutenant Cecily Albrecht

On behalf of Her Majesty the Queen's Personal Guard

"That's the woman who interviewed you last month, isn't it?" Grace tapped the name at the bottom.

Harper nodded, the letter's contents doing little to relieve her fears.

"Good. You might learn something. Just be careful with your eyes. Wonder if they're going to ask you to hunt something."

"I hope not," Harper said fervently.

"Aww, but it might give you an excuse to go to A&E." Grace's face sparkled with a wicked grin.

"Why would I *want* to go to … *Gray!*"

"Still trying to set her up?" Saqib tore his eyes from the envelope. "Even though she stood that nurse up, what, three times now?"

"Yeah. That's the one. Think she may have blown her opportunity there, but he's still the only opportunity she's had in months." Grace leant back and smirked.

Harper sighed. "It's not a big deal, Grace. There are ethics about going out with patients anyway, and we're there so much I don't think we could date even if I didn't have to keep cancelling." She tapped the envelope. "This is more—"

Grace grinned as she cut her off. "Fretting about that letter doesn't change anything. You haven't had a steady boyfriend since uni. He's cute. He likes you."

"But he might have been put off by the fact she's been to A&E three times in as many months," Saqib argued with a mischievous grin of his own. "And your inability to actually get to a date."

Harper threw up her hands in disgust. "You two gossip like fishwives. I am not going out with Theo. End of story. I'm lucky if he doesn't want to stab me himself. I'm going to bed. AJ doesn't care, do you?"

Having made his coffee, AJ looked over at them, a frown creasing his brow. "Don't care about what?"

"Exactly. Goodnight, I'll leave you to it."

"Did I miss something?" AJ asked as Harper left.

"Mate, you really need to leave your room now and then."

AJ glanced at Harper's red-specked shoes by the back door, Grace's greyish hue, and the deep circles under Saqib's eyes. "Nah. I'm good."

As the sun rose, Zero curled up in a patch of weak light that fell across the foot of his master's bed. He licked his paws mechanically, too tired to flinch as his tongue rasped over deep cuts. It was inexcusable to have messed up the banishment circle at the hotel. Almost inconceivable that something had come through. A banishing circle and a summoning circle couldn't exist in the same place. They couldn't. Yet something had come through and someone disappeared.

He'd watched seven humans die. Two witches, five mundanes. His changes should've meant the witches were transported to the dungeons in his master's castle. Instead, they'd been consumed by a creature of blood and electricity. That he'd been able to activate the banishment spell himself and send the creature to his master was a small relief. Aside from the imperative command that anything new be brought in, the thought of what such a creature might have done if left to run amok terrified him more than the pain of his subsequent lessons.

A shiver poofed Zero's fur. A muted mewl escaped as pain scrunched him in on himself again. He licked his paw on autopilot, cleaning blood magic wounds. His master was right to make him practice drawing banishing circles. Again. And again. And again. Until he worked out what he did wrong. Which he hadn't. Zero screwed his eyes shut. It would all start again once his body recovered enough. He had to learn. Failure was unacceptable. Seven people died because of it and the eighth …

What did happen to the eighth? The woman who'd come in first, 'Edie' the man called her, young with raven hair and shadowed eyes. The Guard spy. The demon hadn't killed her, Zero was certain. As certain as he was that she was the third witch. *A Guard witch?* Another impossibility. Where had she gone?

A foot nudged him through silk sheets. His master's multi-tonal voice was quiet, the echoes of others reduced to a background buzz as they prepared for sleep, yet zir disappointment still cut deep. "Zero, your mind is too loud. Cease your mewling and hissing. Go to sleep. It does not behove little cats to be so noisy. You have much learning to do later."

Zero swallowed a whine at his master's irritated tone. Dragging himself on his belly, he crawled up the sheets to lean against his master's chest. Metal-tipped fingers furrowed the fur down his back.

"There, there, my pet. I will help you. We shall practice for as long as we must. I shall be with you."

His master's arm wrapped around him and an unspoken command zinged through Zero's collar. *Stay here. Don't move. I have you.*

Content that he was safe from the horrors of demons, humans, and the outside world, Zero drifted into a sore and uneasy sleep. He limped through the dreamscape, ostensibly searching for powerful dreams or nightmares that might return him to his master's good books, but in his heart he looked for something else. The pretty arty human's dream was waiting and he sank into it, a sense of true safety settling his soul.

CHAPTER SEVEN

A Nest of Snakes

"Good morning, Lieutenant Albrecht." Harper tried to keep the quiver out of her voice as she leant around the office door and gave a small wave. The woman behind the desk gestured to an empty chair. "Good morning, Ms. Ashbury. Please, take a seat." The warmth in her voice didn't reach her hazel eyes and her grey-streaked hair was pulled back in a bun so tight her face stretched as she gave a crocodile smile.

Harper blinked, hoping the burning in her own eyes was imagined. She squinted as she sat, trying to adjust to the bright light behind the Guardswoman. Mists avoided the wall-length window as though even the weather was wary of the lieutenant. "How can I be of assistance?"

Albrecht raised an eyebrow. "Straight to business." She folded pink-nailed fingers together on the desk as she leant forward. "We wish to know the progress of your investigation into the disappearance and subsequent murder of Agnes Clark. You were the one to find the body, after all, and given our previous discussion, I know you are more than happy to share your findings with us."

Harper rolled her shoulders as a shiver trickled down her back. Their previous conversation had been in an interrogation room and she'd feared herself discovered until the Guardswoman's unexpected offer of cooperation. Not that either of them believed the cooperation was honest and open.

"I did. I was heading to the cathedral to drop off some research materials." A little truth to hide a bigger lie. She stuck to the story she'd concocted with the archbishop. "I saw Agnes sitting on a bench and she was all slumped over so I went to check on her. I thought she'd fallen asleep waiting for the bus. When I shook her shoulder, her body fell to the side and I saw her eyes. There wasn't anyone else around, but Doctor Siddique said the coroner confirmed she'd not long been dead."

"You were very lucky."

"Yes." Harper held her gaze in an attempt to channel some of Grace's arrogant authority. After over a decade living with De Santoses, she still hadn't gotten the knack of it.

"What have you discovered since?"

"Other than what's in the coroner's report, not much." *I'm working on a theory the killer got into the archives via another realm and I'm studying a book on the matter, but I can't exactly tell you that.* "As I'm sure you're aware, Doctor Siddique has not been able to detect anything supernatural and the writing from the previous similar victim is missing. Possibly, I interrupted before the ritual was completed. There's nothing in Agnes's personnel file indicating any enemies, and her friends and family have no reason to suspect anyone either. She'd not mentioned any brush with the supernatural. Her job at the cathedral is to catalogue books brought in and note what kind of destruction should be used. Fire, mostly, but some have to be disposed of in other ways. It's possible something she catalogued cursed her, but no other archivist has gone missing and her injuries are too similar to the murders last year for that to be probable. Saqib is looking into two other disappearances that might be related but is struggling to get unredacted files. Maybe that's something you can help with?"

"I shall see what can be done." The lieutenant made a quick note. "And you yourself have seen nothing unusual?"

The choice of words caused Harper's eye to spasm. She covered it with an unconvincing sneeze. "Nothing at the cathedral or related to Agnes's death."

"What about last night?"

Harper shuddered at the memory. "As far as I know, that isn't related. The demon that killed those people has returned to where it came from, as best I can tell. If it was loose, I'm sure we would've heard by now."

"Very well. Please keep us appraised on your investigation into Mrs. Clark's death and don't make us summon you in. I expect more progress on our next update."

Harper stood, dismissed, then paused. "Actually, I have a question for you."

The Guardswoman raised an eyebrow. "Indeed?"

"Is Edith Moore assigned to York now? I thought I saw her a couple of days ago. I haven't heard from her since we graduated but, if she's in town, it would be nice to catch up."

Albrecht's expression darkened. "Guard Moore was indeed here in York but …" Her lips pursed as she thought, then reached some internal decision. "She has … gone missing. We would appreciate if you kept an eye out, especially if there is a potential serial kidnapper or killer being investigated. A Guardsperson disappearing takes the matter to another level."

Harper bit back a retort, as if a Guard going missing was so much more important than anyone else. "Of course. I'll talk to Saqib." *If you think Edith might be missing, you don't know she was there, unless you're bluffing too.* "Any information you can send over to us, her file for example, would be helpful. With the meticulous records you keep, it might give us a break in the case."

The Guardswoman's jaw tightened. "I'll see what I can do. I trust you will be discreet in this matter. It would not do for people to believe the Guard vulnerable. It may cause panic."

Harper kept her expression bland until after she'd left the room. The Guard wanted to seem impervious to all supernatural harm and trickery and it had nothing to do with making people at ease. Fear suited them better. The thought wormed in her gut, lingering even after she left the precinct. Her hands kept drifting to rub her eyes, even though she didn't think she was using magic.

As she walked back to the cathedral, Harper's mind wandered to her nightmare of the day before. The bloodbath at the hotel had driven both the strange dream and the subsequent attack on the house out of her mind, but Albrecht's questions about Agnes brought it all rushing back. The book Alfred gave her could be the key to solving both mysteries.

The next morning, Harper worked from home, pouring over the book Of Realms and Shadows while she was very awake and had a pot of strong coffee to hand. Heresy sat in a fuzzy ball on her bed, his attention riveted on where Harper sat on the floor in hopes the hardwood boards would dissuade her from sleeping.

Harper skimmed through the contents. Each chapter detailed different realms. Some she'd heard of—the mortal realm, Faery, the Otherworld—

although she had believed the latter to be a myth. Others she hadn't realised were realms at all—within the Veil, the dreamscape and the wakening, the Void. Yet others were complete mysteries—Saol Eadrainn, the Inferno, Melltach and Slibhin. The penultimate chapter was labelled simply 'Shadows.' As she reached the end of the list, the final chapter sent a chill down her spine—'Travel Between Realms.'

An ashy tendril snaked over her shoulder to tap chapter seven. "This is where I dwelt before you summoned me, if that word is even applicable for the awkward magic you did."

"Melltach and Slibhin?" Harper's tongue stumbled over the unfamiliar words, assuming them to be Gaelic in origin.

"Lands of the deceitful and sly," Heresy purred, his Cheshire Cat grin wide as ever. "Many who live there are considered 'demonic' by your kind, as though humans are inherently more honest." He huffed a chuckle at the hypocrisy. "Language is such a fickle creature. Once the word meant 'spirit' or 'supernatural being' although we take umbrage at being thought of as unnatural. Human hatred for things beyond their ken and control warped it to mean 'evil' and imply we are against the creator deity, whomever you may believe that to be."

"Heresy, I know all that. May I remind you that you chose 'Heresy' as a moniker?"

He chuckled again and rolled off the bed to sit on her shoulder. "Your sister named me. It is not up to me to disagree with a De Santos on the subject of demons."

"Do you think whoever killed Agnes could've entered the archives in a similar way to how you got here? That would mean someone had to be in the archives performing a summoning spell, wouldn't it?"

"Are you sure Agnes didn't have magical abilities? If she had a book such as this or uttered a spell like you did, she may have drawn something to her inadvertently," Heresy pointed out.

Harper flicked through the book to the final chapter.

While some methods of travel are unique to the point of origin and destination, and are detailed in the relevant chapters, other methods are standard and can be used to cross between most realms unless a barrier is erected.

"Does that mean the Veil is between here and the rest of our world, Faery, and maybe some other realms, but it's not between here and where you came from? If the folk at the cathedral think the Veil separates us from all these realms, then it could explain how someone got through our anti-magic defences. Does it also mean the incursions we fight off aren't breaching the Veil but are from these realms that overlap ours? So the Veil isn't torn it's … circumvented? Like the Maginot Line? Why fight through when you can go around?"

"Be careful, Harper dear, you are at risk of sounding astute." Heresy patted her head causing her hair to frizz. "You did not really believe your paltry spell pierced the Great Barrier Veil that humans put so much faith in, did you?"

"I was somewhat distracted at the time," Harper grumbled under her breath, blushing for not having considered the implications earlier. She took a deep breath, then asked, "Are any of these safe to visit?"

"None are 'safe,' not even the realm which we currently inhabit. There is one you already enter with ease, that the book sent you to before, yet I would not recommend it for the thing hunting you walks there also."

"The dreamscape?" Harper flicked back to that chapter. "You said it would take a powerful dreamwalker to find me in the wakening. Does that mean the thing pursuing me might be a lesser form of dreamwalker? What is a dreamwalker anyway?"

Heresy flicked her ear. "What is your job again?"

"Or I could benefit from the firsthand magical knowledge that's supposed to be the reason you're sticking around." Which probably isn't any more reliable than a human account, but at least I can cross-reference.

"It may be a lesser dreamwalker," Heresy conceded after a long silence. "Or it may be a creature of the dreamscape."

"Which is different how?" Harper asked, pen poised over her notepad.

"One is born here, the other is born there."

"So a dreamwalker is from this realm and physically enters the dreamscape? Could they have travelled through it to kill Agnes?" A more worrying thought struck Harper. "Could they pop out in my bedroom?"

"Dreamwalkers' bodies do not leave this realm any more than your bed is empty when you have a vision." There was a distinct disappointment in Heresy's voice at having to explain something he thought was basic. "They could not 'pop out' in your bedroom nor could they step out of the dreamscape into the cathedral as if through some magical portal. This is why the thing hunting you sends these carpet bombs. It can only have your mind in the dreamscape, and a less-than-focused version of it at that. Not that your wakening focus is good." Heresy snorted. "My magic helps conceal you from it, and something else, possibly whatever made you forget it also hinders its access to you. It seeks you physically, and every time it sees a little more of your mind, it gets closer to following your consciousness back to your body."

Harper's shoulders slumped. It was both a relief and an annoyingly dead end. "Unless someone killed Agnes in her sleep, which I guess is possible, then somehow took her eyes, which I guess isn't, I'd say the dreamscape isn't helpful here." Nonetheless, she rubbed the page between her fingers, tempted to read more. Realising what she was doing, she scolded herself. What kind of archivist rubs pages? She returned to the final chapter, studying the drawings of labyrinths, spells, and rituals.

"I want to find out what happened to Edith too," she said slowly. "That was some kind of banishment circle, but ... that creature came through from somewhere. I was assuming it was from somewhere else in England, or at least a place on Earth where they allow supes, but could it have come from the same place you did? It seems a bit blunt for a deception."

"Most likely it came from Inferno." Heresy poked the book. "See if any of the descriptions on how to access that realm match anything we saw in the hotel."

Harper opened her sketchbook to the relevant pages and sat it next to the book from the archives. She pointed at areas on her sketch she'd already circled with red pen. "Here, here, and here are marks consistent with the banishing spell you taught me, the one that sends something elsewhere in this world. All of this around it is nonsense, as far as I am aware, although some of it has markers of a summoning spell as if someone erased one but didn't remove it all, just enough to invalidate it. But since something did come through, either they didn't do a very good job or there's magic here I'm not familiar with."

"Both ideas have potential," Heresy said.

Harper shot him a glare.

Despite spending hours examining and cross-referencing each diagram, Harper couldn't work out what had happened. The only parts of the spell that were valid were banishing elements. So how had something overridden the banishing circle to let the creature through?

Eyes and mind both tired, she took a break to fix a cup of tea and brought the pot on a tray up to her room. She took her violin out of its case and traced her fingers over the white roses painted on it. Letting her mind wander, she placed the instrument under her chin and played. There was no set piece in her mind, no specific tune to guide her fingers. Allowing the violin to play as it wished often soothed her and allowed her mind to see things it couldn't before. The haunting tune she played was reminiscent of the strains of music flowing down the Ouse, yet she couldn't place why she knew the song. With a sigh, she set the violin aside. It was distracting her, and right now the murders were more important. Finding out how someone breached the cathedral's security was a higher priority than solving an earworm.

"Maybe the creature didn't come through this magic at all," she said to Heresy. "Maybe it was brought here another way." She rubbed her eyes as she returned to looking at the book and her sketch. Her back cracked as she stretched and hastily covered a yawn. Despite putting her violin away, the music lingered. Each blink took longer.

"Harper. You must not sleep with the book."

The sharp shock of static in her ear jolted Harper awake with a curse. She rubbed her jaw, her teeth zinging from Heresy's tentacle poking through to her eardrum.

"Never do that again," she snarled.

Heresy chuckled. "A zap from your familiar is better than being caught by that which hunts you. This book is drawing your mind into the dreamscape. I can hide you in your own dreams, but when you call to it like this, I am powerless to do aught but watch and enjoy the entertainment."

"If it was just funny, you'd let me go to sleep," Harper pointed out. "You don't want to go back to where you came from." She waved a hand at the book. "I wish I could …"

"Could what, Harper dearest? Enact a simple spell?"

"Shush." Harper riffled through the book to the chapter on shadow realms. "It says beings inhabiting shadows over realms can see everything in that realm but can't be perceived or interacted with. A bit like living in a Hiding spell, I guess. Maybe whatever killed Agnes is in a shadow. It came into the archives, left the shadow to kill her, then went back. Our defences couldn't even see it. Entering the dreamscape is dangerous for me, but my best tool in solving this is to try and have a vision. What if I go into a shadow of the dreamscape? So I can see my visions without something in the dream seeing me?"

Heresy's smile faded, a sign he was ruminating, not that Harper had seen it often enough to draw a decisive conclusion.

"If you can find a way to do that, if such a thing exists, then it might work. But the testing would be a great risk."

"You can wake me up again if there's any sign something has perceived me." Harper bubbled with excitement. If this gave her a way to have safe visions, maybe it would also help protect her from human detection.

Maybe it would let her stay in the dream long enough to get to the end and See whatever clues it might offer as to the path home.

Before she could second-guess herself, Harper flipped through the chapter on the dreamscape and the wakening.

"Yes!" Harper held out her fist to Heresy who bumped it with one of his tentacles. "It says a lucid dreamer can manipulate the dreamscape *or a spell can be used to create similar effects if enough about the dream is known*. It goes on to give examples of how this is useful, like controlling repeating nightmares or ensuring you don't wake too early, but it also has a version about making your consciousness invisible so you can watch the dream as if from the outside. If you help me, I think we can adapt that to make it so I only enter a shadow of the dream."

"I shall tolerate you and laugh at the wrong bits allowing you to extrapolate their inadequacy," Heresy corrected.

Harper rolled her eyes. Her teacher would help in the end, no matter what he called it. He had a vested interest in keeping her alive and whole.

There were aspects of the rituals described that reminded Harper of her brief view of the spells in the Hiding tome in the cathedral archives. Although she hadn't been able to read the words, the diagrams of sensory objects like eyes and fingers were similar. Harper tapped a diagram of an eyeball over a labyrinth. "This is the one that talks about not being perceived." She read through the details. Then read them again. *Eyes blind shut*. It *was* a hiding spell. The irony sent a frisson of ice through her.

It took a few days to assemble the necessary items without provoking Guard suspicion, or at least what Heresy claimed were necessary since Harper was avoiding using her Sight on the book after the nightmare and magical carpet bombing that happened last time.

Harper laid out the ingredients of the ritual. Heresy said what something seemed to be was as important as what it was, and this definitely seemed like magic. Every part of her bubbled with anticipation. She was happy with what she'd put together and confident she'd escaped notice. A frisson of doubt muttered, *so is everyone, right up until the sack goes over their head.*

"Focus." Harper pinched her arm. If her mind wandered and this went wrong, Heresy would never let her live it down.

The labyrinth etched in chalk on the floorboards looked good, salt neatly following its lines. White chalk and white salt, as per Heresy's insistence pastels were inappropriate for magic. It meant bland food for a while—the Guard used excessive salt purchasing as 'evidence'—but for a spell this big, Harper was willing to impose minor discomfort on the household.

The sheep's eye in the centre of the labyrinth gave her a baleful stare, its cloudy cornea in strange juxtaposition to the bright eye of the peacock feather she gripped between two fingers. Heresy wanted her to call it a 'wand' but she couldn't quite bring herself to do it. It was just a feather from one of the birds living in the archbishop's garden.

Harper hadn't wanted to ask Saqib why he had a sheep's eyeball. She hoped he had a good excuse ready as to why the lab's inventory was off. She also hoped the spell wouldn't make her invisible to sheep. Not that she encountered many in central York, but it would be weird nonetheless.

Straightening her spine, Harper held her left hand over the eyeball. The sticky sap of hogweed coating it glistened like vitreous humour and made her stomach roll. She swallowed hard. "Ready?"

"About as ready as I can ever be for the disaster that is your magic." Heresy waved a smoky tentacle over the salt. He swelled up, little puffs of static zinging off him, then chuckled, sharp white teeth slicing through his sooty body.

Harper closed her eyes and took a deep breath of the incense-laden air: minty pennyroyal to ward off the evil eye; rosemary, normally used against physical invasion; myrrh for protection against attack. There was always the possibility the pungent mixture was Heresy's idea of a joke.

As Harper breathed in the smoky air, heat expanded in her core. A tingle of anticipation spread over her skin and goosed her bare arms. Her ribs ached as the magic within her inflated, begging to burst free. She'd spent so many hours sitting like this, learning to locate it, learning to contain it. She imagined a thin tendril, like one of Heresy's tentacles, leaking out and travelling through her heart and down her arm to flow into the peacock feather's brilliant eye.

A breeze snuck through a crack in the door, gambling between her toes and tickling her soles.

Harper …

Annoyed, she opened her eyes and glared down at Heresy. "What? What was I doing wrong this time?"

He waved a dozen tentacles in the air. "Nothing. No more than usual. Why did you stop?"

"You said my name."

"I said no such thing. Concentrate."

Static crickled against her foot and she bit her lip to hold back a yelp. It didn't do to provide the little demon with entertainment.

Closing her eyes, she summoned the magic again. In her imagination, it pooled a lurid purple. Even Saqib's equipment couldn't detect it and he'd tried until Harper had fallen asleep with exhaustion.

Just as the book directed, she swept the feather widdershins over the labyrinth. Her hand was chilled as it passed each of the cardinal points, as though she'd brushed up against ice.

Harper …

Ignoring the voice, she made the sweep three times, then returned to the centre. With her other hand, she followed the path of the labyrinth, keeping the dream of the forest in her mind. Her body was heavy yet distant, the same way it felt in the last moments before sleep. Her consciousness looked down at her body, even though it still moved and spoke as if she was in it.

"Eyes blind shut." She Heard it in English but the words her lips formed were unfamiliar. Reaching the centre of the labyrinth, she held her empty hand several inches higher than the eyeball, then clenched her fist. The eye squelched between her fingers. Her palm burned as though she'd grabbed something hot out of the oven. Tears filled her eyes and she clamped her teeth against the pain and the acidic churn of her stomach. It was almost enough to jolt her back into her body, yet it was if a barrier separated two consciousnesses that were both her. Her hovering spirit could See glimmers of lilac magic in the air and Smell pine and farmland. Ghosts of trees bordered her bedroom.

Harper pressed her palm over first her left eye, then her right, grinding the heel against her cheekbones as she repeated the phrase from the ritual. "Eyes blind shut."

More voices filled the room, the cacophony of whispers she remembered from her dreams, repeating, echoing, rebounding. *Eyes blind shut. Eyes blind shut.*

Her eyelids were leaden, eyelashes glued together. Vitreous and aqueous humours slid down her cheek and pooled at the corners of her lips. The heat passed from her palm and into her eyes, far hotter than the burn of Sight. Breaths came sharp and shallow. The fire seared through her irises and permeated her cornea, coursed through her retina and flooded her brain. A scream built at the base of her throat, choking her.

The house juddered. It knocked her consciousness back into her body as it lurched to the side. Her head clonked against the pine bedframe.

"Eyes. Blind. Shut." She shoved the words through gritted teeth. The pain vanished.

"Well done, Harper," Heresy purred. "That is the first time you have done an acceptable piece of magic."

Harper tried to blink but her eyelids were too sticky. She forced her lips closed as she patted around for the towel she'd left out to clean the circle. There was a distant thud and the stomp of feet on the stairs. Probably Grace getting home from shiftwork at the vets. Harper rubbed her eyes frantically, trying to get rid of the slime coating them and her hand before her sister could see. The door burst open.

"What the hell, Harper?"

She blinked up at AJ's lanky form silhouetted in her doorway. Globs of red clouded her vision, beyond that his normally pale face was almost paper white. She followed his appalled stare to the remnants of sheep's eye coating her hand.

Hot bile flooded her mouth and she leapt to her feet, diving for the Jack-and-Jill bathroom she shared with Grace. She barely made it to the toilet before her breakfast spewed from her mouth.

"You need to warn me when you do blood magic. You've completely mucked up my program." AJ came up behind her and ran water into the sink. A moment later a damp towel was draped over her neck. "Clean up, then come see me." The door clicked closed as he left.

Harper leant her head against the cabinet next to the toilet, shaking arms braced around her stomach. Her whole body quivered as though recovering from some long illness. The tremors seemed to leak out of her, jangling the floor and jiggling the doors. Her stomach heaved with the wish-wash of travel sickness that hadn't plagued her since she was a little girl out boating on the river with her brother.

She straightened, eyes screwed closed, trying to cling to the image in her mind of two children in bright clothing, steering a boat with a long pole. A white kitten sat in the bow, one paw raised as though directing. The vision slipped away like a dream until she could remember none of it save she'd experienced a memory from before the day she emerged from the mists.

"Heresy?" Her voice came out a croak. "Heresy? I—"

The house quaked again. Her shoulder rammed into the corner of the cabinet and she bit back a cry. The spell had been designed to hide her from whatever hunted her, whatever attacked the house before. It must be AJ's spell gone wrong. *Please let it be AJ's spell gone wrong.*

Harper stomped downstairs and flung open his bedroom door. "AJ, what are you—"

"Harper, whatever spell you're doing—"

They stopped, glaring across the screen-lit room. Their eyes went wide and they both spoke at once as the house gave another tremendous shake. "That's not you?"

AJ's chair slid across ash floorboards and Harper clung to the doorframe to stay upright.

"Earthquake?" AJ asked.

"In York? What do you do in an earthquake anyway?"

"Unscrew a door and hide under it?"

"I don't flipping know."

"Where's Heresy?"

The tremors subsided and Harper righted herself.

AJ's face was pinched, annoyed, the most emotion she'd ever seen from him. "What did you do?"

When she told him the ritual she'd performed, he raised an eyebrow at her, then looked back at his screen. "Nah, that spell didn't do this. I don't even think it's what messed up my program."

"I … might know what it is." Harper paled and sank onto AJ's bed. "There's something chasing me in my dreams. The spell I did was *supposed* to stop it finding me in the dreamscape, and Heresy protected the house, so it shouldn't be … but …"

AJ stared at her blankly for a moment, then frowned. "You're only mentioning this now? How long?"

"Since the Hiding started failing. I've been having dream visions of … I think it's of home but I don't remember much when I wake up. Heresy said there's something hunting me. It's attacked the house before. Heresy called it magical carpet bombing. It doesn't know my precise location in the wakening, but every time it's in my dreams, it gets closer to finding me here. It makes no sense for it to attack the house now. We designed the spell carefully, we followed the book, Heresy said I performed it well and you know how hard it is to get praise from him."

Heresy curled around Harper's ankles and slithered up her body to drape himself around her neck. "I give plentiful praise to those who earn it."

"Play nice or I'll lock you up again." AJ waved his phone at Heresy. "I coded you into a cage before, I can do it again."

Heresy bristled, little puffs of static zapping Harper's neck. "It is not my fault I was summoned by an incompetent witch who seems to have made a straightforward Hiding spell do the exact opposite of intended."

"Wait …" Something tickled the back of Harper's mind.

"You said it went well, so she can't have done that badly," AJ pointed out.

"She did it amusingly …"

Something was trying to snag Harper's attention but their continued bickering was driving it out. "I said 'wait.'"

AJ and Heresy fell silent.

"Heresy, you said the spell did the exact opposite. It was supposed to hide me in the dreamscape and instead it made me more visible, yes?"

"The attack on the house despite my spells would suggest that conclusion, yes," Heresy said haughtily. "Although it appears to have stopped for now."

"And the magic at The Grand was supposed to banish something, but a demon *appeared* instead. What if it *did* come through a banishing circle."

"You think there's a pattern? Two instances is hardly conclusive." AJ folded his arms over his chest and leant back in his chair. "But it is weird. I'll check in with the coven and see if anyone else has had the same problem. It's probably coincidence, but let's make sure."

"Thanks, AJ." Harper smiled at him and got up. "I'll let you get back to fixing your spell."

She wandered back to her bedroom via a strong cup of tea and cleaned away the dreamscape hiding spell. The tidying was on autopilot, despite the risks if she left anything out. Her mind was abuzz with possibilities and fears.

CHAPTER EIGHT

Voices from the Past

Dense silence pooled between dim wells of undulating light in the stacks of the Third Vault. Mahogany shelves huddled together, leaning overhead like the eaves of the Shambles. Scents of paper and glue weighed down the atmosphere.

The Third Vault contained items relating to supernatural creatures and non-redacted history of the human realm. The main library area held oft-requested texts and the most aesthetically pleasing. The stacks held everything else, miles and miles of it, or so it seemed. There must have been over a hundred small, climate-controlled chambers.

Harper wasn't sure if the information she sought would be in the Third Vault or locked away deeper in the archives. Maybe something here would tell her about the vision she had outside or about a creature that could've breached the cathedral security to murder Agnes. She worried the end of her braid, conscious she wasn't living up to the archbishop's expectations or the admonitions of the Foss.

Saqib had received the autopsy reports for the other missing women, the Guard's efficiency working in their favour for a change. While neither body had been checked for runic writing, those corpses had also been eyeless. Saqib was trying to verify if the Hiding symbols were present but it seemed more likely they were related to Agnes's death and Edith's disappearance. A serial killer with a penchant for eyeballs. Harper ground her fist against her stomach and swallowed the rising acid in her throat. Her skin still felt icky from the sheep's eyeball. How could anyone want to deal with that sensation on a regular basis?

She'd commandeered a quiet nook and piled all the relevant books she could find around her, a barrier should any other archivists happen past. Weary and disgusted from her reading, with no clearer idea as to what may have killed her friend, Harper turned to the smaller stack of books she'd gathered for personal research. Maybe there was something about dreamwalkers or dream creatures that would give a clue as to what hunted her.

She flipped through, skim reading as she searched for key words. None of the books used Heresy's terminology, however, one passage with potential caught her attention.

'Throughout history, humans have claimed to encounter supernaturals who could appear in or influence dreams.

'Angelic beings who bring prophecies and warnings to God's favoured while they sleep.'

Harper swallowed a bitter laugh. If she tried to tell anyone her visions might be a warning from God, she would be mocked all the way to the noose. At some point in history, people stopped believing in miracles. She read on.

'Oneiroi, the Greek personification of dreams, brothers of Sleep.

'Somnia, their not-quite-equivalent in the Roman world, who were Sleep's sons.

'In the far east, we see tales of Baku, who eat nightmares, and yume no seirei, who cause them. Likewise, in German and Slavic lore we find creatures such as mares and nocnitsa who sit upon the chest of sleepers and cause or consume nightmares.

'Certain animals are associated with the ability to see things humans can't perceive, including into the land of dreams. These include ravens, crows, owls, cats, and spiders, amongst others.

'It is now widely accepted that these are all superstitions and dreams are the province of your own mind. They can be influenced by outside factors, just as any psychological condition or mental health problem can, but they are not something other beings can wander into, see, or eat.'*

Harper skimmed down to see what the footnote said.

**This is refuted by various supernaturally contaminated peoples such as the Japanese and tribes of the Northern American and Southern African continents. However, their policies of welcoming creatures who benefit from humans being ill-informed means such opinions hold no scientific weight.'*

Magic deniers infuriated the normally easy-going Saqib with their claims science belied the arcane. Their arguments were no use when searching for the real-life creature hunting her. Nonetheless, she noted down the beings they mentioned so she could look into them more later.

She tapped the word 'cat' with her pen. Maybe the occult symbol on the collar of the cat in the cathedral hadn't been someone's foolishness. Maybe it was a warning. If cats could see into dreams, it was possible the murderer was using the one from Saqib's photos to move between realms. It seemed a little far-fetched to go from 'seeing' to 'moving.' She could See, but it didn't mean she could magically transport herself elsewhere. Yet at this point, she couldn't afford to dismiss any possibility. Perhaps Heresy would know.

Mind focussed where it should be, on the deaths of her friend and those poor other women, Harper returned the stacks to reshelve her books and find new ones. A few, she took down to skim without going back to her desk. A few mentioned the creatures she'd already read about and she made notes on any differences or new information, but none of it answered her questions or shed light on the dead women.

Hearing no shuffle of footsteps or other sounds of people nearby, Harper let her Sight play over the books, hoping for a revelation amongst the memoirs and diaries around her. Her thoughts were elsewhere as she wandered, attempting to unravel the tangle of murders. She was good at finding her way and knew the stacks well. Once she'd been somewhere, she could always find her way again. Almost always. As she walked, she hummed absentmindedly. The tune from the river still played, so vivid it was like her ears could hear it.

Down on the bottom shelf, peeking between dislodged books, a pair of brilliant blue eyes tracked Harper's progress through the stacks. The cat tried to hold still but couldn't suppress a twitch as she neared his hiding place. Only the deepest shadows could dim his floofed white fur, so he relied on large tomes for concealment.

Books around him wiggled like fishes. Zero nudged those next to him back into place before they could disturb the spell he'd drawn. His paw smarted from the bite to draw the blood required to sketch the spell. The books shoved back and he slashed at them with sheathed claws. A warning. They continued to rustle but stayed away from his spell. As if human books could intimidate him after so many years in his master's library. It wasn't as if the books themselves possessed any magic or intelligence, just a little of the cathedral's mighty presence and cognisance rubbing off on them.

As Harper approached, Zero shrank against the leatherbound tomes, lips drawn back in a silent hiss. He still wasn't sure who she was, but he knew *what* she was. Her blood sang to him. His creator. Memories didn't penetrate the gloom of the years before he was taken in by his master. Nonetheless a sanguimancer's instinct insisted this was true. He didn't know how, but he was made of this woman's blood. She didn't have the overwhelming magical presence his master did, and even ze's copies lacked the magical potency Zero had. They were all jealous of his place at their master's side. Especially One. Zero's ear flicked. If he could find out how she made him, his master would be pleased. For now, helping Harper pleased both his master and his own selfish desires.

Through his connection to Harper, he could hear a drone note and the faint strains of a lullaby. The music reached for her, but it wasn't the comforting nuzzle of a mama cat. There were claws hidden beneath its pretty surface.

He'd seen her dreams, though he could never remember the details other than a sense of fear so acrid in his stomach neither fish nor cream could placate it. Something hunted her, something bound by blood to both of them, and if it succeeded in catching her, she would die. And if she died, his master would die.

He didn't know why or how these apparent strangers were connected, their links to an insignificant cat like him not enough to explain why they'd shared a fetch. One creature foretelling two deaths. If his master knew how that was possible, or what the cat's vision meant, ze hadn't seen fit to share the details. Despite the fetch, Zero couldn't believe that was true. His master had lived for centuries. How could the death of a mortal witch affect zir? Ze wanted her alive, her abilities as a Seer too valuable to let die, but ze only really needed her eyes. If they were removed before death, the rest of her should've been unimportant.

Zero squeezed his eyes closed as he almost choked on a lump of nausea. Sometimes it was better to let his mind fracture and hide away the feels his master's work stirred. He couldn't help those folk. The work they did helped more than the few it harmed. He'd never *seen* his master cause real harm to anyone other than zir familiars, not anything more than a little laceration to get their blood, but he couldn't pretend he didn't know. It hurt more than any nick of knife or claw. *Master is trying to keep everyone safe. Bad folk need lessons. Like when I'm a Bad Cat. Master teaches me because ze loves me, so I can be better.* A tiny voice he could barely hear whispered, *I have no choice.* He raised a leg to scratch his collar, then remembered he was hiding. The dark thoughts slithered back to the locked-off parts of his mind.

Ears flat back against his skull, Zero arched his back and retreated as far as possible as Harper neared. Their other encounters could be explained, but no mere house pet would be here by accident.

Harper's violet gaze swept the shelves as she padded between them, humming softly under her breath. The melody called to him, jangled his nerves almost as much as the flickering lights. There was magic in it, old magic, older even than his master. It staticked his fur. Her feet kept time with the tune as she walked in a daze. One of the books on the shelves above called to his blood, but her memory was buried so deep she couldn't feel the pull of it. Before she'd arrived he'd found it and magically bookmarked what he thought she needed to know. Maybe if she could unlock the past they'd both forgotten, at least one of them could escape the nightmare of it. Regardless of what his master wanted, Zero wanted her to be safe. Specific memories couldn't pierce the haze, but emotions were still there. He loved her. As much as he loved his master, maybe more. He owed her his life, and he wanted to give hers back.

He almost darted out of his hiding place when Harper stumbled and clutched her chest. He could see the magic strings tightening as barbed hooks of music dug into her heart and mind. They yanked her forward. Her tears tore at his heart and his eyes stung with tears he could never shed for himself. She did nothing to free herself from the magic's grasp. If she couldn't disentangle herself, he feared where it would drag her.

Just as Harper was about to step level, Zero batted a pin under her falling foot. She stopped with a bitten-off curse and the cat allowed himself a small glow of pleasure at the success of his plan. Portalling in the tiny sharp from his master's desk had been Useful. As she stooped to remove the pin, he slipped behind the books and waited.

Harper's eyes swept the shelves. His spell gleamed as her violet gaze passed over it, the combination of her Sight and his magic, the silver of a river rippling in the moonlight. Her attention snagged, the spell settled to the deep garnet of dried blood. It would become part of her, his blood to her blood to the blood he sensed long dried on the shelf above. Satisfied his magic would lead her to the right history, Zero knocked on the air to open a portal home and slipped away.

The familiar static of magic heated the air and pricked Harper's skin. Cold fear gripped her belly. An image hovered in the air before her. It wavered like a mirage and dimmed but radiated heat like a bonfire. At first it appeared to be a single rune, but then it shattered, fragments flying in every direction like sparks of fire. The books on either side trembled, packed so close together they were almost climbing over each other to get away.

There couldn't be magic here. Not in the Third Vault.

"What are you?" The spell gleamed brighter, fanned by the oxygen in her breath. In response to her question, an image unfolded, rings and points of light rising from the floor. At the centre, a ball of fire inflated, almost the size of her fist, with nine smaller balls looping it and a glittering belt of diamonds between the third and fourth. Other tinier spheres, connected by luminous trails, formed familiar patterns.

As the image grew, Harper was able to trace the paths of the planets and glimmering lines of constellations. They surrounded her, expanding to the ceiling and drifting through bookcases to fill the stacks. Harper watched in unafraid wonder. It was awe-inspiring magic yet something familiar niggled at the back of her mind.

Heat crackled against her face as the sun expanded, flares so real she wondered that the books didn't catch fire. She flinched away, unable to run, feet stuck to the floor. Tears formed and dried instantly, her eyes seared open. Flames danced all around her. Heat smothered her lungs and caressed her body. Almost too hot to bear. Surely her skin would blister and blacken. A hell she'd Seen before.

Pain erupted at the back of her head, as though her skull hit stone from a great height. Her bones shattered to dust. Fire closed over her head, the last of her oxygen spent. A scream died in her throat as her soul was dragged into the inferno.

The magic vanished, leaving Harper shaking and breathless on the floor. Tears beat down the dust cushioning her face. A date lingered in her mind, like the whispers of the Hiding. October 31st 1555.

She inspected her arms, not quite believing it was all a vision. Her shirt was still radiant yellows and oranges with no sign of burning and her skin was unreddened. Each panting breath was easier than the last, the air a cool balm in her aching lungs. Nothing made sense. All that magic, the whole solar system, a whole universe of stars, was to tell someone a date five hundred years ago? Had it triggered because of her magic or was it there to catch anyone? *How did it get in here? Was it a trap left by the same person who killed Agnes? But why?*

October 31st 1555. Too early by centuries to have been the ghostwalker's demise she'd Seen in her vision outside. Too early to be Chester. What could've happened during the Purge that had any bearing on the women being murdered now? Hauling herself up on the bookshelves, Harper scanned the memoirs housed there. She ran her finger along them until a prickle of magic zinged up her arm.

Her hand rested on a small book with no title or author noted, likely an original diary. It was bound in skin—not cow leather although she wasn't sure how she knew—with a cord of the same origin wrapped around to keep it closed. A thrill built in the pit of her stomach as she drew the volume from the shelf, unwound the cord, and opened it. A paper insert showed the date and place the book was found and the name of the archivist who brought it in around the turn of the last century. A handwritten title page stated:

Diary of Leonora Sonata Ashbury
Year of our Lord Fifteen-Hundred-and-Fifty-Three
to Fifteen-Hundred-and-Fifty-Five

Her breath hitched when she saw the name and her fingers trembled as she flicked through the dates looking for October 31st 1555. She didn't stop until she reached the last inscribed page. All Hallow's Eve. Although several blank sheets remained, there was no entry for All Soul's Day, November 1st. She looked again, willing her Sight to see that which her eyes couldn't, but the paper remained stubbornly blank.

Harper read over the last entry, grateful she'd spent so much time with texts of the era that she could decipher the archaic handwriting. The book's existence and categorisation told her plenty: her ancestor, if the name was not a coincidence, had been well-off and educated, was somehow involved in the Purge, and her witness contained no practical information on magic. She skimmed through the entry, heart pounding.

The thirty-first day of October
Tomorrow is All Soul's Day. Though I know it to be a Sin, I pray God forgives what I must do. I will not be consumed by their flames. I will not be imprisoned by his falsehoods. If all the choices remaining to me lead to death, then I will make a choice with my head held high. I would end my own life rather than see it used for the corruption of others. And this I know in my heart for my Dreams have foretold it: should I take my own life, I will not be alone. My kin's Sight shall let her ride with me, centuries away though she may be, and she will learn from my mistakes. It will be a long road for our

people, but it is the only hope my visions offer. She may walk my path and prevail. There are no certainties of success, but she is the sole one I See who may have a chance of it. May God grant mercy on my soul and save me from the Fires of Hell.'

Harper slammed the diary closed. She no longer doubted that Leonora was her ancestor, or at least a relation. The stacks cooled. Ice blossomed on the stone flooring. Breath hung in the air. Her fingers froze around the book, her lips tinged with blue. Harper stood still as a statue as the full weight of Leonora's words sank in. Then she clutched the book to her chest and sprinted out of the stacks.

Harper fled the vaults, hands clammy, heart racing in fear she would be stopped, that someone, or something, would prevent her taking the diary from the archives. She sped through the misty streets of York, not caring about alarmed glances or the *tsking* of the people she passed. When she reached her house, she dashed up to her bedroom and barricaded the two doors, unwilling to share her find even with Grace. Not yet. Not until she knew more.

The secret was both delicious and terrifying. Harper hugged the book to her chest, eyes bright with tears. The ache in her heart longed for a mother's arms, a father's embrace. The diary seemed to wrap itself around her soul, a lifeline to a drowning child cast adrift in a tempestuous world. She wanted to savour each word. Draw them out. Analyse them. Interrogate them.

Half buried in a rainbow of pillows, she read hungrily, ignoring shouts for dinner and Grace's concerned knock on the door save to say she was busy and to go on without her. It wouldn't placate Grace forever, but for once her sister read her tone and didn't insist on being let in. Even Heresy stayed away. Cautioned by Grace or still fretting about the wider defences of the house, Harper neither knew nor cared. All she had eyes for was Leonora's handwriting.

As she read, she scribbled key points in her notebook, careful not to leave so much as a smudge on the original record. When she came to musical annotation, she got out her violin, the painted white roses and verdant leaves on its body fluttering in the candlelight. It was well after midnight by the time she fell into an exhausted slumber, sticky notes, pencil sketches, and a map of Yorkshire strewn across her bed. Her cheek rested on the final entry, her fingers on the violin strings, as the dreaming took her.

Each footstep took a century. Mists billowed out of the way in slow motion. No path was discernible, assumed only from the absence of trees along a narrow route. Charcoal shadows from looming firs appeared, then faded as she passed. Branches blocked out light from the sky, day or night she couldn't tell, but the mists roiled with their own pearlescence, both lighting and obscuring the way.

Whispers floated under their own power on the still air. Familiar words she'd spent all night poring over spoken in an unfamiliar voice that resonated with her soul.

Wanderers

Seers

Starbearers

Protector

Daughter'

With each whisper, the light blazed and her feet grew heavier as though wading through a swamp. Eyes opened at each word, hovering around her, guiding, forcing. Human eyes, some gleaming violet like her Sight, others brown, blue, green, or grey. Some unnatural colours she shied away from, the colours of fire: reds, oranges, and yellows. More and more clustered around her. An old dream. She pushed past them, strangely detached from her body's revulsion at their slick surfaces and the gelatinous ooze that clung to her. The churning of her stomach and the lump in her throat seemed unreal. Her body was the dream. Her mind was reality. This was real, somewhere behind all the theatre the dreamscape masked itself in.

Harper shoved through, blocking out everything but the sense of self deep in her core and the dulcet tones of Leonora. She followed her ancestor's voice and the melancholic backing of a solo violin.

The forest fell away and the world fluttered open like a storybook. At Harper's feet, a broad valley stretched and rolled. Mists cascaded over the meadows to wash up against stone barns and cosy cottages. Overhead, a billion stars twinkled and the full moon bathed the valley in silver. Snow crunched underfoot, but the cold was distant despite her bare toes. Gleaming sprigs of snowdrops adorned her way. The stares of the glowing eyes followed her as she descended.

The glee of children splashing in a stream rolled up the hill. Leonora's voice faded as the laughter grew louder. Harper headed towards it; the first sign of human life since her dreams brought her to these woods. She trudged downhill, following the sound until she reached a plateau where the river ran smooth. In the moonlight, she could see two children on a boat halfway between the two shores. Déjà vu. Her earlier vision came back to her and she clung to the image, hoping it would not slip away again as soon as she awoke.

"Push harder, Dorian," a little girl shrieked as their boat veered off course. The taller silhouette shoved his pole into the water and the boat straightened.

"You're pushing too hard," the other youth replied. "We have to stay in this section. We don't want to get too far from home."

"Merow." A tiny, white cat, almost hidden in the bow of the boat, raised a paw.

"See, even your secret cat agrees with me." The boy gave the kitten an appraising look.

"I know, I know." The girl's long plait whipped out as she looked around. "If we stray from the Protector's sphere we'll be caught by humans. Bad humans." She stuck her tongue out.

"He's already gonna be mad we're beyond the village boundaries and out at night."

"I don't care." The stubborn edge to the girl's tone brought a nostalgic smile to Harper's lips. "I want to know what's down there."

There was a long pause, then a sigh drifted on the breeze. Harper's ears burned with magic as she Heard the boy's whispered response, too low for the little girl to notice. "So do I, Harper. So do I."

Her heart caught in her throat and tears blurred her vision. She rubbed them away, trying to keep the pair in sight as long as she could. The girl looked up, eyes gleaming violet as she stared across the river at Harper.

"What are you looking at?" The boy twisted round.

"Nothing." Young Harper broke her gaze with her older self as she guided her pole through the water. The cat mewed again, a sharp sound so full of disagreement Harper could almost swear she heard it say, 'Liar.' The cat, too, stared at her, brilliant blue eyes more piercing than the girl's violet. *Certain animals are associated with the ability to see things humans can't perceive ... including cats ...*

Harper remembered this moment. Not a dream. A memory. Of boating with her brother, something they'd done so many times, when she'd looked up and Seen the shadow of a woman on the shore. She knew the auras of everyone in their village and this person was different. She'd Seen, but not recognised, herself, assuming it was some spirit out at night or one of the humans she'd been warned about. The Protector didn't allow them out at night and she'd taken the vision as an explanation of why, but she'd never told anyone what she'd Seen either. Only …

Her mind scrambled for the rest of the memory, but it went no further than that moment on the river. It offered no path home or knowledge of her family. But she did remember one thing more. There had been someone else there that night.

Harper scanned the tree-line on the opposite bank, then shrank back against the bole of a large wych elm. A shadowy figure was barely discernible on the other shore. As soon as she Saw him, she could Hear him, too, the faintest trace of violin music on the breeze. A different hand than the music that accompanied Leonora–this violinist played as though one with his instrument. His music consumed her mind and soul, poignant and ancient. This was the one Leonora feared. His instrument gleamed like starlight. Clothes of flowing greys and blacks obscured his physical features save for long, bony fingers and his height, far above any human's.

"Mrow." Something soft rubbed against her ankles and Harper looked down into the wide turquoise eyes of the cat. Her eyes flicked to the river, wondering how it reached her, but the boat was gone.

She turned towards the violinist again. His head twisted to meet her gaze.

Something gouged her ankles, hard, and she glanced down in time to see the star-white cat's bloody claws.

She woke up.

The bed quaked beneath her, almost tossing her out. Harper clutched the diary and her violin to her chest as her scattered notes tumbled to the floor. Her head ached. Her ears rang like she'd stood in the belltower at noon. Grace gripped her shoulder, in the bed with her, scarlet-painted nails digging into her flesh.

"Did you feel that?" Harper panted.

"Feel what?" Grace asked with a frown.

"The house …"

The tremors subsided and with them the throbbing in her head.

"Harp, your eyes are violet. What were you dreaming?"

Fully awake, buoyed by a joy unlike any she'd ever known, Harper dropped the book and violin into her lap and grabbed Grace in a bear hug. "I Saw what's hunting me, Grace. I Saw part of my way home."

CHAPTER NINE

The Lure of the Present

"In a dream? Harper, Heresy said something is hunting you and you said before something has been attacking you in your dreams. What if it's a trap?"

Grace's words brought the reality of her body back to Harper and her spirit settled into her bones. With it came a smart of pain in her ankle. She pulled down her sock to reveal long scratches oozing blood.

"What did you do?" Grace asked as she grabbed a small first aid kit from the bathroom. She cleaned then bandaged the cuts with the same care she might give to deep sword wounds, her brow furrowed in concern.

"I think it happened in the dreamscape." Unlike her other dreams of the past, this one stayed with her. Not exactly clear, but even the shadow of memory was better than nothing. Harper explained everything she'd Seen in the dream, including the voice of Leonora, while Grace fussed over her. "I'm fine really."

"This diary is why you were so unsociable yesterday? Let me see it." Grace held out her hand. The trademark De Santos imperiousness amused Harper rather than irking her. She was used to it and saved her arguments for when it was important.

As she handed the diary over to Grace, she summarised, "The writer is an ancestor of mine, or at least in the family. She was a Seer too. Gray, she

Saw me having a vision of her death. That fall from the tower? That was her, not the ghostwalker. Her people were nomadic, travelling through England at the time of the Purge. They'd been in Scotland and were trying to get down to Glastonbury Tor before heading over to Wales and sailing to Ireland. But they got trapped here when the Bloody Queen closed the borders. As an inherently magical people, they were in trouble. Several were caught and killed. Leonora said they were also cursed, as if the Purge wasn't bad enough. A mare had been drawn to their dreamings and was corrupting their magic. They couldn't sleep nor See a way to escape it."

"A mare? Like … neigh?" Grace slipped a question in as Harper paused for breath.

"Not a horse. A mare. Like nightmare. It hounded them across Europe. Miguel caught one that time while travelling the Baltic countries, remember? They thought crossing the sea would get rid of it, but it followed them to Scotland. In York, they met someone Leonora refers to only as 'Protector.' He promised to vanquish the mare and take them to a place they'd be safe from the Purge. She described him as a creature of the dreamscape and of music but doesn't record who or what he really was. Possibly a powerful human, or maybe one of the Folk. It put me in mind of the 'Magician' the fae woman at the paper shop mentioned."

"They decided to trust a supe?"

Harper raised an eyebrow. "Other humans were trying to slaughter them. Also, hypocrite much?"

Grace had the decency to blush, a sight not often seen. She jutted her chin, stare hard. "Continue."

"Well, not to say you're right, but Leonora didn't trust him. She thought he was as bad as the mare, if not worse. She was in the minority, however. Everyone else decided to go with him. She made the heart-breaking decision to leave the family. Fearing a slow death at this 'Protector's' hands or the fires of the Purge, she jumped." Harper sighed, her eyes misting. "I don't think it helped. In my vision of her death, she was consumed by flames as she died. She feared God would consign her to Hell for committing suicide and hoped to earn forgiveness as all her choices led to death."

"Don't be misled by the beliefs of the time." Grace's eyes narrowed. "They were ignorant. Barely any of the common populace was literate, let alone able to read a Bible written in Latin. They believed what they were told to. Real Christianity would never condone burning humans at the stake. I don't think God sends all suicides to Hell either. Would you, if they were your children? Maybe what you Saw were her fears. Or maybe there were fires there, human fires."

Harper gave Grace a hard hug. "Thanks, theologian."

"More importantly, do you think this 'Protector' is the one Heresy senses hunting you?"

"It seems likely. Which definitely makes it a supe if it's lived this long, unless it's a descendent of the original. Heresy said we share blood, which implies a common ancestry."

"Or blood magic," Grace pointed out. "You and Heresy share blood too."

Harper hugged her arms around her waist. "True. At least we know whatever is hunting me and my path home are the same mystery."

"Don't even think about letting it find you." Grace waved a finger under Harper's nose. "That better not be what you meant by 'Saw part of my way home.'"

Harper swatted her hand away. "No. In my dream, I was in the countryside watching child-me. We always assumed I came from somewhere in the Dales because of where your father found me. It did look a bit like Swaledale only so much bigger, with the river starting up in the hills." *Another realm maybe?* Harper's eyes strayed to her desk where the book *Of Realms and Shadows* nestled in a drawer. "Leonora knew about me. She knew I'd See her death. She thinks … she thinks I have a chance to save my family."

"But we searched the dale so many times, and the ones around it. If there was a whole clan of people, we'd've seen them."

"Not if they're hidden," Harper countered. "This 'Protector' promised to save them from the Purge. They had to be somewhere the Queen's Guard couldn't find them. Leonora thought that meant he had a way to get them out of the country. But supes are still here, hiding, what if he found a way to keep them in England, in Swaledale, but completely imperceptible? How else did I get there?"

"I don't know," Grace admitted. She turned the diary over in her hands, a thoughtful expression on her face. "Harper … you know what today is, right? I want to say it's a coincidence you found this now, but what if it's not?"

The realisation crashed over as if she'd been plunged into that icy river. Harper had been aware of the date in a vague sort of way, but she tried so hard not to think about it that her mind glossed over the import of it. Her phone to confirmed it was after midnight. Three a.m. January 17th. Thirteen years to the day since she'd been found by Father De Santos. Thirteen years since she'd lost one home and found another. Based on her assumed age at the time, she'd now been part of Grace's family for as long as the one she'd left behind.

Grace set the diary aside and squeezed Harper in a tight hug. "I know, sis. I know." Heads leant together, the two women sat in silence as they contemplated all that had happened since that day.

"How can we find them?" Grace asked, determination lacing her tone.

Although she didn't know the details yet, there was a way. Harper had never been so certain of something. Between Leonora's vision and her own determined desire, nothing would stop her. Her whole body thrummed with surety of it. "I will find a way. Not by using myself as bait, don't worry. I found a way out. I'll find a way back in."

Much as Harper wanted to dream, sleep eluded her for the rest of the night. The vision of her younger self played over and over in her head as she grasped for details that faded as soon as she woke. She had a brother. *Does he miss me? Did he search for me when I disappeared or was he too afraid of leaving the Protector's influence? Is leaving that sphere what stole my memories? Did I do this to myself?* Fear and hope mingled in her gut, raced through her veins, and set every nerve on fire. Even the touch of the blanket irritated her skin. Eventually, she got up and went to sit at the kitchen table with Heresy and a pot of tea.

"Do you sleep?" Harper had never asked and, as he had no discernible eyes, there was no easy way to tell.

"I am unconnected to the dreamscape save what little I can view from the outside. I cannot see your dreams or the thing hunting you, I can only sense a sinister presence near you."

"That's not what I asked," Harper pointed out. "I already knew you couldn't see the details of my dreams or you could've told me more about what's hunting me."

Heresy grinned. "Assuming you asked me, that is."

Harper *tsked* at him and took another sip of tea, returning to the diary and the notes and photos scattered across the table. "The white cat is bothering me. It's a huge coincidence for there to have been similar cats in the areas of those other women's deaths and for me to see one at the cathedral the day after Agnes died. Plus, there was one in my dream. Pure white cats aren't *that* common."

"There's one that lives a few streets over." Heresy contorted to peer at Saqib's photos.

"Heresy, are you possessing the neighbours' cats again?" Harper sighed. Grace would have a fit. "They don't like it. Stop it."

There was a pout in his tone, even though his Cheshire Cat grin remained undimmed. "You would not want me to get bored while you are at work. Who knows what mischief I might cause."

"*Heresy.*"

He chuckled off her scolding. "Cats can see that which others cannot, that much is true. It would not explain how someone reached into the cathedral's secure vaults and plucked out a woman's eyes. Yet it may still be a spy for someone. Cats lack the intelligence to do things of their own accord, though they are arrogant enough to believe themselves in charge."

Much as she wanted to, Harper couldn't argue. She kept reading until she heard footsteps shuffling upstairs at which point she tidied everything into one corner of the table and put veggie sausages on to fry. Since she was up ridiculously early, she may as well make a nice breakfast for everyone else. When Grace came down, she made no mention of the date again.

The first couple of years Harper lived with Grace's family, her sister had tried to celebrate her found date. It was down on her documentation as her birthday, after all. Over time, Grace had come to accept Harper would rather ignore the date entirely, and so gave her presents randomly in the summer instead.

After breakfast, Saqib and Grace left for work. AJ hadn't even come out of his room, most likely asleep having stayed up all night too. Harper spent most of that morning sitting at the kitchen table with Heresy, drinking too much caffeine, and poring over the diary. Occasionally, her head would droop towards the table, eyelids heavy, but each time a slight tremor beneath her feet jarred her awake. Something was searching for the house. Sometimes it was stronger, sometimes barely perceptible, but it always returned.

After lunch, Harper hid the diary upstairs and packed her bag. Running out had been odd behaviour. If she accompanied it by not showing up at work, questions would be asked that she couldn't answer honestly. Despite keeping a massive secret from the archbishop, or maybe because of it, she hated lying to him. She stuffed the notes she'd made about Leonora's diary inside another notebook. So long as she was in the archives, she may as well cross-reference a few things.

Harper couldn't remember dropping off. She certainly hadn't intended to. The last time she'd fallen asleep in the archives, she'd had the vision of the dead girl in the tree. Yet she wasn't awake, unless someone had brought a lot of trees into the vault without her noticing. She pinched her arm, hard, but the scene didn't so much as waver.

The forest around her was dark, not lit by soft snow or luminescent mist. Neither stars nor moon breached the swaying branches overhead. A light coating of rain sprinkled her skin and freckled her face as she gazed upwards, hoping for stars to orientate herself by. The spray against her face felt real, not disconnected as her body had been the night before. She didn't even feel like she was dreaming save for the separation between her and the heart-pounding fear she usually experienced in the dark.

Boles of firs, spruce, and pine pressed close around her, uniform in lines, almost military where normally the forest she dreamt was chaotic. A wood farm, maybe, or Christmas trees. It was the same in all directions, for the short distance her Sight could penetrate.

"This is what humans want the world to become." The speaker had a low, musical quality, soothing like a lullaby. Trees passed the words between them, diminishing echoes, flat, in a minor key. Faint violin music twined through the branches, a familiar, forgotten tune.

"Who's there?" Harper's voice was swallowed by the rain and the trees.

"Where are you, my Seer? Why do you hide from me?"

The questions left her cold. The Protector? She huddled against the trunk of the nearest tree. Her clothes were grey and black. Grace's, not her own, provided by the dream to help conceal her. Part of her wanted to confront the speaker, this thing who chased her, hounded her, but more of her was a child, terrified, hiding. Again.

She pulled her legs up to her chest, small as she could be. Pudgy fingers clasped together around her knees. Bare toes dug into mud. Pigtails caught at the bark of the tree. She screwed her eyes closed and hoped to remain unseen.

Something warm pressed against her thigh, soft, furry. She opened her eyes to see a white cat curled up against her, its trembling body mirroring her fears. Its tail was fluffed up like cotton candy, its lips drawn back in a hiss. A black collar cut around its throat like a noose.

"Where are you?" The singsong voice sounded nearer and farther.

"Wake up, Harper." Another voice, inside her head maybe, or right in her ear. So familiar yet she'd never heard it before. Cold fingers clasped hers and she looked up into a human face with dazzling blue eyes slit by voids and framed by delicate white hair. "I'm sorry, Harper." Pain scored the back of her hand. She sat up with a gasp.

Harper curled up with the book she'd been reading hugged to her chest like a shield. The scent was reassuring, grounding. She screwed her aching eyes closed. The details of the dream once again slipped from her mind like moonlit river water, always flowing away, never to return the same. She clung to them, but they slithered through her fingers and left her hands, and her heart, empty.

CHAPTER TEN

A Family Visit

With curfew in full effect, Harper waited until after dawn to head home. She'd forced herself to stay awake with caffeine, sugar, and research. Heresy's protection would allow her a nap, but when she got in, AJ's bedroom door was open. The normally bright array of monitors was dark and he leant back in his chair, feet up next to his keyboard. He beckoned Harper in, gesturing to the bed where she perched on a corner. She eyed the heavy blackout curtains but decided against tampering.

She shot him a questioning look and he pointed to his earbud then to her ears. When she frowned, he gave her a look of exasperation and tapped the corner of his eye then the earbud again. Catching his meaning, Harper heightened her Hearing in the same way she used her Sight. The fizzle on the small bones in her ears was unpleasant and she sat on her hands so she didn't stick her fingers in her ears.

A woman was talking, her tone scathing, with a northern upper-class accent and a hint of broad Yorkshire creeping in as her irritation grew. "It is preposterous that you should ask such a thing of us. Perform magic. In the streets of York. With the Guard everywhere. For strangers. Alastair Jeremiah—"

"I live here, too, you know." AJ cut her off before she could get through his pompously long name. "What about family?"

"You *left* the family. At a critical time, no less."

"You gave me the stupid assignment of monitoring Harper in the first place. If you hadn't, do you think I'd've left my room? I had to dismantle and re-set up everything. It was a nuisance. I'm not doing it again so get your asses over here and fix it or you're going to lose your Network protections."

The woman on the other end of the line gave the most elegant snort Harper had ever heard.

"Unless you can get the whole family to stop using the Net, you need them," AJ warned. "That or you'll be getting a special note through the door."

"You *dare* threaten your family?"

"Just calling out certain people's internet addiction, Mum. Anyway, what do you call your refusal to protect me from something that is an active threat to my work and the place I'm living?"

"Three hours. Be prepared."

There was a ding as the call disconnected.

"Guess I'm meeting your mum at noon?" Harper asked, trying to keep the smirk off her face.

"This isn't a joke, Harp. Remember, they sent me to kill you a few months ago."

Usually laid-back to the point of absurdity, AJ's agitated tone, furrowed brow, and jerky movements unsettled Harper. "What's going on?"

"While you were off gallivanting in the gloaming, something hit the house. Hard. Heresy sensed anger. A lot. Why weren't you home? Whatever the reason, it's not more important than your responsibilities here."

His accusation stung. "AJ, I wasn't out gallivanting. I was at work and lost track of time until it was too late to leave. What is with you?" His agitation was so unusual. It wasn't like him to throw out half-cocked accusations. Her eyes were drawn to the dark monitors again. Another anomaly. "What were you doing that it disrupted?"

His shoulders sagged. "I'm sorry. You're right. You wouldn't. But you and Saqib both being out meant I got stuck listening to Grace tell me about some girl she met on the bus. It's not that though. I was fine-tuning a program I've been working on for *months*. It's all in pieces. The code is scattered across the bottom of the screen. I might have to wipe the whole thing and start from scratch. But even that's not the point. I put my neck on the line to save your life. Left my home. Put up with all the crap that goes on around here. I didn't do it just to get killed by some *thing* attacking *you* because you refused to ask for help."

Harper winced. "I'm sorry. Can I do anything to help with your broken code?"

"Keep *him* away." AJ glared through the open door at the front peephole.

"I'll do my best," Harper promised. Despite AJ's anxiety and the attack on the house, excitement bubbled through her at the thought of witnessing real witches. A coven that pre-dated the Purge and had faery blood must be a match for whatever 'Protector' Leonora feared. "Can I watch what your coven does? It's safer for everyone the more I learn."

He hesitated. "They might not like an outsider seeing their magic. Especially a De Santos, which you are in all but name. But I'll ask them. Now, clear off. I have stuff to prep and you need to hide anything you don't want them seeing. Get Heresy to cloak that book you've got lurking under the floorboards."

"Thanks, AJ." Harper patted him on the shoulder as she got up. "I really appreciate it."

"Especially don't let them see Heresy," he warned, shrugging her off. "If you thought Grace reacted badly to that demon, you'll quake at what my coven would do to him."

Harper sensed the approach of AJ's coven before she heard the knock at the door. She'd never detected anything unusual about AJ, even while he was performing magic, but the combined power of several high-level witches advancing smothered her like ash. Static-filled air resisted being dragged into her lungs and clogged up her throat with sparks.

They hadn't survived for centuries by walking around in pointy hats and flowing black robes, but she looked out her window anyway. Instead of the neighbours' houses stretching down the street, she was faced with a thick blanket of grey, as though someone had erased all the world beyond their house. The fog was so dense neither the near-noon sun nor the lights from the house next door could breach it.

Figures clawed through it. Not AJ's coven. Something else, trapped and desperate to escape. She'd Seen it before. There was something alive in the mists. A face of holes and shadow howled. Spindly fingers grasped her window ledge. Harper jerked back. Its face pressed against the glass, fog writhing under translucent skin. She whipped the curtains closed. Even with her multitude of lamps lit, the dull greyness outside weighed her down. Rolling her shoulders couldn't rid her skin of the sensation of being stalked.

Despite being expected, the knock on the front door made her jump. She bunched her skirt in balled fists, fighting the urge to run downstairs. Heresy lay beneath the floorboards, blanketing her magic paraphernalia and the books in his subtle illusions. AJ had warned she should stay in her room until—*unless*–he told her it was okay to come out. Right on cue, her phone buzzed.

Come down. Alone. Kitchen only.

The text message released her like a pent-up greyhound and she darted down the stairs two at a time.

Five strangers sat around the kitchen table whispering to AJ. A susurration of voices rose and fell from the lounge as well. They all turned as she thumped to the bottom of the stairs. Her sneakers slipped on the tiles as she came to an abrupt halt. All five wore black robes with deep hoods, black gloves, and masks of churning monochrome, obscuring their build and features. Black, white, and greys swirled together in perpetual motion.

Harper raised a shaky hand. "Hi. Welcome to the house."

All five turned as one to AJ. Harper shuddered as their eyes slid away from her, relieved to no longer be pinned by invisible stares.

"They'll let you observe," AJ said, "but you can't talk or ask questions, even afterwards. They've compensated for the protections we cast on the house before, but don't use any other magic, not even your Sight."

Harper swallowed the lump in her throat and gave him a thumbs up. One of the figures pointed to a corner of the kitchen by the backdoor and Harper shuffled over to stand there. It took all her willpower not to bow her head like a disgraced child. Four of the strangers left, heading upstairs, while the fifth took up position by the fridge.

AJ opened the door to the lounge and gave a signal. A moment later, a sixth person came through and exited into the fog-clogged garden. The front door clicked open and closed. That meant there were probably two more, one in the lounge and one in AJ's room. She assumed the four upstairs would've taken a bedroom each and the attic. The stray thought occurred that she hoped they protected the bathrooms and she stifled a giggle.

If this protection failed, whatever was hunting her could kill her friends, her sister. The sobering thought chased any humour away, leaving her nauseated. She sucked her lips closed and leant back into the corner, fingers clasped behind her back.

The person by the fridge stepped forward and removed a candle, mirror, incense burners, salt, and red thread from their bag. Their head turned, assessing the room, then they placed the mirror on the floor in the centre with the candle on top of it. They warded the back door, the door to the lounge, and the bottom of the stairs with sticks of incense, which filled the air with the familiar scents of sage, rosemary, frankincense, and myrrh. A line of salt went across the threshold of each door and window.

The red thread was unwound and circled around the room first clockwise, then counter-clockwise. It hugged the walls, even when tugged, indicating some magic was already at play. Harper shuffled aside to let the person pull the thread behind her, resisting the urge to clasp her throat. The last time she'd seen thread like that, it had been closing around her neck. Once everything was in place, the caster resumed their place by the fridge, arms folded in voluminous sleeves, and waited.

Harper sucked in miniscule streams of air, afraid any movement, even the rise and fall of her chest, may upset the balance of the spell. She was desperate to See, to understand the magic, but she wouldn't do anything to jeopardise this. Not if it might save someone's life. Not if it protected Grace, Saqib, and AJ from becoming collateral damage.

At some unheard signal, the witch stepped forward again. They knelt by the candle and a low sound with a familiar cadence emitted from behind their mask—a multitoned chant in a foreign tongue, as if all those present were singing through one body.

As they chanted, the caster lit the candle with the touch of a finger. The flame stuttered, then grew, slender as a knife yet reaching higher than the head of the kneeling witch. They leant forward, mask almost touching the fire. What had been blacks and whites morphed to reds and oranges.

The chant continued and the flame turned yellow, then blue, then green, the mask mirroring it, and Harper recognised elemental magic from her university studies. Lastly, the fire became brilliant white like a magnesium flare before vanishing without even a puff of smoke. The witch rocked back on their heels, shoulders slumped.

Magic settled around the house. The air hummed with power. *Would Saqib's instruments be singing with it?* Harper could sense the weight of presence from the coven. The sensation was unfamiliar yet comforting. Except ... Her head twitched. An irritation, an itch, a burr beneath her skin. The magic didn't feel quite right. It was the tiniest thing, so small she almost missed it.

"Something's wrong." The witch spoke solo for the first time. Their voice was a light tenor, young-ish and local from the accent. "There's a crack."

Harper opened her mouth to ask, then remembered the terms of her presence and shut it again. The strange mask turned towards her, black-and-white once more.

"Do you have a summoning circle active in this house?"

Harper shook her head.

"Speak."

"No. No magic, just as you asked. Other than the protection and concealment spells already cast."

"Are you certain? We must know what it is before something comes through."

"Something comes through?" She gulped, remembering the bloodbath at the hotel. "There's no magic now, I swear. All my spells were dismantled and washed away. I've not even done any magic today."

"She's telling the truth." Harper had forgotten AJ sat in a corner of the kitchen, watching like she did. "There's no magic interference here." Their eyes met and flicked to the stairs. Heresy wouldn't put them all at that much of a risk, would he?

A scream echoed down.

AJ and Harper dashed up, leaving the caster in the kitchen. Through Grace's open doorway, another witch pointed towards the corridor ceiling. The ladder to the attic was extended and Harper, then AJ, scurried up.

A tawny-haired woman lay across the boards. Her mask had been flung across the room and her robes torn, exposing a pink dress and skin beneath that. Harper was acutely aware she'd dashed up without a weapon. Her eyes swept over the shadowy room in quick assessment but she could see no corporeal threat. Magic fizzed behind her eyes, begging to be let loose, but she couldn't risk it. Not with the air still laden with the coven's magic.

AJ was crouched over his family member, examining her wounds. There was very little blood and she was breathing. When he probed her skull with frantic fingers, she responded with a low moan and her eyes flickered open. All the cuts seemed superficial, as though whatever attacked her merely wanted to be rid of the mysterious robes instead of seeking to cause her harm.

"Fallen and bumped her head against the support beam." AJ pointed to the nearby beam where a few ginger hairs clung. His pale skin was whiter than paper, cobalt eyes wide, calm façade cracked for once, and Harper reminded herself he rarely came with them on missions. He knew nothing in a fight.

"Stay with her." She tried to channel Grace's easy authority as she ran back to the ladder.

"Wait, me?"

Harper was already down on the first floor. She dashed to her room and threw open the chest at the foot of her bed, ignoring the masked stranger sitting beside it. She grabbed her machete and a set of knuckledusters as well as a handful of powder bags, then scrambled back to the attic.

"You okay? Take these." When AJ nodded, she passed him the bags of powdered pepper and herbs. "Grace and I don't reckon these work like the sellers say they do since they don't work on me, but a face-full of pepper will make most things pause regardless. If you see something that isn't us or your coven, lob it."

"Harp, I can't—"

"If Saqib can, you can. Watch my back."

She scanned the shadowy attic again. Their landlady had boarded the floor before they moved in but never finished transforming it to a real bedroom, a fact for which Harper was normally grateful as it stopped someone trying to rent it. As if anyone wanted to bunk with a De Santos and a man who worked for the police anyway.

An unshaded bulb in the centre of the room piled deep shadows behind the wooden pillars and beams. The new boards were firm beneath her feet, no creaks or groans to give away another presence. Harper searched every shadow, weapons ready, but there was nothing there. When she reached the skylight, she opened the shade, steeling herself for the spectres in the fog. Instead, she blinked into a clear blue sky.

Harper leant through the trapdoor, addressing the witch still standing in a corner of Grace's room. "Did anyone see anything leave the attic?"

The caster shook their head. Harper scowled. At least the one in the kitchen had spoken, hadn't tried to preserve anonymity at the expense of the rest of them. She dropped down to the floor and crossed Grace's room in a few short strides. The familiar perfume of coffee, vanilla, and musk settled around her shoulders like a mantle, letting her channel the famous De Santos confidence.

"Look." She poked a finger at the mask, which jerked back. "One of your family is up there with a concussion. We can't call an ambulance because it would get her hanged, so you're going to have to find some way of getting her to a hospital without drawing Guard attention. Whatever attacked her is still out there and it might come back. Your spell failed. One of you better start talking, right now."

"Apologies, Ms. Ashbury. My name is Leslie, ze/he. I'm AJ's fifth and sixth cousin. I think. It's easy to lose track in our family." The witch from the kitchen interrupted from the doorway. Zir mask was removed and Harper could see the family resemblance to AJ in zir mousy brown hair and bright eyes. As soon as Harper's attention was diverted, the one she'd cornered slunk around her and clambered up the attic ladder. "I'm sorry for all the secrecy. There are those amongst our elders"—the young witch flashed a glare over zir shoulder—"who believe a witch in our territory is a threat to us and should be annihilated despite having been overruled following your actions with the Ouse. They therefore wish to keep their identities secret. However, I agree with you that it's better to unite against a common threat."

"Is this a by-product of the spell?" Harper didn't relax her stance, despite zir laid-back posture and tone, so similar to AJ's.

"It's not part of *our* spell. I have no idea what attacked. Hunting that shall have to be down to the De Santos family. It is not our … strongpoint as it is theirs. There has been something amiss since before the Hiding was disrupted, although the lack of magical protection is making it more obvious. That being said, if it had affected the Hiding, the results of it infecting a ritual that powerful could have been catastrophic, so you may have done us a favour by interrupting it."

"Get to the point, Les." AJ clattered back down the ladder to stand with his cousin. "Mel's okay, by the way. She's getting first aid healing as we speak, but she'll need the full works later to be safe. She didn't see anything. She sensed something enter the room, turned to run and tripped over her own robe into the beam. Stupid dress up."

"Certain spells and rituals have had *unintended* side effects," Leslie said delicately, ignoring AJ's criticism. "Not dissimilar to the two you've observed, where the spell worked but also produced an opposing effect. Newtonian physics doesn't customarily apply to magic. I would surmise here that our attempts to keep something *out* of your house have drawn something else *in*."

"Like the hotel bloodbath we're investigating?" Harper asked. "The magic was to banish something and it summoned something else instead." *Maybe that's how Heresy got through too. He said it was difficult and I certainly hadn't intended to summon him. I was trying to See something related to me and I got something unrelated that helps me hide instead.*

Leslie inclined zir head. "It's likely. We don't know what it is or what's causing it. Evidence suggests it shouldn't happen twice in quick succession, so we should be able to complete the ritual. Mel will have to continue on the power of the healing. Leaving the spell with a hole in it would be … problematic." Ze gestured to AJ to follow as ze left the room before Harper could ask what ze meant. AJ threw her a shrug, then went after his cousin.

After completing the ritual, they tidied away the incense, mirrors, and candles, and brushed the salt away from the doors. The red thread was rewound and left with AJ with strict instructions they should all wear a little of it somehow, and to keep as much around the house as they could without suspicion. He went around, binding herbs with the thread and tying it behind pictures on the wall where no one except the most rigorous searcher would look.

The rest of the ball was left on the kitchen table for Grace to sew inside their clothes later. As a vet, she was the only one whose stitches were neat enough, although she would've died had Harper told the two men that Grace was also an excellent embroiderer and secretly rather enjoyed the pastime.

After the coven left, with a lopsided grin from Leslie and a cold shoulder from everyone else, Harper returned to the attic and used her Sight in hopes of glimpsing whatever hurt Mel so she could track it. Guilt gnawed her gut. Once again, her safety had come at the cost of someone else's.

Figures shimmered in the air like ghosts before her burning vision. Mel completing the ritual. A dark swirling hole in the air, no bigger than a dinnerplate. Mel turned at the disruption to the magic, got tangled in her robes and fell, exactly as AJ reported. Something tumbled out of the portal, splatting onto her. It was almost like a white version of Heresy, all static and fluff, then legs splayed and the image resolved itself into a confused cat with a dark collar. Harper couldn't see the details of the disk hanging around its neck, but she was sure she'd See a triquetra there if she could.

Panicked, the animal scrabbled away, claws ripping Mel's robes. It dashed into a corner, eyes wide, chest heaving. The vortex by Mel closed and the cat's lips drew back in a hiss. Then it tapped the air with one paw. Another swirling void appeared and the cat leapt through seconds before the images of her and AJ appeared at the top of the ladder.

"What the heck's with that white cat?" Harper muttered to herself.

Although she and Heresy spent the rest of the day trying to scry for it and searching old children's stories and folktales for mentions of white cats, she was none the wiser by the time she went to bed.

Zero huddled against a tree, shivering in the bitter cold of English hills plagued by January snow flurries. He'd been here. And then he'd been inside somewhere. Then he'd portalled back here.

He clawed at his collar, then hissed as it zapped forks of electricity down his spine. Even thinking about taking it off hurt. Nothing else summoned him like that before. His master summoned him through their shared blood magic. This had been more like a portal opened next to him and sucked him through. But portals didn't do that. Not to him anyway.

He rubbed his head against the bark of a wych elm to try and scratch away the itch that persisted beneath his skin like scarabs scuttering over his skull. Even his marrow itched, his teeth poised just shy of sinking too far into his leg as he tried to reach the discomfort. He'd been unsettled being here anyway. The river in the sweep of the dale sang to him. He chittered at it with guttural hatred. His earliest memory was of that river. Wet. Cold. Trapped in a water-clogged crate. Shipped to his master as tribute by he knew not whom.

The continual low vibration of his collar helped him put aside the sensation of being thrown into a pit of a million fleas. While his master would grudgingly teach him how to ignore such distress, he didn't want to bother zir. A treacherous part of his brain whispered that he didn't want the lesson, although his master's teachings were a blessing. One his rival familiars craved. *I'm lucky. I'm useful.*

It was why he had been sent for this task that his master could entrust to no other. Pride flickered in Zero's chest. Despite his screw up at the hotel, he was the one chosen to prepare the site of the half-moon ritual. Blood would bless the land. The pain of one now would ensure the safety of thousands.

Zero and his master travelled the country repeating rites in different places to hallow the land and ward off the worst of the weather. The magic saved the lives of livestock and farmers alike, although humans never knew how supernaturals aided them. It was part of the Accords that they never find out. Nothing could be allowed to disrupt the spells. Without them, sheep would be lost in snow and shepherds consumed by blizzards. Crops would whither. Starvation.

When the work hurt, Zero leant on the knowledge that they served the land and that, small as his part was, his blood allowed crops to flourish and other folk to live who might otherwise have perished. It was a worthy and noble cause. He was blessed to play a part in it.

He returned his attention to the wych elm. It was the only interesting thing in the immediate vicinity. The disused mineshafts nearby unsettled him almost as much as the river. Dark. Damp. His two least favourite things. Zero circled the tree. Its roots ran deep and faint traces of magic lingered around it. He sniffed it curiously. Another zap of his collar, along with a scattering of rain that made him hiss, reminded him time was short.

It didn't take long, difficult as it was to extract sufficient blood. Zero was almost finished when whistling drifted up the hill. A human hiker, braver than most, straying from their settlements. It was best not to be seen in a place where a house pet wouldn't normally be found. The blood around the tree was unlikely to be noticed. If the hiker saw a darkness out the corner of their eye, they'd assume it was sap or water.

Three knocks on the air opened a portal back to his master's castle and Zero disappeared through the swirling vortex of silver and lilac before the hiker's head crested the hill.

He therefore missed the screaming when the hiker reached the warped elm tree.

CHAPTER ELEVEN

An Untimely Reminder

"You're just in time," Harper greeted Saqib as he came into the kitchen. Grace and AJ were already at the table helping themselves to the bolognaise Harper had prepared.

Saqib gave them a weary wave as he pulled up his chair, rare lines of worry etched across his face. "I have news. After dinner though, so we can all stomach it."

"Hey, Harp's cooking is getting better."

Harper threw her sister a glare. Grace winked at her.

"Heresy and I had an interesting day," AJ said through a mouthful of pasta. Harper rapped his knuckles with the serving spoon and he grinned at her.

"You found something on the dark net," Harper said. He only looked that pleased when he'd done something techy.

AJ smirked and took a large bite of pasta. "Mhmm."

Grace kicked him under the table and he almost choked. Once he cleared his throat, he explained, "Heresy and I have been taking a look around since the coven left. It took some digging, but we found chatter about magic going awry. These are non-human creatures practicing some pretty dark magic to start with. *They're* worried. Most of the occurrences that aren't obviously due to incompetence are being blamed on the Hiding being interrupted. However, we found a few examples that imply there was something wrong before that, like Les said."

"What does Heresy think?" Harper asked.

"Why not ask me?" a voice interrupted from under the table. "I do so hate it when people talk over my head. It is like I am not even here to you."

"You're too bloody here if you ask me," Grace accused as a fine mist rose to settle in Harper's lap.

"Which is why no one asked you, Graceless."

"*Heresy.*" Harper's warning tone elicited a soft growl of satisfaction.

"I do not think this is the work of a single consciousness," Heresy said, returning to topic.

"Either way, it is far beyond anything we can do something about." AJ gestured to the group with his knife.

"Is there a pattern?" Saqib pulled out a notebook and pen and scanned his notes from the hotel murder. "Some similarity behind the magic it's disrupting, or the beings it's targeting?"

"We're still working on that," AJ said as Heresy said, "No."

"You sound certain." Harper looked down with a frown.

"I am certain because I am always right." Heresy's Cheshire Cat grin split his ashen body.

Grace rolled her eyes.

"You've seen this before," Harper accused.

"Now, now Harper dear, there is no need to get prickly. It so happens that I have, or something similar anyway."

"You couldn't have told me earlier?" AJ swatted a hand through the demon who flowed away and reformed on the other side of the table.

"You did not ask."

"What have you seen before, Heresy?" Saqib chewed the end of the pen in his right hand, not noticing he was trying to write with his fork in his left.

"Many, many things," Heresy replied.

"That's because you are hell-spawn," Grace interrupted. "Get to the point."

"It was during the era you refer to as the Industrial Revolution. I was working with a de … spirit on a minor matter involving a child called Eric Wei … something. It was hilarious. The little thing really thought he could fly—"

"The point?" Grace snapped.

"I checked in on the child a few years later. He was working with a despicable man, Rinn, so I was prepared to take my leave rather sharply, when I noticed magical energies gathering around their hocus-pocus."

"What exactly did you sense? Maybe I can work out how to measure—"

"Not now, Saqib," Grace interrupted.

Heresy chuckled before continuing, "Somehow real magic was infecting the falsehoods. I left then, before some human idiocy took place, but I knew someone in the market for mysteries, so I sold it to him. We ran into each other a few decades later and he told me all about it. A local coven let a spell of theirs reproduce like rabbits.

"The hotel disaster is much the same. It is possible these problems are occurring because something is infecting non-magic and making it work. It would certainly explain how this terrible witch managed to summon me."

"You think an accident summoned the demon at The Grand?" Harper asked incredulously.

"A poor combination of spells by someone playing make-believe," Heresy confirmed. "It has leaked into proper magic and causes the world at large to react to the magic, fight it if you will, like an infection."

"Did your 'friend' mention how it was fixed?" AJ asked.

"He did not and I am not interested in methods to stop fun."

Grace's lips turned white as she held back a reply at his casual use of 'fun' to describe something that killed people.

"For now I suggest we leave this alone," AJ said. "The coven are looking into it and none of us have the magic expertise. If Saqib's experiments worked—no offence, mate—maybe we'd have something to offer, but we have enough on our plates trying to find a serial killer before any more women go missing. Harper, Heresy, and I need to be careful what we cast."

"Agreed," Harper said. "So, what about the murders? Now we've finished eating."

Saqib flicked back through his notebook. "I've gone through the full files of the two from North Yorkshire, but they weren't looking for the stuff I look for. Still, the basic similarities to Agnes and Edith are there. Similar physical description, missing for two weeks, eyes gone. Also, I found white cat hairs at The Grand. Not that Edith has been missing two weeks yet but from what Harper Saw, it seems like she was taken by the same thing. Which means it's likely killing them straight away and preserving the bodies somehow, since Harper Saw Edith without her eyes. And there's been another. Same MO. She was missing about two weeks. Young woman, dark hair, brown eyes …" He stuttered off, eyes darting between Harper and Grace, aware his description could be their doppelgänger. "One-hundred-percent sure it's supernatural. Her body was found in a tree but then, well, the tree ate it."

"Ate it?" Grace leant forward in her chair, reflexively reaching for a weapon.

"It's a bit like the girl Harper found in the Tower Street Gardens," Saqib continued. "The tree had a massive hole that wasn't there before. Unlike the one here, this tree closed before the medical examiner got there. The victim is—was—a park ranger in the Dales. She was doing some conservation work and didn't report in at the end of the day. There was nothing for two weeks or so until a hiker found the body."

"Did the Guard cut down the tree?" Harper asked.

"What do you mean?"

"I mean, did they cut it open and check if a body was inside?"

"Not yet. They want us to be there." Saqib gestured towards Harper and himself with his knife. "Apparently they've done a big search of the area and found nothing else tangibly supernatural but the rangers who went highest in the hills around reported having strange dreams afterward. Since visions and dreams are part of your thesis, they hope you'll know something, Harp."

Harper barely heard his words, breath caught in her throat. Liquid, red and bright, slid down the knife in Saqib's hand, lumps and clots oozing as they dripped to the floor. The blade reflected rough-hewn stone. A different hand gripped the hilt, the knife sharp and pointed like a misericord. The image overlaid reality like a daydream no amount of lucidity could control. Her mouth formed words but no sound came out. Her eyes burned and she screwed them closed until gold and green flashes of light formed.

"Harper? What's wrong?"

Saqib's voice was distant. She remembered red glistening, dripping from her fingers, dropping through the mist to disappear before it hit the ground.

I will find you …

The words echoed through her head. Harper pushed herself away from the table with a cry. Her mug was knocked to the ground where it shattered, spraying hot liquid and shards of porcelain.

She looked at Saqib, her eyes bloodshot. "Where was it? Where was she when she went missing. Where?"

"Harper, are you okay?" Grace's voice seemed distant, her tight grip on Harper's shoulders unreal.

"Where?"

"I don't know exactly. Somewhere in Swaledale south of the river."

Harper slid off her chair, clutching her head as images rushed in. Trees, snow crisp across dark branches. Mists swirling around her, filling her lungs with icy droplets. The river gushing around her, rapid but shallow as her bare feet splashed through it. Her lungs aching with exertion, stitch lancing through her side. A voice telling her to keep running.

Then, suddenly, nothing. Nothing but white.

She felt numb, as though she were a construct of flesh without a soul to give it life. The terror of a moment before was gone, both from her body and her mind. She had no past, no future. Just the endless white of mist and snow.

"What are you?" A voice shattered the white, a dark form appearing before her. A voice in her mind, far from the warm kitchen of home.

"I'm a … I'm Harper." She remembered the words, remembered this meeting with Grace's father even though she could recall nothing before it.

"Where have you come from?"

"I don't know."

"Harper. Don't make me throw water over you again." Grace pressed a cool, wet towel to Harper's forehead. "Come back to me. Please."

Eyes scrunched closed, Harper nodded. The memory of Father De Santos faded, his shadow in her mind replaced by Grace's solid presence in the now.

"Sorry, Gray. Everyone. It's just … that's where I came from, we think. It was a vision of an old memory, not anything useful in the now. I'm sorry."

"Nothing to apologise for." Grace hefted Harper back into her chair and Saqib pressed a glass of water into her hands, echoing the same sentiment.

While the others planned and discussed the case, Harper stared at her fingers, only half listening. One word echoed over and over in her head. The place where her life had begun and this ranger's life had ended.

Swaledale.

CHAPTER TWELVE

The Maw of the Wych Elm

The broad dale stretched out before them. Wind ruffled Harper's hair. Light sprays of rain caught on the strands and sparkled in the morning sun. Music haunted the air, whether a true song or the wind whistling through naked tree branches, Harper couldn't say. The village of Reeth lay below them. Smoke from cottage chimneys mingled with the mist and hung over the village like a cloud of wraiths.

She leant against the car as she drank in the landscape, glad to have left the Guard outpost at the Catterick Garrison behind. They were suspicious of everyone going over the top between Wensleydale and Swaledale, yet it still felt as personal as the first time she'd been through the checkpoint. Then, she'd been on her way out of Swaledale, an undocumented child believed to be possessed and only allowed passage because of Father De Santos's strict watch.

Grace stood next to her, arm around her shoulders to provide a shield against the bitter wind as they contemplated the view. Worms wriggled through Harper's stomach and her bones were made of water. To return now, so close to the anniversary of the date she was found, filled her with terror so deep she couldn't force her feet onwards yet hope battled it. She might finally find the answers she sought. Shame clawed at her heart. If she did find the answers, it was a victory that came at the cost of someone else's life.

The blankness of Harper's memories frightened her as a teenager. Deep dread had spread roots and grown through her chest, warning her to stay away from the seemingly pleasant dale. Every nerve in her screamed it could kill her. Despite this, her yearning for home drove her back there again and again, until there was nothing left to explore. When hope fled, she'd been left with emptiness and fear.

In the daylight, Swaledale gave off an air of benign pastoral calm. It was deceptively spacious, broad and without guile. Sweeping fields rolled down to a slow and steady river. Scattered clumps of evergreens were dwarfed by the lush green of farmland. At its height the dale turned wild with mourning purples, greys of heather, and bare rock showing where humanity's docility ended. This early in January, frost swept its icy fingers over the road and snow clumped between shoots of grass and the roots of wych elm and ash.

The main roads were considered safe, the few villages untroubled by supernatural occurrences. During the day, people tended flocks of sheep and herds of cattle. The hills came alive with the sound of bleating and the calls of shepherds to their dogs.

But at night … at night, they locked their doors. At night, no sane farmer set foot outside, no matter the pleas of the herd. At night, they pulled their curtains closed and huddled by their fires, or cowered amongst their livestock in stone barns, isolated pools of life dotted across the landscape.

At night, mist owned the land.

Harper turned away from the view and collapsed into the backseat of the car, letting Grace take the front seat next to Saqib. She was desperate to find a way home, but a sense of impending doom tightened her chest and jellified her limbs. The pull to go and the pressure to stay caught her mind in a web of indecision.

As the engine growled to life, the choice was taken from her, and they descended into Reeth. Beyond the picturesque village, the land sheered upwards and the wild of the Yorkshire Moors broke through. Saqib drove cautiously around black-iced puddles made visible by the collar of frost at their edges.

In the village, they met a group of park rangers. Saqib got out, exchanged a few words with their leader, then returned to the car. They followed the rangers' jeep over bumpy back roads and tractor tracks towards the last known location of the missing woman. The deeper they travelled into the dale, crisscrossing its eponymous river, the more Harper's apprehension grew. It scratched like nails in the back of her brain, clawing, fighting to keep her away. Anxiety coursed through her.

Sweat dripped down her back. Hairs on her arms and neck prickled. Breaths came in short, sharp bursts. She shouldn't be there. It was too dangerous. She'd be killed. She'd be taken back and …

Harper held her breath, staring at the river flashing between the trees as they ascended the southern hills. Scudding clouds were left behind them, fleeing east while the convoy headed west. Weak winter sunlight turned the river scintillating neon and gave the fields an ethereal radiance, as though the boundary between one world and the next was thin. *Maybe it is.* Maybe that was her problem. Maybe she *had* come from somewhere else, somewhere beyond.

Father De Santos's first words echoed in her mind. *What are you?*

"What am I?" she whispered to the steamed glass as she rubbed a patch clean to stare out.

"What was that?" Grace demanded from the front.

"Nothing. Just …"

Grace reached back to squeeze Harper's knee. "Nothing's going to happen to you. Not while I'm here."

Harper's confidence and sense of equilibrium trickled back. Whatever else she might be, she was Grace's sister, and nothing would ever change that. The thought brought a smile to her lips and her apprehension settled to a background niggle. She might not know who she had been, but she knew who she was now. Long ago, she had decided she couldn't put her whole life on hold because she was missing the first thirteen years or so. People changed a lot in a decade. Even if she hadn't lost her birth family and home, that thirteen-year-old wasn't the person she'd be now.

Not far beyond the hamlet of Crackpot, the road could take them no farther and they got out to hike. Snow piled on the uneven drystone walls and frost muted the usual greens of the fields beyond. It was like stepping into a black-and-white photograph. Within minutes Harper's cheeks were numb and her fingers were sore even through her gloves. Cold and music struck her, both tied to the soaring wind. It was the same tune she'd heard the day she met the Foss, the one calling her North and was so familiar for all she couldn't remember why. It no longer came from the river but flowed down the hill like a waterfall.

Some of the park rangers went ahead while others brought up the rear, leaving Harper's team and the medical examiner bunched in the middle carrying the two scientists' equipment. For once, Grace didn't try and take command, graciously allowing the experts to organise and lead.

When Harper raised an eyebrow in shocked question, she replied, "It's a poor general who doesn't use the expertise of her people."

Harper could think of a few choice examples where Grace hadn't followed that advice, but she held her tongue. It had taken a lot for Grace to let her take the lead with the Ouse.

They continued to climb, following Thorn Sike up to its source, then higher, through the Shake Holes and past Hog Gill until they were almost at Tarn Seat at the top of the hill. The moon, a sliver past half full, was a pale memory of zirself as though it hung over another world glimpsed through the Veil. The walk brought back memories for Harper, but not the ones she wanted. Memories of searching these hills for answers, fear of being sucked back into a past that hurt her all the while driven by the unquenchable need to know more. She balled her fists in frustration, quickening her pace. The silence of the hills reproached her. The eyes from her dreams weren't visible in the wakening, but their gaze raked her skin and bored into her heart.

When they reached the top, the rangers fell back to a defensive perimeter. Looking at them properly for the first time, Harper noted one who looked winded from the climb and kept silent. The rest of the rangers shot nervous glances his way. Not simply a newcomer then. Harper gave a small snort. Of course the Guard sent someone.

She turned her head away, talking out the corner of her mouth. "See him?"

A chortle from beneath her hair, at the base of her neck, confirmed Heresy had. "Long before you did, Harper dearest. Do not worry. I can conceal you from such a poor adversary."

While Grace talked to the head ranger, Harper helped Saqib set up his equipment. He'd brought the lights that had been so effective at illuminating the writing on Usa's victims, as well as cameras and other gadgets Harper hadn't seen before. The Guard's financial assistance was one of the few perks to their association.

"They said she last reported in from near these disused shafts. That tree is the one the hiker found her in." Saqib pointed to a gnarled wych elm. "Even though there's no visible trace of the hole, I want to examine it before they cut it down to see if she's still inside. We'll start here and work our way towards it so we don't step on any evidence, if there is any left."

As he tweaked the final details of his setup, Harper stepped aside, her back to the humans. She closed her eyes, willing magic to come to the fore. When she opened them again, dim green was coated in a lurid ultraviolet-esque glow, the result of Saqib's lights. As he cycled through different frequencies which had revealed the lettering on different victims of the Ouse, Harper concentrated on the tree. She stared at it until her peripheral vision blackened and the surrounding countryside turned static and stiff, like the thin card pages of a pop-up book. Her breath curled through the bitter air. Clouds closed in again. There should've been a rainbow to brighten the monochrome world but, if there was, Harper didn't see it. All her concentration stayed locked on the tree.

"Anything?" Saqib asked. "I thought I saw something on this wavelength but it might have been my imagination. It was very faint, and I can't see it now."

His voice was no more than a breath on the breeze that flushed her skin and toyed with her hair. The world glittered, each droplet of rain refracting the lights as though she stood in a hall of disco balls. Everything slowed, the rain suspended in the air. A river crashed down the hill, broader and deeper than the trickles they'd passed on the way up. Like the river she'd Seen herself and her brother on. The dale stretched. Longer. Deeper. Vaster.

Run, Harper. A voice from her dreams. It twisted into the image in her mind of two children and a cat boating. It wasn't her brother's voice, nor the Protector's. Had she missed someone else being there?

The wych elm creaked and bent against the pressure. Its roots strained through the muddied ground. Shadows of its branches swished over Harper's skin. The fear of sheep and cows was drowned out by the mournful tune of a violin, a half step out of key and a semiquaver out of time. Waves of dissonance beat at the droplets of water in the air, a shimmer rippling around her.

Run, Harper.

Darkness billowed through the dale. Fog, black as soot from the coal mines, devoured everything in its path. It rolled up the hill, the music amplified as heavy charcoal clouds descended to meet it. The world disappeared. Everything save the tree, a crooked crack in the darkness.

Darkness.

Harper's chest tightened. Her heart hammered against her sternum and crushed her lungs. Rain plastered her clothes to her body, tight, constricting like a mummy's bandages. Hair slapped against her face, sticky, sodden.

The tree groped towards her, grasping across an impossible distance. Twigs snagged the buttons of her coat and the ribbon in her hair. They tugged her forward, chitinous mandibles dragging in their prey. The bark of the tree trunk split, dark sap gushing like a severed artery.

Run.

"Run!" A sharp electrostatic shock to the back of her neck snapped Harper back to reality. She stumbled back as she reached up, her fingers touching something vaporous, almost intangible in the heavy rain, hidden against her neck by her pulled up collar. Heresy.

Harper looked at the tree, half the distance away it was before. She rubbed the back of her neck, her hair all on end, trying to ease the soreness at the base of her skull from Heresy's rude awakening. Rain whipped in a frenzy. The sun had vanished behind dark clouds that appeared as though summoned. *Something's wrong.*

"Harper? Is everything alright?" Grace called through the storm. Her sister battled her way over to stand next to Harper. Grace's nails dug into her arm even through her thick coat. "Did you See something? The rangers think we should go back. This sudden storm. They weren't expecting anything worse than some showers. They think the site is cursed."

"She's still in the tree," Harper shouted over the wind's howling. Beneath it, through it, she could hear the violin. It wrapped around her, binding to her soul.

"Harper, it is here." Heresy had never sounded afraid before. "We have to leave. Now."

"What's here? What is it?" Harper twisted, trying to See.

"Eyes. Harp. We have to go." Grace dragged Harper back by the arm, towards where the rangers were helping Saqib bundle his equipment in waterproof tarps.

"No, Gray, wait." Harper tried to yank her arm back but her sister's grip was too tight. For once, Grace's heeled shoes proved an asset as she pushed them into the mud like grappling hooks, where Harper's sneakered feet slipped and slid treacherously. "She's in the tree, Gray. She's in there."

Grace spun, her nose an inch from Harper's. Rain drove between them, trying to push them apart.

"She's dead." Grace shouted. "We can't reach her. The storm is too heavy for the equipment. We must go." Wind buffeted them, thrusting them closer to the tree. Grace dug her heels in, leaning against the wind. Wet hair cut across her face like gashes, glistening like blood.

Lightning crashed on the hilltop, thunder a heartbeat later, galloping down the dale like an army. It illuminated every raindrop, brilliant white almost blinding them. When their eyes cleared, they could no longer see Saqib nor the rangers. The raindrops hurtled so fast and close it was as if they stood under a waterfall.

The heel of Grace's shoe snapped. She yelped as she slid. Her grip on Harper tightened further, dragged them down together. Mud slicked their descent. They tumbled down the hill, clinging to each other. Harper hit a protruding stone. It knocked the breath from her. Pain lanced through her ribs. She dug her nails into her sister's leather jacket but she couldn't see Grace anymore. The world tilted and spun. Something hard hit her temple. Hands clawed up her arm to grab her shoulders.

Grace pulled Harper to her, protecting her sister with her own body. She twisted, turning them feet first, taming their mad tumble, yet still they slid. They smashed into the tree. Lightning struck it at the same time they did. The electric ripple burnt through them. Thunder rang in their ears. The maw of the tree opened. Then Harper knew nothing but darkness.

CHAPTER THIRTEEN

Buried Alive

"Grace? Heresy?" The darkness swallowed Harper's trembling words. Earth had closed over her head, muzzling both storm and violin. A presence lurked in the inky silence—watching, waiting. Sentient. Putrid odours of flesh, faeces, and fruit saturated the space, forcing themselves past Harper's lips and down her nose and throat. She gagged, covering her mouth with a sodden sleeve. Every nerve sang of danger. Not just her fear of darkness nor of being alone. An active sense of death hovered over her goosed skin and breathed down her spine. Eyes bored into the back of her neck. Incisors poised to sever her jugular.

"Harper?"

A hiccupping sob escaped as her sister's voice squeezed through the silence. Harper reached out, blindly patting the earth around her. The squelch between her fingers and each shallow, panting breath brought fresh waves of nausea. She closed her eyes, shutting out the darkness. When her fingers encountered a human hand, she clutched at it. "Gray? Are you hurt? Do you have Heresy?"

"I am here, Harper dearest," Heresy purred in her ear. "What an interesting shelter you've found for us."

"Harper, where are you?" Grace's question was almost a demand.

"I'm right here. I'm holding–" The words choked off in her throat. The hand beneath hers was cold and clammy. She'd expected that, with the storm, the January chill. But it didn't move, the fingers stiff and unbending. The stench struck her again and her stomach heaved. "Grace? Whose hand is this?"

Grace's voice was measured, cautious. "Well, it's not mine, so I suggest letting go."

Harper dropped the hand. Her palm stung with the need to scrub away the slimy substance coating it, to strip down to the skin and then remove even that to be rid of the taint. She scrabbled back. The soles of her trainers kicked something heavy.

"Grace? Where are you? Please …" Harper's voice cut off in a strangled whine. Panic washed over her. Drums pounded against her skull as her fists pounded the earth overhead. Her chest was too tight to breathe. They were inside the tree. With a dead woman. Like the one she found in the park. Only this time there were no stars or moon. No police would come to her rescue with flashing reds and blues, and brilliant white torches.

"Harper, close your eyes." Grace sounded unruffled as ever.

There was a click, then a thunk, once, twice, then warmth on Harper's eyelids and the pitch black took on a hint of amber. Grace shuffled closer. The hand wrapping around Harper's ankle almost sent her into a spiral until she recognised her sister's touch.

"You can open them now, but go slow," Grace cautioned.

It took a moment for her eyes to adjust. When they did, Harper almost wished Grace left it dark. Almost. It was impossible not to see the tangled corpse in the centre, but Harper tried, casting her eyes across the root-lined walls and packed earth ceiling. She wondered how she could've groped for Grace and not found her in the cramped space. Her sister was covered in mud, and Harper was sure she looked equally monstrous.

Unable to avoid it any longer, Harper swallowed the lump in her throat and forced herself to look at the fourth occupant of the nightmare. Grace had positioned herself between the person's head and Harper, so all she could see were legs, waist, and a hand. She recognised the uniform, even covered in mud. It was the same as the rangers' who brought them there. She turned to crawl around Grace and get a look at the woman's face but Grace moved with her, blocking the view.

"Harper." Her voice was gentle.

Harper looked up at her, brow furrowed in confusion. "Grace, it's okay. I know she's dead."

"No. Harp. It's …" Grace pursed her lips, then took a deep breath and continued. "She's a little older maybe but … she looks *just* like you. Not only like Saqib was saying, because dark hair and eyes isn't uncommon but …exactly like you. She could be your … your sister."

A roar filled Harper's ears. The ground slid beneath her again. Green and gold lights filled her vision. Then the world went dark.

"Shit. Sorry."

The vulgarity, a rarity from Grace, cleared Harper's mind. She patted the ground around her carefully, until she found something metal and cylindrical. Grace's torch.

"Graceless, such language," Heresy scolded.

Harper scowled. He was enjoying this far too much. He must not have a sense of smell.

"I've got it." When Harper switched it on, the light flickered and stuttered like a candle in the wind. She leant against the earthen wall, counting her breaths until her racing heart wasn't quite so likely to explode.

"We need to find a way out." Business-like. Abrupt. That was Grace and it improved Harper's mood no end. "There can't be much air down here and this torch won't last long. Something's affecting it, magic maybe. The batteries were fully charged."

Harper's insides twisted at the thought of plunging them into darkness again. It frightened her more than suffocation. With the light, the prickly sensation of being watched receded. If it went dark again, the hunter would return. She knew this in the pit of her stomach despite the logic of her eyes. Something was waiting.

"Heresy, do you sense any magic?"

"That was no normal storm. I warned you it was there, and you did not leave."

"What was there?" Harper asked. Anxiety bubbled in her core.

"Your hunter. Whatever it is, its magic is all over this place. It appears to have left a trap for you." Heresy slithered down Harper's arm, leaving a trail of prickled hairs. He contorted to peer around Grace at the deceased. "If this one does share blood with us, it is so many generations ago that I cannot sense it now she is dead. Alive, maybe, I could tell or see if she possessed latent magic, but magic leaves the body with soul and thought. Their similarities may be a coincidence, but her presence here is not. She is a lure."

"By what?" The torchlight glinted off Grace's knuckledusters.

"Something ancient. There was blood around this tree as well as within it. Blood that is not hers. Saqib may be able to tell more." Heresy sounded unusually serious as he slithered around their earthen prison.

"We need to find a way to get out first," Harper said. "We should disturb her as little as possible. Saqib will already be upset we've compromised evidence."

"Hardly something we could help. Our lives come first, Harp." Grace removed her jacket and lay it over the face and shoulders of the dead woman. "We'll come back and give her a proper burial once we work out how to get out. This looks more like a badger sett or fox's den, rather than a grave the killer dug. The rangers would've noticed that in a heartbeat." As she talked, Grace took back the light and crawled around the space, prodding the wall with dirty fingers.

Harper opened her mouth to disagree, then thought better of it. 'I think the tree opened up and swallowed us' wasn't helpful. Instead, she closed her eyes, summoning her magic. If the tree had swallowed them, it wasn't a trick of the lightning or some natural phenomenon. Heresy said there was magic and, while he could be annoyingly deceptive with the truth, he'd never been caught in a lie. Magic brought them there and it would take magic to get them out. The fizzle of arcane power dug behind her retinas and scratched down the optic nerve but when she opened her eyes, nothing looked different.

Harper sidled closer to the body and peaked under Grace's jacket. Dark voids gaped back at her. Like the girl in the tree. Like Agnes. Like Edith. Grace was being paranoid, Harper decided. The woman's dark hair and athletic build were hardly uncommon features. She looked to be in her mid-thirties, almost a decade older than Harper too. The killer had a type, another clue this was not another Hiding but something else. Something relating to Sight, maybe? Harper was certain there weren't another six women in Yorkshire with her ability but maybe they had the potential. If magic wasn't banned and someone could unlock it.

"Ignore her." Grace snapped her fingers under Harper's nose. "I can't believe I'm suggesting this but try to See something."

"I cannot believe I am saying this, but I agree with the snippy one," Heresy chortled.

Harper swallowed a retort. Her irritation was for the darkness and frustration with the murders, not for Grace. She'd been close to something.

"Harp. Try to See something. We need to get out of here."

Harper tore her eyes away from the corpse and cast her magic gaze around the small space again. "I can't See anything, Gray. I-I can't. I—" A dull roar filled her ears as flickering lights zinged before her eyes again.

Grace gripped her wrist. "Don't panic, Harp. Remember Gabriel's story about the guy who got trapped in the mine when he was hunting a mad tommyknocker? The way out was there, but he was too panicked to see it. We'll find a way out. Keep trying."

Taking a deep breath, she looked again. There were no signs of disturbed earth, which supported her theory the tree ate them. She studied the mess of roots around them. Pulses of green flashed along them, sickly to her violet Sight. Her gaze snagged near the middle of the mass.

Ghostly hands reached past her, bloody fingers clutching something angled and white. They pressed into the earth with a click that rattled through her. A key. A single note wavered, setting her teeth on edge, as a singsong voice whispered in the back of her mind.

Fire to light our path,
Earth to join our bones,
Air to cry our songs,
Water to find our home.

The vision left her shaken. Had she been here before or was she Seeing someone else? Another ancestor like her vision of Leonora? She pinched her arm. There wasn't time. "Grace, Heresy, take a look at this. I think I found a keyhole."

"I don't see anything." Grace pulled a set of lockpicks out of the pouch on her belt and swapped them with Harper for the torch. "These have been blessed to work against magic. Give it a go."

It had been a long time since Harper used a set and her fingers felt chunky and heavy. She inserted the picks into the lock, muttering, "Open, open, open." She tried to draw from the magic within her, as Heresy taught her, and envisioned the symbol on AJ's desktop for opening a new magical program. The picks burned her fingers, glowing red, and she dropped them. The dry grass lining the hole caught. Grace pushed Harper aside, stamping out the flames before they could spread.

The singsong voice still echoed in Harper's mind, a song from a dream. A child's song, maybe, a nursery rhyme with a grain of truth. *Earth to join our bones.* The hand had clasped a white key. A shiver skittered over her skin.

"Think, Harper." She tapped her forehead, forgetting the filth clinging to her hand. "Think. 'Fire to light our path.' Well, you have the torch and your Sight and you Saw a way out. 'Earth to join our bones.' We need to join a bone key to open the earth. 'Our bones, our bones.'"

'No, Harper. That was the past. Do not believe the lies of those who deserted us. You know the truth.'

'Yes. Somnia sunt clavis. Somnia sunt libertas. Somnia sunt salus. Somnia sunt veritas. I See the truth. I won't stray from the Protector's path.'

"Harp, what are you muttering about? Is this some spell?" Grace asked as she checked for any last traces of fire.

"When did you learn Latin, Harper dear?" Heresy's sharp smile luminesced in the shadows. "Are you falling into its trap? I would not go to sleep in a nest made by your enemy."

"I'm wide awake," Harper snapped. She'd heard a woman's voice, not Grace, and the voice of the little girl on the river. Her younger self.

"It does not sound it, deluded one," Heresy said. "'Dreams are the key. Dreams are freedom. Dreams are salvation. Dreams are the truth.' It sounds like the indoctrination of one who wishes you to sleep and never wake up."

The only time Latin was used anymore was in church, and even that was rare. She knew a smattering from her studies—it was a common arcane language—but not enough to speak it. Had her ancestors used it as a universal language on their travels? Or did the spell date back further, to when Rome ruled here?

"Harp. Focus. Academic questions later. Getting out *now*." Grace interrupted her thoughts with the accuracy of a rapier stab.

"I … remember being here before, or somewhere like this." Harper rubbed her forehead again. Holding onto the memories was giving her a pounding headache. Her eyes dragged themselves over the corpse and she felt ill. They couldn't defile the woman's body. Could they? If the alternative was death?

Heresy flowed over to inspect the corpse. "You were also murmuring about bones."

"I've Seen a way out," Harper said reluctantly. "I think this is how I escaped before." Despite their desperate situation, hope fizzled in her chest, leaving her lightheaded. "I had a key, a bone key. The spell says, 'earth to join our bones' so I think I need to use a bone to open the earth over us."

Grace's eyes darted to the corpse as well. "No."

"It says '*our* bones' …" Harper petered out, looking at her fingers covered in mud and gore. The ethereal hands overlaid them, the bone key resting across one palm. They floated away, unattached to any body, then turned, palms down, and the key vanished as it dropped. Harper scrambled past Grace and around the dead ranger. "Over here."

She dug through dead leaves, squelched mud between her fingers, clawed at roots, until she encountered something hard and smoother than bark. It had been buried deep, lost in the years and drowned by the storm, but it was still there. A finger, bones held together by thin metallic wire.

Left for the one I expected to follow. A dull ache formed in her chest at the unbidden thought. Whom had she expected? Had they followed and she'd forgotten them, or were they still trapped wherever she'd escaped from?

Run, Harper.

The same voice she'd heard outside. A boy's voice, unbroken and full of tears. Not the brother she'd heard on the river. *Did they stay to protect me or are they out there somewhere?* Her hand clenched around the bone and she jammed the key into the lock she Saw, turning it this way and that like a lockpick. The bone caught on something solid and stuck fast.

"Air to cry our songs." Harper swallowed her revulsion, not wanting to put her face closer to the old bone or slick mud. The torch flickered, sending tentacle shadows slithering across the walls and quickening Harper's breath. She wouldn't be trapped here in the dark, with a body, and air running out. She screwed up her courage and quashed the rising gall. Placing her lips to the hole, she blew around the protruding bone, singing wordlessly to capture the note she'd Heard in her vision. When she found it, the vibrations rattled her teeth and shook the ground. Purple light flashed and there was a click behind them.

"Not sure how we explain, but for now I'm just happy to get out of here." Grace headed straight for the opening, knife in her hand. Harper scooped up Heresy and crawled after her, following the thin light of Grace's torch.

The tunnel wound through the hill, sloping downwards, rivulets of water marking the way. Dim light, when it appeared, took them by surprise. They emerged on the banks of the Swale, muddy and exhausted, out of what appeared to be the entrance to a foxhole.

Harper knelt next to the river, rinsing her hands then splashing water across her face. "Thank you," she whispered, hoping the river spirit would hear.

The broad dale swept up behind her, the tree they'd fallen into lost to the hills and descending fog, but Harper noted the place. The river was familiar as a dream. Some real memory of time there with Grace's family, no doubt. But overlaid now was the image of the young girl and her brother steering a raft with two long poles. It wavered, but held in her mind, opaque.

Water to find our home.

CHAPTER FOURTEEN

Taking Action

Zero prowled the beams of the castle's main hall. From this angle he couldn't see the wall tapestries and their deceptively serene scenery that masked a macabre torment of humans and folk. All he could see was the dais with his master's throne, the emptiness of the pillared chamber, and the deep shadows waiting. Magic fizzled under his skin and rippled a rainbow through his white fur. If One wanted to play cat-and-mouse, he refused to be the mouse. First he had to find her, though, and his master had forbidden him to use magic.

Direct magic, anyway. The castle liked Zero. Stone scraped over stone as the castle created a slender staircase for him. Each block slid out no more than the width of a paw, then slid back into the wall as soon as Zero passed it. He left the main chamber behind, staying high up as the castle created pathways for him. It had been One's undoing in more than one of these endless challenges. She didn't think multi-dimensionally. Still, Zero wasn't going to be complacent. Precedent that she didn't normally look up didn't mean she wouldn't start. Her apparent foolishness might all be part of a longer plan. He had to be vigilant or he could lose more than the privilege of assisting their master. One wanted his place at their master's side, and if that meant 'accidentally' maiming or killing him, then she'd see it as a bonus. She *was* allowed magic.

As he stalked through the vast castle, Zero used all his senses to search for her. A rapidly fading botanical scent hung in the air. A little bit of abnormality so far underground. While the castle above nurtured a sweeping wildflower garden where its moat had once been, the parts of the castle Zero and the other familiars inhabited was deep underground. Zero followed the scent of hare. Without magic, she had the advantage. Her brown fur blended better with the stone walls and she moved almost silently. As surely as he was hunting her, One was hunting him. Zero had long since stopped regretting his part in helping his master create the other familiars. It was One's choice to make herself a hunter, a fighter. It was her choice to enjoy it when she hurt him.

'You are naturally a lazy cat, Zero. Allowing One and others to challenge your position as prime keeps you from getting complacent. Our magics are too important. I must have the strongest and most committed of my familiars at my side.'

Zero's chest swelled with pride for being the one allowed this honour. Yet, there had been times where he'd failed. Declawed and with his magic blocked, One had almost beaten him. That was part of the lesson for both of them. For him, that he needed to do better next time, and for her, that she was still inferior. *'Inferior.'* Zero shied away from the word. His master used it often but it created an uncomfortable lump in Zero's throat. One wasn't inferior. She was what she had been created to be. A prototype. A throwaway. The first experiment that worked as his master's tried to make more of Zero.

How Zero had been created was one of the few things his master didn't know. All Zero knew was it involved *her* blood, the woman he saw in dreams that slipped from his memory as soon as he awoke. No other dreams did that. Only hers. Seeing her in the wakening hurt his chest and filled him with a longing he couldn't explain. He couldn't remember ever being a kitten, his memories began the day he met his master, but when he saw her, he felt like one. Like she was the mama cat he'd never had, or the sibling One could never be.

Zero shook himself. If he daydreamed, One would catch him. A hare might lack the hunting prowess of a cat, but she made up for it with scheming and stubbornness. She wanted his place at their master's side more than anything. Sometimes, Zero wished he could give it to her, selfish and lazy cat that he was. *It's an honour to give blood and magic to protect the land.* His master used his blood to make One. *If she's less magical, less strong, then I'm to blame for that too.*

The scent led him deep underground. *Definitely a trap.* She wouldn't have come this deep into the bowels of the castle. One wasn't an explorer like he was. She followed the rules. A good familiar. The sadness of 'Bad Cat' slowed Zero's steps, but he trudged on. If he occasionally took a little time at the end of a mission to fish or to listen to art at a gallery, that didn't harm anyone. Did it?

There. A movement on the ground caught his eye and all feels vanished. He focused on his prey. The large hare hopped cautiously down the corridor, her nose twitching. Despite a decade of animosity, Zero wanted to bap it. His whiskers quivered and he crouched low against the stone walkway the castle provided for him. Closer. Closer. Still she didn't look up. It must be a trap.

Zero pounced. One looked up a fraction of a second too late and he bowled her over. Tooth and claw dug through her fur into flesh. His teeth closed at her throat, his weight pinned her to the flagstones, yet she didn't give up. She fought his hold to the point of exhaustion. Another reason Zero always won, magic or no magic. He always outlasted her, no matter what damage she inflicted on him. She couldn't handle the high magics of the New Year rituals and other similarly draining rites.

While Zero acknowledged this was a lesson One needed to learn, he didn't appreciate being his master's method of demonstration. It made his fur icky and his skin prickle.

"Here, kitty, kitty."

Zero sprang back. No one in the castle would ever address him thus. Only one person ever called him kitty, and even that was in their dreams. If the beautiful dreamer he visited ever ended up here, then Zero would die of remorse. His mind fractured for a moment, a rare glimpse of the horrifying truth of the agony his master could inflict. Then those shards buried themselves deep in his brain again. His master looked after him, and he must look after his master. He crouched and hissed, eyes sweeping the corridor.

One used the opportunity to kick him hard in the ribs. She boxed his ear at the same time. Bowled over, Zero hit the wall. He was on his feet again in a second. One aimed another kick, which Zero dodged. He tapped the air twice and a swirling vortex opened. As One aimed another kick, he pounced, knocking her backwards. The castle heaved under her feet and tipped her through the portal. It vanished as soon as she did.

Zero mewed soft thanks to the castle. It recognised there was an intruder here even if One didn't.

"Here, kitty, kitty, kitty."

This time he spotted it, a black-clad, masked apparition he'd seen before. Zero cursed his wandering mind. He should've noticed when he'd entered this part of the castle. The figure stood exactly where he'd seen it last time, its back to an impossible sunset that streamed through an open door. Rather than fight it, Zero knocked another portal and darted through, straight into his master's lap. He grabbed zir sleeve in his teeth and tugged.

It's back. It's back. Come see.

For once, his master didn't question the interruption, though a quick glance at zir desk showed neatly stacked notes and bubbling alchemical apparatus. Zir mask was glittering gold and carmine, long fingers stained the same colours, matching the science and blood magic ze mixed.

"The fetch again? Show me, Zero." Ze stood, with the cat cradled against zir chest.

Upon hearing his master's real voice, it became obvious what had bothered Zero about the spectre's. His master's voice was made of myriad tones—old, young, all genders, north and south—but the creature he'd encountered was decidedly feminine. It added the witch's voice to his master's.

Zero knocked a portal back to where he'd come from. The creature, so like his master at a first glance, was but a watery reflection next to the real thing.

"Show yourself," his master commanded.

"Here, kitty, kitty." It held out a hand, rubbing its fingers together as it attempted to entice Zero over. His master's grip on him tightened and a warm sense of safety cushioned Zero. *Master is here. Everything will be alright.*

"Show yourself." His master's tone lost its usual calm veneer, showing the sharp edges underneath. Ze never needed to repeat an order. Except to Zero because Zero was a Bad Cat.

The phantom lowered its mask to reveal his master's face. Only it wasn't quite his master's face. The myriad folk in zir features were all there, shifting beneath zir skin, but there was another. Her appearance was too fleeting to pin down features, but Zero knew who she was. The eyes always gave folk away for none but the most powerful could disguise them fully. Out of the doppelgänger's shifting gaze, violet eyes stared. The fetch wasn't solely a portent of his master's death. It foretold Harper's as well.

Harper's hard, metal chair squeaked in protest as she squirmed under the rigid gaze of Lieutenant Albrecht. The Guardswoman's eyes reflected nothing of the office they sat in. The image in them was one of a swinging noose.

"We sent a team of specialists to retrieve the body and the tree in which it was interred and you return empty-handed, put off by some inclement weather?" The woman arched an eyebrow. "I thought park rangers and the De Santos family were made of sterner stuff. Your reputations must be nothing more than your own gross fictions."

Harper gave a thin smile. Insulting her family may make her stomach roil with anger, but she wasn't going to give the Guard the satisfaction of knowing it. Church and State had an old rivalry and she refused to fall for petty politics. "Don't think I didn't notice your 'undercover' guy pretending to be a ranger. If we were fobbed off so easily, why didn't he retrieve her body?"

"The storm wasn't natural," Saqib cut in before the lieutenant could retort.

Saqib, the medical examiner, and the rangers had been forced to flee, then found the storm abated as soon as they reached the cars. When they turned around to go back, it resumed.

"My apparatus detected unexplained radiation," Saqib continued. "Nothing harmful with short exposure, but not natural for that area. The spectrometer picked up some odd stuff too. We were so close to the lightning that it appeared white, but it was actually on the purple end of the spectrum. While not rare, purple tends to mean drier air, definitely not the case here. It could also be indicative of higher levels of oxygen and nitrogen."

"Which signifies ...?" Albrecht asked.

Saqib shrugged. "Could be low lightning, there's more oxygen lower in the atmosphere. It might mean nothing. I try not to make assumptions."

Or it could be purple because my magic is. Harper didn't want to make assumptions either, but there were an awful lot of coincidences happening. She tagged herself in to take the heat of Albrecht's stare off Saqib.

"Grace and I saw the body but we couldn't drag it with us through the foxes' tunnels," she said. "That would've been disrespectful and potentially destroyed evidence Saqib and the doctor needed. Now we know we're dealing with an area of high magical intensity, we can go back with more specialised equipment to withstand the storm."

"It is no longer your concern." Albrecht sliced a hand towards the door.

"Wait a minute." Saqib stood, leaning over, hands pressed against her desk. "This *is* my concern. People are going missing, then showing up mangled. We intend to stop it, with or without your help, but we both have a better chance of success if we work together. Wasn't that the deal?"

Harper's eyes widened at his abrasive tone, so unlike his usual positive self. He stared the Guardswoman down with an intensity he usually reserved for willing his machines to spit out a result.

Lieutenant Albrecht's eyes narrowed. "We'll send you a report on our findings."

"I want samples of physical evidence." Saqib didn't blink. "Untampered with. This is a confirmed magically affected area. I want soil samples, water samples, everything. To develop a way of finding magic after the fact, like we can do with blood, I need examples of materials known to have been exposed. I may even be able to work out what kind of magic or a potential source. It could narrow down the suspect list or give us a clue why this is happening. It will tell us whether the hue of the lightning is significant. What if lightning colour isn't merely a result of science? What if it's indicative of magic as well? We need to do further testing."

Albrecht's lips were so pursed tight they'd turned white. Harper gripped the back of Saqib's shirt, ready to drag him away from danger.

"You'll get them," the lieutenant growled. "But supervised. A member of Her Majesty's Guard will remain with them."

Saqib stared back at her a second longer than was necessary then nodded.

"Have the files you've been given aided you in finding out what happened to Guard Moore?" Lieutenant Albrecht followed up with.

It took all Harper's willpower not to snort. Albrecht knew they hadn't. The file hadn't even mentioned Edith being in York, let alone why a Guardsperson was at a witches' ritual. All Harper's own avenues of investigation had led to a dead end on that front. Not even AJ's coven were aware.

"Nothing." Saqib's jaw twitched. "If I find anything that's useful, I'll tell you."

When he turned to leave, Harper was surprised at the hostility in his eyes. He marched towards his lab and Harper jogged to keep up.

"What was that about?" she asked when they reached relative safety.

"You're okay with them taking our evidence?"

She placed a hand on his shoulder. "No, but … Saqib, I've never seen you this upset before. You're clearly not okay."

He took a deep breath and his shoulder loosened as he sighed. "I'm … No. I screwed up, Harper. There was all that magic, and the rangers rushing us away, and … I left you two. I should've stayed and searched for you."

She squeezed his shoulder. "You wouldn't have found us and it would've put you in more danger. You were right to get out of there. Grace and I can look after ourselves." *A darn sight better than you can,* she didn't add.

"We need to find who's killing these people, Harper. And why. Why might be as important as who. I hate these disappearances. I hate them."

"Your grandmother?" Harper guided him over to a stool, then fetched a glass of water.

Saqib gulped half the glass. "When we found that faery ring in the park, I thought I might find a way to break through, to find her, even though that's silly because she was taken before I was born. But I didn't find anything. Then you and Grace almost got taken away right under my nose. People in our line of work don't make a lot of friends."

"We love you too." Harper wrapped him in a warm hug.

Saqib squeezed her back, then stepped away with a quirked smile. "I want to solve this before anyone else goes missing or ends up dead."

"I've got a hunch, almost. Let me work on it a bit and I'll let you know later. I need to think. You okay here?" Harper checked.

"I'm fine." Saqib held out a fist and she bumped it. "Let's solve this thing."

"Heresy, I need you to let me dream." Although it was mid-afternoon, Harper sat in her bed, PJs on. Heresy huddled on her pillow, idly poking it with one tentacle.

"If you dream of it, it may find you." A brief grin split him, then was swallowed by ash.

"Not with all the protections you, AJ, and the coven put on the house. Plus, I did that spell so I can be in the shadow of the dreamscape, basically invisible." It felt like an age ago now. "I don't think it can find me."

"It attacked the house after you did the spell," Heresy pointed out.

"But it couldn't find me in the dreams. When I dreamt, I could hear it searching but it didn't find me. The last attack on the house was when I wasn't even here. It's still carpet bombing. Heresy, if I don't dream, I have no way to solve this. I need a vision."

Harper flopped back on the pillow. Heresy oozed out from under her loose hair.

"I do not condone this recklessness," Heresy said with uncharacteristic seriousness. "When the others blame me for not protecting the house, you must tell them it is your fault."

"I will," Harper agreed. "I'm so close to something. I'm sure what's happening to me is linked to these murders. It can't be a coincidence that the park ranger was buried in a place I've been before. Or that another victim was my coworker. And maybe another was a woman in my class at uni. It may be a coincidence, but what if this is my fault somehow, Heresy?"

"You are certain it is not part of another Hiding?" Heresy asked.

"I'm certain. The symbols are missing and they're *all* eyes."

"It could be a partial Hiding. Hiding something from sight alone."

"Hiding from sight ... Heresy, what if it's hiding something from *my* Sight?"

"It is possible, however you did have a vision of the earliest one we are aware of."

"No, I didn't." Harper rolled onto her side to stare at him. "The earliest we know of is the woman up in Scarborough, near where we captured that kelpie a couple of years ago. I didn't have a vision of that."

"Poor, Sightless Harper."

Harper wanted to smack the grin right off Heresy's face. "Spit it out."

"You had a vision of the woman found in the tree on the banks of the Ouse."

"She was part of the Hiding," Harper protested. "That was ... Wasn't she part of the Hiding?" She tried to remember the exact words. *Never scream, never tell, never taste, never smell. Never smell.* "The girl in the tree was killed *before* the janitor. Her murder was out of order? Usa didn't kill her?" Harper slapped her forehead. "That's why Usa asked for my eyes. Because she didn't have any yet, not because mine were better. These disappearances and murders started *before* we stopped her."

"She had the markings," Heresy pointed out.

"You're the one who said she was different." Harper flicked him in exasperation. "Maybe because the killer wanted people to think it was Usa."

"Then this proves the other deaths are related to you by coincidence." Heresy poked Harper between the eyes. She blinked as static tickled her eyelashes. "You do not know the girl in the tree. No one does. Therefore, she cannot be related to you or the weirdness which sent you here."

"I guess." Doubt entered her voice. "But all the others have some connection. The second one lives near Meredith. You remember, that little girl Grace and I 'cured' of possession? What if they knew each other? What if there's some connection to the unknown girl in the tree and I just don't know it yet? Maybe it was some kind of self-fulfilling prophesy. Like … I had a vision of her death therefore we were connected, even though the vision hadn't happened yet. Regardless, we're no closer to catching the killer. I need to use my magic."

"Very well, Harper dearest. On your head, or rather on your eyes, be it."

This dream was different. Instead of the forest, she stood in a windowless hall. Limestone blocks, stained with some unknown substance, arched over her, points almost invisible in the green glow washing over them. The room seemed to go on forever, like mirrors in the Hall of Testing, and the chill air held a sense of vastness that seemed real, despite the dreaming.

In the centre of the hall, a cauldron bubbled toxic green. Several metres in diameter, it dwarfed the young girl standing next to it. By Harper's estimate, she couldn't have been more than ten or eleven.

Ten. The knowledge came to her with certainty. She blinked and she could see through the girl's eyes. The cauldron evoked future memories: classes with her sister, the witches of Macbeth, insulting stereotypes, hiding her personal indignation. Recollections and visions of the future blended as the thoughts of her past and present selves entwined.

The wooden spoon she held was rough against her palm yet she felt disconnected, as though the body were not her own. The girl stirred the mixture. Music escaped from each popped bubble, a screeching tune that set Harper's teeth on edge, as if someone were playing on the wrong side of a violin's bridge.

Standing on her toes, she leant over the cauldron, cautiously sniffed the mixture, then recoiled, nose wrinkled at the foul scent.

"What is it, Seer?" A deep voice wended its way out of the shadows. Harper desperately wanted to turn around, to face her foe, but the girl didn't move. It hadn't happened then, so it couldn't happen now.

"It smells bitter and sour, Protector." The child's high-pitched voice was a year or two older than when Harper Saw her on the river.

"Smell it again."

The vapours rose around her, forcing their way past her defences. A smile spread across her face. "It is sweet, Protector."

"Taste it."

Trembling hands brought the wooden spoon to her lips, her tongue darting out to catch a drip of the luminous liquid.

"It tastes like the sap Papa draws from the trees." She slurped the rest of the spoonful, not caring about her sticky chin. The taste hit Harper like a ton of bricks crushing her chest. An image flashed in her mind of a dark-haired man with a neat beard teaching a pair of children how to make candies by pouring sap onto fresh snow. An almost invisible white kitten watched from a distance, sadness in its penetrating stare. The man laughed as the boy snatched up a hardened sweet. Guilt and joy mixed in equal measure as Harper grabbed her own. She slipped another into her pocket to share with the cat later.

The vision disappeared, leaving only the faintest of memories like the after-gleam of lightning. The man's face was gone, but his laughter remained in her soul.

"Good. Good, my dearest Seer. Eat well."

The girl looked around, dragging Harper's consciousness back to the younger body.

"Would you like some?" She held out the spoon in the direction of the voice. A deep sense of trust and wellbeing swelled in Harper's chest. Something was there, beyond her Sight, but she trusted in the Protector who'd guarded her family for generations. Child-Harper was so confident in his protection that adult-Harper's distrust and fears were smothered. She wanted to See the creature hiding in the darkness, not to confront or berate it, but to welcome it and bring it joy.

"This drink is for the Seer alone." Adult-Harper detected an edge to the voice her younger self missed as she sipped more of the liquid. Magic burned behind her eyes, stronger than ever before.

"Mrow." A white cat rubbed against her ankles. Kneeling down, she held the spoon out but the cat wrinkled its nose and backed away.

"It is for the Seer alone," the voice repeated, even young Harper catching the sharper edge this time.

"But Fionn is my friend. He's magic too." Harper could sense the surety of her younger self even more strongly as she patted the cat, who purred and rubbed against her hand. Her fingers tightened in long, snowy fur. She knew this cat, not just as her past self. She'd Seen it before in the dreamscape then forgotten. It didn't have the collar of the cat in Saqib's pictures, but its eyes were the same turquoise as the cat from the cathedral.

Harper wanted to check the back of her hand and her ankle, each scored by sharp scratches. How could she have forgotten the cat that caused them? She stared at him, willing herself to remember when she awoke. He was another connection between her and the murders. If he'd been in her other dreamings, if he'd woken her up, then he was still out there somewhere and he knew something. She wasn't sure how, but Grace's family encountered too many strange creatures for her to dismiss the animalistic appearance.

Her younger self fought for dominance, memory winning over Harper's control of the dreamscape as she released the cat and straightened.

"You will learn," the voice continued. "The Seer is alone and above. She must guide and be without bias. This creature is not your friend."

The cat hissed, stretching up his paws against the cauldron to bat the spoon out of the girl's hand.

"Fionn?"

The cat hissed again. His long fur prickled as he pushed against her legs to force her away from the cauldron.

"Enough." The voice thundered through the dome sending tremors of fear through both Harpers. "Begone."

For a moment, Harper thought it perceived her. Panic seized her body. Had she been wrong about the spell concealing her presence? Had it found her?

A deep growl rumbled behind her. The girl spun. Myriad eyes blinked in the darkness. Not the human eyes that followed her in the forest. These were red as glowing coals and there was nothing human in them. Padded feet slapped against the ground. A black dog separated from the shadows. Its fangs gleamed in the green light. Shoelaces of drool pooled at its feet. Harper craned her neck to look at its face as it stalked towards her.

The cat leapt in front of her, hissing, back arched, claws out.

The dog pounced. A scream tore from Harper's throat at the bright flash of blood, child and adult both horrified. There was a heart-rending yowl, then the dog turned its gaze on her.

Run, Harper.

Harper had heard that voice in her dreams, always telling her to run, but her past self knew it, too, and trusted it implicitly, even more than the Protector. She ran. Through endless stone corridors, the walls getting rougher as brick turned to natural cave. In the distance she heard the swish of water and the song of a violin. It picked up the tune of the cauldron, the music tainted with inhuman laughter. Primal fear bound Harper's past and present self together, the instinct to flee overpowering her rational adult mind.

Footsteps echoed behind her, in front of her, everywhere. Never hurrying. Never dropping behind. Inevitable. The ground beneath her vibrated with growls so deep she could barely Hear them.

Ahead, she spied a door and found a burst of speed from deep within. She fumbled at the catch until the door swung open and cool night air rushed in. Above, a net of stars twinkled, lifting her heart.

Sharp fingers pierced her shoulder, cold as the deepest night of winter, and wrenched her backwards.

The door slammed closed. The sky disappeared.

"Never forget, Seer, you are my beloved and by my side you will remain as starlight is extinguished and dreams rule all."

Harper awoke with a shout. Her shoulder ached and she yanked aside her shirt expecting to see claws embedded under the bone. Still red, the scar from the fight with the Auctioneer was nonetheless closed and healing. Nothing else was there. She took deep breaths to calm her thudding heart, taking solace in the thin rays of sunlight splayed across her bed. Heresy was nowhere to be seen. Down in the peephole guarding the house, she hoped. There were no thuds or tremors to indicate anything had attacked the house. Maybe her spell worked and all that had been missing was her intent to hide in the dream's shadow.

The dream hadn't been the one she'd tried to invoke. Already details slipped from her mind so she snatched her notepad from her bedside cabinet and wrote down everything she could, sketching tiny fragments of her dissolving memory.

It wasn't much. A cauldron. A man's warm laughter against cold fingers. A tune she'd already forgotten, humming inaudibly at the base of her skull. Shimmering blue cat eyes.

Lingering claustrophobia gripped her body so once she'd noted down all she could, she sat out in the back garden. She laid on the lawn to watch the sky turn rosy, then to darken. Faintly, the bells of Saint Peter rang followed by the deep toll of the Guard's curfew. The muezzin's call marked the Maghrib prayer which Saqib would be in his room observing before coming down for dinner. Grace would be in soon, if she wasn't already.

It all seemed distant as stars twinkled to life overhead. A clear night, for once. She reached out to touch the grass beside her without thinking. The ghost of a hand was almost solid under her fingertips. The dreamscape lapped at the edges of the wakening.

The sensation of two Harpers in one body lingered, as though her past self had returned with her from the dreamscape. Clouds scudded across the sky and mist invaded the garden. Chatter filtered from the house as everyone congregated in the kitchen for dinner.

"I don't have time for this." Harper beat away tendrils of mist. Despite her earlier desire to be alone, she now craved the light and normalcy of being around people.

When she entered the kitchen, Grace and Saqib's conversation cut off as they both turned to stare at her.

"Any news?" she asked.

"Nothing," Saqib said as Grace rooted around in the fridge for dinner. "The Guard delivered the samples as promised but I've not started anything yet. I was tempted to pull an all-nighter but the supervising guardsman made me leave. Did you manage to put your finger on what was bothering you earlier?"

Harper plopped down in a chair next to Saqib. "I worked out something that's bugged me for a while." She explained about the girl in the tree from last autumn and her discussion with Heresy.

"Let's try and enjoy a nice, normal dinner," Grace suggested as she browned mince for a cottage pie. She gestured to a pile of potatoes. "Get AJ and get on with it. Please."

Harper caught Saqib's eye and they both smothered a laugh. The normalcy of Grace's brisk efficiency released the tension inside her and the last of the other Harper's presence melted away.

The three of them were about halfway through their meal, AJ having refused point blank to answer his door, when the kitchen flashed with blue light and an alarm blared.

"Warning … Warning … Warning …"

All three jumped to their feet and ran out into the front corridor where AJ was banging on the front door.

"Shut up. Your stupid alarm made me spill coffee on my keyboard."

"Warning … Warning … Warning …"

Grace pulled AJ back while Harper stepped forward to peer through the peephole.

"We're all sufficiently warned, Heresy. Maybe you could knock the alarm off, please?" The sudden silence left her ears ringing. "What happened?"

"Something hit the house's defences and I saw something in the street," Heresy hissed.

"Can you be more specific?" Saqib asked. "We didn't feel anything."

"If I could be more specific, I would be," Heresy snapped.

Harper and Grace exchanged a glance at his impatient tone and uncharacteristic declaration.

"What did you see?" Harper asked gently.

"I am not sure," Heresy grumbled. "It disappeared before I could make out what it was."

"You think it was attacking the house's defences from across the street?" Grace asked.

"No, that was something else, something far away," Heresy said. "They must be working together."

"Mundane and magical sight," Harper theorised. "Are the defences holding?"

"For now, Harper dearest. They cannot get past me and a swarm of witches." Heresy's normal self-confident, sleek tone was back and Harper relaxed a tiny bit.

"I'll see if any local tech caught anything on camera. The coven defences should hold." AJ disappeared back into his room.

"Harper, if something was physically across the street, whatever is hunting you knows where you are. You *must* stay in the house. Actually, no. We need to go home." Grace's brow creased in worry, her hand tight around Harper's.

"I'm not running back to Father because something rattled the door. We have a case to solve and we need to do it before more people end up dead." Despite her words, Harper's body was tight with tension, a taut string ready to snap. Grace's idea had merits and at least her sister would be safe back in her parents' home in Canterbury. If they could get there. If the hunter had sent someone to watch her in person, Grace and the others were in grave danger. Harper's conscience sank to her stomach. If it had found the house, her spell to hide her there hadn't worked after all.

CHAPTER FIFTEEN

Elemental, My Dear Harper

Despite proud words, Harper sat in her room the next two days pouring over old books and sheafs of notes, the butterflies in her stomach keeping her housebound. All the house's protections, and AJ and Heresy both downstairs, soothed her fears of discovery. She studied the book *Of Realms and Shadows* trying to work out what she did wrong that the creature in her nightmares had still found her. There'd been a delay, but it had known she'd been in the dreamscape. Was it part of whatever was wrong with magic or had something else gone wrong? The pattern indicated that even if the problem occurred the original spell should've worked.

The jangle of her phone broke through her single-minded studying. Her eyes didn't leave the page as she answered and tucked it between her ear and shoulder. "Hello?"

"Something's come up," Saqib said in a rush. "Can you come down to the lab?"

"Are you alright?" His normal excitement hadn't returned since his confrontation with Albrecht.

"I'm fine but I would really appreciate a second pair of eyes on this. Someone with your expertise? Who might See something I've missed?"

"On my way."

Harper hung up, stashed a torch and her blade in her satchel, just in case, and ran out the door with a quick wave to Heresy. The door smoked as she locked it—he wasn't happy with being confined to the house but she couldn't take him into the police station with its Guard overseers.

A worried Saqib greeted her at the station door to sign her in. When she entered the lab, Harper gave an appreciative whistle at the whirring machines and pristine instruments. "Where'd this all come from so quickly?"

"They let me have a mass spectrometer, Harper." Saqib pointed to a white-clad machine covered in screens and buttons. "Have. Not borrow. I've been trying to get funding for one for ages. I want to try and upgrade it to search for traces of remnant magic."

"This is a more sensitive version of the ion mobility spectrometer you used on the stuff you collected near the faery ring?"

"Not entirely dissimilar." Saqib pointed at one of the screens. "Look at this."

Harper scanned the room. "I thought Albrecht said the evidence had to be accompanied. Are they watching us remotely?"

"Probably." Saqib tilted his head towards one of the new pieces of equipment. Their funding of his apparatus gave them the perfect way to bug his lab. "There is someone here in person, too, but he's popped out. I've worked with them before, remember? I get a little leeway."

"Where'd he go?" Harper asked. Her shoulder blades itched as she turned her back on the door to study Saqib's machine. If she was going to try and See something, she'd be more comfortable knowing the Guard overseer wouldn't be back for a while.

"I needed Albrecht's signature on some documentation. It 'accidentally' got left blank when the evidence was given to me. Not that I'm going to be taking any of this to court, but they still have to follow proper procedure. It shouldn't take long though."

"I'll try to be quick then." Harper gave him a wry smile. She didn't care if they heard she was avoiding them. What sane person didn't? "What am I looking at?"

Saqib gave the machine a gentle pat and swatted away an imaginary speck of dust. "This baby uses energised particles to ionise atoms transmuting them to gas-phase ions—"

"Saqib, assume I'm an idiot," Harper jumped in before he could explain further.

He quirked a smile. "Sure. This machine tells me the atomic composition of a sample."

"Was that so hard?"

"Last time I asked you a simple question, I got a lecture on the importance of triangles in pre-Purge magi-science."

Harper laughed. The weight she'd been carrying since Swaledale lifted a little. Chatting like this was as close to normal as life had been in days. "Fair. So, again, what am I looking at?"

"What do you See?" There was a slight emphasis on the final word. When she glanced up, he raised an eyebrow, his eyes darting to the screen and back to hers. She gave him an almost imperceptible nod and looked again.

Magic fizzed up her optical nerve and spread over her cornea. Heat pooled in the corners of her eyes, gathering teardrops. She refused to blink. As she watched, the graphs and numbers slithered across the screen, changing into semi-familiar patterns of protons, electrons, and neutrons. She breathed deep, holding the magic as it tried to break free. It pounded against her eyes and burned through her brain. Tears spilt down her cheeks as the images on the screen morphed into words:

Hydrogen. Argon. Phosphorous. Erbium.

Her knowledge of chemistry was limited but they didn't seem like they belonged together. She hadn't even heard of erbium. Maybe that's what Saqib hoped she'd See. The source of this strange combination.

"Doctor Siddique?" A brusque voice disrupted her concentration and the image flickered back to the spiked graph before she could See what those elements were part of.

Saqib jumped. "Sergeant Blue. That was fast. What did the lieutenant have to say?"

Harper managed not to roll her eyes. "Blue? Really? Ow."

Saqib stepped on Harper's foot, stopping her incredulous mutter. The man before her could not have looked more like a stereotype if he tried. Eschewing the Guard's usual long tan coats, his dark suit, earpierce, and square jaw nonetheless marked him. The Guard had never been good at subtlety.

"Who is this woman?" The sergeant glared at Harper.

"Harper Ashbury, she/her, of the De Santos family. I'm sure Lieutenant Albrecht has mentioned me." Harper stepped forward to offer her hand, which he ignored.

Blue's brown eyes narrowed as he listened to his earpiece. "Do you have any results yet, Doctor Siddique?"

"I'm still double-checking them." Saqib stalled but Blue was already peering at the machine's display.

"Explain." He pointed at the screen.

"You can't rush these things, Blue," Saqib huffed. "Science is ready when it's ready. Just because I have the breakdown of what was in the sample doesn't mean I can explain it. I do have some results from the blood analysis though. The soil samples from around the wych elm contained cat blood. Samples within the tree contained blood of an unknown origin. None of the blood collected belonged to our victim which is consistent with the previous crime scene evidence and the coroner's reports; no visible trauma and their organs were excised in such a way that didn't cause bleeding."

"If not the victim's, whose blood was in the tree?" Harper asked. While she and Grace had undoubtedly tampered with the sanctity of the evidence, she was sure neither of them had been bleeding. She was equally certain no one other than Heresy had been in there with them.

"That is the question. The DNA is degraded, but I thought I might be able to recover enough to see what it belonged to. If it's fox or rabbit blood, it's not worth spending more time on. I won't bamboozle you with the specifics." Saqib shot Harper a quick eyeroll. "The outcome is that I've found a very slight hiccup in the DNA."

"Could be a minor mutation," Harper hazarded. But if not … if Saqib actually found scientific evidence of a magical creature, it would be a first, in English history at least. Academic excitement clashed with the fear of discovery, but she was careful not to let it show in front of the Guard stooge.

"It's possible but unlikely. It's almost like it's a sample from something with a common ancestor to humans but that isn't human. It doesn't match anything in the database before you start rattling off primates."

"What does this tell us?" Blue asked, his monobrow a 'V' of concentration.

"For starters, that my modifications to this gel electrophoresis machine are paying off." Saqib rested a hand on said machine fondly. "But other than that, not much."

Blue folded his arms over his chest. "So, you have nothing."

Harper ground her toe into Saqib's foot before he could protest Blue's dismissive tone. The less the Guard thought they had, the better.

"I expect something more concrete by the time I return from lunch." Blue turned on his heel and stomped out.

When he was gone, Saqib slipped a vial out of his pocket and pressed it into Harper's hand along with a note. "If you could check your research for anything relating to those results, I'd appreciate it."

"Will do." Harper tucked the sample into her pocket. "Don't hold your breath though. My research deals more with fire and earth type elements rather than hydrogen, helium types."

"I'll take whatever you can find. I'd say brush up on supes that have a similar ancestry to humans but that would be a lot, potentially, wouldn't it?"

"A *lot*," Harper confirmed. "Especially if we go off human-morphs and human-esque creatures. Whether they actually share ancestry, you'll have to tell us if we ever get their DNA."

"I'll catch up with you at home." Saqib's eyes drifted to her pocket, then back to her face, slightly widened.

"I'll See what I can do." Harper gave him a quick hug before she left.

She wandered down the road, crossing to take the Ouse path towards the cathedral. Once she was satisfied she wasn't being followed, she sat down on the bank and pulled Saqib's note out of her pocket.

His hasty scrawl was awkward to decipher, almost as good as a code.

Harper. I've given you a sample of the unknown blood so you can try and find out what it belongs to.

He'd written on the back of a periodic table with four elements circled and a scrawl: *In case you didn't work this out from the mass spec. read out, these things should not be found together.*

Any lingering doubts the murders were related to her forgotten past were gone as she gazed at it. Hydrogen, Phosphorus, Argon, and one of those new-fangled elements people only saw in labs, Erbium.

H. P. Ar. Er.

HArPEr. A message. Someone left her a message. They knew she would come. They knew Saqib could read it. They knew *her.*

Her brain screamed to run home and lock herself away, but her body was frozen, limbs rigid with fear. The swaying shadows of the trees stretched and sharpened like grasping claws. The chill January air sliced through to form ice within her bones. Melancholic music surrounded her, the lament of a violin wafting downstream. Drifting from the Northwest, from the Swale into the Ouse, to surround her and imprison her. She couldn't breathe. The music infiltrating her lungs left room for nothing else. Mist rose from the river and slithered over the path. Gold-and-green motes obscured her sight and her head spun as she tilted towards the water.

"I will take your fears, little one."

Harper felt rather than heard the words. They banished the music and her vision cleared. She scrambled back from the river and looked around. Sight bled through, and the world altered.

"Here, little one."

Standing behind her was a wizened woman. Gold rings clattered on her stick-like fingers, her bony knuckles stopping them sliding off as she gestured. She wore a scarlet scarf over her head and silver bells tinkled on a violet skirt.

"Who are you?" Harper asked. Her hand drifted to her bag where her machete lay at the top.

"The answer." The woman's voice was deep and smooth.

"To what question?"

The old woman leered, her teeth broken and yellowed. "The one in your heart." A hand shot out and grasped her arm.

"Leave me alone." Harper yanked away. The woman's nails left marks but didn't break skin. Harper cursed, rubbing her arm. When she looked up, the woman was gone.

A clawed finger tapped her on the back. "You wanted to be rid of your fear, did you not? You wanted to know how to be brave."

Harper spun, jumping back, drawing her blade.

"Too bad, too bad." The old woman turned to walk away. "Come back if you change your mind, little one. I am always hungry."

The colourfully clad woman faded from view and Harper's shoulders slumped. Before she could relax, a cold sweat broke out and she turned again, expecting to see the woman. Sight or no Sight, there was no one there. She bent over the river to wash the ink from Saqib's notes, then let the paper disintegrate. With another worried glance around, she hastened home.

Harper's hasty form left a dark trail in the mists behind her. A white cat stretched a paw over the path, then yanked it back as the old woman reformed, perched crow-like on a twisting laburnum. She whacked the bush with her stick, catching the cat in the ribs. With a yowl of pain, he jumped onto a low branch, reproachfully licking away the dirt. He scowled, chunnering in his throat, as the woman peered, then smiled.

"Ah, you're one of zir pets, aren't you? What does ze want, I wonder?"

She patted the cat on the head. Zero flattened his ears, tail flicking. He didn't like the word 'pet' and he didn't like this old hag interfering in his master's business. If he wasn't discreet, he'd be given more lessons. A high-pitched mewl escaped his throat as he batted her hand away, claws peeking out. Hurting people hurt his heart, but he would if he had to. She had no business trying to steal from his Harper.

"I'd run along if I were you, little one." The woman gave the cat a sharp push and he dug his claws into the tree to avoid falling. "You'll lose her elseways, and I am sure you don't want to be on zir bad side, do you? Now there is a fear which may finally satiate my hunger. Would you like me to take it?"

The cat hissed and the woman cackled to herself before fading from view once again. When she vanished the second time, the mists receded into the river and Zero trotted off, nose in the air, following the whispers of magic lingering in Harper's wake. Her blood called to his, and he would always find her. He knew where she worked, where she lived.

For once, his master's needs lined up with his own selfish desires. *Follow the witch. Find out how her image appears in my fetch. Set aside your personal yearnings, Zero. It is a mystery we must unravel. For if I die, the magic of England will die too.'*

Conflicting love warred in his chest. The mama cat feels Harper stirred clashed with his devotion to his master: the one who fed him, slept beside him, taught him, and cared for him. The image of a misty dale formed in his mind: not green, the air filled with the bleating of sheep, but barren and dark, their death moans carried on the winds. If he could protect both Harper and his master, he would, but his duty to the land came first.

When Harper reached the house, the front door was still smoking. She rapped her knuckles against the sunny blue wood. "Stop throwing a temper tantrum."

The door swung open and she slipped inside, closing it behind her before she addressed Heresy again, "I was at the police precinct. It's too dangerous for you to come along. There's too many Guard around. What if Saqib's equipment did pick something up?"

"His equipment does nothing. This was not part of the deal," Heresy hissed. "You are my sole concern, not these other mundanes nor this pile of bricks."

"Aww, Heresy, do you care?"

"If you die, I go back. I do not 'care.'"

"Well, as you can see, I'm fine and you're still here."

Heresy oozed out of the peephole and wrapped himself around her neck. "You encountered danger. Blood danger. But since you believe my skills are better utilised on bricks and mortar, you may vanish to your doom without a concern from me. Saqib will keep me, if I ask him. I should transfer my contract."

"There are more important things than me in this house." *My sister lives here too.* "Also, if anything happens to me, no one else here can summon you. Maybe AJ, but he *wouldn't* summon you."

"Fine. At least let me provide security in my own way." Heresy puffed up, floating out of the door to buzz around Harper's head like a swarm of hornets. Before Harper could object, he wafted through the open door to settle in the neighbour's cat. The poor possessed creature walked off with its back arched and tail bristled. Harper leant around the door to check up and down the street, but no curtains twitched. Her eyes lingered on the old wall that circled the city centre. It stood opposite the house, up a gentle slope that would be bursting with daffodils come spring. Neither she, Heresy, nor AJ should've been able to perform magic within its boundaries. Despite the Ouse's murders, most people still clung to that comfort. For Harper, it helped that no one lived opposite.

Heresy would get over his tantrum. The neighbourhood cats might have a rough evening, but she had more important things to deal with. He needed her and, since she would be home, it meant he had to keep the protections strong around the house. With her sister living there as well as close friends, the house had to be kept safe, whatever happened to her.

A vague stirring in her chest sent an ache through her nerves, stiffened her muscles, and squeezed her heart. Part of her didn't care if she was attacked, so long as Grace and the others were safe. The old lady by the river couldn't be the one who had attacked the house—Harper was sure there would have been more fireworks and the woman would have tried to stop her leaving if that were the case—but the close encounter with another supernatural barely bothered her. She knew they were about, she'd seen them in the Shambles, and her fears weren't for her own safety. In fact, she'd welcome an end to this decade-long circular chase. She wanted answers. Wanted to go home.

CHAPTER SIXTEEN

A Cat or Not a Cat

It took Harper a long time to get to sleep that night. She lay in bed, spinning the sample of unknown blood between her fingers. Despite her desire to find home and prevent any further murders, using her Sight on it seemed hazardous and logic had prevailed. If it had laid a trap for her, that might be exactly what it wanted her to do.

There was a thud at the front door when Grace came home sometime after midnight, but Harper didn't get up. Her sister's heavy footsteps indicated a long day in the clinic, so Harper let her be. She lay in bed staring at the sky through a crack in her curtains. All the lights were out, even her night light, as she searched the vapours for the merest glimmer of a star. She wasn't sure why it was so important, but the ache in her chest demanded it, not letting her close her eyelids and find a dream. A peculiar déjà vu prickled. Not just from stargazing. She'd done that plenty of times, sweaty palms clenched in her clothes and thudding heart shattering the stillness of the night.

Despite her fear of the dark, there was a comfort in glimpsing the stars. Orion brought peace as he peeked at her between shimmering strands of mists. Ghosts of calloused fingers twined through hers and a whisper of soft hair brushed her cheek. She didn't blink, didn't look. The presence beside her was ethereal, a memory of a rare happy time. A solitary tear gathered in the corner of her eye, then trickled down to her ear. That presence was something more than déjà vu. Her throat clogged with the grief she usually damped down in the bottom of her stomach.

A rumble rippled through the house and the spectral presence vanished. There was a crash from the back garden. Harper sat bolt upright and yanked back the curtains.

Heresy flew through the window, not slowing as he phased through the glass. He circled her, sparks crackling within his ashen body, his grin nowhere in sight. "Not a cat. Not a cat. Not a cat."

The door to Harper's room flew open with such force it rebounded against the wall. "What's going on?" Grace panted. Her hair was dishevelled from sleep, her eyes too wide, but she gripped a crossbow in one hand and her belt of bolts in the other.

"Not a cat. Not a cat. Not a cat." Heresy flew over to buzz around her.

She swatted him away and he vanished through the floor as Saqib appeared behind Grace, half asleep.

"Get back," Grace ordered Saqib as Harper joined her, machete in hand.

"We've got this, Saqib." Harper flashed him a reassuring smile as the two women raced downstairs after the panicked spirit.

Heresy buzzed by the backdoor, puffed up like an angry feline, repeating the same three words over and over. Then he zipped past Harper and through the door to the lounge.

Grace pointed to herself and the backdoor. Harper gave her a thumbs up and followed Heresy to the front. He was contained within the peephole, muttering angrily to himself. The door swung open as she approached, though Heresy made no other acknowledgement of her presence.

Harper slunk down the alley next to the house, keeping her back to the wall as mists caressed her feet. Once at the back gate, she waited until lights flashed on, then dived into the garden, blade drawn.

Grace hit the backlight, illuminating the garden. Looking for something cat-like, Harper almost missed the intruder in the roiling mists, but Grace's crossbow threatened unwaveringly. Huddled in the middle of the lawn was a man. Arms wrapped around his legs, head buried in his arms, he rocked back and forth, whimpering. Star-white hair curled over his face. Harper stopped and looked again. Protruding from his hair were the tufty ears of a cat and a bristled tail swished behind him. And he was naked.

Grace gave a sharp gesture, glaring at Harper's indecision. Keeping her guard up, Harper approached on the balls of her feet. She crouched next to the man and gently placed a hand on his bare shoulder.

"Hello?"

A shudder almost rattled his flesh from his bones and she snatched her hand back. His heaving chest stretched skin over protruding ribs. His head snapped up. Bright turquoise irises locked onto Harper's violet-flecked eyes and he hissed softly. She startled back, jaw slack with surprise. Those eyes were so familiar, though she was sure she'd remember if she'd met a man with a tail before. *You'd remember if you'd met him in* this *life. There was a white kitten in the boat you Saw.*

"It's okay, we aren't going to hurt you." Harper held out a hand, rubbing her fingers together like she was enticing the neighbour's cat. It was tempting to *pss pss pss* at him. The other hand, the one holding her machete, she tucked behind her back. At Grace's sceptical look, she amended her statement. "We don't want to hurt you."

He was young despite the white hair, although his age was difficult to guess. Younger than her, Harper thought as his eyes drifted up and down her and a frown creased his brow. His cat-like ears twitched towards Grace but his eyes never left Harper.

"Is it gone?" His voice was a warm tenor, rasped raw by nerves and fear. Dark smudges made his eyes all the more radiant.

Harper touched his cheekbone without thinking, the purplish hue there not caused by weariness. "Is what gone?"

"Heresy," Grace supplied. "*He's* gone. Who, or what, are *you?*"

Harper knew. A dark collar bound his neck and a triquetra disk dangled against his chest.

"I'm …" The man's eyes filled with tears. "I … I wasn't … I wasn't supposed to get caught … but …" He sniffed, rubbing his nose with the back of his trembling hand. "Ze'll be mad … But … I'm so glad to see you."

He pounced, wrapping his arms around Harper's neck, fluffy tail encircling her waist. Her weapon dropped to the grass as she wrapped her arms around his shaking shoulders. Grace darted forward but Harper held her hand up, warning her sister away.

"It's okay," she said again, running her fingers through his hair as he clung to her. "We won't hurt you."

Whatever her suspicions about the cat's involvement in the murders, she was certain he wouldn't harm her. She couldn't explain it anymore than she could explain why it was safe to tell Saqib about her magic, or that she and Grace had to take this house to rent. It was like her magic not only recognised him but embraced him. If he *was* tied up in the deaths of Agnes and the others, she was better off not spooking him. *Let him get comfortable, then see what he knows.* It was a thin excuse. The wash of big-sisterly feelings his presence evoked wouldn't let her do otherwise.

An upstairs window opened and Saqib leaned out, staring down at the scene below him in confusion. "Is everything okay? Who on earth is that?"

"A very good question." Grace's eyes narrowed as she watched Harper try to comfort the crying stranger. "You better get down here, Saqib. Oh, and bring some spare clothes."

"What?"

"Just do it. Before he wakes the neighbours," Grace ordered. Saqib retreated, closing his window behind him. Grace continued to glare at the intruder, foot tapping against the soggy grass.

Half an hour later they had managed to convince the sniffling stranger to come into the house and Heresy to leave the peephole and join them. They also managed to persuade their guest into a pair of Saqib's PJ pants, clutched with one hand to keep them up, and a hoodie that dwarfed his slight frame.

Harper tried to catch a closer glimpse of the pendant as he shuffled into the lounge, tripping over the long pants, but his hair and the hoodie covered it. His ears drooped and his tail hung limp behind him, poking out between bottoms and top. With his eyes downcast and his hair still over his face, he looked like nothing more than a half-drowned kitten. Harper resisted the temptation to pat him on the head.

He stared at their feet in silence, then Harper, Grace and Saqib all started to talk at once.

"Who are you? Why are you following me?"

"Why are you in our back garden? Was it you Heresy saw outside before?"

"What's with the tail, mate?"

The man looked up with startled eyes and cringed away from their barrage of questions.

"Give the poor cat a chance to speak," AJ said from the door.

He leant against the doorframe, looking for all the world as if cat-boys dropping in after midnight was a perfectly normal occurrence. In his coven, maybe it was.

"You must be freezing." AJ's voice was soft, kind, as he walked over and placed a reassuring hand on the stranger's shoulder. "Tea or coffee?"

"You alright, mate?" Saqib asked AJ, raising an eyebrow.

AJ gave him a pointed look, his hand still resting on the man's shoulder. "Least you could do is offer the guy a cup of tea. Falling into you folks' world isn't exactly easy."

"But he's already a supe," Saqib said weakly and AJ's eyes narrowed.

"Checked pronouns but not names?" AJ asked.

Saqib blushed.

Harper stood up and put her arm around the stranger's shoulders, giving him a squeeze. "It's okay, AJ. We're sorry. We'll be nice." She introduced all of them, then asked their uninvited guest, "And you?"

"Zero. I'm a tomcat."

"Yeah, we saw that," Grace muttered.

Harper glared at her. "But we don't assume."

"I'll go make some tea now that's out of the way." AJ shuffled off to the kitchen, wiping the hand that touched the stranger against his trousers.

"Don't any of you remember our house is under attack?" Grace jumped to her feet. "He's not a pet, Harper. He's probably responsible, and you invite him in, introduce ourselves all polite, and make tea?"

The man flinched again and his ears drooped even farther. "I'm sorry."

"*You* are responsible?" Harper's arm dropped and she backed away.

His beseeching look twisted her heart. "I wasn't trying to hurt you. I want to protect you."

"Protect her from what?" Grace grabbed his chin, forcing his eyes up to meet hers. "What is hunting Harper?"

His eyes rolled, looking anywhere but at Grace. "I … I just know she's in danger. I … I didn't want to hurt her. Something else was coming."

"Grace." Harper rested a hand on her sister's wrist.

Grace released the stranger with a snarl. He scurried to the side of the room, pressing his back against the wall, eyes guarded. One hand lifted towards his throat, then jerked back.

"Here you go."

He jumped as AJ shoved a cup of tea under his nose. Glancing at Harper, he leant forward and sniffed the brew before taking it warily, his hands lost in the long sleeves of his top. "What is this?"

AJ rolled his eyes. "It's tea. I'm going back to my room."

The stranger gave his cup another sniff, then hesitantly lapped at the drink. His eyes widened and drank faster, until his face was firmly pressed into the rim of the cup. He pulled away as he stretched his tongue and examined the mug with a frown. "Why are your bowls so narrow?" He jerked back when Grace laughed. The sudden movement slopped tea on Saqib's hoodie.

"Fair enough," Grace said. "I don't think the guy who can't work out how to use the cup is a threat."

He looked at Saqib's grin and Harper's suppressed smile, then back to the drink clutched in his hands. "Humans are weird."

"Since you're obviously not human, what are you?" Saqib asked.

"I'm a cat." He looked at them as though they were stupid and Harper suppressed another smile. "Clearly."

"Not a cat." Heresy waved a sparking tendril out of the shadows. "Not a cat."

The cat-boy hissed at him and cringed back.

Grace raised her hand to hide her smirk. "I hate to agree with Heresy, but I'm a vet and you are *not* a cat."

"I am too a cat," he muttered, tail swishing.

"It's just we've never met a cat with, well, you're basically humanoid. Take a seat." Harper guided him to a chair.

"Still a cat." He gingerly touched the back of the chair, then gripped it and tried to lift. "Where do you want me to take this?"

"Just sit in it." Harper pushed him down by the shoulders. He tensed, then perched on the edge of the cushion.

"Why are you protecting me?" Harper asked, her hands still on his shoulders, both to stop him running away and from an instinctive desire to quell his frightened trembles. "Who sent you?"

"I asked to come." He swivelled his head to look up at her, eyes pleading something she couldn't interpret.

The sensation of déjà vu enveloped her again. Every time he looked at her, flashes of memory assaulted her, fading too fast to make sense, leaving the lingering look of sad eyes. "Why? Who am I to you?"

"Your blood sings to me. It's part of me. You made me."

Her fingers tightened in his shoulders and he squirmed against the plush cushions. "Made you? What do you mean? Where are you from?"

He cuddled his tail against his chest. "I don't remember. It's a dream. But I know blood and yours is part of mine. We … I … I can't remember. I just … know."

"I told you I sensed others of your blood," Heresy said.

"Are you the one who has been watching me?" Harper asked. The so-called cat nodded. "For how long?"

"Since a little after the autumnal equinox last year."

"What?" Grace jumped to her feet, a snarl on her lips. "You've been following her for *months*? Tell me why I shouldn't hand you over to the archbishop right now."

"Because I know what she is." A sly smile flashed across his face, gone in a blink. "*I know I wouldn't tell anyone, but you don't believe it. If I wanted to hurt her, I wouldn't have protected her all this time.*"

"Why did you follow me and not tell me I'm in danger?" Harper waved Grace away. "Why are you coming forward now and not earlier?"

His fingers tightened in his fur. "I didn't want to interfere in your life. At first, I didn't know who you were, only that you were fighting the Hiding. Then I had a … a vision I guess you'd call it. I had seen your face before but I never remembered when I woke up. Being near you now, over these last few weeks, some things are coming back to me. I can't pin them down. It's like I'm waking up."

Harper grimaced. "I know the feeling."

"You don't remember me," he whined. "Not even a face from a dream."

"I think I do. A little." Harper wiped her eyes. She wasn't ready to tell him about the cat on the boat, if he didn't remember it. It was just an assumption anyway. Saqib would scold her. Coincidences did exist. She reached down to touch the silver disk dangling from his collar. "You were at the cathedral."

"Do you believe I'm trying to help you?"

"No," said Grace and Saqib in unison.

"If you're the cat from the cathedral …" Disbelief edged Saqib's tone. "… then you're the cat at the other murders too. What do you know?"

The cat-boy bit his lip and squirmed under Saqib's unusually hard stare. "I … I don't know anything. My master … I don't know what's hunting Harper. Please?" He looked up at Harper, tear-filled eyes wide. "Please believe that I'm trying to protect you. Please? Believe me?"

"I'm not sure if I do or not." Harper released him and moved to sit on the edge of the table instead. She twisted her fingers through the end of her braid. She wanted to believe him, so desperately it was as though her need bored a hole straight through her chest. But Saqib was right and she had to be practical. He'd been spotted too near too many of the dead women. Maybe he lured them into trusting him with his pathetic mien and sad eyes.

"Would you use your magic to get the truth from my mind?" Zero asked.

Harper and Grace exchanged a look.

"If you could mindread him, do you think you'd be able to tell if he was lying?" Saqib asked.

"I don't know." Harper wracked her brain trying to remember if she'd read anything about it in the archives. "It sounds invasive. I'm not sure it would be ethical to do it."

"He is volunteering," Saqib pointed out. "And you might find out about Agnes's murder and the others. But I agree. Mindreading is a slippery slope. I wouldn't want to know how to do it."

The stranger grasped Harper's wrists and pulled her closer, eliciting a grunt of disapproval from Grace. Despite appearing weak, his grip on her was iron. Harper fought the urge to yank her hands back, not sure she'd win. She wasn't sure she wanted to. Kneeling before him, uncertain, she searched his face. He rested his forehead against hers as he gazed into her eyes. His breath was warm against her skin and his hair tickled her cheeks. She held her breath as he nuzzled her nose, then he smiled, eyes brightening.

"I trust you, Harper."

"Ahem, well, I, um … thank you." Harper rocked back, cheeks flushed deep red at the smirk she could sense on Grace's face. Aside from the compromising look of things, she didn't like the way her heart thudded when he looked into her eyes. It could be another trap, or just too long since she'd had a boyfriend. "I'm uncomfortable reading your mind even if I knew how to do it. Heresy?"

"This *thing* is indeed of your blood as it claims. That gives you power over it. I was only summoned by your blood, this creature shares a bloodlink. With suitable magical reinforcement, it will be compelled to obey you over anything but the strongest of counter-magics."

"I can show you how to do it." Zero's eyes gleamed, sending cold trickling down Harper's spine. He might look scrawny and somewhat pathetic, but there was strong magic within him. Stronger than hers, maybe. "You won't See in my mind, it's more like a truth spell, only we don't need all the usual magic paraphernalia because we're already linked."

"What do I do?" The words slipped out before Harper thought them through. Enforcing her will on another sentient being sounded wrong, almost as bad as mind reading. Yet he seemed so eager for her to do it. If he consented, and it might save lives, was it wrong? *Yes. But is there a right?* Like her dilemma over Usa, Harper wasn't sure a 'right' existed.

"Harper, no. It could be a trap." Grace grabbed the man's wrist and he paled, eyes watering.

Harper placed her hand over Grace's and looked her sister in the eyes. "People are dying, Grace, and someone is attacking us. If we can confirm or eliminate him as a suspect, that's something. Maybe he can help. If he wanted to hurt me, he's had ample opportunity, and Heresy said he has to obey me."

Grace held Harper's gaze for a moment, jaw set, then she flung Zero's hand away from her and collapsed back on the couch with her arms crossed over her chest and a scowl on her face.

He rubbed his wrist, eyes downcast, until Harper took his hands again. His slender fingers trembled within hers, so fragile she feared she might snap them.

"Your own blood must answer you truthfully," he said. "Ask me what you want to know."

Harper summoned the tingling burn of her magic. He blurred around the edges and she could See both the cat and the man. Every vein was etched on his skin like a network of roots, visible despite clothes. She Saw him stripped away without pretence. "Who are you?"

"Zero. Nothing. A forgotten memory. An apprentice. A familiar. A warning." A list poured from Zero's mouth, drawn into the light by her magic. "A mistake. A sacrifice—"

"What's your name?" Harper interrupted.

He squirmed on the chair, breath coming in short pants. "We have no names. Only designations. I came before the others. Before One. I am Zero. Nothing."

"What others?"

"Like me. Shifters. My master makes them to serve zir."

"Who is your master?"

"Ze's—" Zero choked, shaking his head. The skin above his collar blanched white as it tightened. "Ze is … no name … is …" He stopped breathing, his eyes unfocussed, hands tight and rigid in Harper's.

"Stop. It's alright. Ze won't let you answer. I understand." Harper took deep breaths for him although his panic and pain pounded her head. If whoever put that collar on him could stop him answering, she wondered if ze could make him lie. Zero's battle over whom to obey had been so visually obvious, Harper hoped it meant any falsehood would be equally apparent. "Are you or your master responsible for the deaths of the women who've had their eyes taken?"

He flushed as his blood was allowed to flow again and he took several deep breaths. "I'm not."

"But your master is?"

"I don't … I don't know." He forced the words through clenched teeth. "My master means no harm to you. I cannot say who ze is. It is forbidden. Most of the folk know. Ze is no threat to you, nor have I been sent to harm you. My master wants you protected. Ze ordered me to guard you."

That, at least, was the truth though Harper's brain tingled with curiosity. If most of the folk somehow knew, maybe AJ would, though it was not like he was always forthcoming with information. Not wanting to harm Zero, she moved on with her questioning. "What caused you to come here?"

"Your fetch."

Harper couldn't repress a shudder. She and Grace had encountered the doppelgängers before and she'd never heard of one that didn't portend the death of its double.

"Where?" she asked.

"Deep under my dwelling, underground but framed against the sunset, a place which was and was not."

"Where are you from?"

His muscles spasmed and Harper gripped his hands tighter. His mouth opened and closed soundlessly, her power not enough to See the answer within him.

"Why would my fetch appear to you?" she asked instead.

"I am made of you. Blood to blood."

"What does that mean?"

"It's how ze makes us." He wrinkled his nose and ghosts of whiskers twitched. "We start as animals, we become shifters through blood. We don't know how I was made. We can't replicate it perfectly."

"How did you get my blood?"

"I don't know. I've been like this since before I remember. I came to my master this way. Ze made the others, but I was there first. Zir Zero."

"What is hunting me?"

"Something we can't remember. I can't … I can't … I can't …"

Blood thudded through Harper's body, pounding her brain. Her own breath came in short bursts, mirroring his. Nails extended into claws as he gripped her hands. She could See the fight in him as the images flickered. Man. Cat. Man. Cat. Child. Kitten. Eyes like the ocean threatened to drown her. She couldn't breathe. Her chest ached. She couldn't hear over the roaring of her heartbeat. Her brain beat against her skull, desperate to burst free.

She dropped his hands and the connection broke. Tears flowed down her face as she knelt at his feet, trying to catch her breath. She balled her fists in frustration, resting her head on her knees. Warm hands stroked her back and she looked up to find Zero's wide eyes centimetres from her own. A pink tongue darted out and rasped against her cheek, scooping up her tears. It startled her into looking up.

"What are you doing?"

His breath tickled her lips as he asked, "Do you believe me now, Harper?"

"I believe you, Zero. When I Saw you, it was like there was a memory trying to claw its way out of my brain. It hurts." Harper ground her teeth together. She wanted to keep going, demanding he tell her everything he claimed to have forgotten. But pain and exhaustion held her back. Pity and remorse soured her gut and left her drained. She'd experienced so much more than his words told her. A requiem deeper than human hearing. A cry for help. And more agony than she'd ever endured. A magic stronger than hers imprisoned his memories and held his soul captive. To force him to speak against the magic would break his mind and kill his body. Harper clutched her aching head. It might kill her too.

"What are we going to do with him?" Grace asked.

Harper startled; she'd forgotten the others in the room. She blushed, embarrassed at the intimacy she'd shared with a stranger.

Grace added, "I still don't think he's safe."

"I could stay with you." Zero's ears perked up, then dropped again as he fingered his collar. "Now I'm here, it seems the most efficient way."

"We could lock him in the attic until morning and ask Heresy to keep an eye on him," Saqib suggested. "I'm not sure I believe he isn't an accomplice in these murders."

"Heresy?" Zero scowled and the trembling beneath Harper's hands increased, all the fur on his tail standing on end. "That thing is an abomination."

"Why thank you," Heresy purred.

"I don't think that was a compliment," Saqib pointed out.

"It sounded like one to me." Heresy chortled, recovered from his earlier panic.

"You keep that molester away from me." The cat scrambled out of the seat and darted to hide behind it, a horrified look on his face.

"I won't let him possess you again as long as you behave, which includes no licking anyone again please, and don't try anything overnight," Harper promised. She spoke with confidence but a quick glance at Grace's anger left her stomach churning. "We can't let him go, Grace. We can't give him over to your godfather or the zookeeper either. He knows too much, even though he's forgotten it. And he has strong magic. For now at least, it sounds like he wants to stop whatever is hunting me as much as we do. If his master's death is linked to mine, he has to keep me alive."

Grace huffed, her body tense. "If he sets one foot outside the attic, he'll have me to answer to." She made a slicing motion, knife in hand, and Zero cowered.

"C'mon then." Harper tugged him towards the kitchen door. "I'll grab some spare bedding for you. If I order you not to leave the attic or contact anyone, and Heresy keeps watch, we'll be safe."

"One thing's for sure," Saqib muttered as Harper left, their latest addition trailing behind her, shoulders hunched. "This house just got a bit weirder, and that takes some doing."

CHAPTER SEVENTEEN

Walking Old Paths

Harper and Zero sat facing each other on her bedroom floor, palms pressed together. Sunlight streamed through the open window, the mists from the night before vanquished. Chatter from the street and the hum of engines faded as Harper concentrated on her Sight and Hearing. Calloused and lined with thin silvery scars, Zero's hands nonetheless warmed Harper's, leaving a tingle in her fingertips as magic flowed between them.

The connection stuttered as he wiggled his hips, edging across the floor.

"Stay still." Harper opened her eyes as the magic slipped away once again.

"But … sunlight."

Harper took him by the shoulders and slid him back into position. When they started straight after breakfast, he had sat in sunlight but the intervening hours left him in shadow.

"You can sunbathe in the garden later," she chastised.

His eyes widened and his mouth fell open. "I can?"

"Just don't draw attention to yourself. I'm not locking you up. I said I believed you and I meant it."

"You locked me up last night." Zero's lower lip jutted out. "You ordered me to stay in a dark room and left the creepy shadow to punish me."

"Guard you, not punish. We don't know you. Even though I—" Harper bit her lip. She did trust him. "It will take the others a while to get used to you. If you can tell us what you know about the murders, it will help."

"I don't know anything," Zero protested.

Harper gripped his hands tighter. "You've been spotted in the area of several of them."

"Because I was going to places where scrying found our blood."

His panicked eyes filled with tears again and he turned his head, flinching, like she would hit him for repeating the same answers she'd heard all morning. That he'd also been photographed at the home of an unrelated victim did make his answer plausible. He'd been at the house of the mirrorling's victim because he'd followed Harper, not because he had anything to do with Alice's disappearance.

"Could your master have had you spy and scry so ze could find them? Did ze kill them?" *Is ze going to kill me?*

"I don't know." Zero's eyes rolled back in his head. A white light surrounded him.

"Stop it. No magic unless I say so," Harper snapped and the glow faded.

"I'm sorry. I'm a Bad Cat. I wasn't trying to run away. It's instinct. To shift. When there's danger."

Harper softened her voice. "You're not in danger from me. Tell me what you do know. You're not outright denying it, so you must think your master capable of having killed them."

Zero ducked his head, hair falling across his face. "Ze must deal with threats to this land. It's why ze exists. To protect."

A shiver ran through Harper at the word. Could Zero's 'master' be Leonora's 'Protector'?

"Can you think of any reasons why your master would want to kill these women or how they might be linked to my blood?"

Zero shrugged. "Ze doesn't tell me everything. I'm a Stupid Cat. I don't understand even when ze tries again and again to teach me." A judder ran down his arms and tears caught in his lashes. "I don't know why your blood led me to places where you were not. It's possible there's something mixed in with my blood I haven't identified yet. Maybe you aren't the only thing that made me and my magic is linking with something else. It's …

possible that could be my master. Ze didn't make me but we are ..." He raised a hand to fret at his collar. "We share blood too."

Which made him a threat no matter what he said. Harper brushed away his tears, the sibling-esque affection undimmed by the realisation. Heresy said the thing hunting her shared her blood. If Zero had her blood and his master had his blood, it didn't eliminate zir as a suspect.

Without thinking, she scritched behind Zero's cat ears. Whatever threat his master might pose, he was trying to cooperate and she'd seen too many people under pressure slip into panic attacks. He needed a break or he'd be unable to answer anything.

"Thank you for telling me the truth. Maybe I can persuade the others to let you sleep in the lounge if you prefer." Harper extended him a metaphorical carrot.

"Do you have any boxes?" Zero asked. "May I sleep in the kitchen with the warm and the bacon smells?"

He'd wolfed down turkey bacon and veggie sausage sandwiches that morning like he hadn't eaten in days. Despite Grace's frown of disapproval at his lack of table manners and general presence in their house, Harper had seen her sliding food from her plate onto his when she thought no one was looking. She'd known Grace wouldn't be able to resist a cat for long.

"If that's what you want, and the others don't mind," Harper agreed. "Do you think we can try scrying like you did before?"

"I will do whatever you order." Zero averted his face, jaw tight.

Harper carefully cupped his chin and turned him to face her. "You're safe here."

The wariness didn't leave his eyes and she was excruciatingly aware of the dark bruise smudging his cheekbone. Pity formed a lump in her throat and a swell of protective anger rose in her chest.

She opened her mouth to question him further, then snapped it closed again. He would share when he was ready, if he was able to. For now, she had as much to prove to him as he had to prove to her.

"I won't hurt you if this doesn't work," she added. "Show me, please?"

Zero cuddled his tail in his lap and fiddled with his fur. "I need to get some things."

"Sure. Check the chest there or—" Harper cut off as he knocked three times on the air and a silvery whirlpool formed. "That's how you got in and out of the attic?"

"Out, yes. In, no. Something pulled me. Scary." With a scowl, Zero reached through and rummaged around. "That was your attic?"

"Yeah. Sorry about that. The spell was supposed to keep whatever haunts my dreams out." But it pulled you in. Does that mean you're the opposite of what haunts me or that you are what haunts me? She glanced at the scratches, almost healed, on the back of her hand.

He extracted a black glass knife, obsidian Harper guessed, with flecks of red and gold in it. Next came an iron flask, a concave dish small enough to sit on a palm, a stand for the dish, a pair of tongs, and a leather pouch. The swirling portal diminished and disappeared.

"Hydrargyrum," Zero explained, holding up the flask. "Don't be afraid, there's not really water in it."

Harper frowned. "What's 'hydrargyrum' and why would water being in it be scary?"

Zero gave her a perplexed look. "Unless it's for drinking, water isn't very nice. You like water?"

"Well, yeah. As much as anyone. I shower most days and take the occasional bath, if that's what you mean."

The cat wrinkled his nose. "Icky. Humans are weird. Anyway, hydrargyrum is this." He drew a circle on the floor using Harper's chalk, then sandwiched it with a semi-circle on one side and a cross on the other.

"It's associated with the fastest planet, so it's written that way. It's the eightieth element, one of the transition metals, the only metal liquid at room temperature, which makes it perfect for scrying. The fact that it also represents life and death, as well as feminine, may be why my search led me to where women had died recently, or were about to."

Harper blinked at his 'explanation.' She'd done okay in science at school, despite starting from way behind her peers, but most of what he said made no sense to her. "You need to talk to Saqib. Wait. 'Only metal that's liquid at room temperature?' Mercury, right? Which is also the planet closest the sun and presumably the fastest." Despite a tinge of annoyance at his cryptic answer, Harper was quite pleased with herself for working it out.

"This one is dangerous." Zero pointed at the bag. "Phosphorous burns if it touches oxygen. The bag is spelled to keep air out, so it doesn't have to be kept in water. It's the fifteenth element, non-metal, and represents light and spirit. This is taken from owl bones. Phosphorous is the light bringer and owls are the night seers. Basically, this phosphorous helps someone See." He put a second line through the cross under the circle and drew an equilateral triangle intersecting the circle with its base meeting the cross. Then he drew a larger triangle to encompass everything he'd drawn so far except the top semi-circle. "The second triangle represents water. It will keep the phosphorous from igniting."

To Harper's mundane sight, it looked like a chalk scribbling, but when she summoned her magical Sight, the sigil's brilliance caused her to squint and look away.

"This is how you do magic, Harper dear."

She hadn't realised Heresy was watching, the strength of the magic enough to capture his curiosity despite his aversion to their guest.

"The not-a-cat seems scarily proficient, at least as far as drawing geometric shapes goes." He bared his teeth at Zero who shrank back, a chunnering noise in his throat.

"Don't touch my magic."

"He won't." Harper reached out and touched Zero's arm as she glared at Heresy. "You won't."

"I would not wish to dirty myself." Heresy snaked up to sit territorially around Harper's shoulders. "Pray continue. Please try not to accidentally kill Harper if the magic reversal infection takes over."

"I would never hurt Harper!" Zero protested. His tail fluffed up, shaken by Heresy's abrupt appearance. "We're doing a looking spell and the opposite of Seeing something is not seeing something, so at worst, nothing will happen."

"Or you'll blind her," Heresy pointed out with a chuckle. "Blind seers are a thing. It could be entertaining."

Harper fervently prayed the spell didn't blind her, her faith in the cat shaken.

Zero hissed at Heresy and continued, but his voice trembled, his previous confidence diminished by Heresy's scepticism. "Now the water is keeping things safe, we take these tongs and sketch the phosphorous over its own symbol like so, and then we set the dish up over the point here where the circle and semi-circle meet and we tip the mercury in. Then we add blood. In this case, we're looking for something with Harper's blood, so it's doubly important, but even if we weren't, blood or other parts of a living creature make the magic stronger."

"Hence why Usa took body pieces for The Hiding," Harper said, to show she was keeping up. Alchemy had never been her field of study, though she'd taken a few classes about it in uni. Enough to recognise that what Zero was doing had the hallmarks of the pseudo-science. Or maybe not so pseudo if this worked.

"Exactly." Zero held out his hand and Harper hesitantly placed hers on it. He pricked both of their fingers with the knife, squeezing a few drops of blood into the mercury. Harper snatched her hand back and sucked her finger as soon as he let go. He held out his hand again. "Good instinct to stop unwanted blood being taken. I'll heal you."

"You can do that?" Harper's eyes widened.

The complexity of the spell he was showing her paled in comparison to being able to heal with magic, reportedly one of the most difficult of all the arcane arts. Then again, he did seem to have knocked a hole through reality without any prep or aids at all. She gave him her hand. Her finger prickled as he pressed his to it, and when he withdrew the small cut was gone.

"Um. Thank you."

"I can only do little heals," Zero shrugged modestly. "Anyway, we're all set up to scry now. The rest is will. Take my hands and think about Seeing the one who killed your friend."

Harper pictured Agnes as she had last seen her. Tears formed, a mixture of burning Sight and emotional bruising as Zero's magic twisted through hers. The symbol on the floor burned so brightly she feared oxygen had gotten in. The mercury rose to form a swirling silver ball, like the crystal she'd accidentally summoned Heresy through. But instead of a reflection or even Agnes, the image of hilly countryside appeared on its surface and a woman walking along a path by a river. It wasn't Agnes, but she did have dark hair and eyes.

Harper recognised the village in the distance. She and Father De Santos had stayed in an inn there the night after he found her. Her grip on Zero's hands tightened to hide her trembling.

The young woman skipped as she walked, her long brown hair dancing in the breeze. Although there was no sound to the image, her mouth moved in song. Then fear clouded her features as something beyond the vision caught her eye. She turned and sprinted back up the path. Reeds tangled around her feet and she fell. She screamed.

The mercury crashed back into the dish and the phosphorous flare turned the world white. Pain seared Harper's eyes as though fingers gouged through her retina. Skeletal hands wrung her heart. Music, too sharp, sliced her brain. Piece by piece by piece, it cut slivers from her, flayed her mind like carpaccio. The song set her teeth on edge, prickled through her veins, crackled along her nerves. The same words. The same command. *Show me the Seer. Show me the Seer. Show me the Seer.*

Zero leapt over the spell to catch Harper's convulsing body as she fell. Her limbs were rigid, her eyes gleaming violet and wide open. He could sense another presence, one that set all his fur standing on end and made him want to hiss and yowl. It wasn't in her, not yet, but it was close, battering on the door to her soul and demanding she surrender.

"Don't give up, Harper." He lifted her onto the bed, then nuzzled her cheek. "Don't give up. I'm coming."

A soft glow surrounded him. As it faded, Zero's borrowed clothes crumpled to the floor. With a wiggle, he squirmed out of the pile, then smoothed his fur. It felt good to be back in this form. He hadn't spent so long in human form for years, but he'd been afraid Heresy might invade his body again if he shifted overnight, which made sleep an impossibility.

Although he wanted to get to Harper quickly, basic safety had to be observed. A glittering silver-and-turquoise shield appeared around the spell.

"Hurry up, not-a-cat," Heresy snapped. "You did this to her. Undo it before it finds her. I will conceal this ill-conceived magic."

Zero hopped onto Harper's bed and curled himself around her on the pillow. Entering the dreamscape wasn't hard. All cats knew the way. The wakening world faded into the dreaming as silver, violet, and turquoise lights drifted through the air. Firs grew beside him, seeds, then saplings, then mighty trees that blocked out the watery light of the moon. Mists permeated the landscape, swallowing the intermittent starlight. Too dark. Too dark.

'Fraidy cat. Fraidy cat.' The taunt galled him. Stupid One, always mocking him. Cats were supposed to be crepuscular so the light waning shouldn't alarm him. He was the hunter here. Yet the darkness terrified him like

nothing other than his master's presence. It scared him more than One's bullying. He wanted to flee for kinder dreams, but the dreamer who was his refuge wouldn't be asleep yet and, anyway, running away would be selfish. He had to try and stay. For Harper. For his master.

Snow crunched underpaw as he forced himself to keep moving. Trees swayed overhead, ghastly shadows surrounding him, clawing at him. He shied away from them. Their needles caught his fur, yanked it from his flesh, knocked him off course. His claws passed through the shadows harmlessly. He howled, canines bared.

He could sense Harper nearby, though he couldn't see her through the mists. The dreamscape wasn't linear. It twisted and folded. What was sought might be forever within reach and yet unobtainable. He latched onto her pain and fear, letting them drag him towards her like a leash.

He blinked and she was there.

Curled up foetal, a young child with long pigtails and a polychromatic dress. Zero took a step forward. Snow tumbled onto his head and he sank. He clawed his way free, spitting as the wet stuck to his fur. Paws too large for his body scrabbled at the snow and a kitten's whine escaped his throat as Harper's stiff body drew no closer.

"The Seer is mine, mewling." Music surrounded him, a voice, or a memory of one, carried within it. Ears flat against his skull, Zero scanned the dreamscape, lips drawn back in a hiss as the music continued its assault. "Begone from my dreaming and trouble me no more, lest I regret my leniency with you."

Claws extended, he slashed at the darkness. He hissed and spat, back arched. Harper was his and he wouldn't abandon her.

A sharp tug yanked the scruff of his neck, almost lifting him from his feet. Strange fingers digging into his spine hurt no less for being a dreaming. He twisted in the air, unable to see what held him.

"I will warn you no more, mewling. Tell your master to cease zir interference. The Seer must return to fulfil her destiny. I will find her and I will bring her home."

The music stopped with the twang of snapped strings and Zero fell to the ground. His form writhed, unable to maintain solidity as cat or man. His fingers dug into the snow. A midnight shadow hovered over Harper, almost touching her tear-stained face.

"M-m-m-i-ine," he whispered, cracked lips protesting as he pressed them together. His memories were no clearer but, here in the dreamscape, the emotions were crystal. Whatever past this reflected, he and Harper had belonged together in it. Zero forced claws to extend. "Mine."

Harper woke with a start, bolt upright, chest heaving as she struggled to breathe. She clutched the sheet under her to steady herself as her thoughts raced. Her hand throbbed. When she looked down, she saw stripes of seeping blood. The white cat bent his head and gently licked it away. When he lifted his head, the scratches were gone. Then he limped into her lap and placed his head against her chest as he stared up at her. His whole body trembled against hers.

Harper screwed her eyes closed, trying to clear her head. All she remembered was dark and pain and a solitary violin. Then voices, speaking words she couldn't remember. A shadow and a white cat. Zero.

"You scratched me." Harper looked down at his shivering form and any irritation fled. "Are you okay?"

"Mraow," he mewed up at her, eyes wide.

"A nightmare? Do you remember what happened?"

"Mrow." Zero licked her hand as she patted his head.

"Who warned you to stay away from me? Wait. Are you speaking English? How——?" She pinched the bridge of her nose. Her ears heard a cat's meow but her magic Heard his words. "Can I understand all animals?"

"Mraow." The quivering lessened as he rubbed his nose against her fingers.

"Yeah, I don't remember either. I just … we had a vision and I think … I think blacked out?"

"Mau." His whiskers quivered. "Mraow."

"I'm forgetting." Harper thumped the mattress. Zero scrabbled away and zoomed under the bed. With a sigh, she clambered after him, laying on the floor to regard the dusty, shivering tomcat. "I'm sorry. Please come out. It's just frustrating."

"Merow-ow?"

"Not you. Just. Everything. Actually, yes, you too. All of it. Can you please come out and be human again? Talking like this is giving me a headache. Also, I don't care what shape you are, I better not catch you in my bed again. Got it?"

He gave her a plaintive stare, then slunk out from under the bed, skirting around her until he reached the pile of discarded clothes. When a white glow surrounded him, Harper threw up her hands.

"No. Nope. No. Wait until I leave."

A door slammed downstairs.

"I'm going to see who's home," Harper said. "You get dressed *after* I've left, tidy up the spell, then come downstairs and join us, okay?"

"Mrow."

"Yes, you do have to, we need to discuss what we Saw. We can try and find a sunny patch in the garden."

Downstairs she found Saqib putting on the kettle.

"They found Edith's body," he told her. His skin was ashen and he looked irredeemably tired. "Like the others. Eyes missing. No other trauma. I don't know where, they wouldn't let me go so I'm guessing some secret Guard place. I should get evidence to process in a day or two. Have you found anything helpful?"

Harper blanched when he said they found the body. Even though she'd known her old classmate was dead, even though they'd never been close, it hurt. "I think we may have Seen the next victim. I promised Zero we'd sit outside. Come on, I'll fill you in."

CHAPTER EIGHTEEN

Star-Clad Memory

It had been a couple of days since their shared vision of the girl in the Dales, but further magical searching wasn't getting them anywhere and Saqib had yet to turn up anything via his police contacts. The dale already crawled with Guard. 'Anonymous tip' was the phrasing they'd agreed to explain Harper and Zero's vision, citing a Council source when the Guard questioned further. It was enough. For now.

At a loose end, the household regrouped in the garden. Everyone huddled in large coats, hats, and gloves. Zero was grateful they'd come outside for him. Being in a place where he could go outside at will caused an ache in his chest. He thought it might be 'joy.' *I want to be helpful. I want to be a Good Cat. I'm letting them down.*

"There is one thing we could try." Zero shrank back against Harper's legs as everyone's eyes turned on him.

Even AJ looked up from where he sat cross-legged on the grass, laptop on his knees. As evening fell, thin mists reached for the device and he waved them away. Solar-powered garden lights flickered on and the curfew bell rang funereal in the distance.

The impending night thrust daggers of fear through Zero, stiffening his limbs as he smothered the instinct to flee. Harper's hand on Zero's head calmed him and he purred softly, rubbing his ears against her fingers.

"What's that, Zero?" Saqib pulled a notebook out of his pocket and sat on the edge of what he called a 'deckchair.' After seeing how it snapped flat, Zero called it 'deathtrap' and sat on the grass.

"We can ask an information dealer."

AJ inhaled sharply and Zero cringed away from him. His cheek twitched, waiting for the sting of a slap, but AJ didn't move, despite his apparent displeasure.

"Is that what it sounds like?" Grace asked.

"Worse." AJ spoke before Zero had a chance to respond. The cat pressed his lips closed and lowered his eyes, giving way. "They charge steep prices and can be deceptive. They won't tell you anything untrue, but they don't tell everything. We avoid them. Whatever they can tell you isn't worth what they'll charge."

"Sounds dangerous." Grace's stare itched the back of Zero's neck, but he kept his head bowed before her accusation.

"I'm trying to help," he muttered.

"Then help me with my magic." Harper's fingers tightened in his hair, a reflex, he hoped. Not an admonition. "Help me find her before it's too late."

"I did help. I broke the rules. I did help." His collar choked back his protests. Tears stung his eyes. No matter what he did, it was wrong.

"Zero." Harper's patient tone stung even more than Grace's harsh one. He was failing her. "What about your master. Can ze help? Who is ze anyway?"

Zero tugged at his collar as he bent over, grass tickling his forehead. Voices filled his head. Orders. Reprimands. Commands of his master that must be obeyed, even if he was forbidden from speaking of them. Electric stings zapped down his spine, a reminder built into his collar. He flexed his fingers against the unfamiliar coarse covering they made him wear, missing proper claws to dig into his leg.

"You wouldn't … like zir … price …" he managed to stutter out. His nose was pressed into the ground. Cold. Wet. Dirty. He hated it. He waited for the blow to fall, the physical manifestation of her wrath, her disappointment.

"You keep saying you're here to help, but you've just added more questions," Grace accused. "For all we know, your master is the one who was attacking the house. It hasn't happened since you got here."

"I don't know. I don't. I don't. Why would I lie? I can't lie to Harper." He looked beseechingly at Harper but she turned her face away. Tears pricked the corners of his eyes again. Harper's mistrust stung more than a thousand needles.

"To get inside her defences?" Grace hypothesised. "To disrupt something? To divert attention?"

"Gray, leave it." Harper reached a hand to her sister but Grace batted it away.

"I'm here to protect Harper," Zero protested.

"Who else are you protecting?" Grace's fingers dug into his arm as she yanked him up. "Who is your master? What is hunting Harper?"

"I don't know!" A knot tightened in Zero's chest as a blunt ache built behind his eyes. He should know. He should. But he couldn't remember. It would be his fault if she was hurt. She was the only thing from his past he remembered anything of. Littermate and Mama in one. *I need her. She needs me.*

"You need a better excuse than that," Grace warned.

"Zero, tell us what's going on, please." Harper's quiet plea cut worse than his master's athame.

He looked at her, at the confusion and doubt in her eyes, and wished she held a knife instead. He could bear any punishment but disappointment. "I already told you what I can. I already broke the rules."

"That's not the same as 'I told you all I know,'" Saqib pointed out.

"Fine, don't believe me." Zero was sick of this shape and all the complications of being human. At least with his master's lessons he knew what to expect and why it happened. He shifted, the world warping around him as he shrunk, scents growing stronger, sight growing dimmer. With a snarl at the tangled clothes, he fought free and darted between Harper and Saqib's legs, through the cracked open doors until he reached the locked front one. Heresy drifted over him and he twisted to bat away the demon.

"Just opening the door to get rid of you." As Heresy settled in the peephole, the sky-blue door swung outwards. Zero darted out, leapt the garden wall, and dashed down the street. He could hear Harper calling him back, but her voice was drowned by the ringing in his ears.

Heresy drifted back into the kitchen where the others waited and settled on the table. "I do not trust that not-a-cat. His magic is strong. He could be an accomplice."

"Or a target." AJ sat at the table, sipping a cup of cold coffee.

"You think he's innocent?" Saqib asked. "What evidence do we really have that he's here to protect Harper?"

"I think the kid's in trouble and this is what we do." AJ shrugged. "Either way, one of you better go find him before the Guard or something worse catches him instead. He has Harper's blood. His master has probably protected him so far, but zir isn't near now. Zero could be vulnerable."

"AJ, do you know who his master is?" Harper asked with a frown.

"I might," AJ said delicately. He tapped his mug as he stared at the cold brew.

"Feel like sharing?" Saqib prodded.

"If I'm wrong, it's not helpful for you to know. If I'm right, then me telling you could get Zero hurt. He's prevented from saying who he works for. If we confront him directly with his master's title, he might be punished for it."

"AJ." Grace's voice was a low growl as she leant over his chair, one hand on his shoulder. "Do you know what is attacking Harper?"

"No." He looked up to meet Harper's eyes. "I swear I don't. If it was his master, I don't think the house would still be standing. If I'm right about who that is. Whatever is attacking seems to be a thing of dreams. Maybe his master is an old 'deity' of sleep or something and not what I think at all. Whether they're the same or not, ze's powerful. Zero has a shit-ton of magic. You don't want to mess with something that can keep him collared. I'm going back to work." AJ tossed the dregs of coffee into the sink before turning to leave. "You should get him back. If anyone discovers he's not a normal cat, he'll be arrested. Even if they can't catch him, it'll get him in trouble at home."

"You could confront it." A sly grin slit Heresy's body. "Maybe its master will take it away again. Nasty not-a-cat."

"I'll go find him." Harper ignored Heresy and followed AJ into the front hall, Zero's clothes in her arms.

"You're the last person who should go." Grace grabbed Harper's coat before she could pull it off the peg.

"He's *my* friend … apparently. *My* link to the past. And both Heresy and AJ agreed whatever is hunting can't find me, just things close to me. So actually, I'm the safest. Plus, AJ's right. We should give Zero a chance. I was a bit of mess when your father found me too, Gray."

"Yeah, I remember the night he brought you home." Grace smirked. "No clue what a freaking shower was, thought the electric lights were magic, kept falling out of bed." Grace bit her lip, then added soberly, "You burst into tears because you couldn't remember the way home."

"Maybe we were hard on him." Harper grimaced. "He has been here three days and if he's been following me for months, he's had ample opportunity to harm me. He can't tell us everything, and logic tells me to mistrust that, but my heart tells me I'm safe with him. Like it told me I'd be safe with you."

Grace squeezed Harper in a hug. "I remember. I'll trust you, sis."

Harper returned her sister's embrace. "Thanks. You and Saqib check out the house and make sure everything's safe. I'll go bring the cat home. It'll be embarrassing for everyone if we have to put up 'lost pet' posters."

"I should go with you," Grace said.

"I don't think he'll let me find him if you do."

Grace gave a tight nod as she handed over Harper's coat. "Be careful. I love you."

Harper gave her sister an uncertain smile as she left. "I love you too."

Her Sight showed nothing unusual outside, nothing to indicate which way Zero went. The encroaching darkness was cut by the full moon's light, letting her function without the paralysing fear pure black nights could bring. She took a deep breath and closed her eyes. His blood connection helped him find her. That *must* go both ways. Words slipped from her lips, a forgotten spell dragged up from the darkness of forgetfulness. "Blood to blood, I search. Blood to blood, I call. Blood to blood, I See."

Her heart burned and its roar filled her ears. When she opened her eyes, a violet trail of pawprints blazed. Hoping she didn't meet anyone since it was after curfew, Harper followed the magic south. It led her over the protective wall and down the west bank of the Ouse, through Rowntree Park and over the Millenium Bridge. Several times she was diverted, unable to follow the straight line the cat had taken, but each time she was able to pick up the shining trail again.

She eventually found a forlorn Zero by the side of the Ouse at the edge of Danesmead Wood, laying with his head on his paws. There was no mistaking his starlight coat even though his legs were covered in river mud. Harper had never seen a cat look so utterly dejected. She sat down on a rock nearby but he didn't look up.

"Zero?"

He buried his nose under his leg, tail swishing.

"I'm sorry for the things we said." Harper stretched out a hand to stroke him, then pulled back. "You've not done anything to hurt us, we should give you the benefit of the doubt."

His head cocked to the side, one ear pricked.

"I'd like you to come back with me. It's hard for us that you don't remember much but … we didn't stop to think about how you felt about it. When I used my Sight on you, you were telling the truth. I'm sorry, Zero. Will you please change and talk to me? I brought your clothes."

Zero stretched, his legs sticking to the mud. He walked up to Harper and nuzzled against her leg. She leant over and rubbed his head, scratching behind his ears as he purred. When he looked up at her, his eyes held an ocean of sorrow.

"All you want is to be friends, don't you?" The loneliness in him broke her heart. She'd seen it before, many times, for all she couldn't remember when. Her stomach churned with guilt at being the cause of it. "If you come back, I'll make you as many bacon sandwiches as you want."

Zero stood on his hind legs, leaving pawprints on Harper's jeans. He nosed against the clothes in her hand, then jumped up on the rock next to her and waited expectantly.

"I'll leave the clothes here and come back in a few minutes," Harper said.

Zero dismissed her with a flick of his tail, so she placed the clothes on the rock and went a short distance. She resolutely looked away, humming to herself to mask the small noises. When a cold hand slipped into hers, she jumped.

"I washed in the river. It's chilly but I didn't want to make you muddy." Zero spoke to the ground, fluffy white hair falling across his face. The hood was pulled up to hide his ears. He looked pudgy around the waist and it took Harper a moment to realise it was his tail curled around under the hoodie.

"Let's get you home and warmed up, okay?" Harper twined her fingers through his. His hand fit hers perfectly. Touching him was so natural, she wondered how she ever could've doubted him. Linking hands with him was something she'd done hundreds of times before as they scampered through the trees. The memory disappeared before it had a chance to fully form.

Instead of heading back towards the bridge, Zero tugged Harper away from the path and into Danesmead Meadow instead. He gestured to her to sit, then sat back-to-back and leant against her.

"I wasn't not talking to you," he said slowly, "but some things are hard to say in cat shape or when you're looking at me."

Harper reached back and rested her hand over his. "What did you want to say?"

The pressure on her back increased and soft hair brushed against her neck as he looked up at the sky.

"I wanted to say, 'I'm sorry.'"

Harper looked over her shoulder in surprise but he didn't turn. Silver, violet, and turquoise magic glimmered in the air as he stared at the sky, the picture of serenity. "What are you sorry for?"

"For not coming for you sooner. For confusing you so much. For not answering your questions. There are things I *cannot* tell you, not because I don't remember them but because … because I *can't*. Some things aren't my secrets to tell. But none of those secrets mean you harm. I wouldn't allow it." The last words turned hard as diamond and he stiffened, his back like steel.

Harper tilted her head back, resting on his shoulder, and he relaxed. "Oh, Zero. You don't need to apologise to me. It's not your fault. I'm sorry my questions are hurting you."

The only reply was a soft purr. Once again, Harper was engulfed in a strange sense of déjà vu. They'd sat together like this before, back-to-back, watching the stars twinkle overhead while the mists flowed around them. Their fingers twined together as they gazed up at the full moon.

"I used to try and use the stars to find my way home," Harper said wistfully, breaking the long silence. "I was terrified to go out at night, but still I hoped so hard it hurt. Grace's father taught me to live with the darkness, though it scares me. This, with you here, doesn't feel as bad somehow."

Zero squeezed her fingers. "Did you ever come close to finding home?"

"Not this way. I guess I was closest when I was in Swaledale, based on the women murdered there, but there are deaths here, too, so I'm not sure. I always thought, if I could See the stars as they were over my home, I could navigate back to the spot where I'd seen them that way last."

"I like to sit on the roof and watch the stars but I'm hardly ever allowed. When I watch the stars, I dream of you."

"I wish I had dreamt of you, but my dreams never bring anything good."

"Maybe you dreamt of me and didn't know it. Our dreams have overlapped since the Hiding started slipping. I don't remember the dreams but I remember *you*. Maybe it happened before and we don't remember or didn't realise. Like we lost our memories when we left our home, I think the memories of our dreams about it slip away too."

"I've woken up with scratches on me," Harper said. "All I remembered was they came from the dream, but not what caused them. Was that you?"

"Maybe," Zero conceded. "It's difficult to hurt someone through a dream, but a true dreamwalker can do it, with a strong enough connection. I wished upon a star once. I wished I could find you. But that was a long time ago, in another place."

"It came true eventually."

"Eventually …" Zero let out a deep breath. "We used to sit like this and dream better dreams."

Harper could almost See an overlay of the image. Two adults, souls scarred, had once been innocent children longing for something more. Tears pricked her eyes as the memory trickled through, bypassing her conscious mind to appear in her Sight as she spoke. "We dreamt of the stories within the stars and the secrets of the world they could unlock."

"You liked the Greek stories from that book we found in the cave." He sounded younger, smoother, the scars and anxiety gone. "I don't remember why it was in a cave, but it was. Lots of books. In Latin, mostly. It was a happy place."

A laugh bubbled in her chest, the memory of childish levity so physical it almost burst out of her. Harper split, the girl from the river staring at her older self, a faint frown marring her face. Both voices spoke together. "You liked the Egyptian tales because they revered cats. I promised to take you there one day."

"We couldn't leave …" Zero trailed off. He tilted his head, breath tickling Harper's ear. "How did we end up here?"

"It was a very long time ago and …" The memory rushed away, borne on a river swollen by rain. A boy's face, eyes wide in terror, faded into the night. Mist tumbled over her memories, obscuring what was once clear. The little girl was gone, leaving adult Harper cold and shaken.

"We … remembered it?" He lilted at the end, tail swishing.

"We did." Harper leapt to her feet, yanking Zero up with her. "We remembered it. It's fading now, like we were dreaming, but we were awake and we both remembered the same thing."

"Does that mean you believe me now?"

Harper flung her arms around his neck. For the first time, a little of her memory remained. A white-haired boy staring at the stars, hope in his turquoise eyes. She wanted to dance. To scream. Darkness be damned. "I do. I believe you, Fionn. I've always believed in you."

"What did you call me?" Zero put his hands on her shoulders and stepped back. His tensed fingernails dug into her joints.

"Fionn. That's your name. I remember you. Only a little, but I do."

His eyes lit up as he engulfed her with his arms and tail, crying onto her shoulder.

"Do you like it?" She patted his head, feeling more than hearing his purring.

"Thank you, Harper," Fionn whispered. "Thank you for finding who I am. I knew … I knew I was part of you, still."

It took a long time for him to stop crying, leaving her shirt a soggy mess sticking to her skin. As they walked home, Harper didn't have the heart to tell him the rest of her memory: that they snuck out because going outside was forbidden after dark, not just for children but for anyone.

How could she have forgotten? How could she have forgotten her whole family was nyctophobic? How could she have forgotten it was forbidden, on pain of banishment, to go outside during the night, to even look outside? Maybe it was the key to why she left her home. Maybe it was the key to why she never managed to find her way back.

CHAPTER NINETEEN

Fake It 'Til It Kills You

Harper sat at the kitchen table with a map of Yorkshire, Saqib's crime scene photos, and about a hundred notes spread out in front of her. Grace was in her room reading and Fionn was curled up asleep in a cardboard box in a patch of sunlight. He'd been with them a few days now and preferred to sleep in the kitchen, with the smell of turkey bacon and the possibility of milk, and in cat form. They'd been trying to force a vision all morning, leaving them both exhausted. His human form looked paler than usual, the dark circles under his eyes deeper although the bruises were fading. He'd refused to explain them, getting agitated and tugging at his collar, until Harper was forced to drop it. Eventually, she'd insisted he rest. He'd fallen asleep to a lullaby played on her violin, which he was fascinated by.

When her phone buzzed, Harper was so absorbed in watching the sleeping cat that it took her a moment to notice.

"Hey, Saqib. Got anything?"

Harper could hear the rustle of Saqib's lab coat and the click of his shoes as he paced back and forth. "Harper, I've found a match to that 'anonymous tip' we got from Swaledale. Her name's Vanessa Cotterill."

Fionn's head appeared over the rim of the cardboard box. He cocked his head to the side, ears twitching as Saqib continued.

"She wasn't on my list because she's from Lincolnshire. Different jurisdiction and you know what the Guard are like about sharing info. She was believed to have eloped with a young woman of, and I quote, 'dubious background' around ten days ago. Her parents reported her lover to the Guard as a suspected witch. They arrested her a few days later. She claimed not to know where Vanessa was. Said they were supposed to meet in Reeth but Vanessa never showed so she returned to Lincolnshire to look for her. All the file says is 'held for further questioning.'"

"If she disappeared ten days ago, that means we have four days until her body appears if it follows the same timeline as the others." Panic squeezed Harper's chest. She couldn't have another woman killed in her stead. She couldn't. "She might still be alive. We have to find her."

"I've got the park rangers searching. They don't want another death in the Dales and they're eager to find who killed their friend. We have another disappearance closer to home to look into."

Harper's stomach dropped. "Another?"

Fionn hopped out of his box and jumped onto her lap, nuzzling her cheek with his nose. She gave him a pat on the head and he purred.

"Chief Bradford just informed me of another missing woman," Saqib replied. "His officers got a call to Le Page Court at Vanbrugh College this morning. You went to York Uni, right? You know where I mean?"

A lump blocked Harper's throat and muffled her strangled affirmative. She swallowed hard and tried again. "I know it. I lived there. So did Edith."

"Too many coincidences, Harper." Saqib sounded deflated. "Multiple witnesses heard sounds of a fight coming from the girl's room. When they came out into the corridor to see what was going on, the reports vary wildly. Everything from a massive demon, to a giant spider, to a black-clad man with a knife. When the police got there, they found nothing. The on-call person gave them keys to the room and no one was there. Lots of occult paraphernalia though, which is why the Guard got involved and why we've been called in. No bloodbath like the hotel, thankfully."

"I'll grab Grace and meet you there." Harper hung up. Fionn peered up at her, offering a soft meow. "You better come too if you can slip in without being seen. Maybe you'll spot something we're missing or recognise the magic, if the stuff is genuine."

Fionn stretched, claws pricking her knees, then dropped gracefully onto the tiled floor. He tapped the air twice with one paw, the tip of his tail flicking back and forth. A dark light grew, shimmering in the air before him.

"Why is that a different colour to—"

He stepped through. The void disappeared as it consumed the last fluff of his tail, successful in letting him dodge the question.

Fionn debated whether to change to human form as he summoned a portal, but human form was awkward, vulnerable. He targeted his portal at the university but sensed the static of magical wards surrounding the area. The caster's signature was unfamiliar but not dissimilar to the magic surrounding Harper's house. He wrinkled his nose and directed his portal to the edge of the shield, then slipped through before Harper could ask uncomfortable questions. He wasn't sure if it was against the rules to explain the silvery portals went home and the black ones went everywhere else.

His master would be interested to know one of AJ's coven protected the area around the university. If it was undeclared, he dreaded to think the trouble that witch would be in. It was a problem for later. He hadn't dared check in with his master, although the longer he delayed, the worse the punishment would be. Still, if his master needed him back, he would've been summoned. *Not being called home is as good as consent, right?* Fionn irritably scratched his collar, the silver disk heavy around his neck, then trotted in what he hoped was the right direction.

Human-form would've made it easier to read a map. Fionn sat and peered at a street sign. A little boy dragged his father over so he could pat the kitty. The kid's hands were sticky and he stroked the wrong way, but Fionn didn't care. The child meant well. He mewed and nose nudged the boy who squealed in delight before his father said they had to keep going.

Fionn stopped three times to be patted by students who were fascinated by his long, soft fur. He didn't mind. He liked the attention. He liked being wanted, especially after having been ripped from his favourite dreams by Saqib's call. He wished he could visit that dreamer in the wakening. *We spend so many dreams together, surely we're friends?* He worried when the dreamer slept during the day. Fionn wasn't sure they took adequate care of themselves. Although he didn't know their name, pronouns, or even their true appearance, he loved them almost as much as he did Harper.

The dream was indulgence. One his master disapproved of and re-educated Fionn about when he was caught, so he banished his concerns. *Concentrate on your work and on helping Harper. Even if you could find the dreamer in the wakening, master's attention on them would be disaster.* He shuddered, fur bristling at the thought.

As he slunk through the campus, white fur blending with stark, modern buildings, Fionn sniffed the air. A storm was coming. He hoped to be home before it hit. Being wet as a cat was miserable. He wasn't a big fan of it as a human either. Grace's insistence he shower was nothing short of torture. *Surely humans didn't actually stand at length under streams of near-boiling water?* Harper said she enjoyed it but he must've misunderstood.

His master would scold him for being so distracted. Ze didn't like it when his pets took liberties. Fionn's legs locked and his vision swam. Then he shook himself and continued, somewhat woodenly at first, but soon resuming his normal, smooth gait.

When the signs indicated he'd found the building Saqib mentioned, he stretched out in a patch of sunlight and waited for Harper. Police tape crossed the front door and a bored Guardsperson in a long, tan coat loitered nearby.

When Harper arrived Fionn slipped past the Guard, curving his spine around her ankles as he stole through. The static of magic fizzling in the air gave a clear trail to follow as he dashed ahead. The building was split into small groups of rooms, each section hiding behind a locked door. He stood on his hind legs, stretching as high as he could to mew softly to the locks. They clicked open at his command.

The bedroom of the missing girl was obvious from the web of police tape plastered over her door. Nothing in her room seemed inherently magical but his hackles rose, his fur almost crackling. Magic was close. He nosed into each room as he continued down the corridor, even though Harper and the others stopped to cut through the police tape and investigate the bedroom. He turned and mewed at her, pointing down the corridor, and she extended her fist, thumb pointing upwards. It was accompanied by a smile and a nod so he took it as assent.

It was not until he neared the end of the corridor that he found anything amiss. Stains on the floor and the smell indicated multiple floodings, not just a one-off event. The way his pristine white paws sunk into the soggy carpet made his skin crawl.

He nosed open the door to the shower room, whiskers aquiver with distaste. The cubical was stark, prison-like, without windows or much room to turn around, even for a cat. He hissed at the dripping showerhead. Plink. Plink. Plink. Faint strains of music drifted in time to the metronomic sound. He batted at his ears in case of earworms. The music swelled, rebounding in the cramped space. A familiar tune, though his master rarely used melodies. A shadow gathered in the corner of the shower, growing until it filled the tiny space. The voice was one from his dreams, but the shifting face was chillingly familiar. *Master is the one hunting Harper?*

"I warned you, mewling. The Seer is mine."

Saqib finished his initial photos and lifted a wad of police tape to let Harper and Grace into the missing girl's bedroom. Although the furnishings were basic—bed, desk and chair, shelves, and sink—with all three of them in there, it was cramped and uncomfortable.

"I think she was overdoing it a bit." Grace raised an eyebrow at the décor. Black cloth and dribbling candles adorned every flat surface. A recipe book for spells sat out on the desk. "Don't they have room checks anymore?"

"She wasn't a real witch," Harper declared as she flicked through the book.

"What gave it away?" Grace stared pointedly at the broomstick in the corner, which clearly had never cleaned a floor in its life, and the black cape hanging over it.

"That book is a load of crock," Harper said. "Official archivist opinion. No one with any real magical ability would keep such a piece of trash. No real witch would be this brazen either, but I'll take a proper Look just in case."

Harper let her Sight fade in. It was almost ridiculously easy now. After Seeing nothing unusual in the room, she stood to the side of the mirror, in case a mirror spirit had taken the girl, and watched just beneath the surface of the glass. Nothing.

Yet something snagged her attention. She scanned the room again, eyes lingering on the window ledge. An incense burner tilted precariously on one corner, a framed photo on the other. A dark-haired child stood between two adults, all with fake smiles stretched across their faces. Harper tapped the little girl. "Is this her, Saqib? Do you have a current photo?"

"Here." He passed over his tablet. "That's her uni ID picture. Look familiar?"

Harper's hand trembled as she took it. "I met her once. In a bookstore near the cathedral. She saw …" Harper stuttered, dropping down on the corner of the bed. The blood drained from her face and her vision swam, woozy. The walls of the bedroom expanded, bookshelves sliding out of cracks in the plaster, colourful paperbacks popping onto them. Her nose burnt with the scent of decades of dust and her eyes ached. She blinked and the white walls of the residential hall bedroom returned.

"She saw my eyes. I convinced her it was a trick of the light. I was … I was mean to her. Told her she'd end up hanged if she kept pretending to be magical. I wanted to scare her safe. I never thought …"

Grace perched next to Harper and wrapped an arm around her shoulders. "You didn't do this, Harp."

"But she knew me. Agnes knew me. Edith knew me. Two women taken from Swaledale where your father found me. One living in the same area as the child we cured of possession. This girl a pretend witch who saw my magic and one of the others a woman involved with someone suspected of witchcraft. And they *all* look like me. At least a little. Dark hair. Brown eyes. Similar build. My reoccurring visions of my ancestors and my own history. Fionn showing up. It's not coincidence Gray. It's not. Something is killing them because it's looking for me. She saw me and it knows."

"I've been in all those places, too, and they look as much like me as they do you, Harp," Grace said. "Obviously, I think we're pretty hot stuff, but being honest, there are lots of girls like us. Skin tone, hair and eye colour, build … Bigger picture details like that describe thousands of people. Even if these murders and disappearances are related to the attacks on the house, they aren't your fault."

Before Harper could respond, a white blur dashed past them to huddle against her ankles. She scooped Fionn into her arms without thinking, burying her face in his fur. He dug his claws into her arm, shaking all over and mewling. A tremor rippled through her as she grabbed for a slippery memory. Too late.

"What did you see?" Harper lifted him up so she could look into his eyes. He looked straight through her. "Fionn, what is it?"

The telltale white glow surrounded him and she half tossed, half dropped him onto the bed and threw a blanket over him. Cat-ears poked out, then his nose, as he grew to human form. She tucked the blanket around him and took his ice-cold hands in hers.

"I saw it again." His voice trembled.

"Saw what again?" Grace put her hand on his shoulder and he shied away from her.

"Part master, part Harper. Cold. Wet. Soulless. Waiting." Each word seemed an effort to him, unable to form a coherent story.

"You saw my fetch again? The same as before?" Harper's nails dug into his wrists.

"Wetter." Fionn wrinkled his nose in disgust.

"Wetter?" Grace looked at Harper over his head with a raised eyebrow.

Harper stroked Fionn's trembling hands. "Stay here with Saqib. Grace and I'll check it out. Where was it?"

Fionn's hands tightened around hers, his eyes wide as he shook his head. "Don't go, Harper."

"I have to." His nails scratched her hands as she pried them loose. "Where was it?"

"Sh … shower," he whispered, ears flat against his skull.

Grace took point, crossbow notched at her side. Harper grabbed her other arm. "Wait. Gray. Can you really shoot something that looks like me."

Grace's stare was cold but Harper could sense her panic in the quiver of her muscles and the slight tic of her eye. "If I have to. Can you kill something that looks like you?"

Harper glanced back towards the bedroom where they'd left Saqib and Fionn. "If I have to."

"Meow."

Harper looked down to see Fionn sitting in the middle of the corridor, his fur prickling out as he blocked her path.

"You shouldn't come." Harper nudged him back towards the bedroom with her foot. His eyes narrowed as he bapped her shoe away. With a flick of his tail, he turned his back on them and marched towards the bathrooms.

When he reached the end of the corridor, Fionn nosed the door open, hissing at Harper as she got too close. Part of her wanted to laugh at this little cat trying to protect her. Then she remembered the ease with which he'd knocked a hole in space and the sun-bright radiance of the magic scrying. While he was with her, her mind was clouded by hope and desperation to learn more of her past, but Fionn was no innocent kitten. If he could open a portal here so easily, he could've gotten into the archives. He might not have killed Agnes, but he could've given access to whoever did. Maybe this was one of the things he was hiding. A problem for later. For now, there was a fetch to deal with.

His claws clicked on the floor as he set one paw in the bathroom and a shiver rippled his fur. With a yowl he dived in and the door swung closed behind him. There was a splash and a strange gurgling. Ignoring Fionn's warning, Harper slammed the door open, expecting to see a bloody fight. Instead, all she found was a bedraggled and miserable cat.

"Where did it go?" she asked.

"Mau." He pointed towards the plughole with one paw.

A shout ripped down the corridor.

"Saqib."

"Bedroom sink. The pipes must be connected."

They dashed out. Fionn crouched outside the cubicle. The swish of his tail the only movement, his body tensed and coiled to pounce should the creature appear again.

Harper reached the bedroom a hair's breadth ahead of Grace. At first, she thought the room was empty, then she heard a whimper behind her. Saqib was huddled in the nook between the open door and the wall, as far into the corner as a grown man could get. He clutched his notes without seeming to notice, his eyes wide.

"Grace." Harper pointed and her foster sister went to examine the now-empty sink. Harper knelt in front of Saqib. He stared through her just as Fionn had. "Are you hurt? Saqib?" When he didn't respond, she grabbed his shoulders. "Saqib? What happened? Are you hurt?"

His eyes swivelled until they focussed reluctantly on hers and he gave a tiny shake of his head.

"There's nothing here." Grace's face twisted in disgust. "What on earth is going on? Is it in the pipes? Pull it together, Saqib. We don't have time for this. If it's like that demon at the hotel, Harp and I need to catch it fast. What happened?"

"Random." Saqib spoke so quietly that both women leant closer to hear him. "Faeries. Dancing and mocking. Nothing worked the way it's supposed to. No gravity, no Newton's laws, no logic."

"What?"

Saqib grabbed Harper's hands, his fingers as cold as Fionn's. "It was terrible, Harper. There was no science, only faeries with sharp teeth."

"You didn't see a soggy version of me?"

Saqib shook his head.

"Saqib?" Grace squeezed his shoulder. "What are you afraid of?"

Harper tilted her head towards her sister. "A fear metamorph?"

"What would Saqib fear most in the world? The breakdown of his beloved science and at the hand of the thing he's trying to use it to protect the world against."

"And Fionn is made of me, so seeing my death could result in his as well."

"Plus most cats hate being wet, so it being all wet is even scarier."

"Fionn … Gray, it's gone back through the pipes. Stay with Saqib." Harper ran out of the room, called back, "No one should go alone, it will confuse it."

She could barely see Fionn crouched outside the stall. He hissed and spat, hunkered back on his haunches, his whole body tensed. Then he launched himself into the shower.

Harper rounded the corner and for a moment she found herself staring into her own startled eyes. Before she could register what she was seeing, it crumpled in on itself, as if squeezed by a giant unseen hand. Fionn twisted to land on his feet and Harper scooped him up. He hung on her arm, trembling and chittering as a black origami nightmare unfolded. Dissonant music ricocheted around the cubical, cutting into her brain like a scalpel.

The demon's wings scratched the ceiling and blocked out the flickering electric light. It stood at least nine feet tall with bloodshot eyes like a snake's and ashen flesh. The darkness under its bare skin swirled like a stormy night. It grasped towards Harper, pointed claws like a hawk's talons. A long, forked tongue flicked the air with a satisfied smirk. Part human, part beast, part snake, part bird. Its form was similar to the demon she'd briefly Seen at the hotel, but the music was that which had been haunting her.

Her heart flickered irrhythmically. Each beat that clashed with the music stung worse than heartburn. She tried to swallow but her throat was dry, her breath coming in shallow bursts. Her blood burned like frozen fire. She couldn't move, couldn't look away.

Fionn wrenched out of her numb grasp, landing on the floor with a splat. The creature didn't glance at him, its gaze locked on Harper. Her peripheral vision registered Fionn swiping at it fruitlessly, but her mind couldn't connect him with reality. All that existed was the dark and the music. A white glow dimmed pitch black to veiled shadow, letting a trickle of oxygen reach her lungs.

"Harper, wake up." Fionn's shout sent Harper's mind reeling, his nose almost touching hers as he pressed her face between his hands. Her eyes widened, then locked on his.

"Fionn?"

"Harper, use your Sight. This isn't real." Fionn stepped aside. "*Look* at it, Harper. I was wrong. It's not a fetch. It's just a fear demon."

Don't let fear take control. Harper's eyes flooded purple. The creature in front of her faded to a transparent shadow of what it was before. A small, squat creature with mottled green skin looked up at her with a sheepish grin and gave her a small wave, its three fingers curling slowly as it sidled towards the door.

"No, you don't." Fionn grabbed it by the scruff of its neck. "I know just the place for you."

He opened a portal with a double knock on the air. The ease of his magic sparked a brief fantasy of being able to wave her hand and command physics. *Don't be jealous.* Harper grimaced. Fionn tossed the creature through and the portal disappeared. When he turned to Harper his eyes were full of concern. "Is everyone alright?"

Mind still scrambling to catch up, Harper looked away, casting about the cubical in the hopes a towel would appear out of nowhere.

"You need to change back." Harper studied the plain white ceiling. "Saqib had a bit of a scare but he wasn't injured. Grace is fine, she stayed with him. Are you hurt?"

"No, I don't think that thing can hurt us. Not really."

"Harp, we think it's—well, *hello,* Fionn."

Harper turned to Grace's appraising leer. She'd thrust out a hand, shoving Saqib into the wall so he couldn't see into the room. "Saqib, maybe you better go fetch a blanket."

As Saqib hurried back down the hall, Harper's eyes were drawn to Fionn, who stood unabashedly before them. Visible to her Sight, dozens of thin scars crossed his torso and arms. Something dark and twisted pulsed within him. It started at his collar and wormed through his chest, barbed and sharp as if his soul was consumed by rose thorns.

"Are you sure you're okay?" She reached out hesitantly as her Sight faded. He pressed his head against her hand and Harper obliged by giving him a firm pat.

"Just a little soggy." He scowled at his dripping tail, then pinched his fingers together over it. Water droplets flew to form a swirling ball over his hand that he then dropped down the drain. "I've seen these creatures before. They look big and scary to make you go away but they're essentially harmless. I should've realised earlier. I'm sorry for freaking everyone out."

He hung his head. Harper ran her fingers through his hair and he flinched away, then looked up at her when the expected pain never came.

"You aren't mad?" he asked, eyes wide as saucers.

"Of course not."

Harper almost gave him a hug but decided that would be too weird in this shape and settled for awkwardly patting him on the head again. Fionn exhaled slowly.

"Where did you send it?" Harper asked.

"A bog somewhere," he replied. "It's where I usually send wet things. It'll feel at home there. My master is already aware of its kind in this area, so it isn't an anomaly I need to report or show zir."

"Why was it here?" Grace asked. She leant against the doorframe, the smirk never leaving her face, though her eyes didn't dip again. "Is it related to the disappearance?"

Fionn shook his head. "I think it came through when she disappeared. Something took her and, somehow, something came through the other way too. Like at the hotel."

Grace's expression softened. When they'd questioned him about it, they'd all seen how witnessing that massacre had scarred his mind. She grabbed the towel Saqib had been bumping against her arm around the door and held it out to Fionn. "Wrap this around your waist, please."

"I can't go out like this. I have to leave like I came in." Fionn glowed and shrank before any of them could protest, not that Harper tried hard. He was right, and naked cat was much easier to deal with than naked man.

"We'll meet you back at home then."

CHAPTER TWENTY

Invitations

Back home, the two women and human-shaped cat sat at the kitchen table. Saqib had gone straight to his lab. Fionn squirmed in his seat, anticipating a scolding.

"The clock's ticking. We have less than two weeks to find her. We need a plan." Grace set the teapot down in the centre of the table and slid everyone a mug. "Fionn, you've been finding these women either before or after their deaths. Now you have specifics belonging to this girl, can you find her or the kidnapper with your magic?"

Harper inhaled sharply, staring at her sister. Grace gave her a hard look back. "If it saves a life, I'll use it." Some silent communication passed between them and Grace turned back to Fionn. "Well?"

"If I could find it, don't you think I'd've tried to stop it?" Fionn whined into his tea. "If master knows, ze isn't telling me for a good reason. There are rules and protocols. I'm bending them by being here." *Which might be why it hasn't been expressly forbidden. If I'm caught, ze can tell everyone what a mouthy, stubborn, Bad Cat I am. It won't be unbelievable because it's true. Ze stopped the Hiding and used Harper as a shield so no one would know.* That he was forbidden to speak of, ever, to anyone. Even thinking it shot frissons of static into the back of his neck. Tears formed in his eyes, not from a sting so familiar it completed him, but for the hurt his uselessness caused to others.

Grace's hand smacked into the table. "You make portals as if it were no more difficult than snapping your fingers—"

Fionn cringed away from her.

"—and you broke through AJ's Coven's defences, and Heresy's, as though they were nothing. I refuse to believe you can't find these missing women and the one taking their eyes."

Fionn's tail twitched. "I don't know that much magic. I just do what I'm told. But …" He swallowed, glancing over at Harper. "But I do know someone who might be able to help. For a fee."

"Not this again." Grace tapped her foot, pointed shoes millimetres from Fionn's bare feet which he tucked under the kitchen chair. "We already said, we can't trust an information dealer."

"This is … different. This is a sanguinary. She reads stories from blood. Although we don't have any of the girl's blood, we have the unknown blood Saqib found in the tree. As Harper has seen and spoken to this girl in the wakening, not a dream or vision, the blood combined with her memory may be enough."

"Blood magic?" Grace tensed.

Fionn wiggled his chair back. It screeched across the tiles, setting his teeth on edge. "Have you got a better idea? Harper and I tried to have another vision, but everything we do triggers another attack in the dreamscape." He rubbed his head, still pounding from their attempts to trace the missing women without summoning the spirit that haunted Harper.

"Grace, I trust him." Harper stepped between them, and Fionn let out a small hiss of relief. "Stop grilling him."

"I know what I'm doing." He crossed his arms over his chest and bowed his head. His master called it 'petulant' but he didn't care. He was sick of being wrong to everyone. He had to take it from his master, from Harper. He didn't have to take it from Grace. "I wouldn't let anything hurt Harper. Why don't you know that yet?"

"Wherever she goes, I go, to make sure."

His head shot up. "No. Only Harper. If I take a De Santos to the Soul Traders' Market, we'll be literally flayed alive."

"Oooh, I have always wished to see the Market." Heresy poked a tendril out from under Harper's hair and Fionn scowled at it. Harper didn't need that little demon now she had him again. "I am even more of a 'supernatural' than the not-a-cat or Harper, so you can have no objections to my presence."

"Am a cat," Fionn muttered. "And I do object. I have contacts. They won't like a deception spirit trying to confuse them. Don't deny you will. You can't help it."

"Heresy can come with us and he *will* behave," Harper jumped in. "Sorry, Gray, but we're going to a supe stronghold. You and Saqib have to stay here and I doubt AJ will want to come. Fionn, can we go now?"

"At night. It's not there in the day." He buried his chin against his chest. *Why does she have to bring a nasty little possession demon? Because she doesn't trust me.* The thoughts stabbed through him and he blinked back tears.

"Then we'll go when the sun sets," Harper said.

"Come back in one piece," Grace warned. "I recognise that stubborn set of your mouth and I know you'll go whether I like it or not. That's been happening a lot lately."

Harper hugged her sister and Fionn sat on his hands to resist barging in the middle. His master always laughed and called him 'jealous,' but it wasn't that, not exactly. He didn't mind other people having hugs, he just wished he could have one too. Grace was Harper's family and a guilty part of him knew he should try to get along with her. She patted him as a cat and gave him extra rashers of bacon or a splash of milk when no one was looking, as well as tablets she said would stop the milk upsetting his tummy, but when Harper was there, she gave him looks colder than the eyes of a barghest.

"Grace?" He tugged the corner of her sleeve until she looked at him. "I'm sorry I'm not trustworthy to you. I promise, I will keep Harper safe, no matter what the cost. I will. And I'll … I'll bring you back a present since you can't come too."

"She's worried about me," Harper explained.

Grace glared at her but when she turned to Fionn a soft smile flitted across her face and she patted him on the head, smoothing his spasming ear. "Just don't bring me a dead bird or mouse, okay, cat?"

"Yes, Grace."

"I'm going to take a nap until it's time to go." Harper headed to her bedroom and Fionn scooted his chair closer to the stairs.

"Nuh uh, cat." Grace's hand on his shoulder was gentle but firm. Heresy drifted back down, then phased through the door into the lounge. Grace's eyes followed and she gave Fionn a push after him. "Go play for a bit and let Harper sleep in peace. She'll be safe so long as you two aren't actively looking for something, right?"

"Yes, Grace." He bowed his head and received a light pat.

"Good cat."

Her words swelled his chest with pride. *I've been a Good Cat.*

As Grace headed upstairs, Fionn shifted, sick of being trapped in an unfamiliar form, and nosed his way into the lounge. It was empty so he made his way to AJ's bedroom.

"Don't touch any of my tech, you'll static it," AJ said when Fionn nosed the door open. "If you want some place to stay, you're welcome to sleep on my bed. Not allergic or anything."

"Mrow?" Fionn stretched on his hind legs to place a paw on AJ's knee.

"Alright, get up here. Maybe you can see why this program won't work." AJ scooped Fionn up, supporting his back legs, and settled the cat on his lap. Fionn needled his legs a little, then curled up and was soon blissfully asleep, hoping he could find the dreams from earlier, the dreams of the arty person who knew true joy.

Harper hadn't meant to dream, but the familiar forest fanned out behind her and the dale sloped away into the mist. A fine dusting of snow crinkled under her bare feet, toes numb and cerise from the cold. She had no idea how long she'd stood under the stars in nothing but a white linen shift and with no warmth save her dark plait curled around her neck like a scarf.

A little farther down the slope, a lone tree rose into the sky, its leafless branches creating fissures in the night. Stars twinkled between waving twigs. Clouds scuttled and caught on rough bark. The tree was twisted and gnarled, battered by decades of winds. Roots rent the uneven ground as it clung to the side of the hill.

Threads of music twisted through the air, puffs of lilac and sage on the wind. The tune brought an ache to her chest and stung her eyes with tears. It seeped into her bones, jolted muscles begging to dance, and wrapped around her soul, suffocating. Her fingers jerked, tracing out the notes as if her violin were in her hands, not at home tucked under her bed. She knew each note as if she'd played it a thousand times.

Tears left icicle trails on her cheeks as she walked against the bitter wind, searching for the source of the music. She trudged uphill, through the forest. The tune never wavered, never intensified, until her toes snagged on a fallen branch and she tumbled into the dirt.

Roots ensnared her, wrapping around her waist and wrists. Bloodied knees ached as bark scraped over her legs. She lay on her back, pinned, twigs jabbed into her spine. The same tree towered over her. She recognised the pattern it created against the sky.

The music swelled. The steady thrum against her eardrums gave her vertigo. Blood trickled from gashes in her fingertips, muddied by the crumbling bark. It seeped from her ears as the music pried into her brain. Her eyes were on fire, eyelids welded open. She scrabbled against the roots, looking for an opening, a way to escape the tune that shredded her skin and fractured her bones.

Great strips of wood peeled away from the ancient tree. A hole the size of her arm opened and she thrust her hand in. Empty. She tugged at the edges, dragging her body out of the roots' clutches. Her dress tore, scraps of white that fluttered in the wind like dying birds. The roots released her with a groan and she tumbled into the hole.

She landed on something soft. The music followed, filling up the space like river water pouring into a drowning car. Harper pushed her fingers into her ears and closed her eyes. It made no difference.

"There you are, my beloved Seer." The voice was almost indistinguishable from the violin. Velvet tones squeezed her. "Embrace the music and dance with me once again."

The music jerked her muscles like a puppet on a string.

"No." She dug her fingers into the mud. The ground yielded in a putrid stench of decay and syrupy fluid drenched her hands. She opened her eyes.

An eyeless corpse stared up at her.

The woman she and Fionn had Seen fleeing something unknown down the Swaledale path.

"I thought she was you," the voice taunted. "But the magic within her was a mere glimmering. Perhaps from a common ancestor who refused to follow me. You have been awaited through the centuries, my Seer, each generation carefully matched and chosen. She was nothing compared to you. But she was similar enough to bring us closer. The child I See now has seen you, witnessed your magic with her own eyes. They shall become mine and we shall be closer still."

"No." It came out as a whisper. Acid choked Harper's voice, her tongue swollen, stuck to her throat. "This isn't my fault. It isn't."

"Oh, but it is, Seer dearest. You chose to leave the Olympus I offered you, chose to abandon your people to darkness and nightmares. What could I do but search you out?"

"Who … who are you?"

"Embrace the music and know me once again, my beloved Seer."

The violin's voice wrapped around her, coated her tongue and poured down her throat. Its magic mingled with hers, carnelian and violet.

"No." The word was but a whisper. She couldn't feel herself anymore, not even deep down where Heresy said her magic dwelt.

"No." Another voice. Louder. Incandescent silver and turquoise magic sung through her veins, banishing the violin's hold. Fionn. "This is a dream. You can't find her. You can't have her. Harper, wake up."

Something shook her roughly by the shoulder. Claws pricked her flesh. The music stopped. Blankets trapped her hands and she thrashed against them, the sensation of a rotting body not banished from her skin as her spirit moved back to the wakening.

"Harper. It's okay. It was a dream. It's okay." Fionn's eyes gleamed in the darkness. He rescued her trapped hands, his skin feverishly hot against her icy digits. Harper flung her arms around his neck. The rise of his chest pressed against her and she matched her breathing to his until her heart rate slowed. Every beat of his heart thrummed in her body and his magic blanketed her.

"But it wasn't *just* a dream." Her voice was muffled in his naked shoulder.

"It was. Whatever it was that spoke to you had no sway there other than what you gave it. It hasn't found you. Yet. But it is close."

"She's dead, Fionn. It killed her. The woman from our vision. We can't find her because she's already dead. The girl from the bookstore will be next. She saw my magic and it knows. It will kill her to get closer to me."

"Every step it takes closer to you, brings us one step closer to finding and vanquishing it."

Harper was shocked by his harsh tone. She sat back, eyes wide. Her blanket was wrapped around his lap, his only covering other than his fluffed-up tail and shaggy hair. She reached out, hesitated, then placed her hand over his heart. Her flesh was dark against his chest, as though she'd bored a hole straight through him. His skin was warm, soft. Her breath caught in her throat.

"If it catches me, what happens to you?" she asked.

Fionn shrugged, looking away. His tail flopped over her arm and lap, though his fists stayed clenched in his lap. "That doesn't matter. I would do anything to save you, Harper. Anything. I'll kill it if I have to. I'll die if I have to. I'll … I'll defy my master if I must. I'd try anyway, though I wouldn't win."

"Fionn." Tears clogged her throat.

"It's time to go. I'll meet you in the kitchen. Grace will want to say goodbye." He pushed her hand away and a pearlescent light surrounded him. He shrank until all that remained was a white cat. Without another look, he hopped off the bed and trotted out of the room.

CHAPTER TWENTY-ONE

Sanguine

After another lecture from her sister, Harper stepped through Fionn's portal. She glanced back over her shoulder to catch Grace's mouthed 'Godspeed' before she stepped into swirling blackness. Her sister's hug had been rigid, disapproving, but she understood. As the kitchen disappeared, it was as though the ties binding them were physically cut, leaving her adrift in an unknown sea with a stranger to steer her.

On the other side, she clutched her fingers inside her sleeves and wrapped her arms around her waist. Crystals of snow caught on her lashes. The back of her neck itched with more than Heresy's static, as though unseen eyes bored into it for all the ginnel they'd stepped into was deserted. There were no streetlamps or stars. A familiar fear clouded Harper's heart. Dirty brick walls rose high on either side of them, houses straining towards each other over the snickelway, leaving no more than a crack for the sky to peek through. Her breath hung in the air. Mists churned up to her knees. No sound nor scent permeated the alley. It was like an incomplete place.

"Ah yes, you define 'market' like you define 'cat.' As in 'not a.'" Heresy sneered at Fionn from Harper's shoulder.

"Shush," Harper admonished, although she didn't entirely disagree with him.

Fionn ignored Heresy and sniffed the air, the tip of his tail twitching. Harper watched him, wondering how far she could really trust him. Knowing each other as children didn't mean they knew each other now. And, despite his assertion, she feared he'd harm her should his master command it. She wasn't sure he'd have any choice.

Shadows cut across Fionn's face giving the impression of a torn mask, as though she could see the façade and the reality both at once, or two deceptions, layered one atop the other. He'd taken human form for the trip, although that seemed to have given him some slight pause with the portal as he worked out how to make it big enough for him and Harper. He was dressed in jeans rolled up at the ankles and a T-shirt that dwarfed him. Despite the January chill, he'd eschewed to wear a jumper or coat, stating it hampered him too much if he changed shape in an emergency. As evening mist seeped through the paving slabs and glided up the alley, it welcomed him, twining around his ankles and clinging to his tail. He moved through the mist without disturbing it, at one with it.

When he reached the end of the alley, he beckoned them to follow. Mist swirled away from Harper's footsteps, then crowded back in as she moved on. Dark tendrils writhed within it, grasping like the roots of the wych elm. They snagged on her shoelaces, entwined through the eyelets, trapped her, dragged her underground to a hollow grave of dirt and blood.

"Harper?"

Fionn's hand slid into hers and the vision faded. She leant against the alley wall struggling to catch her breath. Tears slid down her cheeks, mixing with the lingering touch of cool vapours. Too dark. The soft touch of hair against her face barely registered, but the warm tongue that delicately lapped her tear made her jump back.

"Harper? What's wrong?"

"Nothing. I …" *You licked me. Again. You're a cat. It's what you do. It doesn't mean anything.* "I just got stuck in a memory. Human don't lick each other, okay?"

"Sorry. I'm not good at human things. You remembered something?" Fionn rested his forehead against hers, his hopeful gaze disarming her once again.

Heresy slithered out a tendril and flicked Fionn's cheek. The cat pulled back with a hiss, rubbing where Heresy zapped him.

"Stop it, you two." Harper took a step back and wiped her eyes. "I was thinking about the park ranger. That's all. Let's get going."

Fionn winced when she pulled away. When no blow came, he took a step towards her, thought better of it, and offered her his hand instead.

When she didn't take it, his ears drooped and he turned away, heading to the mouth of the alley. Heresy mumbled something about 'good riddance.'

"Don't cry once the market gets here," Fionn warned. "There are those who'd pay a high price for a seer's tears."

"Where are we?" Harper asked as she joined him. A closed market spread out before them, but not the Shambles market with which she was so familiar. It was haunted by supernaturals and she'd assumed that was where they were going, but this place was completely unfamiliar. Fionn ignored her, stalking out of the ginnel's scant shelter. She resisted the urge to grab his tail and pull him back. There was no one here to sound the alarm.

She wandered after Fionn, past stalls advertising bakers, butchers, and various crafts, exactly what she'd expect to see in a mundane market. Even her Sight revealed nothing unusual. Heresy continued to mutter about incompetent not-a-cats and whine that they should leave without him. Harper refrained from pointing out it would mean buying a train ticket home from wherever the heck they were, which might lead to some awkward questions from the Guard.

The bones of the market were there, but it lacked life, its skeletal remains clad in ragged cloth and the fetid residues of meat and skin. Even the night predators, the rats and the foxes, were nowhere to be seen. The only sounds were the wind's whistle and the flap of paper now devoid of tender morsels, cast aside by gluttonous hands with no care for the world. The air stunk of stale food and urine.

Fionn seemed unaffected by the abandoned marketplace. He stood to one side, nose raised, eyes darting about. Despite how brittle he looked, there was a confidence to him Harper had only seen when he cast spells.

"What happens now?" She stopped next to him.

He glanced at her, his eyes sharp, black slits barely visible in the shadows. "We wait. They will be here soon. It's easier for the Market to come to a human than it is to bring a human to the Market. Since you're in the space it's trying to occupy, you'll get scooped up by it, but it wouldn't let you in from the outside. A number of homeless humans get caught up in it every year because they're sleeping on its turf. Some are eaten or broken down. Some are ... surprising."

Harper filed it away under things to ask him about later. She didn't like the way Heresy chuckled. The snap of canvas drew her attention as the wind picked up. Stubborn, the lingering fog clung to the stalls with knobbled fingers, thickening as it swelled from the light scattering of rain.

Faint outlines of stock with an eerie, pale blue gleam shifted from one reality to another. The canvas, tied down to protect the stalls overnight, faded away as the world bled through to the other side of the coin.

Vague figures solidified in the mist. Walking, talking, dancing, laughing, they were sketched into the scene by an invisible artist, silent as a painting. Harper jumped when something touched her elbow but it was only Fionn. The pale blue glow enveloped him, too, growing stronger, soaking into his strange eyes. His hand on her arm was outlined by dim light. Harper glanced at her own hands but they seemed as solid and real as ever.

"What is this place?" she breathed, afraid any noise would break the spell.

"The Soul Traders' Market. It's still forming. It will be here soon. It moves around but it's always in progress somewhere. You can buy anything at the Market, if you can survive it long enough." His face was serious as he watched the figures become shaded with pastels, the artist adding layer upon layer, each progressively brighter in their rendering.

The sound, when it came, came all at once. A vast clap of noise louder than thunder. Harper staggered under the blast of it. Folk shouted greetings and hawked their wares. Wild music spiralled like a tornado. Percussive sizzles from woks larger than tables blended with the tinkling of bells falling from the lips of organza-winged faeries. Myriad scents assaulted her: charred, savoury meats and sharp, sour fruits warred with the warming scents of freshly baked bread and twinkling sugar delicacies. Fionn's grip on her elbow tightened, helping her stay upright, but he himself didn't flinch.

"Don't let go of me. Say nothing unless you have to. Don't use my name or give anyone yours. Don't stare at the wares if you can help it, no matter what you see. You don't have to exchange money, or even speak, to make a bargain here and you wouldn't like the payment required. The Market doesn't allow refunds."

Fionn's hand slid down her arm and came to rest in hers. Harper clung to it. No matter her lingering doubts, she had more faith in him than this strange in-between world of impossible creatures. A shadow realm, as the book called it.

"For once, I must agree with the not-a-cat," Heresy whispered in her ear. "Just as with the auction, it would be easy to strike a bargain here that you do not want."

She shuddered. That had been a narrow escape. There was no Grace to fight with her this time, nor Saqib to save the day.

Fionn took a delicate silver chain from his pocket and wrapped it around both their wrists.

"Fionn, what—?" Harper tried to yank her hand back, but his grip was stronger than his slight frame indicated.

Heresy hissed as he slithered down her arm and wrapped himself around the chain. Having him buzzing around her hand made her fingers go numb. "Why do you have binding magic, not-a-cat?"

"So folk know she's mine. They won't mess with her then. They can have you." Fionn glared at Heresy as he tried to shake the spirit off their hands.

"Heresy, stay on my shoulder where I can hear you? Please?" Harper said, then turned to Fionn. "What do you mean 'know she's mine'?" The possessive way he said it prickled her feminist leanings, but the Market so overwhelmed her that there was a guilty relief in him taking charge.

"We can't stand around talking," Fionn hissed. His fur bristled and his lips drew back in a snarl until Heresy withdrew, but the moisture in his eyes caught the glittering lights belying his waspish tone. "Folk here know who I am. They won't harm anything under my protection. It's still better not to invite their interest. Can we go?"

"Yeah. Faster the better, right?" Harper muttered. Heresy's allegiances were never clear, and Fionn's were murky at best, although she believed neither wanted her dead. She hoped they could resolve their differences soon before she got stuck in the middle of a cat versus tentacle creature fight.

Fionn weaved them through the bustling throng like fish through water. The … people—Harper went with for lack of a better word—moved out of his way without looking at him. They bashed into her. Fionn's strong grip kept her afloat in the throng. She clenched her jaw, ignoring the churning of her stomach as her emotions flipped between fear of this alien world and gratitude for his presence.

"I trust you," she blurted out. If he heard, he didn't turn. His ears didn't even twitch. Harper bit her lip, turning her gaze from his back to stare at her surroundings.

"You should not," Heresy muttered.

"You or him?" Harper said under her breath. Heresy's smile widened, prickling the hairs on the back of her neck.

"Both."

She shuddered, turning her attention back to the Market. She didn't need Fionn's warning, not at first anyway. The people distracted her, obscuring her view of the goods on sale. As an archivist of Saint Peter's Cathedral with a degree in Inhuman Studies and the dubious accolade of being an honorary De Santos, Harper prided herself on being well-versed in the supernatural. Yet the people of the Market surpassed even the bizarre creatures from the auction in their variety. The phrase 'folk come in all shapes and sizes' had never been more apt.

Some of the shoppers looked human, or mostly human, but even those had tell-tale signs. Some, like Fionn, had strange ears, tails, or eyes. A bland man, who would not have looked out of place as a Guardsman, paused and stared at Harper. Then he opened his mouth to run his coiled, cleft tongue over three sharp rows of teeth. Harper shied away from him and gripped Fionn's hand tighter.

The majority of the shoppers could never have passed for human. Something wet slapped against Harper's leg. She scuttled back, biting off a cry when she looked down into the bemused face of a fish. Ze had a certain gentlesenly air. An umbrella was tucked under a fin that clutched a briefcase. Ze raised his hat to her, dusted off zir pinstripe suit, and continued zir squelching walk through the market. Many ze passed paused to offer greeting or wave, and each of them received a tip of zir hat or a nod in return. Harper just caught Fionn's mutter of, "Not again," as the gentlesen passed but the creature was gone before she could ask what he meant.

A couple necking in a corner were a mass of arms and tendrils that turned Harper's stomach. An orb the size of a basketball bobbed past, zinging with electricity. She flinched, remembering the eyeballs from her nightmares, all the hairs on her arms prickling. A creature with the body of an eagle and the head of a frog swooped over a food stall, tongue lashing out to steal a fly cake. The proprietor, half-spider, half-human, sporting a dozen mechadendrites, muttered a curse and the thief tumbled from the sky with a deep-throated croak. A trail of smoke followed zir down like a crashed plane, although Harper couldn't tell what struck zir. Ze smacked into a puddle, sloshing putrid water over Harper's shoes and legs. A pointy-eared humanoid sneered at the scene. Ze licked sharpened emerald teeth and dribbled acid over the eyes trailing down zir chest. Harper's ears were ringing and she couldn't look away from the spectacle. Lights flecked her vision and she stopped, frozen, as the chest of eyes turned a wicked leer on her.

Fionn brought her round with a subtle elbow to the side. "Don't stare. They might decide to do more than stare back." His voice was cold and deeper than usual, goosing her skin. She wished to be back home and forget she ever came to this dreadful place. This wasn't the scintillation of danger the Shambles invoked. The Guard were there and humans thronged. Even on the mistiest day, the supes there kept to themselves and remained quiet. Here, there were no such constraints. Here, they belonged and she was the invader.

A fresh breeze floated past, carrying on it a bewitching tune. Harper turned without thinking, scanning the Market for its source. Her grip on Fionn loosened. Claws dug into the back of her hand, drawing a gasp and making her eyes water. His yank on her arm almost sent her sprawling. The world went white as his tail wound itself around her head, covering her eyes and ears. Heresy buzzed around her like a swarm of bees, dislodged by Fionn's sharp movements.

She grabbed a handful of fur, forcing his tail down as she bent over sneezing. "What the heck, Fionn? I need—"

"That's how it gets you." He flapped his free hand around their heads, his tail beating the air. "Not everything with consciousness is visible. Have you ever wondered why humans get songs stuck in their heads? Earworms. Sentient tunes. Parasites who temporarily inhabit their victims. They suck concentration, memory, creativity, whatever they can force out of you. Then they move on, never more than a tune in your head. They can drive you crazy."

"I'm starting to feel like I already am." Overwhelming helplessness sapped the strength from Harper's limbs and her knees buckled. She was lost in a world of folk who would relish her death, and now Fionn was saying she could be attacked by creatures she couldn't even See. Couldn't defend against.

Fionn caught her, half dragging her to the side between a cloak stall and one selling flying shoes. Heresy floated down next to her to rest on her knee. Fionn squeezed her hand so hard her bones creaked.

His face was tight, his eyes cast down as he said, "You're not. Believe me, I have been to that realm and you are not even close."

Once again, he raised more questions than he answered. *Then again, if dreams are another realm, then why not madness?* Harper tried to remember if she'd seen it in the book.

"C'mon. We're wasting time." Fionn plunged into the crowd again, dragging Harper behind him with Heresy clinging to her leg. She kept her eyes on the swish of Fionn's tail as he wove through the gathering. When he stopped, she almost careened into him.

"Are you hungry?" he asked.

"I thought you said we shouldn't buy anything. Isn't it bad to eat foods of other realms?"

Fionn shrugged. "This is merely a shadow. Eating something of the Market will help you blend in. You smell too human, it's drawing attention."

"The *thing* is right. You reek of human," Heresy agreed.

Harper wondered what scent she was giving off which could be described as 'human' but thought the answer would be unflattering. "I don't want some kind of Persephone problem."

"I can get you home, don't worry." Fionn gave her a reassuring smile and Harper was struck once again with how their roles were reversed. The shy, jittery cat was gone. Here he was confident, in control.

Without letting go of her hand, he approached a stall to barter with the fishmonger in a language Harper didn't recognise. He handed the fishmonger a gleaming marble from his pockets, which Harper guessed he portalled in from home. He certainly hadn't been carrying anything when she found him in the back garden.

He handed her a fish bao before chomping into his own with a massive grin. "Eat up. They're really good," he said, mouth crammed full. "They're my favourite. I always get them when I come here."

Harper took a cautionary nibble of her food. It was hot, sweet, and salty. As she ate, tension dissolved and it became easier to make her way through the crowds. "Do you come here often?"

A wary look flashed across Fionn's face, a familiar panic that appeared whenever he was questioned. It was gone in an instant but the twitch in his ears gave him away.

"Quite often," he said with forced nonchalance. "I … trade sometimes."

"The magic you told me about before, the stuff for the land, I guess your master doesn't get paid for that, so is that what you do for a living?"

"Partially. I dabble in a few things. This is a good place to dabble. But yes, I get good enough results to keep living."

"To keep …" Harper bit her lip and decided not to pursue the thought. He was far more magical than she was. AJ was right. She was no match for anything that could collar Fionn. "You trade magic?"

"Dreams, spells, things I build, all sorts." Fionn tugged her hand. "We're almost there."

When he stopped stock still, she hit his back, sharp shoulder blades digging into her chest.

"We're here."

He'd stopped outside a pointed tent of deep scarlet fabric. Tiny shells and bones hung from it on golden threads, clattering together in the wind like a mouth of chattering teeth. A pennant fluttered at the point, a drop of haloed blood that gleamed as though it were still liquid. The iron tang that pervaded the air turned the fish in Harper's stomach sour.

Fionn pulled back the tent flap, then paused, one foot over the threshold. "Don't let go of my hand. No matter what."

The décor inside the tent set Harper's skin crawling and her heart racing. Set in the ground around the edge of the tent were smouldering human-esque skulls. The desk in the centre of the room was made of bleached white bone. A single lantern hung in the centre, a fire flickering within a rib cage. On the desk there was nothing but a writing set and a large set of scales.

Seated behind the desk was a woman. She wore no clothes, leaving her onyx skin exposed. Pulsing under it, a fine network of glistening veins and arteries stemmed from a slowly beating heart. Flames caught in her faceted skin and danced within her. Her eyes were black as the bottom of the deepest well.

Her narrowed gaze cut through Harper, who raised an involuntary hand to her throat.

"An illusion spirit?" A smile slithered over the woman's face. "A curious choice of payment, Cat. Or is it the human morsel you've brought to appease my hunger?"

Heresy prickled and a tendril emerged from under Harper's hair in what was unmistakably an unflattering gesture. Harper scowled at the sanguinary. Her fingers itched for her blade, but even more she wished Grace was with her. Her sister would have her back. She was less confident in Fionn and Heresy.

Fionn stepped forward, his face carefully blank, and bowed so his head almost touched the floor. His tail was curled tight behind him, but one ear twitched. "Blesséd night, Lady of the Bloody Tears. The human is mine and is here to barter. I regret the spirit is a visitor to the Market and also not merchandise."

The being inclined her head gracefully. "Blesséd night, Cat. For what purpose come you to my lair?"

"I come seeking another such as she," Fionn replied as he straightened.

Every part of Harper's body screamed to run as the omniscient eyes of the sanguinary swept over her again.

"Like to like, life for life." Her singsong voice set Harper's teeth on edge, like syrupy cherries cut through with knives of lime. Cloven crystal feet clicked against the concrete floor as she circled them, predatory eyes locked on Harper, who froze when the sanguinary touched one transparent digit to her forehead. Her nerves were on fire, too terrified to register a command to run. Her mind was fogged. Reality twisted. Even the urgent voice of Heresy in her ear and the static buzz his body created were distant. The entrance to the tent seemed miles away, the path lined by the judging eyes of the dead. Harper didn't know where to turn, couldn't flee even if she did. The onyx digit meandered from Harper's head down her arm leaving a trail of vermillion frost in its wake.

She feared this woman even more than the dark. A primal reaction that had never been triggered by the Ouse, not even at the last when the river tried to steal her eyes.

The lady traced the band of silver around Fionn and Harper's bound hands. Harper waited for her sharpened nails to rend the delicate silver. What had seemed like imprisonment was now her lifeline. Magic from the silver pulsed against her wrist, Fionn's heartbeat in time with hers. Fionn gave a small hiss and the lady stepped back, insipid smile never leaving her pristine features.

"Bound to name, bound to fate." Her face lit up with a genuine smile. "Bound to life, bound to death? Only the Timeless One shall know. What payment offer you?"

Harper was caught off-guard by the question but Fionn seemed unfazed by the lady's odd proclamation.

"I offer blood," Fionn promised. Released from the lady's freezing gaze, Harper opened her mouth to protest but his claws dug into her hand. "And a vision of one whose life both may and may not be."

"I deal not in dreams, dreamwalker, and know I your policy on blood." Her eyes shifted to Harper's throat where Heresy curled. "An illusion spirit can offer no more than deception."

Heresy gave a quiet 'humph' at that, but even he seemed cowed by the sanguinary.

The silicate woman inclined her head until her nose almost touched Fionn's, her eyes scrutinising his. Harper guessed she must have been at least a foot-and-a-half taller than the cat-boy. He stared back calmly and Harper wasn't sure whether that was better or worse than him cowering. It was like he didn't see the danger, though a little rational thought at the back of her head knew he must. The need to protect her kitten overwhelmed her fear. *My kitten?* The image of him on the boat floated over the bloody scene of the tent. He had been her cat and she had been his human, a relationship more complex than owner and pet, and strong as the bonds between the closest of friends.

"I have brought you the blood of something ancient and forgotten." Fionn's eyes stayed locked on the lady's. His measured words snapped Harper's thread to the past. "I give you the blood of one who brings death, a hunter of dreams and enslaver of folk. They do not dwell fully within our realm and I would know the path to theirs. I would know the fate of one whom they have taken, for we would save her if we can."

"Have you the blood of the girl you seek?" the lady asked.

Fionn didn't say we sought a girl … Harper wetted dry lips, but Fionn squeezed her hand before she could speak. *Stay out of my head.* Harper tried to think it at the sanguinary instead.

"You know I do not," Fionn answered. "I have brought you a seer who has met the one we seek. She gives you no dream. A memory, fortified by the power of Sight and a connection of death."

Now Harper wanted to argue with Fionn. She could describe the girl, more based on her photo than exact memory, but that was it. Thus far, she had been unable to consistently trigger her Sight without some focus, such as being in location.

As if he, too, could read her thoughts, Fionn turned his unblinking gaze on her. "You can do it, Harper. The lady will guide. Just let it happen. For the missing girl. For our pasts."

Harper swallowed her irritation and fear, then nodded.

As if Harper wasn't there, the lady held out a hand. Her fingers unfurled as her head tilted to the side. "I am intrigued by what you offer. Approach the scales."

Fionn placed Saqib's vial with its few drops of blood on one side of the scales, then reached behind Harper. A sharp pain pierced her skull. Her misgivings surfaced again as Fionn placed a strand of dark hair on the other side of the scales. The lady's dark eyes never left Harper's face. She swallowed her questions. *I trust him.* She repeated the words over and over in her head as the scales tipped, first towards the blood, then towards her hair. *Whatever this is, I* must *trust him.*

The scales stilled.

"A deal is struck." The sanguinary's fingers clicked as they grasped for Harper's hair but Fionn snatched it away. The strand disappeared in a flare of fire from his fingertips. The lady pursed her lips but said nothing. Instead, she waved her hand and a second bone chair arose. She gestured to Fionn to sit and he obeyed, his hold on Harper's hand not slackened.

"Release your pet." The lady stepped between them and gripped Harper's chin. This time flight beat the instinct to freeze and she tried to yank her head away but it was as though her face was caught in a cleft of rock. Heresy poked ineffectually at the sanguinary, who brushed him aside with a wave of her hand as though he were solid. When Harper grabbed the lady's arm, it slipped, cold and unyielding, under her desperate fingers.

Fionn hissed. "You can take your vision without me letting go of her." His grip never eased. Harper clung to him, forcing herself to believe in his certainty, despite everything her senses told her.

The lady's eyes narrowed and her hold on Harper tightened but she didn't contradict the cat. Instead, she stared at Harper until all the world was swallowed by the vacuum of her eyes.

"Think of the day you met the missing student." Fionn stroked Harper's hand with his free one and his tail brushed against her ankles. "Be open. You can do this. The Lady of Bloody Tears will guide your vision."

Harper trembled, every bone turned to jelly. The lady's iron will kept her standing like a suspended puppet. Blackness enveloped her, then gradually brightened to blood red. It wasn't the bookstore she Saw, it was the girl's room. The wrong memory. Panic gripped her. *If I can't do this, is our deal reneged? What will she do if she thinks we lied to her?*

The vision unfurled, no longer under Harper's control. The room was exactly as she'd seen it earlier that day, save a black-clad teen sat hunched over the desk. She typed furiously on a laptop with occasional pauses to check something in one of her textbooks. When the music began, she looked towards her door. A frown creased her brow, probably on the assumption her neighbours were being discourteously noisy. Black starbursts of kohl framed dark brown eyes and tiny diamonds drawn in makeup cascaded down her cheek like tears. With a huff, the student returned to her work. The music swelled, a tidal wave that threatened to wash away reality.

It bore the girl on its crest. Harper had heard the phrase 'the music took me someplace else' but never had it been so literal. The bedroom dissolved and only a sickeningly familiar tune remained. No fear. Not yet. For the music was beautiful and the girl was captivated by its magic. She neither saw nor felt danger coming until skeletal fingers reached inside her skull and wrenched out her eyes.

"No!" Harper screamed with the girl. Optic nerves were torn. Black star makeup surrounded blackhole voids. Excruciating pain flooded their bodies and whited out their brains. There was music. There was pain. There was death. With the last beat of the girl's heart, the vision cut off.

The lady released Harper, who stumbled back, panting, tears streaming down her cheeks. Heresy stroked her hair, frizzing it up, but for once he didn't laugh. Harper hung on Fionn's arm, barely able to stand, fighting for breath. Fionn was on his feet, his hand gripping the lady's wrist in a futile fight for control.

"A worthy payment indeed." The lady's smile was sharper than a knife. "Now as to what you seek, Cat."

"That wasn't what we agreed," Fionn spat, ears flat against his head, tail bristled. He crouched between Harper and the sanguinary. Magic gleamed under his skin.

The lady ignored Fionn as though he were a toddler throwing a hissy fit. After peering into the vial of still-liquid blood, the sanguinary tipped the contents onto her hand. She lapped it up, her spiked tongue turning deep cherry as the blood was absorbed into her body. She turned her gaze upon Harper, the blackness tinged with red at the edges. "You who are cursed with Sight, See where your goal lies."

Harper's vision swam. She doubled over, almost losing the contents of her stomach. She was vaguely aware of Fionn's arm around her waist as the tent filled with the bloody remains of people too numerous to count. Not all were human—some animal, some mineral—yet she knew in her heart all had possessed higher intelligence. In a daze, she followed a ruby pulsing light to where it was buried under a pile of bleeding organs.

"Take it." The lady's voice came from afar. Harper shook her head. "Take it or forfeit. It is the key to unlocking the path to what your heart desires."

"Do as she says." Fionn's voice, closer, almost in her ear, his tone soft and reassuring.

Harper thrust her arm deep into the pile. When she pulled her hand out, she held a dark brown eye, cornea misting.

"Look around," Fionn whispered. "Do you See where she is?"

Trying to ignore the tacky fluid dripping from her hand, Harper's eyes swept the tent. The walls were formed of rough limestone. Water trickled over them, twinkling like stars and tinkling like faery bells. She followed the water, clogged with the lifeblood of a thousand dead. She floated through fissures in rock and into the currents of an underground stream. It dragged her out into the frozen night, near the disused mine shafts where the ranger had last been seen and where Fionn said he and his master completed a ritual the same date her body was found. It swept along the top of the hills where no river ran.

Frost gathered as mist tumbled down the dale. Pine branches swept the stream. Starlight filtered through and the beaming gaze of the full moon lit the way for the ruby-red tributary. Harper tumbled down the dale, sometimes above ground, sometimes under, a path taken a thousand times. The wych elm whizzed by but she stayed with the path of the water until she fell into the Swale. The river, normally browned by peat, gleamed with the offerings of severed veins and ruined arteries. They gushed, growing with every tributary, as the Swale became the Ouse, the Ouse became the Humber, and the Humber became the North Sea.

"Have you found that which you seek?" When the lady spoke, the bloody river faded from view, leaving only the skulls lining the edge of the tent.

Fionn placed his free hand over Harper's, taking a gleaming red gem from her. At its centre pulsed a black void in perfect time with the beating of her heart.

"Thank you for your custom." The lady resumed her seat. She picked up her quill and pulled a scroll out of a drawer, the material more leathery than papery.

"Don't think about it," Fionn muttered, following Harper's gaze. He pocketed the gem, then bowed deeply. Harper was grateful to accept his shielding as he pushed her behind him and he backed out of the tent. Her legs and arms were flaccid and weak, her stomach filled with acid.

The fresh air outside was a blessing. Fionn guided her to the side and she leant against him, head on his shoulder as tears broke through the dam of fear.

"Don't cry here. It's not safe." Fionn nevertheless let her bury her head in his shoulder, tears absorbed in his borrowed hoodie. That he, too, was shaking was not reassuring.

"Well, that was alarmingly interesting." Heresy's voice at Harper's ear made her jump after his near silence in the tent. "An impressive illusion, if I do say so myself as a master of the craft. Harper dearest, are you sure the not-a-cat means you well?"

"Yes." Harper lifted her head and said it without thinking. Despite his pale mien, Fionn beamed at her like she'd offered him the largest fish in the ocean.

Heresy harrumphed again and curled at the back of her neck, muttering to himself.

"We shouldn't linger long." Fionn petted her hair. "Try not to throw up, it's not a good idea to leave a piece of yourself here."

"Why did you offer her that?" Harper choked.

"She is a sanguinary, nothing more, nothing less. She trades in blood and stories. I didn't know she could force you to have a vision of something you hadn't already Seen. I'm sorry."

"She … she's dead. As soon as she was taken, she was killed." Harper tried in vain to swallow her sobs. Too late. Again. Someone dead because of her. Again.

"The killer must be keeping the bodies to strengthen the rituals they're using to track you," Fionn mused.

"How can you sound so … so … academic about it." Harper pulled away from him.

"Because …" Fionn traced a toe through the dust on the ground. "Because sometimes there is so much blood and death that there's no choice but to keep going. Mourning is a luxury we don't have when others may yet share her fate."

His practicality shocked Harper out of her tears. His philosophy wasn't wrong, yet it seemed callous. It echoed the words of the spirit of the River Foss.

'Fight, Seer of York, Seer of the Dales. You took our fate into your hands. You owe us more than self-pity. So, I ask you again, what will you do about it?'

Mourning would let her fight harder. She would not succumb to the weight of it. Not again.

"Take me home," she ordered Fionn. "We're going to find this abomination and stop it, before it kills anyone else."

"There is one more thing we need first. We now have the means to find the evil. You have power, Harper, but your magic is … not very useful in a fight, and you need a weapon that is more than a lump of metal."

"You're suggesting I get a new weapon here? You told me not to even look at the wares."

"Come with me," Fionn said with a small smile. "I'll pay. Plus, I promised Grace a present."

CHAPTER TWENTY-TWO

The Maestro

They left a cheerily red-and purple-tent a little while later with Harper happily clutching a new machete, some fancy crossbow bolts for Grace, and a leather bag of throwing stars. The seller promised the machete had the ability to reflect and capture the prowess of an enemy. Harper was unsure about that, but it had good balance and kept a sharp edge through testing. Fionn had paid with more of the swirling marbles that looked like planets.

"What are those anyway?" she asked once they were clear of the tent. "The spheres you're paying for stuff with."

"These?" Fionn took one from his pocket and held it up to a lantern at the side of the path. "They're dreams. I make them."

"You *make* dreams?"

"Dreamwalkers can make dreams," Heresy said in a bored tone like he was repeating a lecture given a thousand times. "It is not impressive. A simple illusion captured in a piece of crystal. If anything, it is less impressive than a proper illusion because a dream relies on the dreamer, whereas my illusions come purely from me." He bared his teeth at Fionn who stuck his tongue out.

"Well, I think it's impressive," Harper interjected before they could start fighting again.

"Of course you do, your magic is very simple." Heresy sniffed at her, which was a different kind of skilful given his lack of nose. "But by all means, stroke the ego of the not-a-cat that keeps putting you in danger."

"I do *not.*" Fionn's voice went up at least an octave, but Harper wasn't listening to them bicker. Her Hearing latched onto a sound far fainter and more alluring. She paused, pulling Fionn to a stop beside her.

"What is it?" he asked. "I thought you wanted to get out of here."

"Shush."

He frowned, glancing around nervously. "Harper …"

"Shhh." She waved a hand at him. Whatever it was, it hooked into her, an inexorable call. "Can't you hear it?"

Fionn cocked his head to the side, ears pricked. "Hear what?"

"Harper, whatever it is, do not listen to it." Heresy's voice held an unaccustomed, serious urgency.

"Don't you recognise the music?" Harper asked Fionn. Her heart ached to hear it, tears pricking at the corners of her eyes. It sang to her like the music that drifted down the Ouse the day after Agnes died. An overpowering longing stuffed her chest so tight she feared she might burst.

"Harper, I can't hear anything. It's probably another earworm." Fionn flapped a hand at her head but she shoved him away.

"I've heard it before, in my dreams. In dreams of my past. They slipped from my memory but I know this song. It's calling me." *It's the way home. I can't ignore it again. I can't.* The newly bought weapons dropped from numb fingers. The blade narrowly missed her toes, but Harper didn't flinch at the clang of metal on cobbles.

"Harper, no." Fionn planted his feet and tightened his grip. "It's a trap, it's—"

With a sharp tug, she pulled her hand free from his, and the silver chain shattered like glass.

"Harper, stop!"

Before either of her companions could do anything, she dashed into the crowd. They parted before her with the precision of dancers. Faces and bodies blurred until the bizarre became homogenous. Her feet followed the tune as though the music were written in the dirt.

Harper, and Heresy, were soon lost to sight. With a deep growl, Fionn scooped up their shopping and portalled it to Harper's bed, then set off after her, sniffing the air for the lingering scent of human. She moved fast, passing through the Market as if it were empty. Fionn pushed past the densely packed denizens of the Market. A couple of well-placed curses zinged against his magic, but it defended him as it always did and, seeing his collar, no one tried to curse him twice.

The stalls thinned as he neared the edge of the Market. Dark shadows created barriers between them. Scant wares sat out, signs hinting at the goods on offer without explicitly stating the nature of the stalls. Proprietors stared from behind veils and masks, loose flowing garments hiding their forms. Only their eyes were visible, some dark, some bright, all feral.

As they turned their sharp gazes on Fionn, goods disappeared up voluminous sleeves and under tablecloths. He caught scant glimpses: human fingers, a white philosopher's stone, and Venetian masks. All items his master had forbidden trading in England. No wonder they hid from him. If he was able to tag them and report them to his master, they might be banished, if they were lucky. But Harper was getting farther from him, her scent degrading, so he sprinted on as if he hadn't seen. The collar tightened around his throat, a warning. It was one of the unavoidable commands: report any illegal creatures or magic. If he didn't stop to investigate, the collar would punish him until, eventually, its full power would be unleashed and the blood bond would force his body no matter how his mind fought. But he had some time. He would save Harper, no matter the cost. *Selfish Cat, putting one life before thousands.*

Fionn glimpsed her ahead. Never nearer, never farther. No matter how fast he ran, she remained beyond his grasp. He stopped in a deserted ginnel on the edge of the Market, concentrated on Harper, and knocked twice on the air. A swirling vortex opened. It was more effort than portals normally took, he wasn't used to creating them large enough for humans.

Fionn stepped through and Harper ran straight into him, sending all three of them sprawling.

"Fionn, what are you doing?" she shouted. "Get out of the way."

"Harper, See."

The fear in Fionn's eyes and the panic in his voice punched through the music to the rational part of Harper's brain. As she scrambled free of the tangle of limbs, the music wormed in again. She rubbed her ears, her brain fogged.

"Harper. See." Fionn's magic sparked at her fingertips as he took her hands. Her eyes burned as though pepper had been rubbed into them. Through the gathering tears, she took control of her magic, reaching into her core as Heresy had taught her. It hung within her mind's eye like a star, radiant and violet. A thread of silver ran through it.

"Get out." The snarl came out harsher than she intended but the slender tendril of Fionn's magic withdrew.

"You need to See, Harper. Use your magic to Hear and to See." His words forced their way past the music, his breath warm on her ear. Still invading her body. She wanted to shake him off, to run, but she held her ground. The music was too important to turn her back on it. She needed it. Magic gushed through her, ready to embrace the tune. It was home, more right than anything she'd felt before. More right than Fionn's hand in hers or even Grace's strong embrace. It was home, her place in a world that had always rejected her. She needed it like she needed air. It was home.

"Listen to him, Harper," Heresy warned.

An alarm bell rang in the back of her mind at the two of them agreeing.

"It's not really home. It's a nightmare. I promise," Fionn pleaded with her. He was the dreamwalker. If it was a dream, he would know. He would awaken her, as he had so many times before. "Please, Harper. Wake up."

"No." The whispered word fell from her lips as tears spilled from her eyes. Despite her desperation for it to be real, his words rang true. Fionn's pleas and Heresy's static worry wrapped around her and the music lost its hold.

Her mind clearer, she could See the source. A violin hung in the air, its body of silver birch and its strings of ivy vines. Smooth as silk, treacherous as a spider's web, a bow of flax caressed the strings. Invisible hands played with the skill of centuries, the tune too complex for Harper to ever master. Notes doubled and tripled in impossible harmonies.

The music grasped for her again, sharp notes piercing, flat notes punching. They twisted lilac in the air, surrounding her in a whirlwind, then struck a glittering silver and turquoise barrier.

Fionn planted himself between Harper and the violin, eyes like gemstones, and the music rebounded from his magic. The power radiating from him took Harper's breath away with its potency. She could See the maelstrom, but the air was filled with silence.

"Mine." Fionn spoke through gritted teeth. His ears were flat against his head, tail curled around Harper's waist as he shielded her.

"You were to tell your master not to interfere." The voice slithered around them, issued from every compass point. Harper had heard it before. Somewhere. A dream. Her head ached from the strain of trying to remember, but her mind was clearer without the music battering it.

"Mine." Fionn growled the word, his chest heaving with the exertion of speaking. He thrust his free hand forward and the music was pushed back, battering silently against his magic. "You can't have her."

"The Seer wants to come home, little mewling. Do not presume to challenge your creator's wishes. She cannot but obey *her* creator."

"She doesn't want to come to you." Fionn sucked air through clenched teeth, his hand so tight around Harper's she feared he might snap their bones. The discomfort was grounding and the music lost the last of its hold on her.

She grabbed Fionn's wrist and yanked her hand out of his. His magic flickered in the wake of her indignation. Heresy chuckled, always seeking amusement even when he himself warned her of danger. His misplaced mirth fanned her rage.

"*She* will say for herself where she goes. I belong to me, not to either of you. And yes, I want to go home, but not to the demon that enslaved my people and now murders innocent women. I will go home on my own terms. You know where I am now, and you know I will never, *never*, willingly go with you. Your magic isn't strong enough to make me. Leave this realm while you can. Because I have Seen the way home, and my sister and I will vanquish you."

"Did you believe you could vanquish me with a few angry words? If such as that harmed me, all the teenagers of your line, whom I raised, would have turned me to dust on the wind. When your Sight followed the path of blood, I followed your magic to you."

A gnarled hand formed around the neck of the violin. A billowing cloak fluttered in the breeze, drawn in inky blackness. It obscured the creature's translucent shape and being. Where its face should've been there was only void, topping a frame so tall it hurt Harper's neck to stare up at it. A cosy scent of oats and bread filled the air, muddying her thoughts again and forcing a yawn past her lips.

Fionn still stood before her, his back tight with tension, his magic holding the music at bay. His shoulders heaved with the effort, his footing heavy as he kept his body between her and the ethereal musician.

"You interfere too much, mewling. You and your master," the hooded creature spat.

Fionn hissed back, his tail bristling. "What do you want with her?"

"I will tolerate you no longer." A sweep of its hand shattered Fionn's shield. He was yanked into the air and flung into the alley wall. He dropped to the floor with a moan, blood dripping down his neck and staining his hair cerise.

"I have looked for you long, my Seer. By breaking my spell, you became invisible to me, but as the Hiding faded, I began to sense you through those to whom you were connected. I sent your kin to find you, then took her vision when she succeeded. I took glimpses of you from the eyes of those around you and those who walked where your magic had been strongest. I followed your dreams and your blood. You may hide from me in the wakening, but here on the edge of the dreamscape, your little mewling has led me to you."

The creature extended a hand to Harper. She scuttled back. Her stomach churned, her breathing shallow, bile coated the back of her throat. It seemed like a dream, as though it happened to some other body, not hers.

"You are mine." The creature's voice was melodious and smooth. Harper's eyes grew heavy. Her mouth formed a 'no' but her voice was silent. It held out its hand again. "You are mine. I have searched for you so long, my Seer. It is time to come home."

"I …" Harper clutched her hand to her chest.

Fionn threw himself between her and the apparition again. He wobbled, shoulders hunched, blood matting his hair. "You shall not touch her."

The creature thrust forward with its bow. Fionn raised his hands and the bow struck the air centimetres in front of him with a crash like lightning. Sparks cascaded as it fought to penetrate his glimmering shield.

"Get out of here, Harper," Fionn ordered. "If you can get far enough from the Market, you'll re-enter the mundane world. I'll keep it occupied."

"No …" Harper's mouth formed the word but she found she couldn't move, transfixed by the magical battle. Fionn, starlight white, shining with magic, and the violinist, dark as a clouded midnight, surrounded by nothingness.

"Harper, we must run." Heresy wrapped his tentacles around her. "Neither you nor I have the power to defeat one such as this. I can hide you no longer."

The creature drew back its bow again and thrust it towards her eyes though it was several metres away. A black swirl erupted from its tip.

The vortex struck Fionn's shield and slowed. For a moment. It bent, like light through a prism, then it struck Fionn square in the chest. He was thrown backwards into Harper's arms.

"Fionn!"

A scarlet flower bloomed where the magic impaled him. "Forget him." The creature extended a hand to her again. Eyes scraped over her, though she couldn't see a face. They stripped away her flesh and flayed her soul.

"Harper." Fionn's voice was weak. "That thing cannot take you home."

"Silence, mewling." The violinist spoke sharply, then his voice turned sweet again. "My Seer, my dearest, take my hand and return to the home you lost. Forget the cat."

Fionn's blood dripped onto her hand where her fingers were curled into his hair. It was as though she watched through a pane of glass. It was happening to someone else. Wasn't this what she'd been searching for? A way home? The fire within her spluttered, her magic dim and smothered. Heresy's voice, his warning, was distant as though he called to her from the depths of the river.

The creature leant closer. Fionn hissed, his ears flat against his head. The glow around him pulsed, weakening. He crouched between her and the darkness, a barely living shield. Harper looked between him and the billowing figure. Her fingers balled into fists, then she let herself go and grabbed Fionn's hand so they could face the darkness together.

"You're lying." She forced the words past her teeth, biting back the acceptance her heart wanted her to utter. "I don't believe you will take me home. By Moon and Starlight, I banish you."

The creature recoiled as if struck. Its violin hung in the air, hesitant.

"I banish you," Harper said, her voice stronger. "By Moon and Starlight, I banish you." The words were dredged from some forgotten place. They were right, familiar. *We've done this before*. The thought flitted across her mind as she laced her fingers through Fionn's.

"We banish you," they said together. Violet, silver, and turquoise magic glimmered in the air around them. "By Moon and Starlight, we banish you."

The musician shrieked, its voice the high-pitched whine of an out- of-tune violin. Then it vanished, sucked into the instrument. The violin clattered to the floor, shrinking in on itself until nothing remained.

As soon as it was gone, Fionn collapsed. His skin was as pale as his hair, save where blood brightened it. He raised one trembling hand and tapped the air with his knuckles. Once. Twice. His hand fell to his side but the magic listened. A portal opened, flickering and smaller than the one they'd left by, but a portal nonetheless.

"Get out of here," Heresy urged. "The other side is home."

Harper hefted Fionn up. The vortex opened into the kitchen and Harper half stepped, half fell through it. Grace was waiting, sitting at the table reading a book. She rushed over when Harper appeared and grabbed her sister in a rough hug. "What on earth happened? You're bleeding. I told you not to trust the cat."

"It's not my blood." Harper pulled back. Fionn's arm was slung over her shoulder in a limp embrace and she clutched around his waist, too baggy clothing making it hard to keep her grip. His ribs bumped against her arm.

Grace caught him as he fell forward, his knees giving up as the portal closed behind him, the last of his magic consumed. His eyes were closed and his breathing shallow. Blood coated Grace's hands. She helped Harper lay Fionn on the table where a first aid kit waited. "Harp, I can do some, but if this is as serious as it looks, he has to get to hospital."

Fionn's hand raised to his collar, and he whispered, "No."

"Gray, we can't take him to a hospital. He's a cat. You're a vet."

"He's human-shaped at the moment."

"He's undocumented. Even if we somehow hide the tail and ears, he'll be disappeared if we go to the hospital."

"He'll be dead if we don't."

While Harper boiled the kettle, Grace cut away Fionn's hoodie and pressed a wad of bandages against the puncture in his chest.

Saqib burst into the room and stared at Fionn in horror. "What—"

"Later," Harper snapped.

"Get pressure on that head wound," Grace ordered, grabbing Saqib's wrist. "There. Keep your hand like so. And use the other one to call an ambulance."

"No. Wait." Harper clutched his other arm. "If the Guard take him, that's worse than death. They'll execute him as a supe … eventually. I'd die before letting them have me. I think he would too."

"Harp, he's been stabbed."

"By magic. And he's a cat." Her voice raised to a screech as panic gripped her.

To Harper's Sight, the growing pile of bloody cloths was overlaid by the sanguinary's image of a mound of broken body parts.

"Mundane medicine won't cure him." AJ's calm voice cut through the mayhem as Grace worked frantically to stop the bleeding. "Magic wounded him, magic must heal him."

"Your coven?" Harper asked. A thin ray of hope shone through her fear.

"They won't help." AJ's clenched jaw spasmed. "It would draw too much unwanted attention and put him in more danger."

"He'll die, AJ." Harper's eyes overflowed with tears. Fionn would die because she didn't have enough willpower to resist a song.

"The elders don't value the sanctity of life. They sent me to kill you," AJ reminded her. "He needs to go home."

Harper shook her head silently. The marks on his face came from somewhere, and yellowish bruises were visible down his side, behind the blood. She was certain he wasn't fed enough at home. She didn't want to send him back to a master who might punish him more.

"Ha ... Harper ... Is okay." Fionn stretched his fingers out to her. "He's right ... I go home."

Grace jumped back with a shout as he glowed. In a few seconds, the light was gone leaving a rag of cat lying on their table. He raised a paw and knocked three times.

"Mau?" Pleading eyes met Harper's.

"No," she whispered. "You can't go back. Don't make me send you back."

"Mrow?" Fionn nuzzled her fingers.

Tears streamed down her cheeks as she lifted him and passed him through the shimmering silver circle. Something on the other side yanked him away. Harper snatched her hands back and the portal closed.

"Now we wait." AJ put the kettle on.

It seemed too normal, but he was right. There was nothing else to do but brew up and wait.

"Think you can tell us what happened?" Grace held her hand, thumb stroking circles on the back of it.

Harper recounted the story of the Market and the Lady of Bloody Tears. Her memory was clouded after that, flashes of violin music and a soul-deep longing. She remembered standing up to something, challenging it, but vestiges of its music held her bewitched memories captive.

"My kin. I remember ..." Even as she spoke, the words warped in her mind and slid away like a shard of ice grasped too tight. "The girl in the tree in Tower Gardens, she was my kin. I don't ..." It was gone.

Fionn hadn't returned by breakfast. Harper had spent what remained of the night tossing and turning before forsaking her bed to cook. The others joined her, bags under their eyes. Even Grace, who still held strong misgivings about the cat, was worried. Breakfast was a silent affair with little eaten.

They were onto second pots of both tea and coffee, when a silver portal opened by the back door and Fionn tumbled out of it into his box. Harper leapt up.

"Fionn? Are you healed?" She gripped the edges of the cardboard box so hard her knuckles were white.

"Meow." Fionn blinked up at her.

His fur was clean and she couldn't see any lacerations, even when she carefully rolled him onto his back. He purred as she stroked him and craned his head to nuzzled her fingers. He looked fine, but his breathing was rapid and his movements slow and jerky.

Switching to magical Sight, Harper gasped. Every wound blazed and something twisted and spiky swirled in Fionn's chest, an extra darkness to what she'd witnessed at the university. "Something's still wrong. The physical wounds have been healed but that magic is still in him. I can See it. Why would his master send him back when he's still hurt?"

Grace knelt beside her and wrapped an arm around her shoulders. "Maybe ze can't fix it, or maybe it takes time to heal."

Maybe ze can't fix it? If ze can't, no one can. Why return to ... Fionn's voice rang in Harper's memory. *'It's how ze makes us. We start as animals, we become shifters through blood.'*

"Grace, open his mouth."

"What?" Grace frowned.

"Just do it," Harper scrambled up and grabbed a knife out of the block on the counter.

"What are you doing?"

"C'mon, this has got to work." Harper sliced the knife across her arm, blood spilling along its edges.

"Harper."

"Don't let go."

Grace did as she was told, holding the cat's mouth open. Harper's blood flowed over his tongue.

"C'mon. I made you." Harper leant over and whispered in Fionn's ear, "I made you. We're stronger than whatever black magic has you now. Please come back. Please." Her tears dripped onto his face and mingled with her blood. She'd said she trusted him, then she'd turned her back on him and he'd almost been killed. Being bewitched was no excuse. She should've protected him.

He's my cat.

With that acceptance, a knot loosened within her and magic spilled from her core. It ran through her arteries with each pump of her heart. It poured into Fionn to combine with the vestiges of his power.

With a splutter, Fionn dragged himself to his feet. He bared his teeth, stained with Harper's blood, and his fur stood on end. As if he had a furball to hack up, he dry-wretched and threw up the black light. It popped like a bubble made of oil, and he collapsed again. Harper scooped him up in his blanket and cuddled him against her chest. He mewed and rubbed his head against her chin.

"I'll get him some water." Grace guided Harper back to the table. She filled a shallow bowl with water and placed it in front of Fionn, who stood on Harper's lap, front paws on the table, to lap it up.

When he finished, Fionn scrunched his nose, making small mewling sounds, and Grace patted his head.

"You rest. Harper told us what happened, at least as much as she can remember. At least we know how it's been selecting its victims and that it isn't your master." Grace turned to the rest of them, the mantle of general almost visibly settling around her shoulders as she straightened her spine and squared her shoulders. "Harper, hit the archives and see what you can find about this creature. If it was around at the time of the Purge, maybe someone other than Leonora knew about it, or maybe you can find something about whatever spell it cast on you to make you forget and to hypnotise you. You need to find a way to counter that before you can fight it. AJ, you do the same searches online, or into whatever records your family keep. Fionn, when you're able to shift back, write down anything you remember in case there's something Harper forgot. Saqib, you're still running lab tests, right?"

Saqib nodded, then asked with a tired smile, "And you, Grace?"

"Find out what this is and I'll kill it before it hurts my sister." There was steel in her tone, and Harper would've bet on Grace against any supe in the world.

Now Fionn was back, the tension that kept her awake drained away and she yawned. There were still parts of her missing, but between him, Grace, and the rest of the household, pieces of her puzzle were slotting together. "We need to find out what it is fast, before it attacks someone else."

"Before it kills *you*," Saqib said

"Before it kills *anyone*. I won't let another person die in my place." Harper twisted her fingers through Fionn's fur, soft against her cheek as he purred into her shoulder. "The Lady showed me the way the water escapes. We followed something similar last time, through the wych elm to the river. I'm hoping the crystal she gave me will show me where to go from the elm or unlock some door to a shadow realm. Before we go there, I'd like to know what we face. I'm going to head to the archives. Fionn? Will you be alright here alone?"

Fionn pawed his collar, eyes rolling like a cornered animal. Then he closed them, took a deep breath, and nodded. A white light surrounded him.

"No." Grace jumped up and grabbed the first material that came to hand, before realising it was kind of silly to throw a tea towel over him.

"Keep your fur on for a minute. You can stay with me and tell me your side of things directly. Harper, I'll text you any new info."

Harper almost passed the cat to Saqib, before it registered that it was AJ volunteering. With Fionn's permission, she handed him to the techno-witch. AJ ignored the incredulous looks from around the table and left with Fionn purring in his arms.

CHAPTER TWENTY-THREE

Graceless

Harper showered, dressed, and spent some time reading the book *Of Realms and Shadows*, but it offered no insight into what kind of realm she sought other than confirming that the blood crystal could indeed be the key for a door between planes of existence. Before leaving for the archives, she knocked on Grace's door, but her sister's room was empty. Left for work, no doubt. They couldn't afford to act out of the ordinary and risk the Guard's suspicions.

She poked her head around AJ's door to find him deeply absorbed in programming and a human-shaped Fionn fast asleep in his bed. AJ had emerged from his coding long enough to tuck his blanket around the cat-boy. Harper was a little surprised he was unphased by the naked man in his bed, but he didn't seem any more bothered by Fionn's human shape than his cat one.

With a whispered goodbye to Heresy in the peephole, she left the house, texting Grace as she went. Mists hugged Harper's legs and pulled at her hair as she hurried to the cathedral. Despite her lack of sleep, she was wide awake. She needed more than the path. She needed to find out what she faced and how to stop it. The hints didn't add up. Not yet. The Latin she spoke in the tree hinted at a Roman link but there were many beings within Roman lore associated with dreams, visions, or music. Something could've come here when they occupied Britain, but could it have remained for over sixteen-hundred years? Or it could be that Latin was a red herring. Not deliberately, but it was a magical language and an ancient universal European tongue. It didn't have to mean her enemy was of Roman origin.

The trials barely registered as she made her way into the depths on auto-pilot, brain on overdrive with what she'd Seen. When she reached the Fourth Vault—housing books and artefacts relating to rituals, spells, and other realms—she slung her bag on an empty table and threw herself into work.

Since finding Leonora's diary, the archives offered her nothing useful. Acid churned in her stomach, her throat tight as she swallowed the rising bile. If she submitted to the creature from her nightmares, then no one else would die in the search for her.

"But I don't want to die." The words fell flat in the silent vault.

She stared at the pictures spread out on the table in front of her.

The girl from York University, someone who unwittingly saw Harper's magic and who lived in her old halls.

The Dales ranger, consumed by the tree that helped Harper escape.

The woman from Lincolnshire, escaping with her true love, a witch, gone missing on the path where Harper was found.

The women from Harrogate and Scarborough, unfortunates about whom they still knew little, but from places associated with supes Harper had vanquished.

Edith, not a friend with her zealous persecution of supes, but an old acquaintance. Now thought to be a witch as well. Schooled together, both investigating the occult.

Agnes, a friend, a fellow archivist. Her death hurt the most. She should've been safe in the cathedral.

The girl from the tree, not killed by the Ouse but by a copycat. Harper touched the pale cheek of the picture. Her kin. The first she'd ever seen. Murdered as part of a quest to hunt her down.

All looked like her, had been where she'd been. All associated with magic as far as they knew. All killed because of her. Each one bringing something a step closer to finding her. Something she could hardly remember but which her ancestor feared. Something she'd Seen, in her dreams and at the Soul Traders' Market, but that her treacherous memory refused to hold onto.

Harper slammed her hands down on the table, the thud echoing through the Fourth Vault. She'd hoped to find something in Saqib's research and the autopsy reports she could match to a spell or ritual recorded in the vault, but all the books were too vague. None of the memory spells mentioned helped either. They recounted victims of such spells but not how to cast or break them. There were no mentions of music doing the kind of damage she'd Seen in Fionn. She needed a book that explained how the magic worked so she could strategise.

A shuffle and cough called her attention to the other end of the long table. Alfred hovered awkwardly balancing a teetering stack of books. "Can I be of assistance, Harper?"

She dropped into a wooden chair. Her chest was hollow. "Can you get me into the Twelfth Vault again, Alfred? I've tried, but I've never been able to access it again."

"The last time, the archbishop allowed it." He set down his books and perched on the desk next to her. "Since Agnes's murderer was able to breach our defences, the artefacts and books we hold here are no longer deemed safe. The most dangerous have been moved, I cannot say where for even I do not know. Security past the Sixth Vault has increased and access for most has been revoked until we find a way to block further incursion."

"Do you know anything about memory spells?" Harper asked. Her friend's knowledge often surprised her. "Have you read anything on how to reverse them?" His eyes slid back and forth as they scanned text invisible to her.

"Without knowing the specifics of the original spell, the highest chance of success would be to vanquish the caster or confront the trauma. Of course, for that you need to remember enough to find those things."

Harper folded her arms on the desk, head dropping onto them. "Then I guess I have no choice but to go in blind."

A hesitant hand patted the top of her head. "Of all people, Harper, you are one who will never walk blind. You may not be able to remember, but you can See."

Her head snapped up, but Alfred was already gathering his books together again.

"What do you know about me, Alfred?"

He quirked a half smile over his shoulder. "That you are more capable than you know." He jutted his chin towards the strewn photos. "You will not allow more to die, nor will you sacrifice your own blood without a fight. Though you cannot remember, know this: to be here today, you defeated it once. You shall triumph again."

His confidence lightened Harper's heart. She gathered up the papers and shoved them into her satchel. If the archives no longer contained what she needed, she'd speak to the archbishop and find where the knowledge did reside. Then she'd go to Swaledale, stop the killer, and free her family he'd kidnapped centuries ago. As Leonora foresaw, she would be their deliverance.

Harper knocked on the archbishop's door. She paced once, twice, then entered without waiting for an invite. He raised his head from the book he was studying. The fire was the sole light source in the room, casting leaping shadows over mahogany shelves and desk, plush chairs, and the archbishop's frown.

"May I be of assistance, Harper?" There was a slight remonstrance in his voice and Harper bowed her head.

"I'm sorry for barging in."

She could hear his smile in his voice. "It must be important for you to be so hasty. Please. Sit." He shifted in his chair to lean back with his hands crossed over his stomach.

"I …" She glanced towards the door, unsure of how openly she could speak.

"Is it regarding our security breach?" As Archbishop Marshall leant forward, firelight flashed over the surface of the gold cross around his neck. "Grace was going to drop by before work this morning to give me updates but she forgot."

Harper's heart skipped a beat. "That's not like Grace. It … wasn't a normal morning but still, she'd never stand you up. Did she call?"

He twisted his ring around. "No, which is very like Grace. I was unable to reach her phone and her clinic stated they haven't seen her in two days. I assumed her absence was related to your case."

Panic crashed through Harper. Every death got a little bit closer to her. Grace looked like her, enough that most people didn't question them being sisters. She'd seen Harper's magic many times. They'd lived under the same roof for half their lives. No one was closer to her in all the world.

"Harper?" The archbishop's hand on her knee subdued the panic enough to clear her vision and let her drag in a ragged breath.

Her hand shook as she fumbled her phone from her pocket and hit AJ's number. "AJ, have you or H …" she glanced at the archbishop, "has anyone there seen Grace since this morning? Can you locate her phone?"

Her fingers drummed against her thigh as she waited, unable to meet Archbishop Marshall's worried gaze.

"We've not seen her since she left for work," AJ said after a muted pause to check with Heresy and Fionn. "We can't find her phone."

At AJ's words, the pit dropped from Harper's stomach as though she'd fallen from a skyscraper.

"It is not switched off, as is customary for our Graceless," Heresy added, possessing AJ's phone. His harpsicord buzz was too quiet for the archbishop to hear. "It is simply no longer here. She had it when she left. Very rude. Staring at it and ignoring my salutation."

"What do you mean, 'No longer here'?" Harper asked. Grace ignoring Heresy wasn't news, although it wasn't like her to be absorbed in her phone.

"He means it's not in this realm," AJ explained. "Even if it were turned off, I should've been able to trace it via our combined skills. I can't find it at all. Even if the phone was smashed or dropped in the river, my methods should still be traceable. By me. Not by the Guard or other supes, of course."

"And I can't portal to her," Fionn whispered. "That's never ... I tried but ... nothing happened."

"I'm coming home." It took Harper three tries to slide the phone back into her pocket.

The archbishop squeezed her knee. She gritted her teeth as he unintentionally dug his fingers behind her kneecap. "Find my goddaughter, Harper. Whatever resource you need, the Council will provide."

A distant part of her wanted to call out his selfishness but the greater part of her shared it. Finding a way to save her birth family or her own life no longer mattered. She doubted it would've killed Grace immediately like it killed the girl. If she didn't believe that, she wouldn't be able to move. It needed Grace alive. Her sister was bait and she would bite.

She'd find Grace and get her home. Even if it killed her.

Harper ran all the way home. Before she could get her key out. Heresy opened the door with an overly dramatic creak.

She burst into the kitchen to find AJ, Saqib, and Fionn already sitting around the table. Heresy drifted in after her and settled around her shoulders.

"We've already packed for you." Saqib pointed to a rucksack on one of the dining room chairs. On the table next to it sat a torch, the machete

Fionn bought at the Market along with other weapons, and Grace's crossbow.

Harper strapped the blades on, the machete heavy at her waist. What good it could do against an ethereal being was questionable, but having it reassured her. If it really could absorb magic and turn it against the caster, it might be both shield and weapon.

Fionn looked up from his mug, upper lip white with milk. "You shouldn't go, Harper. It mesmerises you. You don't know how to fight it yet."

"I escaped before." She puffed up her chest, trying to make the false bravado real. "I'm sure I'll find a way again. We won at the Market after all."

Heresy floated down to the table, a grin splitting his form. "Because it was on the not-a-cat's turf and he had protection from his owner. Without that, dear Harper, you would have been lost to this creature's charms. You will be on its turf and it will have the advantage. It casts an illusion with its magic, befuddles your already confused little mind. However, I have seen how it works. I should be able to protect you against its deceptions."

Harper slung the crossbow across her back. It reminded her of target practice when she was a teenager. Grace always outshot her. Grace was stronger. Faster. Despair gripped her. If it could subdue Grace, what hope did she have?

A vision clouded out the kitchen and she stumbled. Saqib grabbed her shoulders to keep her from falling.

Grace. Lying in a cave, wet clothes clinging to her shivering form. Her eyes were closed, her skin flushed with fever. Chains bound her ankles and wrists, snaking to the cave wall.

Even as reality reasserted itself, the image lingered, a stalwart shield against her doubts. She would not let Grace die.

"Should you tell her family?" Saqib asked. "Surely her father and mother can find her and rescue her. Nothing could stop the whole De Santos clan."

Harper's stomach twisted. If she told them, they'd find out she was a witch. Tears stung her eyes and her hands balled stiff at her sides. "I don't care if they hang me if it means Grace is safe."

She pulled out her phone to call, clicking the favourited contact near the top: 'Mama Maria.' Fionn snatched the phone from her hands. It crackled and hissed, sparks of electricity spiking off it. The screen went blank.

"What the hell, Fionn?" Harper tried to snatch it back, burning her fingers, but he held on tightly.

"You can't tell them."

"Give me that phone." Harper raised her hand and he cowered into his oversized hoodie.

"It won't work. I stopped it."

"Destroyed it, more like." AJ grabbed the phone out of his hand. "You could've just pressed the red button."

"Why can't she call Grace's mum?" Saqib asked before Harper could say anything further.

"Grace's parents might kill Harper for being a witch. If Harper dies, Grace won't have any value to the creature hunting her. I saw Harper's fetch, her death. I don't know from what but it was coming soon. I won't let her die."

"If Harper dies, do you die too?"

"I don't know." He buried his face in his hoodie so only his eyes were visible and pulled his knees up under it against his chest. "It doesn't matter what happens to me. I want to keep Harper safe. Even if she isn't killed, she'll be hurt and imprisoned. If its life is threatened, or Harper is incapacitated, Grace is no longer valuable. It'll take out her eyes, kill her, and try to find Harper again. Long before any mere human can find it. It's old and it's not been caught yet. The De Santos family already searched that area looking for where Harper came from."

Harper's shoulders slumped. She patted his head and he looked up at her with tear-brimmed eyes. "I want to keep Grace safe. I'm sorry, I didn't consider what the knock-on effects would be for you."

"Or me," Heresy huffed. Harper smacked him.

"You're right," Harper said to Fionn. "If it thinks it can trap me, it's more likely to keep Grace alive. I'll find her my own way. If I have to give it my life to save hers, so be it. I'll do everything I can to make sure you're okay. Both you and Heresy. Maybe you should go back to your master now." Her fingers brushed his collar. She hated to say it, but it might keep him alive.

He laced stiff fingers through hers and clung on. "I won't leave you. Anyway ..." His eyes shifted around as he tugged his collar. "If you die, my master dies too. Not directly, I don't think, but when I saw your death, I saw zir death too."

"Then maybe zir'll help us," Saqib said excitedly.

The collar jangled as he shook Fionn head violently. "You're already getting help. You have me. Ze can't do any more without causing ... other problems."

"It would be a bad idea," AJ weighed in. "If his master is who I think ... let's just say we've had dealings over the centuries—yes, zir's that old—

and it never ends well. Harper's life might not be worth the cost. Sorry, Harper, but there *are* worse things than death."

"I don't have time to debate this." Harper glared around the table. "Fionn, can you open a portal to Swaledale for me? To the wych elm?"

"I can." He was motionless, tensed as if to spring, save the flick at the very tip of his tail. "I'm coming with you."

Harper opened her mouth to object, then snapped it shut again. Last time he'd almost died, but she needed him, needed his magic, if she was to find her sister.

Harper gathered her supplies, tucked Heresy under her hair, and gave Saqib a hug goodbye. AJ retreated to his room and resumed searching for Grace's phone, his way of showing worry.

Saqib squeezed her tight before she left. His worry was obvious in the tension around his eyes and the stiffness of his shoulders. "I will keep you in my duas," he told Harper. It was all he could do, and it meant a lot.

Harper gathered cat-Fionn up in her arms. "Let's go."

CHAPTER TWENTY-FOUR

Tap Your Heels Together

When they stepped out onto the Swaledale hills, Harper tugged her coat tighter around her, wrapping Fionn in it too, cuddled against her chest, as though its bright teal might keep out death. Heresy huddled under her hair. His electrostatic buzz brought warmth, small as it was. Even tucked in Fionn's thick fur, her fingers rapidly lost feeling. Her cheeks were stained pink, her nose numb. The wind smarted against her Sight-filled eyes. Flakes of snow caught in her lashes, whitening her hair to premature grey.

The sun sank low over the horizon. Shadows of trees tumbled down the Swaledale hillside like waterfalls of thick heart's blood. They rent grass and snow with chasms miles deep, cracks leading to Hell. Velvet clouds shrouded the moon, almost full but not quite. The stars remained hidden, smothered in grey, each pinprick of light filled in, smoothed over, and banished forever.

Gold, red, orange, and pink tried to warm the sky, reflecting off snow-fluffed fields and the clouds which threatened more to come. Lightning crackled. A threat. Grasping fingers of pale green. The colours of sunset and storm bled away, dripped through the shadows, and disappeared into the earth.

A low mist churned in the dale. The image of a cauldron flashed through Harper's mind. Something from a dream, or maybe something from a memory. No lights came on as the sun set, no sound filtered up from the stables and homes below. It was as though they three were the last souls alive. Winter concealed the rest in a shroud of mist until spring's thaw might reveal their bodies, grotesquely contorted by ice and snow, bloated by the river, blue-tinged nightmares.

"You must move." Heresy's command tickled her ear.

Claws dug through her top and into her skin as Fionn clung to her, offering what little warmth he had. He would sacrifice himself for her. He'd done it before. Her heart was sure of it. Another life lost and laid on her doorstep like an offering to her selfishness.

"Harper. Move."

She squared her shoulders and held out the sanguinary's crystal. The ruby light within it pulsed as she turned, beating faster and faster, then slower. She turned back to where it beat fastest and headed in that direction.

"We are close," Heresy said. "I can sense it, though I could not when last we were here. We are half in its realm already. Blood of our blood. Stronger than our connection, or you and the cat. Call to it and it will come."

Strangely, this statement brought some comfort to Harper. Maybe those below had not truly perished. Maybe they slept, awaiting the outcome of this showdown. Or maybe they dreamt carefree, all its attention focussed on her.

"Are we dreaming?" She looked down at Fionn. His ears were flat against his skull and his tail swished against her arm.

"Mrow." *Both. Neither.* She could hardly hear him over the wind, her magically augmented Hearing translating regardless. His portal had brought them near to the wych elm, yet the last few metres seemed like miles. He dug his claws deeper into her skin and she gasped as blood welled from each prick.

"*Move.*" The urgency in Heresy's voice forced her to lift one foot from the snow, then the other, then again to trudge uphill.

Snow banked up one side of the elm, the leafless tree stark as a domino mask. Plumes of white vapour condensed off it. As the last spear of sunlight was blocked by the hills at the western end of the dale, Harper laid a hand on the wych elm's trunk. It pulsed as if she clasped its jugular. Her Sight showed a network of crimson through it like veins and arteries.

"Mau? Merow." Fionn waved a paw towards a notch in the bark at the centre of a knot. "Mrow." *Try the crystal. The sanguinary said it was a key. Maybe your heart's desire is on the other side.*

The pulsing of the gemstone from the Market matched the beat of the tree's heart. It fit perfectly in the hole and the tree swallowed it. Violet, turquoise, carmine, and silver tinged the air. A wave of dizziness washed over Harper. If Fionn hadn't been clinging to her, she would've dropped him. The world swam in streams of light like the Aurora Borealis, tipping and twisting under her feet. The tree stretched and a gaping abyss opened once again. Tearing pain slashed through her chest as Fionn was ripped away. The airless atmosphere sucked away her scream. The tree consumed her.

Roots tore at her knees and palms as she tumbled. The fetid fruity smell of death lingered within the tree. It felt like she fell for miles, deeper and deeper to a fate more terrible than Wonderland. Images flashed through her memory. An interminable climb, soaked from her trip down the river, clothes clinging. The water had spat her out and the earth had buried her in darkness. She'd clutched the bone key between her teeth, no pockets, fingers busy seeking scant handholds among the roots. Harper fell through space and time.

When she opened her eyes, Harper found herself kneeling in a grove at the base of the wych elm. The trees hadn't been there before, not in her wakening world at least. In her dreams, they'd always existed. The ground beneath her was dusted with a light covering of snow and heat rippled off the tree.

Fionn stood before her, his nose almost touching hers, eyes wide as he panted. Despite the heat from the tree, he was still trembling, all his fur on end, back arched, claws digging into the dirt as though he clung to it in fear of his life. His rough tongue licked her nose, then he turned and circled the clearing.

"Heresy?" Harper managed a hoarse whisper. She pushed herself back on her knees, brushing the dirt from her hands before reaching up to her neck. It was bare and no static prickled her fingers.

Fionn trotted over to rub his head against her elbow.

"Where's Heresy?" Harper asked him. "Where are *we*?"

He purred softly, then pointed ahead with one pristine paw. "Mau mrow."

"Fionn? I can't understand you. What's going on?" Harper rubbed her ears, fearing the cold had numbed them so much she could no longer Hear. They throbbed, almost frozen brittle, and when Fionn mewed again, no translation appeared in her mind. The burning in her eyes had faded away too. Try as she might, she couldn't summon it back again.

"My magic. It's not working." For years she hadn't wanted it, but its loss filled her with dread colder than the deepest snow drift. "I can't See or Hear." But dread didn't bring despair. It brought anger.

Fionn pawed her leg. When she looked down, he traced a single word in the snow.

Trust.

"I trust you, Fionn." He nudged her hand with his head and she scratched behind his ears. "I know you trust me too. I was dragged here, and I think Heresy must've been thrown off, but if it thinks that makes me helpless, it's wrong."

Fionn meowed agreement, then trotted ahead of her towards a slender path. When he reached the edge of the clearing, he jerked his head uphill.

Armed with her machete and steely determination, Harper followed.

It was the reverse of what she'd dreamt. Almost familiar, like déjà vu but stronger. This wasn't Swaledale anymore. It might lead there, through some twisted nightmare path to the wakening, but it was different. The trees didn't extend so far in the real dale, nor did so prominent a brook cut a path down the hillside, yet she could hear one a few feet away, hidden by the trees. It cackled like a witch from a fairy tale as ice cracked under the pressure of tumbling water and frozen shards.

Pine needles rustled overhead. The snow deepened, pitted with tracks Harper didn't recognise. Thin, dagger-like cuts, too many feet. Heavy webs stretched over the path. Fionn slunk beneath them or dived off the path into the trees, then darted back as soon as he passed the blockage. Harper pushed through. They clung to her, turning her vibrant clothes white; a return to the monochrome world to which she first awoke, all those years ago by the river Swale.

"Fionn?" Her voice rebounded off the trunks. *Fionn … Fionn … Fionn … * In the echoes she could hear a child's voice, high and desperate, searching, crying. *Fionn … Fionn … Where are you? Help me.*

"Mrow?" Although his meaning was indiscernible, the way his head cocked to the side matched the questioning tone of his meow.

"Is your magic working?"

He sniffed the air, turning around twice before looking at her again. His eyes reflected the deep forest green, turning them a dark teal. He shook his head as though trying to rid his ears of water.

"I guess that's a 'no,'" Harper muttered.

He mewed plaintively at her.

"Don't do it, you'll freeze, but can you transform?"

The cat pawed at the ground, sketching something into the snow before swiping it clean with his tail. He turned his back and marched off with his quivering tail held high behind them.

"Fionn? I didn't see …" But he was already disappearing ahead. Harper ran to catch up. "Do you know where we're going?"

He didn't look at her, continuing straight on, no longer following the path. He stuck his nose out ahead of him like a bloodhound, whiskers trembling. Harper hurried after him until trees gave way to a field of poppies.

"We're not in Swaledale anymore, Toto," Harper muttered. Fionn glanced back at her with a flick of his tail, then continued onwards.

He halted at the entrance to a cave, his paws not quite touching the shadow it cast upon the snow. Set a little way into the cave was a door, a perfectly carved gag that covered its whole mouth.

"I've dreamt of this." Harper hesitated, then reached out, touching the wood with one trembling finger. Fionn hissed and retreated, fur bristling, but he did nothing to stop her. When she opened the door and stepped through, he slunk after her.

Torches roared to life along the walls, illuminating the way ahead. The firelight caught on each jagged rock casting shadows dancing behind. It reminded Harper of the demonically carved doom stone in the cathedral undercroft. Fionn twisted himself around her ankles and Harper reached down to pat his head. He nuzzled against her fingers, then resumed his lead, the stiffness with which he walked betraying his distaste for the slick, wet floor.

Fast flowing water echoed deeper in the cave. As they headed farther in, stalactites and stalagmites jutted into their path. Violin music drifted down the passage, melodic yet sombre. The smell of poppies was heavy in the air and Harper's eyelids drooped. She yawned. "Fionn, slow down."

She tried to summon her Sight or any sense of magic, but it wasn't there. No barrier, no blockage, just … nothing. As though it had all been a dream and she never was a witch, only a normal human woman caught in a nightmare. Her limbs were heavy. She ached as though a fever settled in her bones. Maybe this was all a hallucination. Her skin was burning, her throat dry, her lips brittle. Just a fever dream.

Harper didn't hear the sharp crack as her knees buckled and hit stone. She didn't hear the crying that was almost human, didn't notice when her head dropped onto something soft, nor Fionn's sharp claws and teeth as he tried to wake her.

Harper awoke to an unfamiliar face hovering over hers. The woman's dark eyes were red-ringed as though she'd been crying, but she smiled at Harper. Something cool pressed against Harper's forehead and water trickled over her cheeks and down her neck.

"Where am I?" Her voice was hoarse as she pushed aside the woman's hand. Harper pulled herself to a sitting position and looked around. A large tent soared over her pallet bed. The entrance flapped in a cold breeze and the woman hurried over to tie it closed. On Harper's left were more beds, each neatly made with small personal items next to them. By one, watercolour paintings and tools. By another, a violin and pages of sheet music. By the third, sachets of herbs and pages of writing in a small, neat hand. On her right was an open area strewn with cushions and a merrily blazing firepit. From it wafted the aroma of stew. Harper's stomach growled.

The woman resumed her place at Harper's side, sitting back on her heels, watching. "Do you remember?"

"Remember?" Harper rubbed her eyes. "I've never been here before. Where am I? What happened?"

The woman folded her long, lavender skirt over crossed legs. She wore lavender ribbons in her dark brown hair, too, and a wide-sleeved top of blues and pinks. She appeared to be around forty-five to fifty years of age, faint lines of grey in her hair and crow's feet around eyes which once laughed so much.

Harper snagged the last thought, the brief image in her mind of this woman much younger, laughing and clapping her hands as a man played the violin and two children danced by the fire, giggling and tripping over themselves. Grief lanced through her brain, as though someone drove sharp stakes through her eyes. The image shattered. Harper clutched her head, doubling over as the pain ricocheted around her skull.

Warm fingers combed her hair. Feverish reality faded in and out of focus, a memory or the present, she couldn't tell.

"Hush, wee one, hush. The dream will be over soon." A woman's voice, an echo of Harper's tone if not her words, the melodic lilt of her accent at once familiar and forgotten. "Don't fight the current. Flow with the vision, it will bring you home safely."

Harper's forehead rested against a soft thigh, overlaid with cotton. The scent of the moors surrounded her, banishing fir and pine. Half-lidded eyes skimmed over the flamboyant rugs which hung around them, bastions against the cold outside. Crackling fire gave percussion to the gentle strains of a lullaby, an ancestral tongue sung by a low tenor. The words meant nothing, yet Harper heard meaning, the tale of a long-lost child. She couldn't remember how it ended.

"Home, dearheart. It will lead you home. To me."

Memory clutched at a grandmother's skirts as rheumatic hands caressed cold cheeks. Harper recalled her wizened smile, leather-soft skin, and warm embrace.

The flow of memory tugged her. Currents rushed, drowned her as image after image flooded her mind. A little boy giggling as he pelted her with snowballs from behind their mother's skirts. Snuggling in her grandmother's embrace to watch through sleep-filled eyes as the adults celebrated the coming of winter. Calloused fingers pressing hers against metal strings, sliding them to the correct position. The notes set her teeth on edge at first, cats yowling, then slipped to a familiar melody. A white-haired boy, fluffy tail swishing as they stalked through the night until they burst into the clearing of starlight.

Heather. Grass. Bread baking. Stewed apples. Scents of …

"Mama."

Harper opened her eyes, staring up into their twins. Rich brown with veins of hazel, circled like Saturn. The word fell from her lips, fearful, hopeful. "Mama?"

The woman smiled, though tears slipped from her crinkled eyes.

"Yes, my baby. The visions have brought you home, as I promised they would."

The words roared through Harper. Twinkling lights danced before her eyes. Her heart pounded. As her fingers brushed against her mother's braid, she let out a juddering sigh, tears released to pour down her cheeks.

"Are you real?" Harper whispered. "Or are you a dream?"

Fingers twined through hers, so tight it was almost painful. A heart beat in rhythm with her own. Hard and fast. As though both might leap from their respective chests to embrace in the middle.

"I am real, my Harper, my joy."

With a sob, Harper threw her arms around her mother and buried her face in the other woman's shoulder. She inhaled deeply, letting the long-lost scents of home anchor her to this place. If this wasn't real, she didn't want reality. She would live forever in this dream.

Strong arms wrapped around them, scents of sawdust and flame.

"Papa?"

He didn't speak, just tightened his embrace around his family and for the first time she could remember, Harper felt completely safe. But not completely whole.

"Something's missing." She searched their faces for the cause of the pain reflected in their eyes. "I Saw a boy—"

A look passed between her parents, so fleeting Harper wasn't sure she didn't imagine it.

"You Saw that you would return to us first." Her father squeezed her mother's shoulder.

"You never Saw his return," her mother said at the same time. This time Harper was certain she didn't imagine the look between them.

"Who is he?" She already knew the answer. It was there in her father's dark eyes, the shade and wave of his hair. It was there in her mother's delicate fingers, so similar to the child's she had seen wrapped around the snowball.

The joy melted from her mother's face as her lips formed a soundless word.

"We cannot say his name," her father said. "You told us, if we ever said it, he would never come home. You don't remember, do you? You don't remember us. You warned us, when you left, that it would be a long time before we saw you again."

Harper rubbed her eyes, then massaged her temples. The throbbing, stabbing pain returned without her mother's fingers to soothe it. "I don't remember any of this. I can't … I can see images, photographs almost, short movies, but I don't remember."

Her mother's head tilted to the side. "We don't know what those are. Photo … something? Movie?" She reached out to rest a hand on her daughter's knee. "You are here. That is enough for us. The Protector brought you home, as he promised he would. We trust when he says your brother will return one day, also. Nothing else is important."

Harper swayed. Nothing else *was* important. She was home, back to the family she'd ached to find, risked her life for by using magic. She'd found herself in these two people, her parents, her past.

'Something is hunting you. I do not know what, but its intentions are not good.' Heresy's words. The words of a demon. Was she really going to let a deception demon scare her away from the only good thing that had happened in over a decade.

Not the only good thing, her heart whispered. *Grace. You have a sister, another family somewhere out there. You have friends. Saqib, AJ, Alfred, Fionn. Fionn.*

"Where's Fionn?" He had been with her in the forest—small, tired, and scared.

"Who?" Her mother's eyes were too wide. "We don't know anyone by that name." The hand on Harper's knee quivered and her father's knuckles turned white.

Harper scrambled to her feet. "Is this real? Are you? Are you my parents? Are you an illusion? Where. Is. Fionn?"

The heavy rugs baring the cold from entering now imprisoned her in the tent. A hundred exits and none, a maze of brocade and tapestry. Heavy drapes buffeted Harper. They slapped back like waves against the shore. She'd seen the entrance flap before, but it had vanished. No matter which way she ran, she always returned to the kneeling couple, the firepit, the crumpled bed where she awoke.

She grabbed her mother's shoulders, bending over her, wanting to shake her and scream. One look into the woman's eyes and all the fight drained from her. Harper's eyes burned, tears rubbing salt into the wounds of her Sight, the anguish of a lost lifetime. They cannot hide the eyes. She had read it so many times. Heard the Auctioneer say it. Heard Fionn say it. Eyes so like her own. Eyes she remembered, full of joy, full of concern, full of love. They could belong to none other.

She folded into her parents' embrace and wept.

CHAPTER TWENTY-FIVE

One

The next morning, Harper awoke puffy-eyed and tired. The multi-coloured blankets were cosy, the snow a distant memory, but even such luxurious camping felt alien. What was a blessing was the lack of nightmares.

For the first time in weeks, her sleep had been naturally untroubled. It was different to the sleep Heresy granted her. Freer than his sleep which held her within invisible walls. He hid her from the nightmares while here there simply weren't any. She was unnerved by it almost as much as waking up to stare at the peaked ceiling of the tent. Rugs cracked as a strong wind railed against them. Winter raged outside, but here in her parents' home it was summer. A stray thought niggled her about the cold but she ignored it. She didn't have to go out so it didn't matter how much it stormed.

Her skin itched with raw nerves and she wrapped the blankets tighter around herself. A fight-or-flight instinct surged through her only to ebb again like the tide. The small voice of concern was drowned out by a sense of calm and wellbeing. A sense of belonging.

"Breakfast, dearheart?" Her mother's sweet voice brought a smile to Harper's lips. Rich and earthy smells of cooking oats, warmed honey, and strong-brewed tea wafted through the tent. Her stomach grumbled. She couldn't remember when she ate last as she'd cried herself into exhausted slumber the night before.

Her fears vanished, quelled by the thought of food as she tossed the blankets aside and padded over to the firepit in the centre of the tent. A glance up showed no hole to let out the smoke but the air was clear. The cloth shimmered with a lilac glow as she adjusted her Sight.

"You have magic too?" Harper sat cross-legged beside her mother and accepted a bowl brimming with porridge. A dash of milk, a dollop of honey, a sprinkle of cinnamon, the same way she ate it in their home in York. An ache twisted in her chest. *Gray ... I need to ...* It melted away as the first bite passed her lips.

"The Protector does it." Her mother waved a hand to encompass the whole of the abode. "He keeps the warmth in and the cold out and a great many other things to aid us. I have worried about you all these years, wondering how you fared away from his shelter. It must have been terrible for you. So alone in a barbaric world with no magic."

"Oh no," Harper protested. "I wasn't alone. I had Grace." The name clung to her lips and she forced it out. *Gray. Gray. I can't forget. I can't ...* But her sister slipped from her memory just as her dreams of home once did.

"I have no doubt you made friends, precious one, but it's not the same as being with your family, as having your mother."

"No." Harper took another mouthful of porridge. It dropped into her stomach, sludge. "Grace is family." She bit her lip, unsure if the words came from her or not. *My sister needs me.*

Her mother leant over and grasped Harper's hand. Her fingers were like claws, sharp, digging into the soft flesh of Harper's palm, leaving crescent moon marks. Harper yanked her hand back. Oats slopped out of her bowl and into the fire where they crackled and hissed.

She clutched her head, dizziness and nausea rising. "Where am I?"

A heavy hand on her shoulder, grip like a vice. "Calm down, Harper. You're home. You're safe here." Her father's voice, deep and reassuring. Panic smashed through the veneer of calm his words sought to bring.

"No," Harper panted. "This isn't my home. My home is with Grace. Where's my sister? I need—"

"You need your mother." The claws snatched her hand again, nailed it to her leg, pinned her down. "This is your home. Nowhere else. You had no sister. Mother. Father. Brother. We are your home."

With a half sob, half scream, Harper wrenched herself free of their grasp. Her eyes burned with the Sight as she backed away. "I don't believe you."

The words, her own words, ripped her heart into jagged pieces and threw them in the fire. They blistered her throat, acidic in her mouth, splitting her lip, blood dripping, salty tears stinging as they drizzled into the wound. She clutched her belly, the porridge a concrete threatening to burst through the thin lining of her stomach. She doubled over.

The words forced themselves past her lips again. "I don't believe you."

Neither of her parents moved, her mother kneeling by the fire where Harper had sat, her father standing, one foot forward, ready to pursue, frozen. His violin rested, silent, near his feet.

"We may not be here," her mother whispered, "but we are real. We love you. We have missed you so much, dearheart. You must do your duty. Only you can protect our people. Only you can save us." Harper could see the far side of the tent through her mother's dress, through her father's long coat. They faded, as they always had in early nightmares, but unlike a dream the image of them remained in her mind. Their faces were as clear as if they were etched onto her cornea.

A cold wind carved up the tent, the rug-lined walls billowing sails under a heavy gale. Sparks of purple flew off the fire and caught the material. Flames spread through the maze of rugs. Harper raised her arms to shield herself from the heat.

"Mama?" Her pitiful voice barely reached her ears over the scorching flames, a frightened child, lost and afraid. "Where are you? I'm sorry I said I didn't believe you. Please come back."

A scream rent the air, layered and sharp, then the crack of wood. "Papa!" Harper cuddled his violin to her chest. Flames licked her hands. With a sob, she dropped the burning instrument. It shattered.

Then another yowling, this one inhuman. Something more familiar than either parent's voice. The smell of burning hair assailed her. Bright flames of red and lilac obscured her vision. Still no smoke. Harper ducked between two burning rugs, searching for the exit, any gap in the fabric of the tent. Screaming again. Nearer this time.

"Fionn?" Harper shrieked his name. How could she have forgotten him? The one person tying her past and present together. Her friend. Her cat. "Fionn, where are you? I'm coming, Fionn. I'm coming."

She staggered through the tent, following the mewling and screams. She found him, backed into a corner. His bristling fur was no longer pure white but ragged and splattered with burnt patches.

Before him was a hare, larger than any Harper had seen before. It was velvet brown, with a pure white tail, and long ears. Around its neck was a bejewelled black collar. It was fancier than Fionn's but bore the same triquetra. The fire swerved around it, turned aside by a shield of amber magic. In comparison to the hare, the cat looked puny and weak. He hissed at the animal, claws extended. Then he pounced.

The two rolled together, biting, clawing, boxing. Harper grabbed the hare by its ears and it twisted to bite, narrowly missing her arm. Harper dropped it.

The hare warped. The air shimmered around it, pushing the flames back as it grew larger, and larger. Bright light pulsed from its chest. Harper grabbed Fionn. She ran. Dashing, dodging. She threw herself at the side of the tent. For a moment it stretched and held. Then tore. Harper and Fionn tumbled out into the snow.

The cold went through Harper like a plunge into an ice-covered lake. It stole her breath. Seared her eyes shut. It burned her exposed skin and clung to the thin fabric of her clothes. She lay gasping on the ground, Fionn still clutched to her chest. His claws pricked her flesh as he trembled against her, the flicker of his heart faster even than her own.

"What's going on?"

"Merow?"

They looked at each other with wide eyes. Harper glanced back to the tent, expecting the hare to have followed them, but it was gone.

"What the …?" She scrambled to her feet, snow scrunching between her toes. "Where …?"

"He tried to give you what you wanted. A mistake, clearly."

A woman's voice, one Harper didn't recognise. Fionn dug his claws in farther, eliciting a gasp. He hissed and spat, craning his neck to see the stranger.

"Who did?" Harper turned slowly. Behind her, sitting on a slope of snow as if it were the most natural thing in the world, was a naked woman of around Harper and Fionn's age. Her eyes were dark brown, almost black, her hair the same velvet brown as the hare's fur. Two long, twitching ears rose from her head. Her skin reddened where snowflakes floated down on it but she appeared to have no care for the cold as she stood, one hand on her hip, finger tapping against her pelvis in impatience. Harper had no doubt there would be a fluffy tail if the woman turned around.

"Who are you?" Harper winced as her movement stretched her skin against the pins of Fionn's sharp claws.

"Zero knows me." A smug smile played on the woman's lips. "Master is most displeased with little Zero. Little *Nothing*." Her cold eyes narrowed as she spat the last word.

A glow surrounded Fionn and his claws retracted, leaving blood-smeared holes in Harper's top. He grew heavy in her arms, stretching, creaking, and cracking. Harper dropped him and backed away. As Fionn assumed his human form her eyes darted between the two naked shapeshifters.

Unlike the woman, he shivered, and wrapped his skinny arms around his chest. His fluffy, white hair was singed from the fire and his body was smeared with soot. Harper could see raw areas of skin where the fire had caught stronger. She needed to get him to a hospital. On instinct she clutched her pocket but her phone wasn't there. Even if it had been, she doubted she would have signal in this strange demi-world.

"One …" Fionn's voice quivered almost as much as his body, tremors from cold or fear, Harper couldn't tell. He licked dry lips, his rough cat tongue no relief. "What are you doing here? I have things under control."

"Really?" The woman's eyes flicked to Harper, that infuriating smile still twisting her lips. "Then why did Master see the need for me to check up on you? And why did I find you burning in an illusion?"

Fionn's fingers gripped his arms so tightly they left bruises. "The Seer was in the illusion. I went there to—"

"The 'seer.'" The woman raised a hand in air quotes. "Some seer, she couldn't even tell it was an illusion. This pathetic witch is the grand prize you promised Master? Hah. Even you cannot recover from this one, Nothing. Master is … displeased." Despite her cocky demeanour, her ears flicked back and her fur bristled as did the hairs on her arms and legs.

"Hey. Don't talk about me like I'm not here." Harper stepped forward, planting herself between this strange hare-woman and her trembling friend.

"Harper, don't," Fionn hissed. Harper waved a hand behind her back. If this position also meant she couldn't see him, all of him, too much of him … heat rose in her cheeks. Looking at the curves of the human-form hare was no better.

"Who are you and what is this place?" Harper locked violet eyes with brown ones. Her Sight blazed, not solely in her eyes or her head, but electric through her whole body. Hairs prickled with static. Lightning threatened to spark from her fingertips.

The woman before her was both hare and human overlayed one on top of the other like reflections in an infinity mirror. The ground beneath her was covered in snow and yet verdant green, sprinkled with buttercups and daisies. Ash, acrid and bitter, stung her nose and at the same time something sweet invaded her, something so familiar that longing rose in her breast unbidden.

Harper blinked and brown hare eyes filled her vision, tinged with twinkling purple, mirroring her stare. She tried to move, to back away, even look away, but those eyes pinned her. The hare-woman's breath on her lips smouldered hot and intimate. The wind blew fur-soft hair across her cheek and caressed her collarbone. Her throat was dry. Deep inside, something stirred, something primal, ignoring the danger. An intense ache below her gut.

Fingers twined through hers, calloused yet gentle. The light scratch of nails sparked electric. Silken words were whispered by lips that tugged her earlobe. "I will taste you, Seer."

A sharper scratch on the back of her hand. Harper gasped and the musky scent of the other woman filled her nose, sucked down her throat. The grip on her hand tightened like a vice, lifting it. She tried to yank away but sharp fingers dug into her hip and palm. A tongue lapped at her skin, along her finger. The heat melted the snow and burnt through every part of Harper's body.

"*Mine.*" The forceful, commanding cat from the Market was back.

The cold hit Harper like the slap of an angry lover. She staggered back with her hand cradled against her chest. Blood oozed along her fingers. The woman writhed in the snow, tossing it up like a storm as she fought the turquoise-and-silver bands snaked around her body.

"Harper? It's okay. My magic will hold her awhile."

A warm hand on her shoulder, a soft nuzzle against her cheek. Harper pushed Fionn away, eyes darting between him and the bound woman writhing on the ground. The magic bands covered her mouth, eyes, and ears, leaving her senseless.

"Can't you …" Harper flapped a hand towards her. "Can't you change her back or something. This is … just wrong."

"What she would do to you is worse." Fionn took her tingling hand in his. "You're bleeding. That's not a good idea. Not here. She lacks my skill, but a taste of your blood could still give her power."

"Your skill?" Harper stared resolutely at a fir tree.

"In sanguimancy. Although I don't need to taste yours to use it. I'm made of you. I can heal you, and your blood heals me, remember?"

His soft touch on her hand sent a frisson of heat through her. *So much snow pillowed on that branch, surely it will fall soon. So much snow. Why can't it banish this heat?*

The rasp of a tongue dragged over her skin, over where the woman licked.

"Fionn. Fionn, what …?" Harper's voice came out hoarse. The world spun. An arm around her waist lowered her to ground that was soft and springy like new-grown grass.

"I'm sorry. I'm done."

His warmth receded and all the cold and aching rushed back to fill the void. Harper opened her eyes, her magic no longer electric in her veins.

Fionn sat a few metres away, his tail wrapped around him. His hair was once again star white and his skin was pale and clean. Harper glanced over his shoulder to where the bound woman had lain but saw no one. Following her gaze, Fionn scooted to the side to reveal a tussled hare whose hind legs batted against turquoise rings of magic.

"Harper, meet One, she's a doe hare." Fionn gestured to the hare. "Our … our master liked having me as a … liked having me so much that ze made more. One was the first ze created. She's always been jealous of me. Of my standing with Master, of my magic. She thought if she consumed your blood, she would be more powerful than I am."

Harper staggered to her feet, fingers numb from the deep snow. "What is going on here? There were … I mean … My …" Harper trailed off, eyes wet as she looked at where the smouldering remains of the tent fizzled in the snow. Any hint of grass or green was gone, leaving a colourless image of frost and carbon.

"It wasn't real." Fionn shrank in on himself, hiding behind his poofed tail, his voice small. "None of that was real. I tried to get to you sooner but he locked me out."

"Who? This 'master' of yours?" Harper turned on him and Fionn cringed away from her. Guilt coursed through her as watery kitten-eyes stared up.

"No," he whispered. "My master wants you too. Ze wants your power, wants to know the future. The one here … he … I can't remember but I know. More flashes come back the longer we're here. He made you and you made me. I can sense his presence nearby but he's hiding. This isn't real."

"A dream," One said.

Fionn leapt to his feet, darting to stand between Harper and the hare as the magic holding her twinkled out of existence and she stood before them, human once more. Harper was relieved to note he kept his tail wrapped around him, although his slight frame did little to conceal the body of his athletic opponent.

"This is all a dream." One's mouth twisted, half grimace, half self-satisfied smirk. She made no move towards them and her eyes drifted over their flesh as though it were nothing. "But in dreams his power is stronger than any of us. Ancient. Can't you sense it, Zero? Even a kitten wouldn't be so naïve. Maybe it is this place, this magic.

"Did you know it is a place Master cannot see, even in the reflecting pool? Do you remember when you first came to zir, Zero? Ze told me about it. Told me when I was spitting rage at you. You came to zir bound and broken, no memory, almost no fur, no soul. Ze wanted me to pity you, to reconcile, to understand. But all ze showed me was how *weak* you are. You claim to be made of this human girl and this ancient power, yet you can hardly crawl on your own. You don't deserve this power. You don't deserve zir praise, zir love. You are *nothing*. You ..."

As One's rant crescendoed, Harper snapped out of her reverie. Darkness expanded around the hare-girl. It obliterated the bright snow, billowing like a cape in the wild wind. Tree branches creaked and moaned. Ash and snow hung in the air.

"Stop her," Harper shouted. "Bind her again. Do something."

"It's not her." Fionn pushed Harper behind him as they backed away from the expanding darkness. One didn't seem to have noticed.

"Get out of there." Harper waved her free arm but One paid her no heed. The darkness continued to expand. It covered the sky and snuffed out the pale morning sun. One was consumed by billowing nothingness. On instinct, Harper reached for the other woman but Fionn yanked her back. This close, Harper could see all the hairs on his neck standing on end. His ears lay back flat against his head.

The darkness swelled and they ran.

Through the forest. A dream, One said. Harper had Seen it before. A vision of the future? A memory of the past? Darkness cascaded from the sky, flooding behind them.

They ran hand in hand. Spider-webs blocked the path. As they barrelled through, the sticky fibres stretched and snapped. A thousand tiny footsteps tickled her skin as they ran their webs round and round her. Inside her clothes. Crawling over goosebumped flesh. Harper tried to brush them off but Fionn tugged her on, darkness lapping at their heels. He dragged her behind him, a glow pulsing around his form. He would be faster as a cat, more likely to escape, but she couldn't unclench her hand from grasping his. Selfish. Again.

Dark firs towered overhead. Their snow-laden branches allowed no light. Needles caught at clothes and hair, scratched Harper's hand, recoiled and grazed her cheek. More blood.

She tripped. No. A root twisted, dropped her, and she tumbled. Down the embankment. They fell together, a writhing mass of limbs and fur. Rocks cracked bones and tore flesh. An inhuman yowl of terror cut through the creak of pines as Fionn hit the freezing water.

Ice closed over Harper's head. Darkness pounded on the surface. The spiders floated free, black shadows in black water against black ice. Her fingers were slick with blood and numb with cold. She couldn't tell if she held Fionn or not, didn't know where he was. Beside her. Or lost. Drowned.

Her feet touched the bottom and Harper pushed up as hard as she could. Her head cracked through the ice and darkness, water cascading over her as she gasped for air. Somewhere in the back of her mind, she remembered this, as though life now mirrored a dream. She was caught in a fairy tale, the story overwriting free will.

Splashing water over herself to knock off any remaining spiders, Harper staggered for the shore and dragged herself onto the far bank.

The darkness overtook her. Only a few minutes before it had been morning. She had sat with her mother, her father, eating porridge. Then, out in snow touched with the golden fingers of dawn. Now, a starless, moonless midnight.

Harper struggled up the bank, shoulders hunched, skin prickling under the gaze of unseen eyes. Ice trickled down her spine. She was forgetting something. Something important. Déjà vu pounded against the door of her memory. Her shoulder blades twitched and she spun, expecting to see all the eyes watching her.

"I've been waiting for you, Seer."

The voice washed over her like a breath of summer. Verdant green and flowers flickered behind the snow again. She sank into the moss. Trees and roots slithered out of her way. A violin melody wound through her mind. A familiar lullaby.

"Come to me, precious one."

She lay in the moss, staring into the darkness. Her limbs were leaden, as though she visited a place where gravity was three times its normal strength. Her eyes began to close. Through her lashes she could see a cacophony of elaborate rugs. The smell of freshly cooked oats. The song of a violin.

"Submit to me, my Seer."

"No ... Grace ...Fionn ..." She fought, and her mind found cracks through which she could cling to reality.

Pain bloomed down her arm at the same time lightning coursed through her as her Sight blazed. The tent and the forest flickered, the scene shifting between the two images so fast they blurred into a grey nothing.

"Run, Harper."

The voice from her dreams. She'd heard him before, protecting her, saving her. That cold January day when she fled. When she won her own freedom and left him to his fate. In her dreams since, buying her time to escape her pursuer. Every time she had left him. Not again.

"Run, Harper."

"*No.*"

CHAPTER TWENTY-SIX

Where Once We Dwelt

Fionn's eyes stretched almost as wide as the 'O' of his mouth. "Harper. You have to—"

"I said 'no.'" She snatched her hand away as he grabbed for it. "I won't leave you. Not again."

The forest flickered around them. Slick rock jutted through bark and leaf. Harper closed her eyes, taking a deep breath as she summoned her magic. Pain drilled deep into her ears like an infection. Tears leaked between her eyelashes as lightning coursed up her optic nerves, through blood vessels, and arched through vitreous fluid like a plasma ball. Static crackled between her fingertips. Air flowed over her tongue and through flared nostrils, first the earthy petrichor of rain and forest, then the bitter tang of metal and peat.

When Harper opened her eyes, the world swam, a transition from dream to reality, exactly like on TV. Grass and leaf receded, giving way to uncompromising stone. Stalactites dribbled from the canopy as icicles hanging from tree boughs morphed and grew. Roots hardened and stretched upwards transforming into stalagmites. The cave closed around them like toothy jaws, fangs dripping with saliva and anticipation.

In the distance, the brook babbled almost-words, whispered just beyond hearing. A warning, maybe, or an invitation. The air around them was damp and chilled. Mist oozed out of fissures in the rockface, unnatural, a gateway between worlds.

"Where are we?" Harper asked Fionn.

A deep guttural sound emerged from his throat. His ears were back and his mouth twisted in a half snarl as he looked at the water-slicked rock, hugging his arms around himself as though the water might leap over and petrify him.

When he didn't answer, Harper stumbled over and shook him. "Where are we, Fionn? Is this still a dream?"

He glanced around. "No. This is … I think I remember this place. Dark, damp, cold, hurting." Keeping her eyes firmly on the stalactites, Harper gave him an awkward side hug. He was shivering, eyes darting about. Shrugging off her coat, she wrapped it around his shoulders. He gave her a tight smile as he tugged it around himself.

It was better than nothing. At least she could look at him again.

"Sorry I broke the rules." Fionn rubbed an ear with the back of his hand, clutching the coat closed with his other.

"Not your fault." Harper returned his smile. "If you remember this place, I don't suppose you remember a way out?"

"The river." Fionn pointed towards the sound. "That's how … that's how I left before. He sent me in a box on a raft. It's my earliest memory." He scrunched up his nose, his tail jerking. "You should've run when I told you to, Harper."

Harper took his hand and squeezed it. "I'm here to save my sister. I'm not leaving without her. This is the right way. I saw the river in the vision the lady gave me. I've dreamt of running away from a cave exactly like this. You were there. I left you behind. I'm not leaving Grace and I'm not leaving you again either."

Tears glinted in the corners of his eyes. "Thank you." His voice choked as he gently headbutted her shoulder.

A passage led out of the cavern. It would be a tight fit for an adult human. *But a good size for a little girl and a cat.* "I don't think we have long before he finds us again. We need to find Grace and get out of here."

Harper went first, Fionn crawling behind her, hissing like a boiling kettle every time he got dripped on. His nails dug into her ankle, even through her cargo pants, as he clung on through the narrow tunnel. When she halted at its mouth, he waited behind her. His trembling shook her leg. She wasn't any more enamoured of the dark than he was, but his fear gave her strength—she wouldn't let him down again.

The room on the other side, for it was a room not merely another cave, had a small bed with a patchwork quilt hanging askew and a thin pillow at its head. A ragdoll sat up against the pillow, her lopsided smile almost a scowl. At the foot of the bed, a warped wooden chest sat open filled with musty and moulding linens that may once have been bedding and clothes. In one corner of the room, shelves were drilled into the rock. The lowest hung vertically, books scattered across the floor. The other two gripped the wall, the books on them slanted and haphazardly placed. A wooden door was the only other exit. Every reachable inch of wall was covered in images painted by an unsteady hand. The style, though rudimentary, was as familiar as handwriting.

Harper's arms trembled, threatening to give way under her. She couldn't breathe the musty air. Images overlaid each other in her vision, a cacophony of light.

A child, barely more than a toddler, huddled in the corner of the bed, tears streaming down her cheeks. Harper felt the hollow ache in the girl's chest, the fear that squeezed her heart.

The same girl, a few of years older, sitting and reading, a young boy at her side, pointing at letters drawn on individual pieces of paper. It hadn't taken him long to learn basics. Fionn squeezed past Harper, his tail bristling as he entered the room.

Tears as two older children cuddled together in a corner. What had been a place they stayed from time to time became their home. She had Seen it would be years before she returned to her parents' fire. A poor birthday gift. Tears drenched Harper's cheeks and she reached for Fionn's hand. Keeping her cat had been a boon. No one, not even the Protector, had known he was something more than an animal. But he'd learnt.

Painting on the walls. Painting spells. Painting things she Saw. Blood. Death. Power.

Violin music seeped through the air. Whether played now or merely a memory, Harper couldn't tell. It was so familiar. Always there. Her whole life. When she heard it, it made her whole. Overly so. Filled as though she might burst, another presence in her mind, in her skin.

She stood in the centre of the room inside a blood circle that glowed to her Sight. Black vapours rose from it. Something familiar yet alien. Old. Too much. Harper clutched her chest over her aching heart. Fionn wrapped his arms around her, holding her tight as her knees threatened to buckle.

"Harp. *Harper.* Wake up." He shook her urgently, her glazed violet eyes looking straight through him. "Harper!"

Grace's voice, a clarion call through time. *Harper Ashbury, you wake up right this moment.* Her sister, the general, always to be obeyed. The visions shattered, leaving Harper's chest feeling cracked but whole. The music remained.

"We lived here." Harper's fingers curled into Fionn's fur of their own accord and his tail wrapped around her waist.

"I think so. What did you See?"

"Me. Us. Learning from these books. Practising magic. Summoning ... something. We failed. I failed. I think I was ... asleep? Does that even make sense?"

"Not really." Fionn helped her sit up, then walked over to peer at the wall. "These sound funny. Maybe because they were drawn by a child. Their voice is young and incomplete."

"Sound?" Harper joined him.

"Yeah. You can't hear them?" He tilted his head at her.

"No?" She drew the word out, lilting to a question. "You can hear all drawings or just these ones?"

Fionn frowned at her. "All art. I sneak into galleries sometimes. You can't hear paintings and sculptures? Is that something humans can't do?"

"Yeah. I mean no. I mean ... humans can't hear art."

"Oh. Weird." Fionn poked one of the pictures, paint chipped by time but still recognisable as a dark-haired girl and a white cat. Between them an object had been drawn multiple times, overlapping, as though capturing in stills its metamorphosis. On the left, nearest the cat, was a child's depiction of a tree. It thinned in the middle with each subsequent image, the top elongating and the bottom rounding. On the far right, where the girl stood, it became a violin, fully transformed.

"Phantasos."

"Pardon?" Fionn stepped aside to let Harper examine the image.

"That's what I think of when I see this," Harper said, her brow furrowing. "In my vision, we were summoning something old, something powerful, but it didn't work. I painted this to illustrate what we were trying to do ..."

Harper circled the room in search of more clues. Other images were similar, blurred drawings of shapeshifting. Some objects, some creatures, some words—both Latin and a script she didn't know. Cyrillic, maybe, or Greek.

In the corner nearest the bed, were drawings so old they had chipped almost to non-existence. Other paintings disrespectfully overlapped them.

"I didn't draw these." Harper traced a finger around one of the most intact.

"Child, you will be a great Seer one day, better than I. You will go to the hallowed halls and you will serve the Protector where I failed. I am proud of you."

A sob rose in her throat to choke her. Fionn's hand on her shoulder grounded her against the onslaught of emotions from the memory.

"Grandmama. She was here, just like we were. She drew this when she was a child too. Before she married Grandpapa and had my mother and aunts. I remember. She told me about it when I was small."

"She escaped and made a new life and remembered this place? Did she ever tell you how?"

"I don't think she escaped. I think she was sent back to our people. She was proud to have been here, but sad she couldn't accomplish whatever task she'd been set. She thought I could. They gave me away, Fionn. They sent me here. Alone. Sacrificed to their so-called 'Protector.'"

Bile rose in her stomach, hot and acidic. It burned up her throat, sour on the back of her tongue. She clenched her fists, nails jabbing her palms. "They fucking *sent* me, Fionn. All this fucking hell we went through and they fucking *sent* me. They didn't *want* me. They aren't looking for me. They … they … they don't *love* me."

Breath came in choking gasps. Her chest was gripped in a crushing vice, innards herniating. Her throat clogged to bursting. Her brain was concrete sludge. The music swelled, humid and sultry after the cold, wet rock.

"Shut up!" Harper screamed, squashing her forehead to the ground, fists covering her ears. "Shutupshutupshutup." A wave of violet light crashed outward from her prone body. It passed through Fionn, raising all the hairs on his body. It hit the walls and kept going, disappearing to sight, leaving a lingering smell of ozone. In its wake, silence.

As Harper lay on the floor sobbing, Fionn brushed her hair off her face. He gently pried her hands away from her ears and uncurled each rigid finger. Her nails left gouges in her palms. Her own sacrifice for her people, her own agony.

"Harper? I'm sorry. We have to keep moving. We're running out of time."

Fionn's whisper slipped through the smog surrounding her brain. His fingers through her hair soothed her, giving her an inkling of why it comforted him so much to be stroked.

"I want you, Harper. I love you."

'I want you here. I don't care what those kids at school say. You're my sister and you're staying, same name or no. We love you.'

Her sister's voice ringing in her ears, as clear as if Grace leant over and whispered it to her again. Harper remembered sitting in the corner of the schoolyard, hugging her knees, completely alone. The other kids in class didn't understand. They teased her for being behind, for having no parents, no memories of summer holidays, Christmases, or birthdays.

Grace had promised her a million memories to make up for the ones she lost. A new home. A new family. Never alone again.

"Let's find this thing, kill it, and get out of here." Harper almost knocked Fionn over as she pushed on his shoulder to lever herself up.

"Kill it? Harper, that wasn't the plan. Grace—"

Fionn shrank away from her low growl, "It's the plan now."

Chapter Twenty-Seven

A Petal for Every Soul Who Falls

Anger pounded in Harper's skull, a panicked prisoner fighting to escape. She yanked the door open, ignoring its protesting wail and Fionn's corresponding mew.

The room beyond was vast. It could've swallowed the small bedroom many times over. Mist roiled on the ground and rolled down the walls like fine lace curtains floating in a summer breeze. But there was no summer here. Nor winter.

Time froze, as though every cell in her body stopped ageing—the absence of a sensation she'd never noticed before. Then time took a breath and ticked forward once again.

In the middle of the room was a raised dais upon which sat an ebony chaise lounge, a hulking shadow against the rusty stone. Plush cushions and silken drapes spilled over the couch, all black as the coal mines that riddled the hills. Tiny gemstones sewn on their covers caught the flickering light of torches so they sparkled like a star-clad, cloudless sky. Hundreds of blood-red poppy petals splattered across the ground.

As Harper crossed the threshold of the cavern, lethargy tugged at her limbs, muscles strained to take even a single step. Anger was too much effort. She clenched her jaw against an involuntary yawn. Her eyelids fluttered and dropped. Rubbing them hard, Harper forced her eyes open, ignoring the dull ache behind them.

"Fionn?" When she opened her mouth to speak, the yawn snuck out, stretching her lips, cracking them. Harper clapped a hand over her mouth. *A yawn lets the devil in.* Normally, she scoffed at the other archivists' superstitions, but here, in this impossible place, she couldn't dismiss them as easily.

"I'm here." Fionn's quiet voice at her shoulder calmed her. "Do you remember what this place is?"

"The home of sleep." Vague memories scratched at her mind. Forgotten lore and bedtime stories told by her mother. The intoxication of dreaming while lying in that same chaise lounge. Bits of her research in the cathedral archives drifted back to her, and the strange Latin she'd uttered when trapped in the tree. *Somnia sunt salvus.* Hypnos, the Greek god of sleep, and Somnus, his Roman equivalent. She'd read Ovid in school, but scarcely remembered his *Metamorphoses* now. *Sleep lived by a river. Lethe? In a cave surrounded by poppies. Lying in bed surrounded by his children. Why would he have left his cave and come to England? Did the Romans bring their gods with them back when York was Eboracum and leave one behind when they withdrew?*

"Your home, beloved Seer."

One moment he wasn't there, the next he'd been there the whole time. His form lay languid on the chaise lounge. One arm swung free, draped over the end. His feet were curled into the silken sheet beneath him. Humanoid, but nowhere near human. His form rippled with minute changes from second to second. Tall, then short, then stocky, then thin. Hairy, then smooth. Legs of a faun, of a horse, a human again. Five fingers, three, nine. Harper's stomach churned, seasick on the rolling images. Only his eyes were unchanging.

Black irises surrounded poppy-red pupils which dilated, sucking Harper into their depths. She was peripherally aware of a sly smile tugging his flushed lips, of his nostrils flaring, his fingers grasping.

"I always knew you would come home, my Seer." His voice was melodious, soothing. Real, like nothing else about him was, save his eyes.

"This is not my home." Harper dragged each word from deep within and forced them through gritted teeth.

"This is where you were conceived, where you were born, where you grew, where you learnt, where you formed. Generation by generation. Your flesh is of my stone, your blood is of my water, your soul is of my being. This is your home."

"Is that what you do? Keep humans like pets? Some kind of sick breeding zoo? Why?" Even as she asked, Harper knew the answer. To dream. To See. Generation by generation. *Child, you will be a great Seer one day, better than I am.* Each newborn babe destined to be more powerful than her mother and her grandmother, all conceived and born in this darkness. Had she stayed, would she have become like them? Grateful to a creature who kept her captive, who played with her life?

Her anger surged back, breaking the lethargic spell. Her Sight blazed, agonising, keeping her awake. Her chest heaved with forgotten breath. "How dare you? This is not my home. My home is with my sister. Where is she?"

His legs swung free of the couch yet didn't touch the ground or move as he floated to her. "Your family is here, my Seer." His voice was seductive, a purr in her ear. The darkness obscured his body, making him little more than shadow again. A counter-melody jingled, off-key, in the background.

"She doesn't belong to you." Fur bristling with indignation, Fionn grabbed Harper's hand, dragging her out of the cloud of darkness. At his touch, the boundary between dreamscape and wakening solidified further.

"Does she belong to you, pathetic little mewling?" The voice took on a bitter tinge, at odds with the lullaby tone it used on Harper.

"She belongs to herself," Fionn spat.

Harper gave Fionn a reassuring smile. "I do. I left this place and woke up. He is a dream and I've been learning to control my dreams." She turned her gaze on the flickering form. Although it still warped, it seemed smaller, becoming less and less human. It blurred between forms: plant, insectoid, and creatures Harper had only seen in illustrations locked away in the archives. The music grew frenzied, but quieter, as though the thrashing violinist's tune struggled to penetrate the rock.

Harper tugged Fionn closer so she could whisper in his ear, "Get paint. I'll distract him." *If I can use paint and music like the images in our bedroom, maybe I can vanquish him.*

He squeezed her hand, then sidled away. When their fingers slipped apart, the line between realms blurred again. Harper flexed her fingers and concentrated. The strength of Fionn's magic at the Market had stunned her, but here, in a world on the border of dreams, her power blazed as it never had before. She no longer needed him. Magic fizzed in her stomach and raced through her veins. Just as out in the snow with One, lightning collected at her fingertips. Heat stoked behind her eyes.

Faltering before her decisiveness, the figure continued to blur from one shape to another. His physical form might have been weakened, but his voice had lost none of its power. "Are you forgetting your real family, Harper

Rhapsody Ashbury? You do me wrong. The outside world has twisted your thoughts. I saved your people when they wandered lost. I freed them from the grasp of the mare and brought dreams of magic and beauty where once horror reigned. I protected them from the humans who would slay them for their magic. Here, dreamers and seers have been allowed to flourish."

"Flourish for your benefit," Harper snapped. "Whatever that is." *Leonora prophesied I could free our people from your influence. I have to believe that's true. They may have abandoned me, but I won't abandon them. Not even if it means taking down the god of sleep, himself.*

Harper strode towards the form. He splintered into a murder of crows, talons flashing. She raised her hands to protect her face and head from the onslaught of claw and wing. They buffeted and scratched, sharp beaks aimed at her eyes.

"Begone."

At Fionn's shout, blinding light burst over her and the birds vanished. When Harper lowered her arms, Fionn was standing next to her, a silver glow surrounding him. His hands were empty; the paint in their bedroom must've dried and gone years ago. The Protector was once again reclining on the chaise lounge. His form morphed slower and his eyes bored holes through her. On the dais, he was more real, although whether that meant he was more in the dreamscape or the wakening, Harper wasn't sure.

"Would you cast your family to human wolves again?" he taunted. "That is what will happen if you bring them back to the realm you ran away to when you turned your back on them. You have spent your time there in hiding, never allowed to be who you really are. There is magic in all our people. Here, they can practice and enjoy their powers. They have food, clothing, art and music. They love and are loved. Out there, they would starve or become a spectacle. They would be hanged and hated. Stay with me, Seer. Protect them with me."

His words plucked at Harper's heart. Despite her fury, she longed to see her family and there was an undeniable truth to his words. If she saved them from him, the human world offered no kinder a fate. For a moment she was a lost child who wanted nothing more than to run to her mother.

She blinked back tears and threaded her fingers through Fionn's. He was real, maybe the only real thing in the whole cavern. If she let the Protector sway her with his dreams, then Grace would die. Anguish, guilt, and grief rioted inside her, but she forced her voice, and her heart, to be cold. For now, nothing mattered but her sister.

"Whatever magic you're doing isn't going to work on me. I won't let it. I won't be seduced by your lies. Why should I care about my birth family?

They didn't want me. They gave me to you, sacrificed me to keep themselves safe. I just want to get my sister and go home. If they're so happy to use their magic to help you, then why do you need me?"

"Not all are blessed with the gift of Sight. Fewer still are blessed with the ability to Hear, to Touch, Taste, and Smell. You are the first in generations with the true potential to become a dreamwalker. All your senses are attuned, your magic is stronger than any who came before."

"Your brother?" *Phantasos.* The name wandered through Harper's mind again. *Not Somnus himself, one of his thousand sons?* She wished she'd explored the possibility further as she could recall little mention of them.

"You are starting to remember. It brings us closer. I protect this place so none who leave here remember when they return to the world of the quick, but the magic also stopped you finding your way home. I tried to find you—"

"And when you couldn't, you killed women who were like me," Harper spat, rage boiling up again. "My kin, my friends, innocent strangers."

"It was … unfortunate."

"Unfortunate?" Harper shrieked. "You killed at least seven women and you're telling me it was '*unfortunate*'?"

"I came to them in your world, in their dreams, because you forced me to. When the Hiding weakened, I was near to finding you on my own. I visited your dreams. I almost reached you. Until the cat interfered. Then you vanished. I could not find your dreams again. So I followed the path of memory left by your power."

"Why kill them?" Harper asked bitterly. "Why not visit their dreams and see their memories of me?"

"My remaining brothers would have found me had anything lingered, or the dreamings may have been reported to the human authorities. Either would put both us and our people at risk. I needed what they saw, not just what they dreamt. Without a true seer, the magic demands their blood and eyes. Also, I could not wipe their memories as I could those who leave this place. Even the little cat, when I sent him as tithe to the caretaker of this land. Good riddance. He would not reveal your location to me when you deserted your folk, and his blood did not yield the answers I hoped."

"His … blood? What did … what did you do to him?" Harper wanted to punch the devious smile right off his face.

"What did *we* do to him, Seer? Do you remember?"

"I …" *No.* Horrors flashed behind her eyes. *No. I don't want those memories.*

Fionn squeezed her hand as his tail swished against her legs. "Don't listen to him, Harper. We're friends."

Harper met the Protector's poppy gaze. "I won't let you distract me. Stay out of my head."

"Enough of this," he growled, his voice harsh and demanding after the silken tones. "You are here now and we have work to do. In a wait of millennia, your little rebellion is but a snap of the fingers. The wayward child has returned. It is time to embrace your magic again. Completing the ritual will help you remember."

"My magic is fine without you," Harper snarled. Despite her fury, she feared he spoke the truth about protecting folk from the Queen's Guard. His threat hung over Grace like the sword of Damocles, but Harper sensed she had something he wanted every bit as badly as she wanted her sister's safety. *Maybe if I find out what exactly he wants, I can get a bargaining chip of my own.* "How can I complete something I don't remember? If you want my help, you'll have to explain better than that."

"Very well," he said. "You remember Phantasos. He was the last we summoned and caught. My father was the god Sleep. Hypnos or Somnus your kind called him then. He was the son of Nyx, or Night. He had many siblings; among them Death, Darkness, Destruction, and Doom. My mother was Pasithea, goddess of hallucination. As a child of sleep and wakening I may traverse both realms. One thousand sons, my father had, the Somnia. Only three were of import to him. Humans knew them as Phantasos, Icelos, or Phobetor as mortals called him, and Morpheus."

Shadows deepened and lengthened. Torches guttered as he uttered the final name.

"The rest of us were of no concern, delegated to the dreams of commoners, never to enter myth or fable. Each resembled a different aspect. Some took the guise of written words, others the guise of feelings, more still took the guise of birds, beasts, and nature, yet none were so talented or so lauded as those three. I was the dream of music and much beloved of the Muses. I could lure a man from his bed to death on the shore with a siren's song. I could calm a troubled mind, rouse a spirit to battle, or bring ardour to a loveless union.

"I went to the dreams of the Sibyls, in Delphi, in Phrygia, and in Cimmerium, a place I knew well for one of the entrances to my father's lair was there. Each one of them foretold that I would outlast my brothers, becoming more powerful, more beloved, until none but Morpheus and I remained.

"Where once my brothers slept around my father's bedside, now I scatter the ground with petals, one for each of them I have conquered, for each new skill I have learnt. Nine hundred and ninety-seven petals adorn this floor, three brought here by you, my most precious Seer. Your mother had the power, but the dreams were driving her mad. I syphoned it from her into you as you lay in her womb. Your grandmother helped me banish my brother who was most like me, he existed as poetry and had the favour of Calliope. Together they evaded me for many years, but your grandmother Saw him and brought him into my domain.

"My brothers wanted to reign supreme. They were cruel to those with the power to challenge them, those of the Folk and humans who possessed the dreaming. They caused dreams that set humans upon one another and against the Folk. Not so I. I nurtured the talents of dreams to protect human and Folk alike."

"Why did you need human seers?" Harper asked.

"You can predict. My father made it so we could not see each other in dreams, unless we went together and knew the other already there. Few mortals can perceive us and I have chosen the strongest among you to nurture that Sight. Your gaze can pierce the Veil, see truth from lie, even cut through the shroud of death. Your magic can imprison that which is too ephemeral for hands to hold."

"And now you want me to help you destroy the last two?"

"Not destroy. Transform."

"Seems like a fine line to me," Harper scoffed.

"The greater my power, the safer your people. Let us resume your training, I wish to see what you have learnt."

Harper and Fionn exchanged a glance. Her circle had held the Ouse, killed her, but this creature was so much older and had feasted for centuries on his brothers' lives. She didn't know if her magic could beat him, here in his own domain, not even with Fionn's help. Their last encounter had almost killed him.

"I will show you something I've learnt after Grace is free." Harper stood her ground, feet apart, the handle of her machete digging into her spine, waiting. Not that she thought it would help much against a creature with no static form.

"If you want her, then See her. Summon her. You have the power." He gestured towards the back of the room where the ground did not run quite up to the edge, instead being interrupted by a stream over a metre in width. "The river flows through her sleep."

Wary of a trap, she nonetheless approached the stream. If the stream did indeed run through Grace's dreams, maybe she could See a firmer vision of where her sister was imprisoned. Just as with Fionn, she sensed a truth behind all the Somnia told her, even if it was only truth as he perceived it.

As she peered into the water's depths, a black cloud loomed over her shoulder, then Fionn's hand slipped from hers. A skeletal hand gripped her shirt and the scent of poppies clawed at her consciousness.

"Grace." She tried to fight him off but her limbs were too heavy to do more than bat ineffectually at his ever-changing form. Her eyes closed and her leaden body fell.

"No!" Fionn's desperate cry was punctuated by the tearing of Harper's shirt as the cat ripped her from the Somnia's hold. Darkness and water rushed to meet her, but sleep took her before their embrace. The last thing she heard was a pitiful mew.

Harper awoke floating on her back. Everything was black as a clouded night with no moon or stars piercing the stillness. Her usual panic was absent as she drifted. Now she knew the monster who hid in the darkness. No matter what he threw at her, she would look him in the eye and face it.

She was still in the caves, her Sight peered through the darkness at stalactites glistening above her like teeth poised to chomp down. She remembered this water. A stolen boat. Her and Fionn rushing downstream on a frothing current. A failed escape attempt. The stream was calm now, serene as sleep. Her limbs were too heavy to move, clothes soaked through by the frigid water, yet she floated despite all her senses telling her she should sink.

She thought of Grace, cold and damp, alone somewhere without Sight to light her way, and some of the feeling returned to her body. Gravity reasserted itself, her natural buoyancy overcome by heavy clothes. Harper splashed to the side and pulled herself up on a low ledge. It only ran a few metres but she remembered they appeared periodically, each leading to a network of caves deeper in the hillside.

"Where are you, Grace?" It would take years to explore everywhere: she'd barely scratched the surface as a child and Grace didn't have years. Unless this was some sleeping beauty story where she'd awaken after a hundred years not a day older when someone appeared to rescue her. No. No one would come for a De Santos save another of the family, who would fall into the same trap. "C'mon, Harper. Think."

Her necklace. Her hand closed around the silver Celtic cross, a gift from Grace on her eighteenth birthday. A symbol of a faith she was not sure if she believed or not, but she did believe in Grace. If a Hiding spell used representations of the senses it was dulling, maybe a finding spell could use representations of what it searched for. For Grace's sake, and because it couldn't hurt, she said a quick prayer.

Fionn had told her magic could be drawn in water; he used the method to catch fish down at the river knowing the magic would evaporate. Working fast, Harper drew a compass on the ground, symbolic, not caring which way was true north, and dangled the cross over it. The chain stiffened as the pendant swung south-southwest back towards the water. Harper kicked off her shoes and extraneous clothes. She left behind all but a couple of her weapons. Those, she left loose so she could shake them off if the water dragged too much. Taking a deep breath, she plunged back in.

At every waypoint, she repeated the spell until her limbs ached like she'd spent all day in the gym and her eyelids were drooping from weariness. She'd lost count of the number of stops she'd made when the cross swung away from the water, deeper into the darkness of the caves.

Sight burning, she only saw Grace, the image from her vision. No fear was greater than the fear her sister would die.

The path dead-ended. Behind the prison bars of stalactite and stalagmite, Grace lay. Her hair drifted in a stream running by her head. Blood dripped into the water like the red river of Harper's vision. Grace's eyelids were closed, eyes roving beneath them, lost in a dream. Rusty iron bound her to the rock. With a cry, Harper darted forward, but lips of rock closed over the teeth.

"Now you know she lives, you will surrender and stay or she will rot here forever." The Somnia's voice sent chills skittering across Harper's body. Away from his throne, his appearance was closer to the misty form she half remembered from the market. Her Sight edged him in violet fire.

"Where's Fionn?" Harper planted herself between Grace's prison and the fluctuating shadow. "Grace and Fionn and I are all leaving. Together."

"Beloved, I am your protector. I will not harm you. Nor shall any ill come to this human, if you aid me willingly in the protection of our people. She dreams of pleasant things. Your kitten shall be sent home to his master. Keeping him will cause you trouble with a higher power."

His voice held no sway over her here. Although Harper doubted Fionn had intended to topple her into the river when he attacked the Somnia, the act had taken her away from his seat of power. Here, they were on even ground. "Keeping her imprisoned, in a dream and in this cave, is already harming her. I saw her blood. And I will not let you send Fionn back to a master who hurts him. Wherever you have hidden him, I will find him, just like I found Grace. I will banish you. By Moon and Starlight, I will banish you. *I will banish you.* I did it at the Market. If I did the same to your brothers, then I can conquer you too."

His laughter was the fabric of her nightmares. The ground warped at the Somnia's feet and a twisted vine rose from the stone. It held within its grasp a violin, and Harper almost reached out to take it. The wooden instrument was painted with white roses across its body like her violin at home. But it wasn't her violin. She snatched her hand back. She would take nothing from him, enter no covenant unknowingly.

He took the instrument in his long-fingered hand and began to play. She recognised the tune even as her head drooped. She'd heard it in her dreams, on the streets of York, in the Soul Market. She'd heard it as a child, sending her to the dreamscape to See past, present, and future. Within its notes was a command, unspoken words that guided her thoughts. Her eyes closed, vision filled with a purple haze of dancing lights. She could See through her eyelids. Every note glittered in the air between them.

"I'm … not … listening to … you." Harper wrapped a hand around a stalagmite to stay upright. With the other she drew her machete. She let her head sink and stumbled forward as if falling under his spell. Magic tugged her limbs and she landed harder than intended, but training with Grace and her siblings meant she was used to ignoring a few bruises.

Harper drove the machete towards the violin. As it swept up, sparkling notes rebounded off its polished surface. The Somnia faltered, struck by his own lethargic lullaby. Harper smashed the machete through the violin, though it fractured her heart to break any instrument. The music died with a scream as though she'd thrust her weapon through a human chest. When Harper wrenched her machete aside, it yanked the splintered instrument from the Somnia's hand to smash upon the ground.

She swung the machete again, aiming for his arm. Crotchets and quavers trailed in its wake like the light of a sparkler. As Harper feared, the weapon phased straight through him. She stepped back, guard up. "I can still banish you with magic. You have no hold on me anymore."

"You cannot harm me, Seer. I am ancient as the first dream and the first note of music. You destroyed a tool. I have many more." His figure warped, no longer humanoid. The shadow of his form expanded though his eyes and the violin bow remained. Wary of the darkness that almost claimed her before, Harper retreated until her back hit Grace's prison.

"By Moon and Starlight, I banish you." She thrust the words in front of her like a shield, but the shadow didn't falter. Fingers stretched along the wall, groping for her. Pitch pooled at her feet, threatening to suck her in. The violin's bow pointed at her like an arrow about to take flight.

"By Moon and Starlight …"

"… I banish you." Fionn chanted with her. Harper could See him on the other side of the darkness. He was bedraggled, wet hair clinging to his face, tail plastered thin as a rat's, still wrapped in Harper's coat. Blood dripped down one leg. He faced the Somnia, shaking from head to toe, from cold or fear or both, but he held his head high.

Laughter surrounded them and the Somnia's voice echoed, "Pathetic mewling, you couldn't defeat me before and you cannot defeat me now." A new shape coalesced, close enough to reach out and touch Harper. He was as he'd appeared before, shifting rapidly from form to form, save burning eyes that held hers. The bow remained, held like a rapier.

"I held you off long enough for her to escape," Fionn almost spat the words. The Somnia's gaze stayed locked on Harper.

A different darkness spread behind the cat. Harper opened her mouth to yell a warning. Too late. Fionn stepped back into it … and appeared in front of her. Harper reached for him but his splayed hand pushed her back. Although the shadows tried to suck his feet in like quicksand, he kept moving, always staying between her and the apparition.

"I remember, now I'm here," Fionn continued. "I remember all of it. The experiments. The torture. The nightmares you gave us. How you warped her mind to think you saved her people, until her brother disappeared and she realised what you truly were. He challenged you, and you banished him."

Harper's eyes flicked to Fionn's feet as magic tugged at her. His magic, created from hers. Her Sight could perceive what the Somnia could not—a spell traced in Fionn's blood upon the rock.

"Fionn, no." Her hushed voice came out louder than she intended but the Somnia's glare was locked on the cat.

"You lie to all of them," Fionn hissed. "You pay tribute to my master and you will always pay tribute to someone, even if you absorb the whole of the dreamscape. You think you can control everything from there, but the power of the wakening will always be greater."

The bow flashed as Fionn closed his spell. It exploded in light and the wail of sirens.

Harper yanked Fionn back as she parried the bow. Her Sight was dazzled. Her Hearing rang from his spell. A hole opened, the swirling black of Fionn's portals, and he propelled her through. It closed immediately, the teeth of the prison now between them and the Somnia. Harper scrambled to clutch Grace's body to her.

Light and sound faded. Fionn lay on the ground, cat-shaped, swathed in her coat and his own blood. Grace's eyes were still closed, her chest scarcely falling and rising. Harper hurried to pick the lock of the chain that bound her sister.

Darkness gathered, a billowing cloud of the coming storm as the Somnia's energy suffused the cave.

Fionn dragged himself over and tapped the air to open a portal next to Harper. His torn flesh hurt as though it were her own.

"Me … r … ow. Mau." *Go. I'll defend you.*

"Never." She grabbed his tail and Grace's hand and dragged them through the portal. It closed behind her as darkness crashed over it, leaving only angry poppy-red eyes that watched her until all faded from view.

CHAPTER TWENTY-EIGHT

A Deal

Grace lay unconscious on the grass, Fionn beside her, both bleeding.

"Saqib, AJ, help!" Harper screamed towards the house. The neighbours' lights clicked on, but she didn't care. Didn't care what they saw, what they said, so long as Grace and Fionn were okay.

Saqib hit the lights as he ran out. He knelt at Grace's side and shook her. Her head lolled to the side, eyes closed. The light revealed a sticky wound leaking into Grace's hair, just as Harper had Seen in her vision. When she turned to check Fionn, her eyes filled with tears. She'd known he was bleeding, he used blood to draw whatever that flash-bang spell was, but she hadn't realised the extent. Though she'd parried the last blow, whatever fight ensued while she searched for Grace had severely damaged the slender cat. Her blood had healed his magical wounds before—the dark magic from the Market and the burns of the dreaming, yet when she tried to feed it to him, his physical wounds remained.

"Get AJ to call a healer," Harper ordered Saqib. She hoped they would know enough to help a cat as well as Grace, otherwise she'd have to take him to the clinic and hope there was no way of telling he wasn't a normal feline. Assuming AJ could persuade someone from his coven to come out at all.

Saqib dashed in as AJ opened the kitchen door, nearly toppling the taller man. Heresy slithered between them and slunk over the grass to settle on Fionn's wound. It sucked at him, his ash getting caught in the blood. The wound seeped, then the flow stopped.

"How did you …?"

"He and I are both of your blood. I can trick his body into the illusion of being uninjured, for a short time. Much as it distresses me to aid the not-a-cat."

"Where did you go?"

Heresy bristled and Fionn gave a soft moan of pain.

"I could not enter the realm you went to. I returned here." Heresy shrunk, teeth bared. "That was three days ago."

"Three days?! What's wrong with Grace?" Harper asked AJ who was kneeling next to her, checking her pulse and breathing.

"She's asleep." He pinched her cheek but Grace didn't stir. "Possibly concussed. We should take her to the hospital, Harper. Tell them you were fighting something for the Council. The archbishop will back you up."

A glow surrounded Fionn.

"Don't—" Harper shouted, too late. Heresy clung to Fionn's changing form, tendrils spread like Frankenstein stitches.

"She's … she's still under … the spell …" Fionn wheezed out. He tried to sit, but AJ placed a hand on his shoulder. He leant past AJ to stroke Grace's hair, glowed again, then winced, his head lolling like he was dizzy. His eyes were unfocussed as he blinked at Harper. "I healed … her wounds. I can't … heal … the sle-sleeping spell … You must …" He coughed up specks of blood. "You must … defeat the caster … to release her. We … escaped … by luck. He won't … stop … hunting you."

"You healed …?" Harper didn't have time to wonder at his magic. She had to trust him. "Can my blood heal you again? I tried giving it to you, but do I have to do something special?"

Fionn flopped back on the grass, eyes closed. "It healed … some … magical … damage. Not all. Too much … physical … damage."

"Should we still call a healer?" Saqib asked.

"I must … go … home." Fionn's fingers twitched, as though he wanted to raise his hand but couldn't.

"No. Fionn. Don't." Harper grabbed his hand and clutched it to her chest. "Please don't go back to a place they'll hurt you more."

"You need … your strength. I'll … come back." He slipped his hand, slick with Grace's blood, out of hers. The portal he opened was a shimmery silver.

"Fionn, please ..." Harper begged, terrified if he stepped through, she'd never see him again. He came back last time only to get hurt again. His master might not let him go again.

"You have some ... something more im-important ..." He shifted back to cat, then darted through the portal with a speed that belied his injuries. It snapped shut behind him.

Fury burned inside Harper. The Somnia almost killed her sister. He'd wounded her oldest friend and sold him to a sadist. This 'protector' banished her brother, and made her his tool. If she had to vanquish him to wake Grace up, then she would. Ancient godkin or not, he would soon be dead.

"Where are you going?" Saqib asked in confusion as Harper pushed past him into the house.

"Look after Grace," Harper said. "I'm going to find out how to defeat that thing before I forget what I saw there. The Somnia used me to trap his brothers and help him absorb their power. I painted it on the walls. Dreams to find them, music to conquer them. I can control dreams, kind of, and I know who to ask about the music."

She dashed upstairs, strapped her violin case to her back, then ran out the house towards the Ouse. Words replayed in her head, of a meeting not so long ago although it felt like a lifetime.

'Wait. Help us. Please.'

'I am. And I will. When the time comes, you will know what to ask me and I know the price you must pay for it.'

The Foss was right. The time had come and she did know. Whatever the price, she would pay it.

Harper skidded to a halt at the point where the two rivers met. On one side, the clear greyish waters of the Ouse flowed without life. On the other, the mossy green Foss teamed with energy.

"Foss?" She leant over the metal bridge to shout down at the water. "Foss? I need you. You said you'd be here."

"And I am." His soft voice made her jump. He stood on the shore between the two rivers, as beautiful as she remembered.

"You knew," Harper accused. "You knew a music demon was hunting me and killing people."

"I knew your fate was tied to music from the moment I saw you in the Shambles during Advent. The demon you think to defeat will not be the only one simply because it is the most apparent."

"What can you teach me and how fast?"

His face lit with a smile like the sun rising. One's curves flashed in Harper's mind and she repressed the image.

"Typically, I would expect a sacrifice from you upfront to determine the nature of my teachings, but given your skills will benefit us both, I shall waive that for today. That does not mean there will be no price."

"Noted," Harper said through gritted teeth.

"Follow me." He flashed her a smile before he stepped off the edge of the embankment and disappeared into the water without a ripple.

Still wet from the Somnia's cave, Harper stepped into the water without allowing herself to think of anything other than Grace's closed eyes and Fionn's white tail matted crimson with his blood.

Cold shocked through her system, dragging a gasp of murky water into her lungs. A hand clutched her ankle and she kicked out. Something squished as she landed a solid blow. The grip tightened, hauling her down despite her struggles. Her lungs burned and the world went black.

Images flashed before her, a thousand or more yet in a handful of seconds.

Grace, laughing, knuckleduster glittering on her fist. Grace fighting. Grace sparring with her brothers. Grace, a teenager, dark hair sprawled across Harper's pillow as they snuggled together, Harper's shield against dark and nightmares.

She saw Father De Santos emerging from the mists. Her own bare feet, crisscrossed with red, startling in a black-and-white world.

Nothing but mist.

Then eyes piercing the glimmering, every hue, lidless and staring.

Wet feet slapping against stone.

A cat hissing followed by a sharp crack and a pitiful mewl.

A boat rushing downstream, twinkling rocks flashing by like stars.

A cauldron bubbling. Her blood dripping from striped fingertips into the broiling mixture.

A violin in her hands, blood slicking the strings as she played the same tune over and over.

And over.

And over.

And over.

Harper awoke with a jolt to staccato notes. The tune was wild, free. A song of windy hilltops and cascading waterfalls tumbling down a dale. It made Harper's feet itch with the need to dance and her fingers followed the music on an invisible violin.

The Foss played with his back to her. His movements pulled his thin shirt tight across his shoulders. White material, translucent with water, clung to his muscles. Harper tore her eyes away from his bouncing curls and looked around. She was half sprawled on an embankment by a mossy green river. Nearby, a mill stood silent, waterwheel motionless, and behind that a waterfall tinkled, the only movement in the unnaturally still landscape. The other side of the river, and beyond the mill, was shrouded in fog. Harper stared into it, willing her Sight to reveal what lay beyond, but all she Saw were the pinprick lights of wary animal eyes.

The tune came to an end and the Foss turned. "This is my domain. Your magic will not show you anything save what I wish you to See."

Harper clambered to her feet. "Did the Ouse have a place such as this? Somewhere a bit of her spirit might still remain?"

He gave her a mirthless smile. "If she did, do you not think her tributaries would have tried to return her? She was the river and the river was her. I am but a latecomer to this land, brought across the sea by marauding forces. My kind are tied to waterways, mills, and music, but we are not the embodiment of them. The Foss stood empty, banished long ago just as the Ouse stands empty now. I took his role as caretaker in addition to my own as maestro and I made this new land my home."

"You came with the Vikings?"

He inclined his head. "As you call them, yes. Long have I taught music to folk, although customers have been fewer in recent centuries. Yet there are always those hungry to learn. You are not the first of your folk I have seen."

Harper's hand rose to her throat. "You mean my family? The ones kept prisoner by the Somnia? Did you meet my cousin when he sent her?"

"I met one many centuries ago. A seer she was, too, and a talented musician. It was a great loss when she took her own life, flying from the cathedral tower to splatter across the stones below, violin crushed beneath her."

Blood rushed to Harper's head, roaring in her ears. A memory of the vision she'd had in the astronomy tower and then again on the steps of the cathedral.

"More recently another came through," the Foss continued, "maybe five and ten years ago. Merely a boy, still with his voice high as a songbird and his fingers lithe and nimble. I gave him all I had to give and he stayed a year and a day under my tutelage."

"What happened to him?" Harper clutched at the Foss' sleeve.

"I know not where he went after he left me, save the strains of his music I hear on the wind that tell me he yet lives."

Harper's heart leapt in her throat. Her brother had challenged the Somnia. Although an illusion, her parents had spoken of a banished brother too. If he was out there in the world, not under the Somnia's control, he may know how to defeat him.

"Nay, Seer. The boy could not free your people. He came with that thought but Usa told him otherwise. She and the Swale have spoken often of the dreamworld that drifts along through their waters. Only one who can See, anticipate, control the dreamscape, can defeat him."

"Only me." Harper snapped the words, bitter, not against the messenger but against the message nonetheless.

"Only you, unless you would make them wait another five hundred years."

Harper closed her eyes, fists balled at her side. She wanted to seek out her brother lost in this world, but her sister needed her first. "I don't have a year and a day. My sister is still under his control and my family have been imprisoned long enough. They may not have wanted me, but I cannot leave them enslaved to him. I know what you are, a fossegrim, no? My studies say you can give me your gifts in a single night, if you desire."

"And so I shall, but on one condition."

Harper pursed her lips. There was always a condition with supes.

"You shall find a new spirit for the Ouse, as I fulfilled the role for the Foss, and if you cannot find one to cleanse her, then you shall take her place."

"A bit open-ended. How exactly does someone take her place? What do they need to do? How long do I have?"

"From now until the days are balanced once again. This tale began with a death on the night of the autumnal equinox last year. It must be concluded before the moon sets on the vernal equinox else the river may decay past the point of no return."

"That's only six or seven weeks. How am I supposed to find someone to take on a role like this in such a short time?"

"It is my offer. Take or leave it as you wish, but know I shall not make another."

Although the parental warmth she'd experienced up in the hills was no more than a dream, it trickled into the empty spaces in her heart. She couldn't leave her parents or her brother, the boy she'd Seen in the dreamscape. She couldn't leave Grace, no matter if the Foss asked for her life in return.

"I'll do it."

CHAPTER TWENTY-NINE

My Kingdom for a Tune

Harper was bone weary as she turned her back on the joined rivers and trudged home. The finger pads of her left hand were raw and red. Dried blood coated her hands and mingled with the stains of Fionn's left on her sodden clothing. In her right hand, she clutched a violin. It was the lush green of the forest on a wet morning, etched with a chaos of leaves and flowers. Its base was broad and sweeping, with narrow hips and flared shoulders, all more accentuated than on an acoustic violin. The Foss had assured her she needed no amp for the electric instrument. The bow hung from her waistband, glittering emerald matching the instrument.

She'd expected a lesson in how to draw some magic from the violin, a bespelled tune or way of playing. Instead, the Foss had dragged her fingers over the strings of his violin until the wounds were so deep she could see white bone. Her stomach heaved at the memory and she was glad she hadn't eaten since God knows when. *Eat something, you need your strength,* Grace bossed in the back of her mind. Always the general, always the big sister, even when she was pure imagination. In all the myriad universes, Harper couldn't imagine Grace being anything else.

The wounds healed quickly, still itching as tissue continued to knit back together, and by the time she was home they were mere scratches. The

Foss hadn't told her what to play, although she'd begged for a tune, and he hadn't let her practice.

He had handed her the new violin, more the spirit of a violin than real instrument with its strange shape. Harper didn't ask how he came to be in possession of the violin she'd admired in the music store during Advent.

"You chose your weapon well. It is of an era he does not know, crafted by masters. Do not play until you see him or he may learn of your new power. Catch him unawares. Then play the wind in the trees, the cascade of the water, the rumblings of the earth, the heat of the fire, and the sparkle of ether. He is old, but not older than the elements nor than the dreamscape itself. You can align the realms if you so choose."

Harper clenched her fist. She had no idea how to play the elements as he suggested. She hoped he had more to gain than the enjoyment of seeing her lose. It was a roundabout revenge if his hope was to punish her for the manslaughter of the Ouse.

Align the realms … Something clicked in her weary mind. Maybe Alfred had given her the answer without even realising what it was she faced. Or maybe he knew far more than she'd ever suspected.

When she reached the house, all was quiet. No sarcasm greeted her at the door in a silken voice although the peephole was black as night, indicating Heresy was present in it. Harper poked her head around AJ's bedroom door when no one responded to her knock. He was always up at night. Yet he lay with his head on his keyboard, eyes scrunched shut.

In the lounge, Saqib had crashed out in an armchair. Harper knelt next to her friend and shook his shoulder.

"Saqib? How's Grace? Saqib? Wake up, Saqib."

His eyes roved beneath their lids and his muscles spasmed, but he stayed lost deep in a dream.

The kitchen was empty so Harper ran straight upstairs. Grace lay on her bed, still asleep, her condition unchanged. In Harper's bed, Fionn lay curled up foetal, in human form, his tail wrapped around him. Harper touched his neck to check his pulse and he stirred.

"Haaaarrrrrperrrrrr?" His voice came out in a long purr, more cat than human.

"Fionn? Are you awake? Are you healed? I can't get anyone else to stir. Even Heresy seems to be asleep."

He stretched, wincing, his hand flying to his leg where he'd been injured. The clothes he wore were unblemished and Harper couldn't see if he'd received treatment. He blinked sleepily up at her. When he spoke, his words were sluggish and strained as though his tongue were numb. "They are under a spell. He attacked the house while you were gone. Master knew. Sent me back. Heard Somnia's voice in my sleep. Won't let go until you go back." He stretched and yawned, drawing his lips back over sharp teeth, then chittered as the movement pulled at his wounds.

"Fionn." She shook his shoulder as his eyes closed again. He purred and leant his cheek against her hand but didn't awaken.

Harper pulled out the book *Of Realms and Shadows*. She'd studied it enough that now she could skim to the parts she needed–descriptions of how the dreamscape met the wakening and of how a shadow lay over them both, the ever-changing in-between realm, Saol Eadrainn, and how music could be the keystone of a bridge between realms.

Scared, but determined, Harper put the book away, then shook Fionn's shoulder again. "Fionn? Can you open a portal for me? I know what to do. I think. I don't have time to go by public transport and hike. Fionn?"

He rubbed his cheek against her hand with a soft purr. "I'm coming with you." His tongue darted out, licking the dried blood from her fingertips.

"You're injured. I'll do this alone. I just need the portal."

"I'm healed." Fionn pushed himself up on his elbows, jaw tight. His gaze sharpened as he looked at her properly for the first time. "Master healed me and your blood helps keep me with you."

"You're not healed, Fionn. You're clearly still hurting." Harper's throat constricted and she blinked back tears. He was too pale, too thin, wincing with every movement.

"Pain and damage aren't the same thing." He stared into her eyes, his mouth a thin, stubborn line. "My damage is healed. We are blood. I was with you at the start. I will be with you when you win."

A white glow surrounded him as he shifted and shrank into the blankets. Then Fionn opened a portal and trotted through. His gait was awkward and Harper's heart hurt thinking about what he said. *'Pain and damage aren't the same thing.'* What had his master done to him?

Yet, despite the risks, she was glad she didn't have to go alone. Many memories evaded her, but Fionn was right. They were blood. They'd started this together, many years ago, and now they would finish it.

The hill, the woods, and the cave were unchanged. No more than a few hours had passed, the stars wheeling overhead the only indication of time's passage, yet it felt as though it had been years. Fionn nuzzled against her ankles as he pushed her towards the mouth of the cave.

"No." Harper turned her back on the cave entrance and looked up the hill. "That is his place. We must find mine. We need the high ground."

She scooped Fionn up and placed him around her shoulders so her hands were free. Together, they ascended the hill, something in her heart leading her feet. Strains of violin music ghosted on the wind. Not his music with its insidious magic. This was human music; lively and hopeful, flawed and beautiful.

Past the end of the woods, a fire burned at the top of the hill, near the trig point. In the real world, the marker was small, no higher than her shoulder, yet to her Sight it towered several stories high. Shadows of figures circled the fire, their distant voices like the bleating of lost lambs.

"I remember this place." She twisted her head to look at Fionn. He tapped a paw on the air and opened a portal, exiting it at her feet. He tentatively placed his paw on the steps spiralled around the outside of the tower. He glimmered to her Sight, not part of this world anymore.

Harper took a deep breath, letting the smells and tastes of fir, grass, fire, and sheep fill her lungs, fill her soul. She closed her eyes, and birdsong and the whisper of the wind became her heartbeat. The world shifted around her, like standing in the middle of a carousel. She hadn't moved, reality had.

She opened her eyes. "I know what I have to do."

Fionn climbed to head height then paused, watching. He gave a soft mew when Harper opened her eyes and continued, soon disappearing behind the vast tower now standing before her.

Harper looked around but, although the fire still burned, she couldn't see or hear people anymore. *A halfway point. A watchtower.* A memory begged to be heard. Fionn, a human-esque child, holding her hand as they climbed the tower. Their fingers squeezed together as they shifted the world around them so they could See beyond the pocket realm in which they lived. Even then, his magic had been strong. Her Sight alone would never have pierced the illusion.

The memory faded and Harper hurried up the tower after him.

At the top of the stairs, a door led inside. Harper pushed it but it was locked. It always had been. Muscle memory wedged her toes into crevices in the stone, harder now she was taller and heavier. She didn't look down as she grabbed the edge of the roof and hauled herself up. Strong hands gripped her wrists. Then a soft light as Fionn shifted back.

Harper stood on the roof of the tower and gazed across the sleeping dale. It seemed locked in eternal night, but she trusted the dawn would come. Her kin were forbidden to leave the village during the night, tales of the mare the Somnia rescued their ancestors from still frightening them into staying. Yet it was the Somnia himself who stalked the woods, not the demons her family feared. Her brother had known.

"It was him." Astonishment left her numb. She remembered. Her brother had always been suspicious. He'd been the one to introduce her to the night, telling her and Fionn made-up tales of the stars. When she was chosen, he'd fought it. Then the Somnia banished him.

Anger overwhelmed the numbness.

Anger at centuries of lies imprisoning her people so he could feed on their magic, on their dreams.

Anger at being taken from her home as a child.

Anger at the punishment meted out to her brother.

Anger at the torture he'd put her cat through.

Anger at the sleep that now claimed her sister.

"Enough." Her voice shattered the silent night. She lifted the violin to her shoulder, fingers tense on the strings. "This is your last chance. Let my family go. Here and in York. Leave and never return."

Music surrounded her, slips of violet visible on the wind. Fionn cowered against her leg, back arched, fur on end. He hissed as a shape coalesced in the air before them.

"My beloved Seer. I am protector of dreams, composer of melodies. Return to me and live in peace with your kin."

"No," Harper snarled. "You took me from my family. Shut me up in the cave. Punished anyone who tried to help me. You've imprisoned and tortured everyone I love. I will defeat you."

He laughed, the sound like a thousand plucked strings in clashing discord. "You cannot defeat me, child. This is my realm."

Her smile cut through his laughter, knife sharp, learnt from Heresy. "You belong in the realm of dreams, and nowhere else. I am Seer of the dreamscape, Seer of the in-between, Seer of the human realm. I can pierce the shadow between realms. I can change your reality."

She placed the bow on the E string, her fingers high up the neck. One long, keening note, matching the whistle of the wind through the tower's windows. The violin didn't need a hollow body of wood or a mess of wires to roar. The world became part of it and the illusion around them quaked under its power. It amplified her voice over the wind's moan.

"You wanted to use me. You taught me everything and thought I'd forget. I remember now. Everything I learnt from you. But I've been away from your lies for over a decade and now I know more."

It grew within her, the power the Foss had bestowed. No. Not bestowed. Unlocked. It was natural, part of her. Fionn's magic twisted through hers—violet, turquoise, and silver. Her own dreamwalker, her best friend, in control of the dreamscape so she could concentrate on the music. A true partnership.

Harper played the melody of the wind, the grass, the earth. She played the song of the sky and the birds. Starlight danced across the strings, guiding her fingers. She played the warmth of a summer's noon and the chill of a midwinter night. She played the cry of a newborn and the wisdom of an ancient. She played reality, with every ounce of magic her Sight and Senses gave, with all Heresy had taught her of illusions, with all the Foss had reminded her of music. She found the true path, the melody that wends through the world, and she turned the realm in which she stood towards it.

A countermelody intruded. It warped her notes into discord and dissonance. It wove through the illusion, repairing cracks and cancelling reality. A humanoid figure hung in the air before Harper. His body was a mass of swirling notes and lines; quavers, crochets, semibreves, minims, and semiquavers. His true form revealed.

The violin in his hand was made of bones filled with swirling winds of lilac and silver mist, the strings stretched cat gut. Fionn's. From once upon a time. Harper remembered harvesting it, stringing it. It cut her fingers. Fionn's blood and hers in the Somnia's violin. A bow of meteorite strung with black and silver hairs skimmed over the strings. They gleamed to Harper's Sight and she Heard each hair's thoughts whisper in her ear. A hair for every seer the Somnia bred. One from her grandmother, her mother, her.

Despair washed over her with each note from the Somnia's violin. How could she beat something made from her own being and that of her ancestors? Reality flickered, drifted apart as her tune faltered. The Somnia's tune grew louder, rolling over the hills like thunder.

Lightning flashed past her cheek and Harper flinched, her bow screeching over the strings before she realised the blur wasn't lightning, but white fur.

"Fionn!" Harper tried to grab him but it was too late. He launched himself off the rooftop, a hissing ball of fury, straight into the Somnia.

The ethereal being had no true body. The notes swirled around Fionn to trap him mid-air as he tore at them with tooth and claw, but the creature's tune didn't falter. Fionn slashed through the tangled mass of music, swiping at the violin. His claw hooked a lock of dark hair and snapped it from the bow.

Harper's scalp prickled as the loose strand flapped in the wind. The walls of the illusion crinkled.

Fionn swiped again, snagging the E string which broke with a loud twang. Pain sliced through Harper's stomach.

Her blood in his violin.

The Somnia trembled, every note aquiver, as he reached in with skeletal hands made of the slashes and dots of repeats and tore Fionn from his body. He tossed the cat aside as though he were a fluff caught on a jacket. Fionn's howl was swallowed by the mists as he plummeted. Then the Somnia drew its hand over the broken string and restored it.

Harper felt it deep in her gut as the string tightened, tuned, found its place in the song.

Her blood in his violin.

It was made of her and her ancestors. Their hair, their blood, their bones. It wasn't his.

It was hers.

She tucked her emerald violin under her chin. An extension of her body. Her weapon.

Her fingers were still coated in the blood of the Foss's lesson. Her blood. Her violin.

AJ had taught her about lores of affinity to explain the Hiding.

The emerald violin was part of her. The Somnia's violin was part of her.

When she played, both fiddles sang together.

His fingers scrabbled at the strings of the bone violin and the bow of her ancestors' hair dragged over them, but the tune was hers. No matter what notes the Somnia tried to place, the violin sang Harper's song.

She sped up, the music of the dual instruments a celebration of the world and the folk that created them. She played joy where he tried to bring despair. She played love where he sought to create fear. Harper called the winds to her and claimed every sound the violin issued. Its music was hers to play. Its magic was hers to use. He was hers to command.

She played moonlight and sunlight, the emerald violin of forest and water in complete affinity with the stolen violin of blood and bone. The words she and Fionn used at the Market blazed in her mind. She could Hear his voice and turquoise-silver gleamed once again alongside her violet magic. She looked into the soul of the Somnia.

By Moon and Starlight, I banish you.

Dawn's light caught the bone violin as the Somnia's body burst apart and washed it to Harper on a wave. She accepted it, laying the emerald one on the roof at her feet.

The Somnia's violin, no, *her* violin, warmed her hands. It thrummed with a heartbeat and panted with breath. She could sense each of those who came before her, generation by generation. She tucked the violin under her chin and played.

CHAPTER THIRTY

Homecomings

Reality spread out before Harper, thousands of scattered notes awaiting a composer to bind them together into something beautiful. It wasn't her reality but nor was it his anymore. She could bring it back to her realm but she paused, fingers trembling on the string over one sustained note. She could bring her kin back to the real world, release them from the bubble where they'd been imprisoned, but the Somnia had not been wrong. So many people appearing out of nowhere would be accused of magic and arrested. Moreover, something was amiss. There were more notes, more movements to the piece than there should've been. There was more to the bubble reality than would fit in its equivalent place in the real world.

Harper viewed it as a conductor views the orchestra. She could See everything. The river that shouldn't exist and the forest far greater than the one in the mundane world. Tents and fires and children running to and fro. Tears blurred her vision as the form of her mother, made from purest song, left a tent and scooped up a youngster.

The encampment covered the entirety of the inside of the bubble, up its sides and over the arch of the top. To those inside, it seemed flat, or as flat as a hillside could be, but reality warped around them. To lay it out across Swaledale would destroy the dale.

Harper settled back into her own body, separating herself from the violin and its music. She strapped the emerald violin to her hip, and hurried down the stairs, almost tripping in her rush to get to the bottom of the tower. She prayed Fionn had been able to create a portal out of there but her mind saw his broken body on the ground. She let out a sigh of relief when she found him sitting, humanoid, on the bottom step with his tail wrapped around his waist.

When he heard her approach, he scampered up the steps and wrapped her in a hug. "You did it, Harper. You beat him. He's gone. I felt it."

Her knees gave way and she sank into his arms, almost knocking them both down the last few stairs. All the energy, all the power she'd possessed on top of the tower bled away, used up in the magic taken to release it from the Somnia's dominion. Only a little was left.

"We can go to them now," she whispered into Fionn's shoulder. Part of her wanted to run straight home to Grace, to make sure she'd woken up, and the others, too, but another part of her feared if she left this in-between place, she might never be able to return. The Somnia was gone, and with him his spell of forgetfulness, but that didn't mean the path would stay open.

They descended to stand near the fire. Harper closed her eyes and willed reality to change again, concentrating on the voices and the spritely human violin.

"Harper?" A strangled voice told her they'd arrived. She opened her eyes in time to see Fionn shoved aside as a tall man with a dark beard threw his arms around her. The violin in his hand tapped against her spine as the bone one in her hands must've dug into him, but neither of them slackened their embrace.

"Papa?"

A thump on her right, then her left, as others piled into the hug. The sobbing of her mother filtered past her father's broad chest, and the indignant mutterings of a toddler ignored. Hands clutched her clothes, stroked her hair, pinched her cheeks. Family. Establishing the reality that their lost daughter was home.

"Harper, what happened? We all felt it. The earth shifted and the sky cracked then smoothed again." Her mother tugged her hand, wide brown eyes the mirror of Harper's own. "Did something happen to the Protector?"

Disappointment soured Harper's gut and she swallowed a sob. After all this time, no word of concern for her, no condemnation for the one who took her from them. But then, her mother had been a seer too and her faith had been as stalwart as Grace's, albeit in a false protector.

"Mama." Harper wanted to fall into her mother's arms, but the steely gaze held her back. "He wasn't a protector. He was keeping you prisoner and draining your magic. I've banished him, or killed him, or something." She glanced at Fionn who had snatched a blanket from near a fire and wrapped it around himself.

"Banished, I think," he said. "It's hard to kill an ancient deity, but you broke his link to your family."

"*We* broke it. I saw your magic combined with mine." Harper smiled at him, then looked back at her mother's frown. "Mama, I will explain everything, I promise. But for now, can't you be glad I'm home?"

"Mama?" A little girl tugged her mother's skirts. Harper's eyes widened.

"Yes. You have a sister." Her father placed a hand on the child's head and beamed. "The protector needed a seer and your mother's ability was less potent after you were born. We feared another child wouldn't have the full power since so much had been passed to you, but the protector instilled it in her."

The girl looked up at Harper and Harper stepped back on instinct. The child's eyes were vivid violet.

"Mama, Papa, we need to talk."

"No." An iron voice cut through.

"Grandmama?" Harper turned to meet a gaze that made her mother's look like melted butter.

"Be gone," the old woman snapped.

Harper opened her mouth but she had no words.

"You betrayed us once and ran away, leaving us blind. You were always unnatural, tainted. Wanting things that would take you from your birthright. Now you betray us again by fighting our protector. He will return. We can't allow one who vexed him to remain. I am ashamed that you and your brother are my get. So begone and leave us in peace. Or do you refute that the outside world is a danger to us and our way of life?"

"I don't, but that doesn't mean you should be imprisoned. You can stay here. It's safe. We can work out how to leave safely later. I—"

"Enough," her grandmother snapped.

"Mother." Her father stepped forward, placing himself between his daughter and his wife's mother, but she pushed him aside with her cane.

"Child of my blood, betrayer of my kin, I banish you."

Power rose in the old woman, almost as strong as the magic on the tower. Harper searched the eyes of the throng around her. Family. Friends. One woman met Harper's eyes, tears twinkling in her moss green ones, then she turned her gaze to study her feet.

"Child of my blood, betrayer of my kin, I banish you."

Her grandmother's words shoved Harper back a step. "How—"

The world shuddered around her. Fionn grabbed her hand. "I'm sorry, Harper."

"Child of my blood …"

Fionn opened a portal and dragged Harper through before her grandmother could finish the incantation. The image of her family shattered. The spell chased them. As soon as they were through, Fionn closed the portal, cutting it off.

"One day you can go back, but not if she banishes you," he said. "We had to leave before her magic took effect. I'm sorry. But now I've been there and I remember, I can open the portal again. We'll go back once her outrage is cooled. You can write—"

"Write? Write? After all these years apart you want me to send a piece of paper? I should've had longer." Harper sank to the floor, barely registering she was back home in her own kitchen. "I knew I couldn't stay, but I should've had longer."

"*I'm* glad you're back." The most familiar embrace wrapped around her as her sister laid her head upon Harper's back. Harper wiggled around to hug Grace properly, relief flooding her that her sister, her true sister, the sister of her heart, was awake and well.

"You're awake. You're okay?"

"Everyone is," Grace reassured her. "We all woke up when the sun rose."

"That's when Harper defeated him," Fionn added.

Grace cracked a smile. "Very poetic. The guys are waiting in the lounge. They thought you'd come in the front door, but I knew better. I knew you'd come straight to the kettle. Or that the cat would come straight to the cream." She gave Fionn a mock frown, then smiled at his blush.

"I'll put the kettle on and you can tell me why you have two violins I've never seen before. Fionn, go put some real clothes on."

"Yes, Grace."

Once the kettle boiled, Harper, Grace, and the gang sat around the table and she told them all that had happened.

"What do you want to do now?" Saqib asked when she finished.

"Definitely not sleep." Harper hid a yawn. "I almost don't want to sleep ever again. I wonder if I'll still have dream visions now the dream god is gone."

"You will, I think." Fionn sat in a corner by the door, lapping at a mug of milk, in the vain hope sunlight might filter through the fog. "The magic is yours. He bred it into you, supplemented it, but it's yours. The Ashbury's had it before him. It was in Leonora's diary."

"At least those missing women should stop now," Saqib said. "Wonder how we'll square resolving this case away with the Guard."

"A child of the De Santos family banishing a demon is nothing new to them." Grace smirked as she patted Harper's hand. "I'm more concerned about how we're replacing the Ouse."

Harper stared into her mug. "I need to find my brother too. I remember now. In snatches but I think it will all return. I recall the day he disappeared. Mama was distraught. She thought a nightmare had slunk through the woods and stolen him away. That night, Fionn and I searched for him. We found no trace. The tunnel we'd made between the encampment's reality and this one, the path through the wych elm, had been blocked off. I didn't know how to reopen it until I was older. I need to find him."

Grace scooted over to wrap Harper in a tight embrace. "We will. Your brother is my brother, and we will find him."

Fionn rested his head against the backdoor, only half listening to them. Outside, mist piled against the windows. The garden was a blank silver, gleaming in the pale sunlight. Harper didn't hear the voices over the chatter at the table, but Fionn heard what she did not.

Harper...

Harper...

We're waiting...

We're here...

He tugged at his collar, aching at the restrictions his master had placed upon him. He still had an unfulfilled mission, the real reason his master allowed him so much freedom to aid Harper. Her death and his master's were not yet prevented. Magic was still imperilled and broken. The voices called to Harper but beyond them he heard something more.

The plaintive strains of a solo violin, at one with the mist, calling to her. Blood to blood.

Acknowledgements

My deepest thanks to my husband, Chris, without whose patience and sacrifice this book could never have been written. I am sorry writing is such a solitary pursuit. Thank you for the grace and support you always give me. Also, for letting me chatter your ear off about it.

As ever, thank you to my parents for both the gift of stories you gave me as a child and all the marketing you do for me as an adult. Your faith in my abilities is my firm foundation.

To my sister, Chloe, who likewise has unassailable belief in me and always supports me, no matter what. It is you who can do anything you set your mind to. You have my admiration and deepest love.

My Team Tea and Books writing group gave my characters a chance to shine and be thrown into the deep end in many scenarios they would not normally have faced. I know them better thanks to you. Thank you also for your unending support and boosting all my social media.

Special thanks to TTAB's Sarah Fletcher and P.S.C. Willis, whose characters are such an intrinsic part of Fionn's life that he refused to give them up. You have made me a better writer and him a better cat.

No acknowledgements would be complete without my oldest and dearest writing friends—Taylor Grothe, Amanda Casile, Jessica Mitacek, Tanya Pell, and Rae Wilde. You make me a stronger writer and person. I am thrilled that soon so many of our books will be on shelves together.

Thanks also to my amazing beta readers Jon Palmer, Ben Chalfin, Caitlin Colvin, and K. Ryan. Also to Mire Mirke for her Islamic expertise.

Thanks to Heather and Steve of Brigids Gate for all their support of Harper and the team, to MJ Pankey for editing, to Elizabeth Leggett for her incredible cover art, and to Stephanie Ellis for proofreading and formatting.

Finally, just as this book started, to my beloved Sprite. You are my eternal joy. May beautiful stories grace your dreams and nightmares never touch you. Also, thank you for repeatedly convincing people I'm a published author by shouting, "Mommy's book!" and then sitting on the floor and 'reading' said book.

ABOUT THE AUTHOR

Alethea (she/ze) writes various forms of SFF, with a particular love for science-fantasy, dark fantasy, dystopias, and folklore. Many of her works take place at the intersection between technology and magic. Ze enjoys writing stories with subtle political and philosophical messages, but primarily wants zir stories to be great tales with characters readers will love. She also has soft spots for found family, hopeless romances, and non-human characters. Her short stories can be found in a variety of publications and links for these are on her website.

Alethea lives in Manchester, UK with her husband, little Sprite, a cacophony of stringed instruments, and more tea than she can drink in a lifetime.

Bonus content for *The Seer of York* & other works can be found on her website: https://alethealyons.wixsite.com/stories/seerofyork

Social media, newsletter, and to purchase stories: https://linktr.ee/alethearlyons

CONTENT WARNINGS

- Blood
- Death/dying
- Bodies/corpses with no eyes
- Murder
- Spiders
- Violence
- Weapons
- Religion
- Memories/dreams of a child stolen from her home
- Homophobia hinted at
- Injury to an animal (who is a shapeshifter with human level intelligence)
- Domestic abuse (towards said shifter) mentioned but not directly shown

MORE FROM BRIGIDS GATE PRESS

MUSINGS OF THE MUSES

ed. Heather and S.D. Vassallo

Sing O Muse, of the rage of Medusa, cursed by gods and feared by men …
From the mists of time, and ages past,
The muses have gathered; hear now their songs.

A web of revenge spun 'neath the moon;
A poet's wife who breaks her bonds;
A warrior woman on a quest of honor;
A painful lesson for a treacherous heart;
A goddess and a mortal, bound together by the travails of motherhood.

And more.

Listen to the muses, as they sing aloud…HER story.

Musings of the Muses, 65 stories and poems based on Greek myths, is an anthology of monsters, heroines, and goddesses, ranging from ancient Greece to modern day America. They, like the myths themselves, cast long shadows of horror, fantasy, love, betrayal, vengeance, and redemption. This anthology revisits those old tales and presents them anew, from her point of view.dangerous place to live.

DAUGHTER OF SARPEDON

ed. Heather and S.D. Vassallo

Medusa.
Cursed by the gods.
Slain by Perseus.
A monster.

So the poets sang.

The poets got it wrong.

Daughter of Sarpedon: A Tempered Tales Collection is an anthology of short stories, poems, and drabbles, ranging from retellings to completely new stories, from ancient to modern day.

Featuring the talents of Eva Papasoulioti, Laura G. Kaschak, Linda D. Addison, SJ Townend, Christina Sng, Ann Wuehler, Amanda Steel, Ellie Detzler, Elizabeth Davis, Katherine Silva, Megan Baffoe, Rachel Horak Dempsey, Romy Tara Wenzel, Stephanie M. Wytovich, Die Booth, Rachel Rixen, Federica Santini, Thomas Joyce, L. Minton, Catherine McCarthy, Ai Jiang, Katie Young, Lyndsey Croal, Elyse Russell, Deborah Markus, April Yates, Theresa Derwin, Jason P. Burnham, Claire McNerney, Marisca Pichette, Gordon Linzner, Patricia Gomes, Stephen Frame, Sharmon Gazaway, Kayla Whittle, Alexis DuBon, Sam Muller, Avra Margariti, Christina Bagni, Kristin Cleaveland, Eric J. Guignard, Marshall J. Moore, Owl Goingback, Renée Meloche, Cindy O'Quinn, Eugene Johnson, Alyson Faye, Jeanne Bush, and Agatha Andrews.

THE HIDING

Alethea Lyons

Arcane archivist Harper has always been plagued by dreams of grotesque creatures and bloody deaths. When she bumps into a ghostwalker in the Shambles and has a visceral experience of his execution, she knows it's a foretelling. Yet fear of the Queen's Guard stops her speaking out. When her vision indeed comes true, the unusual markings on the ghostwalker's corpse, combined with his neatly excised vocal cords, send a ripple of terror through York.

The witch hunt is on. As the body count rises, Harper knows her magic is the only way to find the killer – if she can avoid being hanged as a witch. To protect both human and supernatural, Harper walks the thin line between their worlds. She and her demonhunter foster-sister form a multi-faith team with a forensic scientist, a spirit Harper accidentally summoned, and a techno-witch, to catch the killer before more people die.

REAWAKENING

Alethea Lyons

After centuries of suppression, the magic of England is

Reawakening

Return to the world of *The Seer of York* with this collection of new tales set in the aftermath of *The Hiding.*

Harper, Grace, Saqib, Heresy, and AJ bond as a team and as a family to save innocents, supernatural and human, despite hunters pursuing them.

Introducing Zero, a starlight cat with a bleak and painful past.

Demonic-possession
Faery circles
Púcas
And more

Visit our website at: www.brigidsgatepress.com